THE ARCTIC FURY

THE ARCTIC FURY

GREER MACALLISTER

THORNDIKE PRESS
A part of Gale, a Cengage Company

LIBRARY OF CONGRESS CIP DATA ON FILE.
CATALOGUING IN PUBLICATION FOR THIS BOOK
IS AVAILABLE FROM THE LIBRARY OF CONGRESS.

ISBN-13: 978-1-4328-8633-2 (hardcover alk. paper)

Published in 2021 by arrangement with Sourcebooks, Inc.

Printed in Mexico
Print Number: 01   Print Year: 2021

For my grandmother

We cannot say what the woman might be physically, if the girl were allowed all the freedom of the boy.

— **Elizabeth Cady Stanton**

The real work of an expedition begins when you return.

— **Louise Arner Boyd**

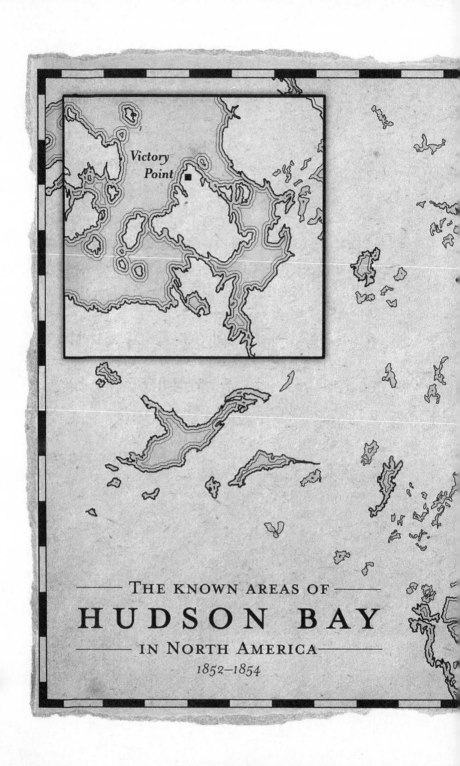

Victory
Point ■

THE KNOWN AREAS OF

HUDSON BAY

IN NORTH AMERICA

1852–1854

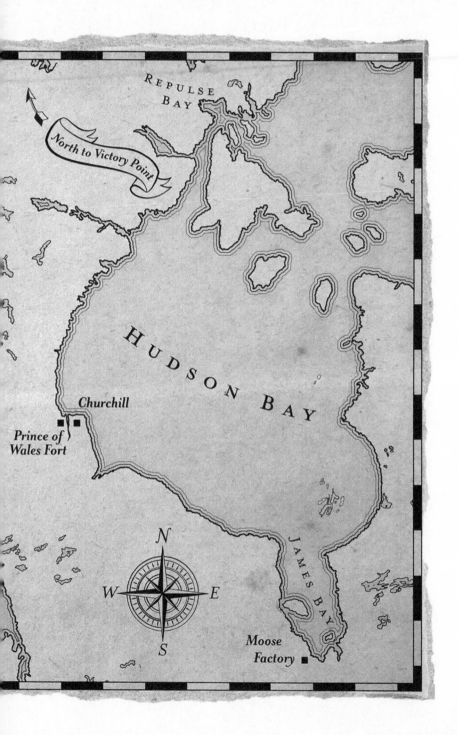

MEMBERS OF THE
WOMEN'S EXPEDITION

Margaret Bridges, journalist
Irene Chartier, translator
Caprice Collins, mountaineer
Dove, nurse
Ebba Green, British Royal Navy wife
Stella Howe, housemaid
Christabel Jones, illustrator
Elizabeth Kent, lady's maid
Ann Montgomery, dog breeder and trainer
Siobhan Perry, medical student
Althea Porter, British Royal Navy wife
Virginia Reeve, leader
Dorothea Roset, navigator

CHAPTER ONE:
VIRGINIA

Massachusetts Superior Court, Boston
October 1854

In the front row sit the survivors.

Virginia can see them clearly from her seat in the dock. Even when she looks away from them — toward the judge, the jury — she still feels their presence. Five women, broken and brave, who came to this courtroom against all odds. She wonders if they feel jarred, the way she does, minding the rules of civilization again: caring what they wear, watching what they say, wondering how their actions make others feel. They were free of all that, not so long ago. Then again, what a steep price they paid for that fleeting freedom.

Only five. Not all who survived, that's a mercy, but all who choose to stand up and be counted as survivors. She feels the ones who aren't there as much as the ones who are. If she closes her eyes, she can see each of the lost before her. One laid out cold and blue as cornflowers. One swallowed by the ice, its hungry maw open just wide enough to devour. One bathed, writhing, in blood. Each a pinpoint tragedy Virginia will never forget, never stop regretting.

Even the ones who sit here today are missing parts of themselves they'll never get back. How many fingers, how many toes? One ear, Doro's. The right, if she remembers correctly, and how could she forget? Also lost: a sliver of each of their souls, including Virginia's. She does not close her eyes to picture any of that, any of those losses. She knows them well enough.

Five women present and willing to be known as survivors of the expedition, not counting Virginia, who had no choice about whether or not to be known. If they had to be counted — in happier times, they joked about it, a welcome thing, an optimist's dream — there should have been eleven. Virginia the twelfth. That was the size of the expedition they'd planned for, though not what they'd launched with, and certainly not what had returned. The numbers don't add up, but then again, the numbers have never added up correctly. That was Caprice's fault. Virginia should be done with her anger at Caprice by now, but she's not.

She may never be done.

"All rise for the Honorable Judge Elton Miller," calls the bailiff.

Virginia rises.

The judge is younger than she would have thought, though not young, exactly. Dark hair instead of white, not a flash of gray among the jet. Her eyes land on a reddish streak along his jaw. Careless with his razor? A stumble in the night? She is sick of analyzing injuries. Siobhan should be here to do that. But Siobhan, like so many others, is not.

"You may be seated," the judge says, and the whole courtroom dissolves into soft rumbles and thumps as they shuffle to comply, exactly like a congregation. Virginia half expects to hear an organ lumbering into the opening strains of "All Things Bright and Beautiful."

Instead, the not-old, not-young judge continues, "We are here today to hear the case of the Commonwealth of Massachusetts versus Miss Virginia Reeve. How do you plead, Miss Reeve?"

From the defense table comes a reluctant but forceful voice. Higher than it should be. Virginia winces at how young he sounds.

"Judge, the charges," says her counsel, whose name is Clevenger. He looks young as well as sounding young, all apple cheeks and skinny limbs. Clevenger is the tallest man in the courtroom, yet somehow, at least to Virginia, he seems to take up the least space.

The judge blinks. "Come again?"

Her counsel shuffles papers, makes another attempt. If Virginia were the lawyer, she tells herself, she would make a stronger beginning. *If ifs and buts were candy and nuts,* Ann would have said to that. Poor Ann.

And poor Virginia. Five faithful, living women in this courtroom form a silent, united line, and it's the voices of the other seven who won't shut up.

"I believe the charges should be read first? And I will tell you how she pleads?" says her counsel.

"Oh, I apologize, Your Honor!" booms the judge, not a whit of apology in his voice. "I forgot to address you as Judge! And in your own court no less. What an embarrassment."

More twitching, more shuffling of papers. "Your Honor, I'm not a judge."

The judge says, with great relish, "Precisely."

Virginia's counsel is silent.

"Now may I proceed?" asks the judge,

16

though it's not really a question.

"Yes, Your Honor."

"Rise," says the judge, though Virginia doesn't hear him until he repeats, more stridently, "Rise."

Virginia rises.

"Read the charges," he says to the bailiff.

"One count of kidnapping and one count of murder," the bailiff says, "in the death of Caprice Collins."

Whispers zip around the courtroom, a handful of flung pebbles skittering on slick ice. But from the row nearest Virginia, there is only a thick, welcome pocket of silence. She feels herself resting on it like a pillow. Shock and surprise may bubble over everywhere else, but nothing surprises the survivors. The capacity for surprise was blasted out of them, frozen out of them, wrenched out of them in the Far North. They froze solid up there. While their bodies are warmer now, something within them has never thawed. She doesn't believe it ever will.

The judge turns away from Virginia, away from the lawyers and the women who sit in the front row, away from the unknown faces who make up the audience for this — what? Circus?

"Men of the jury," he addresses them

ponderously. "Know that the prisoner at the bar, Virginia Reeve, has heretofore pleaded and said she is not guilty of each count of the indictment. For trial, she puts herself upon your good judgment to try the issue. If she is guilty on either or both of said counts, you are to say so, and if she is not guilty on either or both of said counts, you are to say so, and no more. Good men and true — stand together and hearken to your evidence."

Of Virginia herself, he shows no awareness.

His heavy indifference, she thinks, threatens to sink her. She cannot let herself be drawn down. She has endured worse than this man's disdain. And she has a choice in how deeply she lets him cut her. She turns her attention away from him, toward the only people in the courtroom she truly knows.

The five survivors buoy her up with their silence. She fears the words they may speak when called upon later — not to mention the words of others with damaging, dark things to say, true and otherwise — but for now, their quiet reassures her. All she wants from them right now is nothing, and that is exactly what they have left to give.

CHAPTER TWO:
VIRGINIA

Tremont House, Boston
April 1853

As she entered the lobby of Tremont House, Virginia only heard her first three footfalls. One, two, three steps on slick golden marble. The plush, deep carpet smothered the sound of four, five, and everything after.

She moved forward silently in the flicker of the gilt lanterns, the luxurious sofas beckoning with their rich crimson cushions, the cavernous ceiling soaring overhead. Two women sat on the farthest couch with their heads bent together, clearly in conversation, but in such a vast room, she couldn't even hear their voices. *Silent as the grave,* she thought, unbidden. For years, she hadn't felt right in open spaces, either outdoors or in, and she fought back the urge to flee.

Behind the desk sat an attendant in a shirt as white and smooth as fresh snowfall, his eyebrow rising at her approach.

"May I help you, miss?"

"I'm Virginia," she said, and when the hush around her swallowed her voice, she spoke louder the second time. "Virginia Reeve. I'm expected."

The attendant's head went down, possibly checking some kind of list. She saw no signal, but as if by magic, a tall man dressed entirely in black appeared just behind her. In the glimpse she caught over her shoulder, he looked like a crow, and she started, a high gasp in her throat.

Her escort, well trained enough not to call attention to her mistake, merely nodded, clicking his heels together.

"Miss Reeve, it would be my pleasure to show you to Mrs. Griffin's suite," he said.

She trailed him up the stairs and down another hallway of that plush, rich carpet, soft and silencing. The miles she'd traveled to be here exhausted her. The rough wool of her traveling dress made the side of her neck itch, and she longed to scratch the spot. She'd been through far worse, of course, but this always amazed her: how the worst pain, no matter how terrible, could recede into the past. At some point, it no longer breathed into one's ear like a hungry wolf. The minor irritations of daily existence became irritating again. Suffering stayed suffering in all its myriad forms, all its degrees.

She knew not to speak of what she'd been through. No one wanted to hear. What did the mysterious Mrs. Griffin want to hear instead? Virginia had crossed the entire continent to find out.

Her escort rapped lightly on the door of Room 17, bent his ear to the door to wait for an answer, and appeared to hear one. He gripped the doorknob and swung the door open wide, gesturing for Virginia to enter.

"That'll be all, William," said a woman's voice, accented, low, and husky.

"Very good, Madam," answered the escort, stepping back into the hallway and closing the door with practiced care, making no sound.

The entire room seemed gilded. The bright light of day peeked through the gossamer curtains, lighting the white and gold of the room until it glowed. It felt like Virginia imagined a Greek temple might have felt, far back in ancient days.

Virginia turned her attention to the only other person in the room. Mrs. Griffin could well have been an alabaster statue, as still and pale as she sat. Her plush chair curved gracefully around her seated body

21

like a throne.

Though a close observer could see the signs of age on the backs of her hands, Mrs. Griffin had been maintained with great care. Her cheeks were soft with cream, her faded hair still sculpted and pinned as carefully as a bride's. The extravagant folds of her watered silk gown would have offered a litter of collie pups shelter for the night. In age, she might have been Virginia's mother or even her grandmother, but in appearance, it would be obvious to anyone the two never could have sprung from the same family tree.

The older woman spoke without rising. Her accent was clearly British, crisp as a starched sheet. "I must apologize, Miss Reed. I've begun our acquaintance with subterfuge."

Dumbfounded, Virginia did not know how to respond. She latched onto what she could. "Sorry, ma'am. Miss Reeve, you mean."

As soft as the woman's face looked, her eyes were hard and sharp.

"I know what I mean."

"And yet," Virginia said, "my name, begging your pardon, is Virginia Reeve. You wrote to me under that name, did you not?"

"I did," the older woman said, "and yet

names can be deceiving. That is the subterfuge I speak of. I am not — and here I beg *your* pardon, a fair trade — a Mrs. Delafield Griffin."

"Well then, what's your name?"

"Goodness. The Americans of my acquaintance are direct, as one expects, but you — how do they put it? Take the proverbial cake." This in a dry voice, cool and collected, but not without a hint of humor. "The proper way to address me is Lady Franklin."

In wonder, Virginia blurted, "Lady *Jane* Franklin?"

The woman gave a controlled, careful smile. Virginia had the distinct feeling that Lady Jane Franklin rehearsed her smiles in the mirror to choose the most flattering. "It seems that my fame precedes me even to the Western frontier of your wild country."

"A Canadian friend of mine was quite fond of your song," Virginia said. She didn't even really mean to begin singing it, but she opened her lips, and out came the memory:

In Baffin's Bay where the whale fish blow,
The fate of Franklin no man may know.
The fate of Franklin no tongue can tell,
Lord Franklin alone with his sailors do
    dwell.

23

A warm feeling was gathering in her veins — the song reminded her so strongly of Ames — but when Lady Franklin held up her hand for silence, Virginia swallowed down the words.

"I have heard of your many talents," Lady Franklin said. "Singing does not rank among them."

"I didn't mean to upset you."

"You didn't upset me in the least," said the woman, though it sounded to Virginia like a lie. "You are simply a very bad singer. And it is not *my* song, as you style it. It is simply a popular song that purports to speak with my voice, though I gave no permission for it to do so. But let's have done with that. Please, tell me, how was your journey?"

As rusty as her social skills might be, Virginia recognized a change of subject when she heard it, and she took the cue. "Long, to be sure. But far more comfortable than it would have been without your generosity. Thank you for that. If one has a first-class cabin on both the Pacific ship and the Atlantic, the portage in Panama is the worst of it."

She tried to make the journey sound like nothing, when in fact, it might have broken a less experienced traveler. The journeymen

24

who carried her belongings in Panama made off with one of her two precious trunks. A drunken sot on the Atlantic journey mistook her cabin for another's and pounded on her door, shouting and then sobbing, the better part of a night. But she wasn't one to complain. Her neck itched again. She pictured the rash she would find — an inch-thick strip like a priest's collar, all the way around — when she finally peeled the infernal wool dress away. She missed the buckskin trousers and tunic she'd worn as a guide or even the plain cotton hand-me-down dresses she'd worn before that. As dangerous as they were, the wilds beyond the eastern edge of America did offer some advantages over civilization. On the frontier, a young woman in her twenties might do almost anything, as long as she was capable and smart, and if she chose, she could do it dressed in comfort.

"I hope you don't come down with the fever," said Lady Franklin, her clipped British accent brushing away her ending r's. *Feev-ah.* "It might interfere with the plans I have for you." *Int-ah-feeh.*

Virginia smiled. Small talk was done with, it seemed. "Your correspondence referred to a journey, an expedition. And now that I know who you are, I suspect the travel you

25

have in mind is entirely northward."

The older woman laughed, a throaty, husky sound, and looked Virginia up and down. "Do you, now."

"Your husband is lost," Virginia said simply. "I assume you want him found."

"Those are the facts of it, yes. I would expect most young women — or thoughtful people of any age or sex — would phrase it with more care, having some regard for my feelings in the matter."

"Feelings are a luxury, ma'am," said Virginia, respectfully but firmly. She figured Lady Franklin would appreciate a hard head. "Feelings did not bring me here."

Lady Franklin's sharp eyes grew even colder, indicating that she'd miscalculated. "How jaded you are, even at your age. Feelings are what make us human. It is my deep *love* for my husband that drives me to continue to seek him out, despite so many obstacles, so many failures."

Taking a new tack, Virginia tried to appear contrite. "I apologize. I confess I do not know the whole of what you have done so far to seek him. West of Fort Bridger, news is thin on the ground."

"And yet you know that song, the one you referred to as mine. 'Lady Franklin's Lament,' they style it."

"As I said, my Canadian friend was fond of the tune. He was a better singer than I am."

"Was?"

Virginia ignored the question, forging ahead. She had come a long way for this opportunity; she would not let it slip away without knowing what was truly on offer. "If it's a northward journey you have in mind for me, Lady Franklin, I hope you don't misunderstand my background. I have spent no time in the North."

"Your expertise is in leading people. I need people to be led."

"Over land or sea?"

"Both, as it happens. And lakes as well, which may be new for you. Land, lake, sea. Good things, I am told, come in threes."

"And deaths," said Virginia.

"Beg pardon?"

"It's a superstition," she said, feeling her cheeks redden. "I'm sorry. Deaths also come in threes, they say. But I apologize, I should not have steered us off course. Tell me, what sort of people do you have in mind for me to lead?"

Lady Franklin sat up straight in her chair, curling her fingers around its soft arms like an eagle's talons on a branch.

"I have determined," said Lady Franklin,

"a key similarity between all the expeditions — and I now need a second hand to count them — that have failed to find my husband."

"And that similarity is?"

"Men," said Lady Franklin, not with rancor but still investing the word with a sharp importance. "Each of these failed expeditions has been conceived by men, run by men, peopled by men entire."

"Forgive my ignorance," Virginia said apologetically, though she was getting the distinct sense that Lady Franklin may not. "Aren't all Arctic expeditions so run?"

"Yes." Lady Franklin smiled a wry little smile. "They have been, so far. But I have a theory about women. Would you like to hear it?"

"Of course."

"Women can do far more than the narrow lens of society deems fitting. I suspect there is nothing, literally nothing, of which women are not capable."

It was a shocking statement on the face of it. Virginia happened to agree.

Lady Franklin went on, "I myself have done things only a handful of travelers of my generation can lay claim to, man or woman. Sailed down the Nile. Ridden a donkey into Nazareth. Visited a quarantine station in Malta, the docks of Alexandria, the shining Acropolis. Can any man of your acquaintance say he has even been in the presence of janissaries? Bedouins? A pasha? I have met them all."

Virginia's awe was sincere. This elegant, carefully arranged woman — sixty years old if she was a day — bore no signs of such adventure. Her soft cheeks, rich dress, sophisticated air, all seemed at odds with the idea of such unusual achievements. "You are clearly extraordinary."

"You mistake me!" Lady Franklin leaned forward, intent. "I do not argue my own exceptionalism. What I have done, a thousand other women could do, given the chance. This westward expansion of yours proves it. These American wagon trains. Women drive wagons or trek alongside them, learn to shoot firearms, protect themselves and one another, survive the worst storms and the baking sun, shift for themselves through hardships. Over thousands — thousands! — of miles. These intrepid women. At the end of it all, they make it to California or Oregon or Washington Territory."

"Except when they don't," Virginia blurted.

Pinning her with a direct look, still from the comfort of her gilded chair, Lady Franklin said, "Well, yes. To attempt great things sometimes means failure. But even in failure, there are often kernels of success. That party of settlers that went astray on the way to California, marooned in the deep snow of a mountain pass for months, more than half of them dead at the end, you know who survived?"

Virginia held her peace. So many possible answers. Lady Franklin's was the one she wanted to hear.

Lady Franklin said, "The women. If women can live through that, who's to say they can't succeed where men have failed and bring my husband back to me?"

"What if there's no husband to bring back?"

"Girl," said Lady Franklin, her voice turning harsh again, "I said it before, you have no regard for feelings."

She'd spoken too plainly, Virginia realized, and she tried to recover from the mistake without showing weakness. "I understand your feelings, ma'am. Fully. Yet I believe they are not the only reason you called me here. I believe you wanted to offer me some sort of employment."

"I did."

"If you do still," Virginia said, "I am more than willing to listen."

30

Lady Franklin's pause was long, but it ended with clear, steady words. "Simply put, I propose you lead an expedition to the North to bring back my husband. He is a great man, and the world does not yet recognize his triumph. Once he returns, his name will be sung far and wide."

Virginia was eager to embrace the proposal, but she forced herself not to agree just yet. Why her? She had to be clear, just in case. "Leading wagon trains through the pass to California is not the same as leading people on foot through the frozen North. What we were looking for, I already knew how to find."

"But how many people did you take safely through?"

After Virginia had abruptly given up her career as a guide and settled temporarily in San Francisco, a newspaper article — just one — had told her story. Lady Franklin must have seen it, and it included the number she was asking for. There was no reason to hedge. "By my best estimation, 563."

"I believe you have the skill and strength to do what I need, Miss Reeve. The terrain will be different, but the party is much smaller than what you're used to. You have my confidence. I only need your agreement."

Virginia's mind was whirling, starting to seize at the particulars. "You propose for me to lead this expedition alone? Myself?"

"Yes. You will be in charge. At different points, yes, you will need to work closely with others — the experienced voyageurs with the canoes, for example, and the captain of the schooner that carries you north through the Bay. That's why I chose you. You worked with a man to lead those parties through the mountains, if I recall correctly."

And there was the rub. She needn't have avoided mentioning Ames; Lady Franklin obviously knew why Virginia wasn't leading wagon trains through the pass anymore. Why her number of saved souls would never climb any higher than 563. Because she could no longer do it with Ames, and she would not do it alone.

Perhaps this expedition — this mad, ridiculous idea of an expedition — was actually exactly what she needed.

And then she remembered the last verse of "Lady Franklin's Lament," heard it as warm and strong as if Ames were standing right next to her, his scratchy baritone singing directly into her ear. It took real effort to keep from smiling at the memory.

And now my burden it gives me pain,
For my long-lost Franklin I would cross
   the main.
Ten thousand pounds I would freely give
To know on earth that my Franklin do live.

There was a reward. Real money. She would almost do it only for the adventure, but what could she do with that money if she had it? Anything. Nothing. She could live as she liked, where she liked, and never feel even the slightest hunger. Money would free her from so many questions, so many concerns. One could not even put a price on that freedom. There was no other realistic way for her to earn so much money so fast — and become so free. "And if we find him, the reward is ours?"

"Yours alone. To share with the rest of the expedition however you see fit. Like a whaling captain shares with his crew."

"And if we fail?"

"I'm betting that you won't," said Lady Franklin. "You should be willing to make the same bet."

Virginia thought. She was on the cusp of something extraordinary. Whether it was something fantastic or fatal, she did not know. But there was excitement here, and wonder. There was potential she had not thought she could ever embrace again.

At her silence, incongruously, Lady Franklin smiled. "When I read about you, I knew you would be qualified, but whether you'd be interested in taking on the work, that I didn't know. Having met you, talked to you, I'm completely sure you are the right choice. I feel confident no one else could do as well."

Virginia said, "I'm . . . flattered, Lady Franklin."

"Of course you are. You'll leave for the first leg of the journey in a week. I have a few other things to discuss, like some letters you'll carry for me. Very important letters, including one to deliver to my husband when you find him. We can go over the particulars at the desk here, if you'll please?" She gestured for Virginia to sit.

Virginia remained standing. "I said I was flattered. I didn't say I'd do it."

The older woman's brow knotted in discontent. "What could possibly stand in your way?"

"Those particulars you mentioned. We need to discuss them first. Who else will go? And how? How much will you pay if we fol-

34

low the route but return empty-handed? What are the dangers, and how will we be prepared for them?"

Lady Franklin's brow eased, and she met Virginia's gaze with confidence and calm. "I have an answer for every one of your questions, I assure you. I do have certain conditions, which I will spell out. But first, you must sit."

Virginia didn't know why Lady Franklin cared so much whether she was sitting or standing, but she knew that when someone cared very much about a thing and you didn't, you might as well give them what they wanted. Goodwill was a good like any other, to be traded and hoarded and spent.

So this time, when Lady Franklin told Virginia to sit down, she did as she was told and smiled her prettiest smile. "Let's begin."

CHAPTER THREE:
VIRGINIA

Massachusetts Superior Court, Boston
October 1854

"Very well. Proceed," says Judge Miller.

The prosecutor poses in the front of the courtroom as if Charles Loring Elliott himself were engaged to paint his portrait. The man looks like a textbook illustration of an attorney: tiny spectacles, rigid posture. Prominent belly and jowls to match. Virginia's judgment is clouded a bit by the circumstances, but she believes that even if he weren't rabid to see her hanged for a crime he can't prove she committed, she still would not like him.

She likes him even less when he launches into what is supposed to pass for his opening statement. To her ears, it sounds a great deal more like a schoolmaster's harangue.

"Society has rules," lectures the prosecutor, whose name she has not caught. "Some say we should be kind to those who flout them. Forgive them, for they know not what they do, as we read in the Good Book. But those who choose not to move in society are rarely the gems we wish them to be. You have not heard the name Virginia Reeve before. No doubt, before your time in this courtroom ends, you will be sorry you have heard it at all. Nor will you want to hear the details of how our own Caprice Collins, a native daughter of Boston — upstanding and sorely missed — met a horrible death at the hands of this cast-out, unknown girl. I want to thank you, as her family thanks you, for your service. Because you are taking on this unpleasant task, hearing things no good gentleman should ever have to hear, you may be able to stop a fiend from murdering again."

Virginia stays as motionless as a statue. Or a corpse.

"This girl, she claims that her expedition was initiated and paid for by Lady Jane Franklin. But I ask you, why would a high-born British lady do such an outrageous thing? Gin up a misfit band of American women — women and girls! — to search for two British Royal Navy ships that not even the world's most qualified, experienced seamen have been able to find? It's a foolish argument on the face of it. And I tell you, though I regret to do so, there is nothing to learn beyond the face."

He gestures back toward her without fully turning around, without raising his arm all the way. Something desultory about it, almost demeaning, but subtly so. "The defendant, Virginia Reeve, has no family. No history. No one to vouch for her, except for these poor, misguided young women" — he indicates the survivors with a backward sweep of his hand, and Virginia wants to launch herself at him like a bearcat and rake the very flesh from his pompous pink cheeks — "whom she has clearly placed under some kind of spell. As we will prove she did to her victim."

A year ago, even half a year, Virginia would have laughed at the idea that anyone would call Caprice a victim. But the realities of the trial, what's at stake, have sunk in. She does not feel at all like laughing now.

After a stately pause, the prosecutor resumes his address to the men of the jury. "Each had her own reasons for believing the lies Miss Reeve told. But make no mistake, good gentlemen of Boston. She swindled every one of these girls into believing a lie, the same lie she'll tell you — if her counsel even lets her speak."

As much as she wants to leap up and tear

into him, Virginia gazes out from the dock with a blank look, seemingly impassive. For all the terrible things her Arctic ordeal has done to her, not to mention the ordeals previous to it, it has at least done this one good thing: her face keeps many secrets. When she was young, she had a nimble face. Flashing eyes, pink lips quick to smile, the guileless expressions of a girl who wore her heart for anyone to see. No longer.

And so the people in this courtroom, this judge, this jury, will not be able to find any trace of what she feels inside by looking at her outside. They'll see the neat slate-gray dress her counsel shoved through the bars of her cell without comment, neither cheap nor extravagant, blamelessly plain. They'll see the toll that the cold North took on her face, the red bloom on her cheeks that never quite goes away no matter how cold or warm the room might be. They'll see her dark hair parted in the middle and gathered in a smooth, tight coil at the nape of her neck, not a strand out of place, as if she were a painted picture of a woman and not flesh and blood.

But they won't see her anger, the anger that has burned in her for years, unladylike, unquenchable. They won't see how she truly feels about what happened to Caprice, the fierce, haunting regret.

Most importantly, they will never, ever see her fear.

"Thank you. The prosecution rests," says the lawyer, and Virginia stares straight ahead at a knot in the wood of the witness stand, on the far side of the judge's bench. She pretends it's the most interesting knot in the world.

The sound of shuffling papers comes from the defense table. If she could reach, she would slam her hand down on those damn papers to silence them. Her counsel is preceded by rustling everywhere he goes, like a preening debutante who fluffs her skirts to draw attention.

She has spoken with Clevenger on exactly two occasions. Neither filled her with optimism. But she tries to reassure herself: Clevenger is a trained attorney, not a dilettante. The entire purpose of his profession is to protect and defend people like her, and as long as this trial lasts, her specifically. And while she does not feel entirely comfortable in his hands, there are no other hands on offer in which to place herself.

She keeps her body still, turning only her face in his direction to watch him while he rustles, clears his throat, and stands. The assembled courtroom listens with sober attention.

Clevenger addresses the jury, the bystanders, the survivors. In his reedy voice, he says, "My client — Miss Reeve — is innocent."

A long, long pause follows those six words. In Virginia's mind, the pause stretches to fill hours and days of fretful possibilities, of worry and rot, of glaciers and icebergs crashing upon distant shores, of the sun soaring overhead to blot out the blue of the sky until the oceans drain, until the flesh of every person in the courtroom melts away to leave nothing but bone. In her mind, it takes that long. And her counsel isn't even the one to break it.

Long after the silence becomes uncomfortable, the judge says, "And, Counsel?"

Clevenger says, "We will prove it."

Virginia pleads with her eyes for him to say something else, anything else. For him to advance what she's told him about Lady Franklin, about Brooks, about Captain Malcolm. *Is Captain Malcolm here?* she wonders. She will not let herself turn to look. She remembers the five survivors to her right, reaches out for their strength, lets herself rest on it while she waits for her counsel to make her case. Any case.

Clevenger says to the assembly, with a

firm and completely groundless pride, "That is all."

It takes everything Virginia has not to put her head in her hands and weep.

CHAPTER FOUR:
VIRGINIA

American House, Boston
April 1853

After their long talk at the Tremont House, Virginia and the Englishwoman had concluded their conversation with a firm, definite handshake. Virginia had heard enough of the particulars to say yes, she would undertake the expedition for the agreed compensation, and yes, she would await Lady Franklin's designee at her hotel to make all the necessary arrangements.

But it had been three days, days that had suddenly and irrevocably slipped through her fingers. With nothing to do but wait for Lady Franklin's envoy, she could feel her patience dissolving like sugar in tea. On the trail with Ames, she had always been in motion; stops at forts lasted no longer than absolutely necessary, and with California-bound parties coming through so frequently, they rarely waited more than two or three

43

days for a hire. A room this size in Fort Bridger, she thought to herself with a grim smile, would have slept two dozen. Thinking on inequities like this made her want to scream; best, then, not to think on them.

Though it was not as extravagant as Tremont House, Virginia's hotel was by far the most comfortable place she'd ever stayed, and certainly the most private. In the American House, she had two rooms behind a locked door entirely to herself. The indulgence! Virginia imagined Lady Franklin looking down her nose at the relatively stark bedroom and sitting room, not an inch of gold leaf to be seen anywhere. But one's upbringing helped determine one's definition of luxury, and for Virginia, nothing was more luxurious than space.

Virginia's semipermanent lodgings had included two farmhouses, three wagons, and one cabin she barely let herself remember, but in none of these had she ever had one entire room to herself, let alone two. She stood stock-still among all the damask and the chintz, the silk and the mahogany, and drank in the excess. She would have strewn her belongings around if she'd had more belongings. But the lack would soon become an advantage. Certainly, she would not be able to take much with her on the proposed expedition. In some ways, she was perfectly suited for this undertaking, but it would still be unlike anything she'd ever done before.

She was already humming with excitement. The Arctic! The cold was no friend to her, and yet there was a thrill to this adventure that she could not, would not, shake. To seek this lost man and his company and find them when no one else could. The impossibility of it was exactly the allure. The potential reward was enormous, yet the reward was not the only thing that drew her. Going north felt like fate. It felt, in so many ways, like escape.

But before she could begin, Lady Franklin's envoy needed to appear at the American House, and every day, he did not. Even though her surroundings were lush, as each day slipped by, she began to feel more and more trapped. Her logical mind understood exactly why. But in those becalmed, constricting times, her logical mind was not the part of her that writhed and bucked in panic, blind with fear.

So she pushed down the fear and gathered her energy for readiness. The only thing worse than the wait, she knew, would be to miss the envoy when he came.

For three days, she did not leave the hotel, not even for a moment. She took every meal in a room called "the ladies' ordinary," a new innovation of which the hotel staff seemed quite proud. She was unsure how much it differed from a fine restaurant, as she'd never been in one, but in her opinion, the ordinary offered more than enough comfort. Elegant globe lights above the tables cast soft, flattering shadows at night; during the breakfast and noon meal hours, enough daylight streamed in through the windows to tint the tablecloths and china warm gold. For a moment, she thought she might amuse herself by counting up how many meals in her life she'd eaten without even plate or utensils, let alone a table and chair, but then she shoved the thought away. She should focus on where she was and where she'd be going, not where she'd been. God had seen fit to give her a fresh start more than once. It would not honor Him to linger on what she'd needed a fresh start from.

So she focused on the surroundings of the ordinary, its lush fabrics, its gleaming silver. Water beaded on the outside of her glass, and she resisted the urge to swipe it away with a fingertip.

Looking around to find herself surrounded by women was a new, odd feeling for Virginia. She knew the reverse quite well — at any given fort, she was likely to be the only woman for miles — but here, she felt more out of place. She reminded herself that anyone looking at her would see her sober dress and calm expression. Not the fire that burned inside. Not the lingering ghosts of her past. All that, as indelible as it was, was blessedly invisible.

The woman who tended to her table at meals was a dark-eyed, quick-witted woman, likely not much past her twentieth year. She introduced herself as Miss Thisbe. In Virginia's limited experience with those formally employed to serve others, there were two main types: those glad to serve and those who resented being in service. Thisbe seemed another type entirely. She seemed almost amused by her own role in service, lighthearted at every turn. She took Virginia's order with a wink and set her plate down with a grin, as if the fact that Virginia could ask her for things was a private joke between the two of them.

Virginia sometimes lingered over her meals to prolong her conversations with Thisbe, a behavior she also found new in herself. She did not think of herself as someone who wanted or needed company. But then again, she'd so rarely had the choice of whether to be in company, perhaps she'd never been away from others long enough to miss them.

After her fourth supper at the ladies' ordinary, as she returned to her room, she found a strange man lingering in the hallway near her door. Even looking directly at him, she wasn't sure how she'd describe him to someone seeking him in a crowd. He was not particularly tall or short, thin or fat, dark-haired or light-haired. He was not particularly anything.

"Mr. Brooks?" she asked.

"Brooks," he said in an accent that differed from Lady Franklin's. She could tell it was neither American nor Canadian, but beyond that, she could not pin it down.

"Brooks? Is that your first or last name?"

"Brooks will do, Miss Reeve." His voice was matter-of-fact.

She looked more closely at him, observing. Like the rest of him, his face was undistinguished in a way that she suspected made him very good at doing someone else's bidding.

"Will you come in?" she asked. "It isn't proper, but then, we're not on proper business, are we?"

"It's all fully proper, Miss Reeve," he said, the strange accent bending his words, his jaw tight.

48

"But . . . unusual."

"We can discuss whether it is usual in the privacy of your room, please." He nodded toward the empty room behind her, and she opened the door to let him in.

As he entered, she searched his face and body for some characteristic that might help her define him. Was he an envoy or an enforcer? His shoulders were broad under the smooth fabric of his coat. There was a tense strength to his movements, even when all he did was shut the door. Virginia was uncomfortable enough in his presence to hope she needn't find out any more about what he could do with his strength if he chose.

Brooks began, "I've come to tell you about the arrangements that have been made and help you make those that remain."

"Lady Franklin sent you?"

"My employer prefers that no names be used."

"Even here in private?"

"Even so." Though his accent differed, his cadences seemed to mimic Lady Franklin's, businesslike and formal. "From this moment, all dealings will be in my hands. My employer will have no further contact with you. Nor will the financing of your expedition be made public. If asked any questions about this expedition, unless and until you come back successful, my employer will deny all knowledge of it and you. Is that clear?"

Virginia felt a tickle of disappointment to hear she wouldn't be seeing Lady Franklin again before they left, but it wouldn't do to let it show. For his benefit, she gave an indifferent shrug. "As long as she pays when we do come back successful."

"I pray you do attain that success, miss."

She did not ask him to whom he prayed. Instead, she said, "Get on with it, then."

His voice was dry as he responded, "She did say that you were quite . . . straightforward."

"Are women not straightforward where you come from?"

She saw by the ghost of his smile that he understood her gambit.

With a condescending air, he said, "My understanding is that women of good breeding, regardless of what country they come from, know how to conduct themselves in society. Now, you were the one who wanted to, you said, 'get on with it,' am I correct?"

"Yes."

"So let's."

They both gestured to the empty chairs at the same time, and then both sat down, eye-

50

ing each other, wary as dogs.

Brooks drew a map from a hidden pocket and unrolled it on the table between them. He traced the route with a blunt fingertip as he went, hundreds of impossible miles streaming by in barely a sentence. "Train to Buffalo, canoes to Sault Ste. Marie, transport overland to Moose Factory, and a topsail schooner up the west side of Hudson Bay to Repulse Bay, arriving in late July. From there, you'll make the overland trek to the search area. That's King William's Land, specifically, Victory Point. That leaves you four months to trek in, search, and trek out before winter."

"Easy as falling off a log," said Virginia breezily.

"Indeed." He rolled up the map in silence and tucked it back from whence it came.

Virginia wished he would've left the map out to examine further; she wanted a closer look. All this was so new. But in the glimpse she'd been given, she hadn't missed the top left corner where the lines changed from reassuring solidity to ambiguous, tentative dots. They were headed straight for the vague, smudged unknown.

"Nine of the women have been chosen for the expedition," Brooks went on, changing focus. "Our employer felt that you might like to choose the other three. You have a week to do so."

Her head spun with the new information. There was too much to take in, and yet she had to be strategic in her questions. "Three that I choose. In a week. And I absolutely must take the nine — well, eight, besides myself — that she asks me to?"

"That you are asked to take, yes," he repeated, a stone wall. "The expedition in total will be twelve. No more, no less."

"So that's another condition she's set, then."

"Another condition, yes," he said, and she heard his annoyance, but only because she was listening closely. He was good, this one. Fully in control of himself. It was a rare quality and one she admired. She reminded herself to look for it in the recruits she had just been informed she needed to find. In seven days. In a place she'd never been, with no friends or family, no connections.

But that, she would sort out herself. At the moment, she had to stay focused on Brooks and what he could tell her.

Virginia asked, "And what about the rest of our transport? The canoes, the ship?"

"All in good time." He seemed offended.

"When is there a better time than now?" She was particularly curious about the ship that would carry them northward. The ships of the lost Franklin expedition had been Royal Navy ships once upon a time: armored, solid, ready. But the Royal Navy's half-hearted attempts to find Franklin had brought back no news, and Lady Franklin had taken matters into her own determined hands. Would she enlist an American ship? Canadian? What could she get hold of, given her funds and desperation?

He shook his head. "I'll leave you a file with the logistical information. You can read, can't you?"

With absolutely no hint of her aggravation, she said, "Yes. I can read."

"Good. But first things first. Our employer would like you to familiarize yourself with the other members of the expedition. To meet those who are here in Boston. To understand their strengths before you assemble the remainder of the team."

"How many are here?"

"Three," he answered.

"Only one thing, then."

"Yes?"

A hint of a smile crept into her voice when she said, "You'll have to tell me who they are."

"Althea Porter. Ebba Green. Caprice Collins." He consulted no list or paper; the names rolled off his tongue.

"And they are already familiar with the terms of the expedition? They've been invited and confirmed?"

"Yes."

"And told how much they will receive in payment?"

"They are less preoccupied with payment than you are, Miss Reeve."

She squirmed but fought to hide her reaction, balling her hand into a fist. The three he mentioned must be well-off. Only wealthy people thought so little of money.

"Tell me more. I understand you've given me their names, but who *are* they?"

"You're impatient," he said. "I hope you'll be more patient as you prepare to take your life — and the lives of eleven other women — in your hands."

"I hope you'll be more forthcoming with information that will enable me to protect the lives of those women." She let some of her anger show in her voice; she wanted him to know she was no doormat. "That is my top priority. Followed by ensuring we return successful from our voyage, with full knowledge of the fate of John Franklin or, God willing, John Franklin himself."

He inclined his head just a fraction. "Indeed, miss."

"So who are they? These three?"

"Althea Porter and Ebba Green are the wives of two of Franklin's officers, James Porter and Daniel Green, two of his best lieutenants."

"They must be sick with worry."

"They are Royal Navy wives," he said coldly. "They were prepared."

Though she was sure he was correct about the preparation, Virginia doubted any woman could truly be trained not to grieve the disappearance and probable death of the man she loved.

"And these ladies are good adventurers?" she asked. "Strong?"

"You will have to ask them directly. I will give you the address of their hotel."

She should have known. "Well then, I'll dash off a note and set an appointment to meet them. As soon as possible."

He nodded.

"And Miss Collins — it is Miss Collins, yes, not Mrs.?"

"Miss."

"Shall I write her as well?"

"No, that won't be needed," he said. "You're expected at her house in Beacon Hill in" — he pulled out a pocket watch, spit-shined gold, incongruous and gleaming — "just under half an hour."

55

The surprise must have shown on her face. He smiled, a smile without kindness, only superiority, a smug pleasure in seeing someone else's discomfort.

"Better hurry, Miss Reeve."

CHAPTER FIVE:
VIRGINIA

Massachusetts Superior Court, Boston
October 1854

"Call your first witness," says Judge Miller, and despite herself, Virginia feels her curiosity rise. Who will it be? Who will be the first to sell her out, to make her a villain? To name her a murderer?

Of course she has been called a murderer, or more properly a murderess, in the papers. One does not stand trial for murder in Boston without attracting notice.

She had never read a Boston newspaper before she was arrested and locked away in the Charles Street Jail. She had never been much of a reader. Since her arraignment, when it became clear she would stand trial, she has been squirreled away in a private cell, where she sees no one but her two regular guards. One is named Benson, the other Keeler. Both regularly read the newspapers aloud to her, but as they have chosen different newspapers, the effect is wholly different. Benson reads the *Beacon* as reassurance; Keeler reads the *Clarion* as punishment.

Either way, she finds the company better than no company at all. So she listens to the *Clarion* vilify her as "the Northern Borgia" and "self-proclaimed Queen of the Arctic" — a proclamation that has never passed her lips in public or private — almost as reverently as she listens to the *Beacon* praise her as "a noble American Valkyrie" and "the Arctic Fury." At least there are words. At least there are voices.

And now that her trial has begun, there will be more voices and faces than she can stand. She will listen in silence as penance. They would not disdain her if she had not failed; she deserves this. Who will the first one be?

The prosecutor announces, "The Commonwealth calls Gabriel Bishop to the stand."

Bishop? She knows no Bishop. Breath and motion ripple throughout the room while whoever it is comes forward, murmurs tracking him like wind in grain. Again she is reminded of church. Will she ever be allowed in church again? To see shafts of light illuminate stained glass, to feel the utter peace of her soul lifting after confession, the deep rumble of the organ vibrating in her very bones? How long until she's allowed to set foot anywhere beyond her solitary cell and — hardly better — this cavernous courtroom? She does not allow herself to think about where she will spend time or how much of it will be left to her if she's found guilty.

The man Gabriel Bishop steps up into the witness box. He has thinning reddish hair, smoothed sidelong across his forehead all the way down to a narrow, silky-looking pair of brows, incongruously delicate. His sideburns are faint, and he is otherwise clean-shaven. His face is more English than Irish, not a freckle to be seen, and wholly unfamiliar. What Virginia can see of his body is on the slim side of average and as straight as the barrel of a gun.

The bailiff extends the Bible forward, and the witness places his hand atop it without hesitation. He raises his other hand to take his oath. She is still not sure she has ever seen his face before. Then again, she doesn't need to remember him for him to remember her. And she has no idea what he's there to say. What nail has he been called here to drive into her eventual coffin?

The prosecutor opens by requesting his

name and position. Bishop's relevance springs into her brain, too late, just as he begins to speak.

In a firm, steely voice, he says, "My name is Gabriel Bishop. I am employed as a butler in the home of Mr. Tiberius Collins." The British hint to his voice is more a lilt than an accent. *But-luh.*

"That's Tiberius Collins of Beacon Hill, correct? The father of Caprice Collins?"

The butler stares out over Virginia's head and the heads of the women in the front row to gaze farther into the courtroom. "From her birth until her untimely death."

"Her murder, yes. May she rest in peace," says the prosecutor with great, performative sorrow.

To Virginia, the routine playing out here seems as carefully rehearsed as any scene in a playhouse. The actors exchange their lines with precisely chosen inflections. She's keenly aware others will see it with less cynical eyes. And those people might believe it. She wants to leap up. Scream. Give voice to her sorrow, her anger, her fear.

Instead, she sits in silence, not even letting her toes touch inside the closed box of the dock, giving the observers nothing to observe.

The next question. "How long have you

60

been employed by Tiberius Collins?"

"Twenty-two years in that good man's employ, sir, and if I might add, I was employed by his father-in-law before him. The now Mrs. Collins was born a Masterson. Of the Chestnut Hill Mastersons. You know of the family, I presume."

"Oh, of course," says the prosecutor, his voice approving.

"I was established in the Collins household when they married as a bit of a gift, you might say."

"I might," said the prosecutor, smilingly familiar. "I imagine Mr. Collins was thrilled to have a man of your sterling reputation as his butler, with your long-standing record of excellent service. Someone upon whom he could rely."

The butler's eyes return to that same spot in the crowd, and Virginia realizes that Bishop must be looking at Mr. Collins himself. She can't pick him out without turning her head, which she decides against doing, but he must be there. A shiver runs up both sides of her neck. She hadn't thought of having to face Caprice's parents, these people who want her dead for what they think she's done. She hasn't seen them since they had her arrested, months ago.

"I should like to think so, sir."

"So you were in the household when Miss Caprice Collins was born, then?"

"Yes."

"Knew her from a babe?"

"I did, yes, sir. She grew into a fine young lady, fine indeed." His overbearing pride in himself extends, for a moment, into pride in Caprice.

Virginia sees no sorrow at all here, just this stuffed-up, faux-noble arrogance. How she would dearly love to slap him across the face. As if names and places of origin matter. As if any of this matters. If he is going to help them kill her, which it seems he is, she wants him to go ahead and get straight to the meat.

The prosecutor continues. "And though I know she's less familiar to you, I'd like you to tell us now how you know this person here, the defendant at the bar."

Virginia notices he doesn't use her name or even *young woman.* Just *person.* Caprice was a young lady. Virginia is the defendant. This time, he does not even raise his arm to indicate her. He does not turn, even slightly, in her direction.

"That is Virginia Reeve," says the witness, who does glance her way, if only for a moment. "Or at least she gave that name when she visited the house. We had no benefit of a formal introduction."

"She just showed up at the Collins house one day?"

"She did."

Virginia notices the implication that she wasn't expected, though in fact she had been. Witnesses could do equal harm to her through what they said and what they failed to say.

"And were you present for the meeting?"

"I showed her in and presented her to Miss Collins, who received her in the formal parlor."

"You're sure of that?" The prosecutor interrupts him to ask the obvious question, which Virginia wonders at, but she imagines he must have his reasons.

"The day is utterly etched in my memory," the man intones in a serious voice, the picture of responsible rectitude.

Virginia's stomach drops. How much of this have they rehearsed?

"Thank you. Please, proceed."

He does. "After I brought the visitor in, I immediately retired to the hall, to my post at the front door."

"Yet you heard some of their conversation?"

"I did. I did not eavesdrop at all, of course. I would never compromise my employer's expectation of privacy."

"No one doubts your integrity," says the lawyer, as if he can make it true merely by saying it. Virginia fears perhaps, in a way, he can.

"Thank you. I was not listening, I promise you. But when their voices were raised, I could not help but hear. In a fine, well-built house like the Collins home, one cannot hear a typical conversation in the parlor from the front hall. Certainly whispering or civil conversation would not convey."

"So this was not a typical conversation?" the lawyer offers.

"It wasn't. As I said, civil conversation is not audible from the front hall. But shouting is a different matter."

The prosecutor shakes his head, disapproving, rueful. "Shouting, you say."

"I do. That is what I heard."

"And from what you overheard — unintentionally, as you said — the two women didn't seem to get along?"

"No, they most certainly did not. I should say, Miss Collins was perfectly polite. It was this one who was . . . I can't quite find the words, sir."

"Take your time."

He pauses a moment longer, purses his lips, and finally says, "Well, I suppose she was *rude.*"

It stuns Virginia how this lemon of a man, full of sour reproach, can make *rude* sound worse than *murder.* And yet.

The witness's eyes land on her at last. From this distance, in this light, they seem to have no particular color. She returns his gaze without flinching. After the space of a few heartbeats, he is the one who looks away.

The prosecutor says, "Could you share with us some of what she said?"

"I object," says Virginia's counsel, and she winces inwardly. He could not choose a worse moment to speak. She sees the trap before he does. Fool or mouse, he walks right up and springs it.

"Yes?" the judge asks. "Please, share the grounds for your objection."

"Why ask this man what my client said? She will recollect better than he."

"Then when the time for defense comes, you are welcome — encouraged, even — to put her on the witness stand."

The lawyer's silence stretches on, uncomfortable, obvious, until he sits. Then he reaches out for more papers to rustle and fans through them without speaking. Virginia resists the urge to put her head in her hands. She has so many urges in this room she knows she must resist. Civilization is a maze of forced constraints; she almost wants to be out of it. But she remembers, too, how dark the world beyond civilization can be.

Virginia twists the middle of her body slowly until she can feel her stays pressing into her flesh. She does this to remind herself of her own fragility. What a vulnerable vessel the human body makes for the human soul. Puncture the membrane and it all spills out like water.

"Now, Mr. Bishop," purrs the prosecuting attorney, "please do tell us what Miss Reeve here called your client."

Clearly enjoying the attention, the witness puts his shoulders back and says, "I remember her words quite well. She called Miss Collins an 'arrogant, empty-headed fool.' "

"Goodness!" exclaims the prosecutor, his eyebrows raised, prim as a pastor's wife in a pew. "Those were her words exactly?"

"Yes. 'Arrogant, empty-headed fool.' I'd stake my life on it."

Easy for him to say, thinks Virginia. *His life isn't the one at stake.*

The prosecutor sweeps a searching glance across the room, making sure everyone within these walls has had a chance to ponder the witness's words, and then goes in for the killing stroke. "Was that all?"

"No, sir," says the butler, leaning forward with relish.

"What else did she call her?"

"Wasn't what she called her, sir. It was her threat."

"Threat!"

"Yes, sir. She said to Miss Collins, and this is exactly the word of it, sir, I'll never forget. She said, 'If you insist on going to the Arctic, you'll never come back.' "

CHAPTER SIX:
VIRGINIA

The Collins House, Boston
April 1853

Caprice smelled like money. Not the blood-tinged scent of copper pennies, heaven forbid, nor the grimy stink of much-handled bills, but the crisp, almost leaflike smell of a dollar fresh from the mint. When she stirred her skirts, the smell wafted up, settled in. It was the first thing Virginia noticed about her.

The second: she was as homely as a toad.

The third: while she herself was probably unaware of the first point, she went to great expense to distract you from the second.

When the butler showed her into the parlor, Virginia wasn't sure where to look. The velvet couch upon which Caprice was arrayed was attractive enough, an elegant lavender in color, and in a plainer room, it would have been lovely. But it was flanked on both sides by chairs upholstered in a turquoise-and-pink floral pattern, in front of a wall striped with gold and rose in turn, and if the riot of color weren't enough, the stripes gave the whole scene an air of the circus. Then there was the rich, thick carpet, which swirled all the other colors together with ribbons of cream and green, a snarl of flowers the likes of which would never be served up together by nature.

Caprice herself wore a floral pattern that clashed equally with the chairs and the carpet. The skirt of her dress was heavily embroidered with lilies. Her bodice, tapering down to a sharp point at her narrow waist, was a solid green. Perhaps she was supposed to look like a flower herself. She did not.

Setting a careful foot on the outrageously flowered carpet, Virginia extended her hand to Caprice. Caprice did not take it.

Looking past Virginia to the butler, Caprice said, "Thank you, Bishop. That will be all."

Virginia turned her head to see the man, slim and rigid. He bowed sharply at the waist as if it were the only point where his body could bend. Then he backed away and disappeared around a corner, still facing them, until he receded from view. Virginia wanted to laugh, but she could tell from

Caprice's expression that this was expected. She swallowed her amusement and waited instead for her host to speak.

Once he was gone, Caprice looked up at Virginia, appraising her frankly. "So tell me. Who are you?"

The rich girl's glare made Virginia uneasy. If Caprice had any pretty part, it was her muted gray-green eyes, but what she did with them was piercing, not pleasing. The confidence Virginia had felt with both Lady Franklin and Brooks seemed to drain away instantly. Hesitating even as she cursed her hesitation, Virginia began, "I thought Lady Franklin told you. She's asked me to organize the expedition . . . She did mention the expedition?"

Caprice waved the back of her hand once, like a birdwing, and said, "Yes, yes, I know all that. What I mean is who *are* you? Where did you come from?"

"California," she replied.

Caprice rolled her eyes. "No one comes from California."

"People do," Virginia protested weakly.

A rap sounded on the door, and in came a young woman with a tea tray. What they called "tea" on the trail had been brewed from acorns, somehow both flavorless and bitter. This tea tray was piled high not just with a flowered porcelain pot of tea and matching cups on saucers but a tempting plate of little biscuits and cakes, iced with graceful swirls.

The young woman arranged things on a low table, and Caprice dismissed her with, "Thank you, Eleanor. We'll serve ourselves."

Eleanor backed out as the butler had.

Virginia reached for a round biscuit with a perfect little flower on it and had it halfway to her mouth when she heard Caprice chuckle. In the chuckle, there was malice.

"That hungry, are you?" said Caprice.

"I'm sorry?"

She pointed at the sweet in Virginia's hand. "It isn't generally done, just grabbing one's own fistful like that. But I suppose you do things differently in California?"

Mortified, Virginia thought to put the biscuit back, but that seemed wrong; instead, she defiantly popped it in her mouth and began to chew. When she'd swallowed it — so quickly she didn't even have time to savor the taste — she said, "Well, you did say we'd serve ourselves."

Caprice's smile, like her laugh, was malicious. "I suppose you haven't been in a house like this often enough to speak the language. Here, that means that the host serves. The guest waits. It's how polite people do things. But you're self-sufficient, I see, so why don't you pour yourself some tea?"

Once, Virginia remembered, a sudden, vicious wind had whipped up on a sandy trail through the Sierras, blasting their party. Virginia had been shocked at how much a tiny grain of sand on one's skin, delivered with enough force, could hurt. Caprice's obvious condescension, her scrutiny, hit Virginia like those grains of sand.

They should be talking about the expedition, how exciting it was to be included, how they would do what no other women had done. Virginia wanted to find out why this girl was important enough to be a required participant. She was sure Caprice was equally curious about her. They should use every minute to find out all the facts, all the warts, before such things came out on the journey. Then it would be too late.

Instead, Virginia reached out for the pot of tea and found the handle so hot to the touch she had to pull back her fingers, yelping, "Bugger all!"

"Goodness!" said Caprice, sounding genuinely shocked. "Now I'm sure no matter where you were raised, you understand that sort of language is inappropriate for a social call."

Virginia considered fleeing the room entirely and abandoning the very idea of the expedition. It was nearly as tempting as the tray of sweets. But she forced herself to calm down, and in a deliberately deferential voice, she said, "You know, I've decided I'm not really in the mood for tea. Please forgive me. May I sit, or is that something that also isn't done?"

She stared directly at Caprice, who matched the grit in her stare and finally, slowly, gave a nod of approval. "You're right. Let the tea cool. Let's talk about the future."

"Let's."

They seated themselves on the overstuffed couches. This was their last best chance to start over. So Virginia said, "So, Miss Collins, what is your reason for wanting to join the expedition?"

"*Wanting* to join? That makes it sound like there's a question. If I am not part of this expedition, there will not be one."

"Is that so?"

Caprice's chin went up. "I have persuaded my father that the search for Franklin is a noble undertaking. You could say I'm the reason this expedition is happening."

Virginia answered in a dry tone, "I assume Lady Franklin would say her husband is the reason."

"I suppose, in the sense that we would have no one to look for if he hadn't gotten himself lost, along with two very expensive ships and over a hundred other sons, husbands, and fathers. But my father's money is making this female search expedition possible. That's why I'm going."

Virginia's eyes lit on the striped wallpaper, the ornate and expensive surroundings. "And your family will allow it?"

"It appears you don't know much about me or my family, Miss Reeve. Soon, I will be curious to hear what you *do* know, about anything, but I assure you that if I want something, my family will not stand in my way. And I want this."

"But why?"

"Why do you? Why does anyone?" Caprice crossed her arms in front of her. Virginia could see her fingertips digging into the soft flesh of her upper arm, so fierce was her grip. Whatever her flaws, she meant what she said.

Caprice went on, "The North is there. Few have seen it. I want to be one of those few. To be extraordinary."

"There are other ways to be extraordinary."

"I want *this* one," the rich girl said. She might have said the same words in the same voice about any number of things: a toy, a pony, a handsome young suitor. Virginia suspected she'd said it about all three at different times in her life. Odds were good she'd gotten what she wanted each and every time.

Virginia struggled to find her next words. If she could not be genial — and that ship had sailed — she could at least be clear. "Are you sure you're prepared for the difficulty of this journey, Miss Collins? We'll be miles from civilization. From ballrooms and porcelain teacups and silk dancing slippers. I expect it'll be the hardest thing you've ever done."

"You have no idea what I've done, actually," interrupted Caprice. "Did you know I'm a mountaineer, probably the most ambitious one in the entire country? I've climbed Alps that would make your head spin. I'm used to the cold, and I'm used to hard work. I've woken before sunrise to summit some of the tallest mountains in Europe. Clambered over stone. Saw an avalanche rip down the side of Monte Rosa. On Mont Blanc, I collapsed from the insufficiency of the air, and after I regained consciousness, I got right back up and started climbing again. So no, Miss Reeve. I'm not so sure this will be the hardest thing I've ever done."

Virginia was impressed with the litany but couldn't let herself show it; that would feel like backing down. Instead, she pushed harder.

"But we'll be on our own," she said. "No porters or guides. Humping all our own gear. Once we're on the ice, hunting our own food. You've climbed all those mountains, but have you ever climbed one no one else has climbed before?"

Caprice narrowed her green-gray eyes. "I don't see why that's relevant."

"We will be in the complete unknown. No buildings, no succor, no one to catch us if we fall. It's like nowhere else on earth. Frankly, Miss Collins, I don't think you will like it."

"As it happens, Miss Reeve, I don't give a fairy's whisper what you think."

Her euphemism was laughable, but the sentiment behind it was unmistakable disdain.

Virginia answered her disdain in kind. "Shall I speak freely?"

"Oh, you shall," said the rich girl, her chin up, her lovely eyes challenging in her un-

76

lovely face. "I insist upon it."

"Well then. You, Miss Collins, are an arrogant, empty-headed fool."

"Am I?" She seemed undaunted by the insult, the tone of her voice unchanged. "And on what basis do you make this estimation?"

"In these few minutes, you have made your personality very clear. All I have to do is observe your behavior. Listen to your words. I can tell already that you will not listen to me, that you will not follow a leader. On a journey like this, that habit is often fatal."

"Is that a *threat*?"

"No, absolutely not," said Virginia, who certainly had not meant it that way. "But you were not appointed the leader of this expedition, for whatever reason. So once we go north, if you try to substitute your judgment for mine, the outcome can only be . . . imperfect."

"Speak plainly," Caprice taunted. "You said you would."

"If you insist on going to the Arctic and you behave in such a careless and disruptive manner . . ." Even as bold as she felt, she found it hard to complete the sentence, to say what she could not take back once spoken.

"Don't shilly-shally! Be plain." Caprice slapped a delicate side table with a flat palm, the sound of the slap high and sharp in the silence.

"All right then." Virginia's voice was loud and low, sounding to her almost like a stranger's. "I wouldn't give a tinker's damn for your chances. Come to the Arctic, disobey me on the ice, and I'll lay odds you'll never come back."

Caprice chuckled. Something merry flashed in her gray-green eyes, which had darkened to a mossy shade in the afternoon light. With a smile, she said, "Very well then, Miss Reeve. I can't say you didn't warn me, and I'll take those odds. When shall we begin?"

CHAPTER SEVEN:
VIRGINIA

Charles Street Jail, Boston
October 1854

Has the weather turned, thinks Virginia, or is her blood just thinning? When they came back, worn thin by the deep freeze, she'd felt hot every hour of the day and night. She'd slept hot, breathed hot, lived hot. But now, even though her cheeks still burn against the cooling air, her hands and feet feel the chill.

Perhaps it is the jail itself. No doubt they don't want to waste money on heat for the prisoners, although the jail has been built with all the modern principles, incorporating light and air. The cell itself is eight feet by ten feet and made entirely of granite. Stone holds cold, she remembers. Like dead flesh. Once life goes, heat goes, and a human body can easily freeze all the way through once there's no heart to warm it. Everything becomes ice once the temperature drops low and long enough. Tears. Muscle. Blood.

Perhaps this feeling of cold is something to be happy about, Virginia tries to tell herself. Perhaps it means that her body is regaining a range of feelings instead of the numbness of those final months, that constant thrum of cold, exhaustion, regret. But why bother regaining feelings if she'll just lose them again? If her neck will be in a noose before the year's out, better not to feel.

Today's guard is Keeler. Without a word, he slams down her meal on its tray, and she starts at the sound, mostly because she hadn't even heard him approaching.

It isn't like her to be so wrapped up in her own thoughts. But perhaps this, too, is progress. At the end of her time in the North, she was a constant closed fist of worry. She'd flinch at the faintest whisper, even the sound of a needle in hide. Anything louder frightened her clear out of her skin. She slept fitfully, if at all, and the lack of sleep wore her brittle. If her time in this lone, chilly cell has dulled her senses, so much the better. Again she thinks of the possibility of her impending death, its breath on her neck, inescapable.

Keeler speaks, his voice an irritated grumble. The grumble says, "Reeve, you've a visitor."

She welcomes the distraction, turning to see who he's brought her.

Unfortunately, it is only Clevenger, her round-faced counsel. Not high on the list of people she would want to see, not even on the list at all if she's honest. She will keep this honesty to herself.

The guard pulls up a chair for her visitor to sit in, which is surprisingly kind of him, but its metal legs screech across the stone floor, sending twin shivers up the back of Virginia's neck. Perhaps the noise was the point of the gesture.

Still, she smiles sweetly. "Thank you for your kindness."

"Fifteen minutes," he responds. Something in his voice makes Virginia think he doesn't like her counsel any more than she does.

The counsel in question drops himself into the seat, rustling his papers as always, even here in her cell instead of the courtroom, shuffling them into a case that hangs mostly empty. There are not so very many papers, it seems. Then why must they always make so much noise?

"Well, that went swimmingly," she says.

He sighs a grand, theatrical sigh, as overwrought in its way as the prosecutor's sympathy for poor dead Caprice had been. That butler hadn't even liked Caprice, hadn't really known her the way Virginia had. Living under the same roof as someone did not guarantee you understood who they were, the limits of what they might do when the situation demanded it. Virginia herself had known people for years and then one day discovered she'd never really known them. And the prosecutor, that gruesome bullfrog, had never even met Caprice. How dare he pretend to feel even a shred of the sorrow that Virginia feels. She feels other things too, of course, but the sorrow is still there. The sorrow will always be there.

Clevenger says, "You could have told me what to expect."

"Could I? And what good would that have done?"

"I might have cross-examined him."

"You might have. But nothing I remember would have been useful. You're the one to come up with the questions. Hammer at the witness's weaknesses." Virginia wants to leap up and jam her arms through the bars and grip this young pup's lapels in her fists. He might even be close enough. She does not. She doesn't even move an inch, her voice level, her fingers resting lightly in her lap.

"If he had any," counters her counsel.

"Everyone does."

"Well, if you don't know what they are and neither do I, we'll have an uphill climb," he says.

"My climb might be the steeper," she says sharply, "since I'm the one who could hang."

Her counsel says, "I only ask that you be more forthcoming."

"I didn't know I wasn't."

"Miss Reeve. Please. What the witnesses say can't come as a surprise to me. So tell me the truth. You didn't get along with Caprice Collins?"

"Not when we met, no, I didn't."

"Why not?"

"This isn't relevant," she says, her irritation showing. There's nothing he can do with this information now that Bishop has already testified, so by pushing on this, Clevenger is just wasting her time. She may not have much of it to waste.

"I don't get along with lots of people," says Virginia. "I rarely kill them."

He throws up his hands. "Are you attempting humor? Do you think this is funny?"

"I am aware it is deadly serious," says Virginia.

"I don't know what I'm supposed to do."

Urgently, she says, "Fight for me."

"And how can I? When you won't even tell me the truth?"

She looks away from him, lays her fingertips on the nearest metal bar. It is cool to the touch. "I have always told you the truth."

"You have told me nothing. You have said only that the charges are bunkum. You did not kidnap Miss Collins, and you did not kill her. You say."

"Because I didn't. The kidnapping charge is merely a ruse to place the case in the Commonwealth's jurisdiction . . ."

"Yes, yes." He waves his hand. "I'm the lawyer here."

She has to bite back the response that springs unbidden to her lips. *Then act like one.*

He goes on, "But you tell me nothing about the circumstances of Miss Collins's death. If in fact she is dead."

"She is dead," says Virginia grimly.

"So was it an accident? Were you there? Did you see it?"

"I saw it," she said, which wasn't strictly true. She did not stand there and watch Caprice die. She knows there's no chance she's alive either. Death was a certainty. But

84

if she'd stayed long enough to see Caprice draw her last breath, see the last spark of life drain from her eyes, Virginia might have died too, and others with her. "Put me on the stand and I'll say so."

His eyes squint tight, and she is horrified for a moment that he might burst into tears, like a child whose favorite toy has fallen out of reach. "You know I can't do that."

"Why ever not?"

"You're not reliable. Not credible. Not to them. The prosecutor would tear you apart."

"Let him try," she said, lifting her chin.

He balls one hand into a fist, smashes it into his other palm, wraps the fist in his fingers. If another man made these same motions, she might feel threatened, but Clevenger's actions feel more like playacting. His voice is louder, though, as he tells her, "There has to be a better way."

She says, not unkindly, "I very much hope you find one."

"So you didn't cause her death, but you saw her die. Was anyone else there? Anyone else who can confirm your story?"

Virginia says, "No," but of course, she is thinking of Siobhan. Siobhan could, were circumstances different. But circumstances are what they are. No use crying over spilt milk, as the saying goes.

"You are not a foolish girl, Miss Reeve. I know you understand. Your word is all we have," he says, "and your word is no good. You cannot testify."

Some part of her wants to fight. On another day, she tells herself, she'll muster the strength to. But she is exhausted by all this. Not in a physical way — she could endure, has endured, so much more than this — but in her soul. She can just let it happen. Let her fate sweep her away like the current, the eddying motion of water in Hudson Bay that forces ships into the shrinking space between the ice and the rocks and then crushes them between. Better women than she have died on her watch. Perhaps this fate is the one she deserves. If she sits in the witness box, tells her story, she'll just be making excuses. If they don't hang her for Caprice's death, they could hang her for the others. No one's fate was all her fault, but if different decisions had been made . . . but they hadn't been. She knows this. She'll suffer.

And her lawyer, as miserable and incompetent and foolish as he is, is also right. About the testimony anyway. If he knew the whole truth — is there any chance he knows it? — he'd be even less likely to let her speak for herself. Even the truth he knows is too damning. She's an upstart girl from nowhere, an adventuress willing to lead other women into death. What a terrible person she must be. And such a person as that, she can imagine all these upstanding Bostonians thinking, must be capable of anything.

They have no idea what she's truly capable of.

CHAPTER EIGHT:
EBBA

Revere House, Boston
April 1853

Upon meeting Virginia Reeve, Ebba's first thought sang out like an unwelcome star soprano inside her head: *Just who does this girl think she is?*

When she and Althea were first invited to America to help Lady Franklin raise funds, she'd been against it. Althea had persuaded her. She'd spun a pretty picture of the two of them sipping tea and making polite but firm requests, convincing Americans to invest heavily in the next expedition going north, carving out possibilities where the Royal Navy fell short. They'd be such ideal wives, Althea said. No person with a heart could resist their appeal.

In Althea's case, of course, the appearance was reality, Ebba knew. She truly did miss James like a limb. They'd been such a lovely couple, as well matched as a pair of long-legged carriage horses, both so fair-haired and regal. When Althea plucked at the lace on her cuffs and told the Americans how she would give anything in the world to have her husband back on British soil again, her eyes brimmed with real tears. Ebba's perspective was more complicated, but the principle still applied; why not very publicly support one's husband, vanished or no? Even if — especially if — he would never return?

If the men were dead, there would be pensions. Tens of thousands of pounds would be settled on Lady Franklin, who stood to gain the most, though she needed it the least. Officers' wives like Althea and Ebba would still see thousands of pounds, funds they needed to live. Althea, of course, would far rather have her husband than the money his death would win her. Ebba had her own preference.

Indeed, there had been teas, as promised. So many teas. With Lady Franklin's puppetry behind the scenes, the two of them met potential backers in the privacy of their own homes, at clubs, in parlors, even on yachts at anchor. They went to New York, Philadelphia, Washington. They drank toasts to the missing men, shed tears when tears were called for, spoke touchingly of their unsettled, uncertain state. America might not be better than England, she had told herself, but surely it could not be worse. And dear Althea would be with her — without the commitments that usually kept her away, sealed her into her own precious, gilded bubble. So bring on the discomfort, the distance, the Americans. She was persuaded.

But the Americans were harder to convince than Althea had thought. Even in lush surroundings, Ebba had tired quickly of making the same plea to upstart ruffians who had no more sympathy or tenderness than a blank brick wall.

Then they were invited to go north themselves, and Ebba was the one who had to do the persuading. *An adventure,* she said. *We can be bold,* she said. *When will we ever have a chance like this again?* she asked, then answered it herself, *Never.* Althea protested, reluctant, but at length, she had agreed. Having come so far, why not go just a bit farther? Now they were ready to meet the leader of the expedition, whose secretary had written them to set a meeting in their hotel.

When the girl walked in, Ebba assumed she was the secretary.

Virginia Reeve was of average height with

a mass of black curls on her head, imprecisely gathered into a topknot that added several inches to her frame. Her pale-blue dress was neat and clean with a high collar and no decoration, proper and plain. Her face might have been pretty without the broad nose; her eyes were a warm, intelligent brown, drawn down a bit at the corners. She was young, thought Ebba, even for a secretary. When she introduced herself as the leader of the expedition, Ebba was absolutely certain she'd misheard.

"You mean you represent the leader of the expedition, of course?"

"No," Virginia said, making a sound that might have been a laugh.

Althea jumped in, as was her way. She was the diplomatic one, the born mother, though she had not yet been blessed with children. "You'll have to forgive my friend. Her background is very traditional. As is mine, I must confess. Indeed, before this moment, neither of us has ever heard of an expedition of this kind led by a woman. Are you very experienced?"

"Yes."

"In the Arctic?"

"Well, not precisely there, no."

Ebba said, "Then why should we trust you?"

91

Virginia's warm brown gaze, settling on Ebba, became slightly less warm. "Because if you want to look for your husbands, I'm the best chance you've got. Good luck getting any other expedition to take a chance on women. Our journey will include time aboard ship, and from what I hear, our kind aren't generally welcome there. Am I right?"

Both of the wives nodded solemnly. They knew men of the sea by long association. A sailor's superstitions were as fierce and bright as winter sun.

As Virginia went on, Ebba saw a change come over her, her gaze shifting again. This time, it burned bright. Virginia had entered the room looking like a girl of little import, but in less than a minute, she'd transformed into an assured, capable woman. Perhaps she was their true leader after all.

"I've been told to bring you along," said Virginia. "And so I will. But I've already had an unpleasant conversation on this topic today, and I feel it's important to speak plainly. I trust you'll agree."

Althea opened her mouth to protest, but she and Ebba exchanged a glance, and she shut her mouth again. *Let's hear it, then,* read Ebba in her eyes.

Virginia said, her voice clear and urgent, "This journey will be hard and unpleasant at best. If you believe you can undertake it, I trust you; I have faith that you know your own body and mind. But the Arctic does not want us there, and the men we meet won't either. So by all means, if this isn't a trip you are eager to make, do us all a favor and don't make it."

That was the moment Ebba decided she would follow Virginia Reeve anywhere.

CHAPTER NINE:
VIRGINIA

American House, Boston
April 1853

Regrets and worries swam through Virginia's mind as she walked back toward her hotel, the late afternoon light cool on her face as evening approached. The sky was clear yet the air felt heavy, as if threatening rain. She reminded herself to soak up what warmth there was while she still could. Even June in the North would be far colder. Yet today's chill seemed to settle deep into her core. Low spirits, she told herself, let it in.

Why had she agreed to take on this far-fetched, wild enterprise? She'd led countless women and men through the wilderness, yes, but that was a wilderness she knew and not women like these women. The well-off did not board wagon trains in hopes of a new, better life. They already had the life they needed. Perhaps Ebba and Althea were crafted of steel underneath, but at this first meeting, they looked like a pair of matched dolls in their fripperies, Althea the fair English rose, Ebba a porcelain-skinned brunette. An expedition like this had no need of decoration. And that awful Caprice Collins. Trouble from the first word. If she and the rich girl sniped and poked at each other even in the calm peace of an over-stuffed parlor, how fiercely would their tempers flare when things got rough?

But these three were part and parcel of the deal, and Virginia knew that if she presented an ultimatum to Lady Franklin — or to Brooks, she supposed, all she was allowed — she'd be out on her ear. Women as qualified as Virginia to lead the party were no doubt rare, but she was not irreplaceable. Caprice's family's money, on the other hand, was harder to come by. And then there were the officers' wives, younger versions of Lady Franklin herself: tied up in knots waiting for absent husbands, unable to go on without answers. What aging woman would not choose a younger version of herself to represent her on a journey she could no longer take?

When Virginia arrived back at her hotel at last, she found a parcel waiting for her, and she could barely restrain herself from grabbing it out of the desk clerk's hands. Brooks had promised her files on the other members of the party, along with the logistical arrangements, and here they were. She would not meet the other women in person before they gathered in Buffalo to board the canoes for Sault Ste. Marie. A little worry mixed in with the excitement. What if Brooks and Lady Franklin had chosen wrong? What if she was being loaded up with millstones, incompetents, charlatans? Of course they would not do so intentionally, but without the proper care, they could easily have done so by accident. It sounded like most of the other women had been found strictly by correspondence, placing discreet advertisements in frontier cities and combing local newspapers for figures of interest, and there was certainly room for error in that technique.

Virginia took the parcel to her room, opened it, and spread the contents out on the sitting room's low table.

To be contrary, she did not look through the files of the women first but the arrangements that had been made for their transport. The voyageurs who would meet them at Buffalo were led by a man named Thibodeau, and the *Doris,* the topsail schooner that would take them up the west side of Hudson Bay, was captained by a Jacob

Malcolm. There was no further information on either man, just their names, and in Thibodeau's case, not even his Christian name. Virginia had a moment of panic. Would there be more information in the files of the women she'd be leading?

She set aside the sheaf of papers in her hand and reached for the women's files, skipping the list at the front, relishing the shimmer of excitement in her veins as she plucked the first sheet from the folder and began to read.

Dove, the paper said at the top, and in reading, it became clear that this was intended to be the woman's name. There was no information on where this Dove was originally from or the life she'd lived before 1840, but in that year, she had joined the camp followers tracking the American army on the Mexican border. Her husband was a soldier. When that husband was killed in action, she married another.

Funny, thought Virginia, how decisions that must have been devastating at the time could be rendered in prose as merely factual.

The file went on to note in dry, spare terms the heroism Dove had demonstrated: initially hired as a cook, she began to nurse the wounded, even rushing onto the battlefield to retrieve injured men before their wounds bled them dry, even when gunfire still rang through the air. By whatever miracle, she'd survived and taught nurse craft to other women. Then, for whatever reason, she'd left the second husband. Of her life since then, the file gave no more detail. She sounded like a formidable creature, this Dove, thought Virginia, despite her delicate name.

There was no likeness of Dove, but a brief physical description was included: nearly six feet in height, taller than most men Virginia knew. Dark hair, dark eyes, tawny skin. Certainly, thought Virginia, she'd know Dove when she saw her. Surely not every woman would be so distinctive, but still, the descriptions would help when they met up in Buffalo.

In addition to the battlefield nurse, whose expertise would certainly come in handy, the party would also include a journalist, who would record the women's exploits, and an illustrator, who would help gather information about the landscape and flora of the Arctic wilds. These women were both residents of Massachusetts, though not Boston, and their names were Margaret and Christabel. Virginia wondered if they were durable enough for the trip. Could the same fingers that gripped a pen or sketched a scene also pull back a drawstring? Or a trigger? It would be essential for them to hunt their own food once they entered the sledge portion of the journey. There was no doubt in her mind that Dove knew how to fire a gun — her skills were probably superior to Virginia's — but the others' abilities were far less certain.

Did any of these women really know what they were getting into? Some had been recruited, others had volunteered, but most had only corresponded with Brooks by letter, a slow and imperfect method of communication. What would she do if someone decided partway through that she simply could not go forward? There had been few options for women like that along the Western route to California. Virginia had generally been able to cajole them forward or, when worse came to worst, demand that their families carry them on by whatever means necessary. There were no forts between Fort Bridger and Sutter's Fort, and only Mormons felt welcome at the new settlement, Great Salt Lake City, on the shores of the lake from which it took its name. Where they were going now, options would be even more scarce. She doubted there were many havens in the Arctic for women who did not want to be in the Arctic any longer, besides the grave.

She turned her attention back to the files. Who else would she have with her, and what, if anything, could they do?

While her name had been on the list at the front of the stack of papers, she was surprised — and perhaps a little disappointed — that her own file was one mere scrap of paper. She would have liked to know the entirety of what they knew of her. Instead, there was only the newspaper article, exactly the one she expected to see, with her name circled. Even now, she was not sure whether to be angry at that girl reporter or grateful. Could she have just retreated from the world after Ames's death? Would she have gone back to her family, reconciled with them? Perhaps. She had to pull herself back from wondering.

She flipped over the article with her name on it and read on.

Next, she read with curiosity about Irene Chartier, a woman who by all rights was more qualified for the expedition than Virginia herself: she had lived for ten years in the Canadian territories, frequently journeying into the wilds with her trapper husband, and she was familiar with the languages of several groups of Esquimaux.

Virginia wondered why the role of leader hadn't been extended to Irene. Or perhaps it had, and for whatever reason, the woman had refused? It seemed Irene could become a powerful ally — or, if she chose, an enemy.

The last file was for an Ann Montgomery, and her biography was brief: Ann lived on a farm in northern Michigan and had made quite a name for herself breeding, raising, and training sled dogs. *You don't need to know nothing else about me,* she was quoted as saying in her local newspaper. *Nothing else to know but the dogs, and they're the best dogs on the continent bar none. That, you can print.* Virginia could not mistake her importance. Some overland journeys in the Arctic used man-hauled sledges, and others used dogs, and it seemed the women's expedition would be at least partially dog-powered. They would need Ann's expertise to keep them going.

That was it. Nine women, nine files.

But then, as she flipped the pile over and looked back at the first sheet, Virginia noted something curious: the ghosts of each of their names. As if another piece of paper had been overlaid on this one, a list written on it in a firm hand, and then that piece of paper removed, leaving the hard-pressed marks of each letter behind. A faint set of impressions echoed the one in ink.

Only on the ghost list, there were ten names instead of nine, with a single line struck through the very last one.

MARGARET BRIDGES
IRENE CHARTIER
CAPRICE COLLINS
DOVE
EBBA GREEN
CHRISTABEL JONES
ANN MONTGOMERY
ALTHEA PORTER
VIRGINIA REEVE*
~~DOROTHEA ROSET~~

Immediately, Virginia stood.

This Roset woman had clearly been considered as a potential member of the expedition but had been removed from consideration. Why? Was that why Virginia was invited to bring three choices of her own — because several had been struck from the list at the last minute? Brooks had made it sound flattering, the idea that they'd left some room for her to choose her own lieutenants, but when she thought about it, that couldn't really be the reason. It had taken months to get Virginia here. They must have known that anyone she'd had experience working with would still be out in California, a continent away.

Was it a trap, this open invitation to recruit just a handful of expedition participants? Did they want her to fail so they could then add three other women to the roster? But what sense did that make? They could have already added them, presented her with a list of eleven, and been done with it.

Or had they simply found the only women they could — the handful of fierce women who didn't give a fig for society's expectations, the ones whose love of adventure outweighed their desire for safety — and come up short of what they'd hoped?

Wasting her time guessing wasn't going to get her anywhere. But she had another, better idea.

Virginia buttoned her collar all the way up, tugged on her only pair of gloves, and went downstairs.

"I'm wondering if you can help me with a particular errand," she said to the man behind the front desk.

"It would certainly be my pleasure to try."

"I'm in search of a family friend who lives nearby," she said, "though we lost touch some years ago. While I am staying here, I thought I might try to reach out."

"Sounds like a good course of action. How can I help?"

"The family name is Roset. Unusual enough, I think, in this area. Would you know any families by that name?" She knew there was only a small chance the woman was in Boston, but that was no reason not to try.

"Roset, hmm," said the clerk at the front desk, taking only a brief pause before he spoke again. "My apologies, miss. The name is not familiar to me."

More questions were already bubbling up in Virginia's mind — what should she try next? — when she heard a higher voice speaking from behind her shoulder.

"Could be that mapmaker's shop down on Harbor," piped a woman's voice.

Virginia and the man behind the desk both turned. There stood the dark-haired attendant from the ladies' ordinary, a men's wool coat, unbuttoned, pulled over her uniform. Her head was cocked with interest.

"Miss Thisbe," said the clerk sharply, "you have been repeatedly asked not to speak to the guests outside the ordinary. As a matter of fact, you should not be using this entrance."

"I'm terribly sorry, Mr. Davenport," she

said in a tone that made it clear, at least to Virginia, that she was not. "You can absolutely count on me to obey that stricture in future. However, in this case, I believe I can be of assistance to one of the hotel's treasured guests."

The man's face remained skeptical.

Moving quickly, Virginia said, "Thank you, sir. We'll be quick to take our conversation elsewhere." Then she reached out for Thisbe's elbow and guided her, unhurriedly but firmly, into the hallway where the entrance to the ordinary was located.

Thisbe's gaze was sharp and watchful, intelligence shining in her eyes. Virginia suspected the girl was probably bound for far grander things than a ladies' ordinary. If she'd been a man, she'd have had a desk at a trader's already and a far finer coat than the patched hand-me-down she currently wore.

In a weary voice, Thisbe said, "Well, that tears it. I'm not long for this position, a blind man could see."

"I didn't mean to —"

"You didn't," said the dark-haired woman, wrapping her arms around herself as if even the big coat, even indoors, wasn't enough to keep her warm. Away from the punctilious desk clerk, everything changed about her: the way she stood, breathed, spoke. "I do it to myself. I really can't help it."

"I'm sorry," Virginia said, not knowing what else to say.

"In any case. Roset. Near the wharf, on Harbor, there's a mapmaker's shop with that name. I pass it every week after the fish market. May be nothing at all, but it could be what you're looking for. All right?"

"Thank you so much," said Virginia. Upon reflection, she reached into her small purse and drew out a coin, which she extended to Thisbe as she'd seen others do it: fingers down as if pinching the metal, curled in slightly, the coin itself discreetly kept down out of the light to avoid drawing attention.

Thisbe looked down at the coin and drew back as if Virginia were trying to hand her a live scorpion.

"I didn't tell you that for a *tip,*" she fairly hissed. "I did it to help. Believe it or not, even girls who work in ordinaries don't make all their decisions based on who might cast a dirty coin into their hungry hands."

Virginia didn't want to apologize again, so instead she said, "Well, I do appreciate the information. I'll be on my way, then."

She tucked the coin back in her purse when she went. The last thing she saw before she turned away was a flash of disappointment in Thisbe's eyes. She knew what it was like, to be offended by something you saw as charity but still to need that charity and feel the lack when it was withdrawn. Perhaps she should have pressed the coin into Thisbe's hand. Insisted. But she didn't care to repeat the rejection. Besides, now that she had a mystery to solve, she'd best be on her way.

She stopped for a brief consultation with the man at the front desk again. He was more than happy to direct her to Harbor Street and more than happy to take her proffered coin without objection.

Down she went to the docks, the chill reaching deep into her bones again, as if to warn her what she was in for. But her whole body was also fairly humming with excitement. The more she learned about the other women who would be on the expedition, the more she wanted to know. What must the journalist have reported on, far and wide? How had the translator learned and used her languages? And that battlefield nurse, the one whose husbands had both fought on the Mexican front, she must have hair-raising stories to tell.

Virginia allowed herself a brief fantasy of these women's faces in the firelight, gathered on the bank of a river after a long day's canoe travel, listening with rapt attention to one another's exploits. A party like that, there'd never been its equal anywhere in the world. And she would be there, at its head. It was almost unbelievable. The potential of a thousand sunrises lived in that *almost.*

When she saw the mapmaker's shop, *Roset* in large gold letters on its black-painted sign, Virginia shook out her arms until her fingertips tingled. Then she swung open the door and walked in.

The mapmaker's shop was small and close, mostly taken up by a broad, long counter, with crammed shelves on every wall from floor to ceiling, giving the impression the walls were closing in.

Virginia had no choice but to gawp, taken aback. Most of the shelves were stuffed to bursting with maps: rolled into scrolls or bound into books, framed for hanging or folded for use. The accumulated knowledge these maps represented was truly breathtaking. Her own travels had almost entirely followed maps retained only in people's minds, communicated only in words and gestures.

One shelf stood out from all the rest. A foot from her shoulder, she could see a small collection of what appeared to be embroidered globes. The silk spheres ranged from fist-size down to not much larger than Virginia's thumbnail, all with fine, elegant stitching that picked out important geographical features on the surface of the earth. One was pockmarked with mountains. Another sported only the names of oceans and seas, white thread bright against the loveliest blue silk Virginia could remember seeing. She could not help but step closer, then closer still, trying to make out the features of the smallest one, which gleamed a rich purple under its thickly embroidered pattern of silver.

"I see you are drawn to things of beauty," said a woman's voice, with an unmistakably mournful note. "Sadly, beauty is not what interests the world."

"It interests me," said Virginia.

The shopgirl came forward, but she wasn't like any shopgirl Virginia had seen. She was older than Virginia, for one thing, not a girl at all, yet there was something very young about her. The mapmaker's daughter, Virginia assumed. Men who had the choice of who to hire in their shops hired smart men or pretty women. This woman had a long nose, close-set eyes, and frizzed hair that somehow gave the impression of being every color at once. Her clothes were somber and worn, in stark contrast to the elegance of the silk globes Virginia had been examining.

Virginia told the woman, "Your shop is lovely."

"Glad you like it," she responded, leaning her elbows against the long counter. "Wish more did."

"Business isn't good?"

"Business isn't," the woman said grimly. "My father's health keeps him from the shop, and I'm sad to say, I don't inspire confidence in the same way he always has."

"Did you make these?" Virginia gestured to the silk globes.

"I did."

"Well then. I find you delightfully inspiring."

"I suppose that's because you care more about what's between my ears than under my skirts."

Virginia laughed, a little shocked at the woman's directness but amused. "Well, yes, that's true."

"Rare's the mariner who'll come to a woman for his maps, no matter what shape they come in. And my father knows it, but he's got no sons, so it's either put me in the shop or close the shop altogether. So far, you see what wins out."

"I'll buy a map from you," Virginia said. "Maybe even several. Won't keep you afloat forever, but it's what I can do."

"Much appreciated, miss. I'm Dorothea Roset," she said, extending her hand to shake. "People here call me Doro."

Virginia shook it. "Virginia Reeve."

"Pleasure to meet you, Virginia," she said with a bright sincerity. "So what sort of map do you think you'll be needing? An expensive one, I hope."

"Well, we're headed north."

"How far north?"

"As far as it takes," Virginia said, feeling like it was a bit of a boast. "Into the Arctic."

Doro cocked her head. "Do tell! Over land or sea?"

"A bit of both. Travel by ship up the west length of Hudson Bay, then by sledge toward Victory Point."

The change in the woman's face was immediate. The light in her eyes flashed, as if someone had lit an unseen gas lamp inside the dark shop. "Fascinating! That would speed the miles . . . Where do you plan to disembark in Hudson Bay? Repulse Bay, perhaps? Or Chesterfield Inlet, perhaps, to use the river?"

Something unfurled in Virginia's chest at the words, some kind of hope, like a small flower. She had read these words before, seen them spattered across the maps, but

Brooks was the only person she'd ever heard speak them aloud. It felt like a modest miracle to hear them from another woman's lips. Everything felt infinitely more real.

"Repulse Bay," said Virginia, unable to hold back a grateful smile.

"Bold!" said Doro, slapping the counter, returning her smile. "I like it. Don't you love the place names up there? Repulse Bay, Fury Strait. The very maps tell you what you're getting yourself into. No illusions there."

"Have you been?" asked Virginia tentatively.

"Oh, me? No! But I've made rather a study of the ice. Read everything I can get my hands on. Those British sure like to write about everything they've seen. Especially if they overwinter or if they're sailing back home: nothing but time to write. But tell me, are you a captain's wife? What's the purpose of your journey?"

Virginia weighed exactly what to tell her and decided to keep it vague. "We're looking for someone."

Doro slammed her flat palm on the counter again, this time harder, and it made a noise like a shot. "You're going in search of the man who ate his boots! Franklin!"

Virginia was startled. "You know who

112

Franklin is? Is that what he's called?"

"You don't know the story?"

"I know *a* story. Not the boots part."

"This wasn't his first trip." Doro leaned forward with obvious excitement. "Went overland in 1819. Didn't go well, that journey. Took three and a half years to find their way back to civilization. Not all of them did either. Left with twenty men, came back with nine. Starved to bone. And when you haven't got anything left to eat up there, you chew leather. Like your own boots. Which Franklin did."

"Sakes alive!" exclaimed Virginia.

"Not enough alive," Doro said. "But that seems to be their pattern over there. To keep the men encouraged to go, whether or not they come back with anything useful. Anyone who makes it back gets a promotion and a prize. So others will try."

"Try and fail," Virginia muttered.

"Well, yes. It's funny, now that I think of it. Had a man come in a week or so back, asking lots of questions about what I knew of that part of the world, then asked to talk to my father."

"What happened?"

"Nothing," shrugged Doro. "My father said he couldn't get the man what he wanted. Just funny. Life is full of coincidences, I suppose."

"I suppose," echoed Virginia, who knew that there were, although in this case, what seemed like coincidence to Doro was not.

"But I've got a great map of that area. Based on Rae's overland survey. Now he's an explorer. Knows what he's doing. Read him. His work's stunning. Not the words themselves — he's an atrocious writer — but what he writes down about what he did. The amount of ground he covers. Fast as the wind. He lives on the land as he goes, keeps the party small, trades with the local Esquimaux for supplies. Hold on. I'll get it."

She lifted an invisible panel in the counter and passed Virginia on her way to a shelf.

As Doro searched, Virginia pondered. Clearly, Brooks had considered this young woman for the expedition, but he'd dismissed her. Why? What had happened during the conversation with her father? She couldn't ask, because it would seem too strange, but maybe she didn't need to. Brooks had chosen not to include Doro. That didn't mean Virginia had to make the same choice.

"Here," said Doro, fetching the map down and spreading it out. "See here, this is more detail than we've ever had north of Repulse

Bay. He trekked overland up the Melville Peninsula, north almost to Fury and Hecla, then back down and across the Simpson Peninsula too."

"What did you say his name was?"

"John Rae. Wintered up there too, without a ship, if you can believe it. First man to do so."

As she spoke, jabbing here and there with her finger, the young woman's face was aglow, her body fairly vibrating with excitement. Then she looked Virginia full in the face. "He was the first white man, so they say, to see many of these places. Do you have your heart set on being the first white woman?"

"Not exactly," said Virginia. "My patron intends that we search out Franklin first and foremost."

"Well, that's almost as good. Wouldn't mind finding him myself, were I to head up that way. Who's your patron?"

"I'm not to share the name, I'm sorry." She realized she was in danger of telling this virtual stranger everything. It was just that she could tell Doro understood, and she had not, since Ames, felt understood.

"Is he American? British? I heard there's an expedition out of New York that some merchant captain intends to run. More big ships, through Baffin Bay, but if that was where Franklin was, British would've found them by now. Your patron, does he have a better idea?"

"Well, she —"

"She!" interrupted Doro. "Dare I — is it — I won't ask, but oh. *She.*"

Virginia wanted to smile but decided to keep a straight face. "*She* wants to send a dozen women north in search of Franklin's ships."

"The *Erebus* and the *Terror.*"

"Precisely. This will be the opposite of previous expeditions in every way. Small and agile. Over land instead of sea. Instead of men, women."

"Of course! And you can go everywhere these other parties couldn't. Live off the land for longer, if you've got good hunters. That's what Rae did. You said going by schooner to Repulse Bay? Now, even in summer, that bay is full of ice, so you've got to cling close enough to the shore to avoid the ice boulders but not so close that you run aground. Shallow beds there running miles out from shore. If the big boulders are coming at you, they say, sometimes you just have to anchor to a big one and let the little ones hit you."

"I can't believe you know so much about

the Arctic. I wish I could take you with me," said Virginia.

Without missing a beat, Doro said, "Then do."

Virginia was momentarily speechless. Could it be that simple?

Doro said, "There's a prize, isn't there? For anyone who finds Franklin or evidence of him? The latest is that it's risen to twenty thousand pounds. If you could cut me in on that, it'd be more than I could make in six months at this lousy shop."

"It's not lousy," Virginia said automatically, but her mind was still spinning. Doro was practical, knowledgeable. Lady Franklin and Brooks had chosen a group of smart, skilled women, but none of them had any loyalty to Virginia in particular. Doro, unlike the others, would start out owing her something. An instant ally.

"I think I could be a real help to you besides," said Doro brightly. "I know the territory better than anyone else who hasn't been there. Probably better than some who have. I'll bring my maps, help direct the search, though of course, all the decisions will be yours."

"Won't your father object?"

"Oh, he's objected to plenty about me over the years, for all the good it's done him.

He's always jawing about closing the shop for a while, sticking to his private clients. I'll do it and see how he likes it. Is your patron giving out advance payments to smooth the way?"

"She is."

"Then I have everything I need. All that's missing is your invitation."

At that, Virginia was done fighting her instincts. She said with a smile, "Consider yourself invited."

CHAPTER TEN:
VIRGINIA

Massachusetts Superior Court, Boston
October 1854

When they all file into the courtroom to start another day of questioning, Virginia looks at the five. Like rosary beads she goes over them, one and the next and the next and so on, only without touching them. She would if she could.

Doro is all the way to the far end, closest to the center aisle, solid, strong. Her hair is styled over her missing ear, smoothed over her temples and pulled in an unusually low knot to hide the lack. It does not look fashionable, but Doro was never one for fashion. Her countenance is not as impassive as Virginia's. Worry is written into every muscle of her face.

Next to Doro sits Althea, her ringlets of shining blond hair the only aspect of her appearance unchanged by the journey. All the women are far worse for wear, but since

Althea started out the prettiest, she lost the most. While she once had the complexion of an English rose, her cheeks are now chapped and worn, making her look older than her true age. Virginia can see her gloves from here but not her boots. Inside the boots, she knows, there are not as many toes as there used to be. If Althea were the joking kind, she would laugh that at least it was easy to hide the lack. But she has always been sweetly serious, for as long as Virginia has known her, and from what Ebba said of their shared history, she was that way long before.

Poor Ebba.

Foolishly, when the police took Virginia into custody for the murder of Caprice Collins but didn't mention any of the other women who had died or disappeared on her watch, she was initially confused.

"What makes that one so special?" she asked her counsel the first time they'd met.

"I think you know," said Clevenger, the most — or possibly the only — intelligent thing he'd ever said in her presence.

Of course. Money. No one was asking about Stella, who had been only a maid. No one knew where Ann had come from, so there was no one to wonder where she went. There had not even been questions about

Elizabeth, whose fate the Collinses must certainly be curious to know. They only sought vengeance for the loss of their daughter, who Virginia had not returned to them, and it seemed they would satisfy themselves by taking anything and everything she had in compensation. Including, if they could manage it, her life.

As civilized as Americans liked to think themselves, she reflected, they were not so far from the primitive rituals of, say, old Scotland. There, a village's sin eater would consume bread and wine from the chest of a dead person to absorb and carry away that person's sin. That way, the dead could ascend unencumbered to heaven. This, in Virginia's opinion, is what the Collinses are doing to her: using her to erase Caprice's mistakes. Sin eaters, like Virginia, were outcasts. And the prison's bread can't be much worse than an ancient Scottish crust. She's only missing the wine.

The prosecutor wakes her from her reverie by booming, in his customary imperious tone, "The prosecution calls to the stand Mr. Tiberius Collins."

Caprice's father is a smaller man than Virginia thought she recalled from the one time they met, but every inch of him looks the born aristocrat, slim-hipped and perfectly fitted in a fabric that even Virginia can tell is a fine weave of rare quality. His hair is paler than his daughter's, his complexion a touch darker, though still no darker than an egg's shell. He does not have her lovely gray-green eyes, which must have come from her mother's side. His eyes are dark-blue marbles in his patrician face. His hands are soft.

He takes the witness stand with a rough energy; even the way he stands is commanding. Virginia does not want to hear what he has to say, but she will have no choice but to listen. *Penance,* she thinks again. Her sentence has already begun. The judge and jury are mere formality.

"Sir," begins the prosecutor, "I am so sorry for your loss."

"Thank you," says Mr. Collins stiffly. "You are kind to say so. My wife and I are grateful for the support we've received from the community."

"In the wake of this disaster."

"Yes."

"Could you tell us about Caprice?"

"I could tell you everything."

"Yes." The prosecutor allows himself a mirthless chuckle. "Of course. Let me be more specific. Could you tell us about her personality? How she spent her time?"

"She was an excellent daughter. My wife did a superb job raising her."

He leans forward, indicating someone in front of him in the crowd, and Virginia realizes it must be the wife he's mentioned. Without moving her head too far — she doesn't want to be seen gawking — she manages to catch a glimpse of the woman.

With the angle, it's hard to make out the features of her face, which she has raised a handkerchief to partially cover, but her jewels are plainly visible. She wears a spectacular necklace of gleaming pearls — three strands, if Virginia's not mistaken — interrupted with inky jet beads, perfect spheres. Virginia is momentarily distracted, wondering how many pounds of pemmican one could trade for a necklace like that, but she forces her attention back to the witness.

"She was a gem," Mr. Collins concludes, "and she never gave us even the slightest cause to be ashamed of her."

"Some would say that she was unconventional," the prosecutor says, his tone a bit more critical. "She wasn't married, despite her age, and she had some . . . unusual hobbies. Yet this didn't change your good opinion?"

The fact that Caprice's father is not charging out of his seat, shouting at the prosecutor for impugning his daughter's legacy, is the tell. Virginia sees it all clearly. They have planned this, rehearsed it, down to the gnat's eyelash. The prosecutor will air all Caprice's dirty laundry so her father doesn't have to, and the old man will claim he never had any second thoughts about his daughter's reputation. Even though those are all lies. Virginia knows how Caprice's father felt about her. She heard it from Caprice herself.

"My good opinion of her was unblemished. Unusual hobbies did not make her less of a sterling daughter, a young woman of whom I am — was — utterly proud."

The prosecutor presses. "Even though she hadn't done what you would expect a daughter to do by her age?"

"She was young yet. So young. And she would have — she would have settled down and gotten married. She would have been a wonderful wife, a wonderful mother. I would have liked to have seen that. But her whole future was stolen away by that woman."

His trembling finger points at Virginia, and even though part of her wants to roll her eyes at the cheap theatricality, there is also something terrifying in that accusing finger. She feels like a Salem witch on trial.

124

Those women were innocent too, she recalls, for all the good their innocence did them.

Mr. Collins is saying, "My daughter never would have gone with this stranger willingly. Someone without pedigree, without reputation? Never."

"How do you think she did it?" asks the prosecutor, sounding more than mildly curious.

"God only knows," the witness answers darkly. "There's nothing to which people like this won't stoop. Perhaps she had some associates threaten Caprice? Threaten us, her family? Caprice would have done anything to keep us safe. I think that may be why she went."

Virginia wants to leap up and shout, *Lies, lies, all lies.* He is simply fabricating stories to make what has happened make sense, even though it never will. She can't help but wonder whether he believes any of this, but on the other hand, does it matter? What matters is what the jury believes.

"To what end?" asks the prosecutor. "Why would the defendant want to spirit Caprice north?"

"For one thing, Caprice was an excellent climber, proven to be able to withstand hardship, so any party of adventuresome women would be incomplete without her. An intelligent organizer would put her at the head, in fact. But I think they were using her just to get to our money. A great deal was taken from our accounts; we believe a male associate of the defendant impersonated me to make those withdrawals."

"Wouldn't they have spent all the money on this expedition?"

"What expedition?" guffaws Mr. Collins. "I'm not convinced there ever even was a party to the north."

The prosecutor speaks Virginia's thoughts when he says, "There will be witnesses who say so."

"But how are we to know whether they can be believed?" Mr. Collins takes his time, letting his words sink in. "Unless you know where someone comes from, their family, how can you know whether to trust them? I don't know these people. I don't know what their word is worth."

"If anything," adds the prosecutor helpfully.

Judge Miller says simply, "Counsel." His voice is perfectly steady, but it might as well be a growl; the rebuke is clear.

"Go on, please, Mr. Collins," the prosecutor says, signaling that the judge's message, however subtle, has been received.

"If there was . . ." begins Mr. Collins but trails off, reconsiders. "But no. No journey of hers would have ended this way. It wouldn't. My daughter was headstrong, but she was a survivor."

A loud sob erupts from the gallery. Mrs. Collins, no doubt, with her kerchief and her gems. The silence after the sob hangs in the air for a moment. No one calls attention to it. The sound does not repeat.

Mr. Collins goes on, his tone forceful, determined. "No matter who else didn't make it back, Caprice should have. Caprice should have survived."

So he will simply lie, Virginia realizes. That is the sum total of his strategy. He knew it all, but because he doesn't like how it ended, he'll pretend he wasn't part of it the whole time. He'll pretend the money was stolen, not given. He'll pretend Caprice was kidnapped, not sent. And if her own counsel will not protest — why doesn't he protest? — there is nothing, nothing Virginia can do. Not until the Collins family decides that she has suffered enough.

And she reminds herself that yes, perhaps it's right that she suffers. This was the decision she made — they made — to keep this secret, no matter the consequences. So she bears it, her face a mask, her heart thumping inside a chest that might as well be made of stone. She feels like stone most days anyway.

After Tiberius Collins testifies and it is time for her to go back to her cell, this time, she does not look at the five women in the front row. She can think only of those missing. They should extend to the right and the left. They should take up an entire row. If the women of the expedition have to be here at all, watching her fight for her life — or refuse to fight — they should all be here together. Ann with her gruff focus, Dove with her arrogant swagger, Elizabeth with her ever-watchful eye. Yes, even Caprice with her bluster and that nasty laugh she sometimes had, the one Margaret once likened to hot vinegar. They should all, one way or the other, be together.

As she shuffles back from her wooden cage in the court to her iron-and-granite cage in the jailhouse, the one who consumes her thoughts is Siobhan. Siobhan, with her smattering of freckles like tiny, glowing suns. Siobhan, with her capable hands. Siobhan, one of the only women on earth who could stand up in front of this room and swear to the absolute, absolving truth: she saw exactly what happened between

Caprice Collins and Virginia Reeve out there on the ice northwest of Repulse Bay. Siobhan, who had cried with her, laughed with her, starved with her as the sunlit nights gave way to colder, dimmer days and the light itself waned into nothingness.

Siobhan, who is not here.

CHAPTER ELEVEN:
SIOBHAN

Harborside, Boston
April 1853

The classmates spilled out of the front door of the tavern and into the street, raucous and wild. They were drunk enough not to notice that one of their number, the stout young one they knew as Perry — Christian name Sean, not that they used Christian names — was not nearly as drunk as the rest. And Perry was an excellent actor, pretending to be woozy, shouting along with the crass drinking songs, letting out a well-timed belch.

She'd honed her craft well. There was too much at stake if she didn't.

The young men at the front of the pack straightened themselves up, dusted themselves off, laughing. Warren, who'd gotten them ejected from the tavern, called back to the rest, "Their loss! Shall we progress to the Green Dragon?"

"Long way up to Union."

"But the barmaid there's sweet on me . . . two ales for the price of one." Warren held up two fingers to illustrate, squinting to be sure of his count. Without asking for confirmation, he proceeded, though the young men toward the back of the pack were still milling. The group began to stretch out until they were only loosely a group, flirting with the edge of entropy.

The one they called Perry dragged her feet. She'd taken a risk joining them in the first place. It was time to end the ruse for the night, get home to her parents and Sean, who at this very moment inhabited the role of Siobhan in the way she inhabited Sean's role. They shared a fear of discovery for each other as much as themselves, their twin spirits fused in a way no one who was not a twin would ever understand. She had to keep herself safe, undiscovered, for both their sakes.

She had lingered so long that she was the last one standing in front of the tavern, one fellow lingerer beside her, and she'd come to his notice.

"Perry!" shouted Bergin, clapping her on the back. "One more, y'think?"

Siobhan Perry was still forming her answer when the shape of a dark-haired young lady, clearly unaccompanied, came toward them in the dark. Siobhan felt a knot gather in her stomach.

Her fear was justified when Bergin, drunk, slurred, "Miss! You lost? Lemme help you!"

He lunged for the unknown young lady, who twisted away in surprise. She managed to evade his grasp, but her sudden movement took her over a loose stone, and she fell, tilting, plunging.

She hit the street and cried in pain.

"Lemme help you!" said Bergin again, but his words were slurred into a heavy burr, and the leer on his face suggested he had more than one type of help in mind.

"No," said the young lady from the ground, her voice clear and firm. The dark curls in her topknot were dislodged, one tumbling down along the length of her face, but she did not lift a hand to fix it.

"But you're so lovely! I jus' wanted to tell you. Nothin' wrong with admirin' a fine woman, is there?"

"Sir, leave me alone," said the young lady crisply, struggling to get back up. She was moving her ankle with care — it had likely been twisted in the fall — and when she found it would not bear her weight, her anger was undercut by her low moan of pain.

Siobhan could not stay back any longer. Keeping her voice in its lower register, the voice she thought of as Sean's, she said, "The lady said to leave her alone, Bergin."

She knelt next to the dark-haired woman and laid a hand on her elbow. The young lady clearly wasn't a doxy or a shipyard slattern; she must have gotten lost after visiting one of the shops in the more reputable section of the docks just to the south. Siobhan made her grip gentle but firm. She didn't want to scare the young lady any more than she'd already been scared, but she didn't want Bergin to make the situation worse either, so she had to lay claim in some way, as a man would.

"Begging your pardon, miss," she said in Sean's voice. "I'm a medical student at Harvard College. If you'll agree, I could take a look at that ankle, make sure it's not seriously injured."

Before she could answer, Bergin was squatting next to her, so close she could smell his ale-laden breath. "Now, now, Perry, I'll handle this. Miss, ignore 'im. I'm the man you want. I've looked at more women's ankles than I can count."

"It's true you can't count that well," muttered his classmate. "I don't think she's looking for your kind of attention."

"Women love my attention! I ain't had no complaints."

The young lady looked back and forth between their two faces. Siobhan kept up the pressure on her elbow, steady but light, willing her to make the right choice.

Bergin butted in again, saying, "Don't let this one fool you. He's a lady-killer for the ages. Just wants his own private viewing."

Raising her chin, the curly-haired young woman said defiantly, "No one views anything I don't want them to. Not unless they want to lose an eye. Or both eyes."

"Ho-oh!" said Bergin, raising his hands and backing away. "That kind of woman we have here, then? I thought she was a lady!"

"She's a patient," said Siobhan in Sean's voice, "and it sounds like if she doesn't like you, you'll be one too. How about you catch up to the rest? I'm going home from here."

"Suit yourself," Bergin said with something bordering on a sneer, and then he was gone.

When it was just the two of them, the young lady said, "Thank you."

Siobhan took the young lady's ankle in both hands. "I apologize for Bergin. He's an oaf."

"I've heard worse. You don't need to apologize for your friend anyway."

"Oh, he's not my friend, I assure you. A classmate."

"At the college?"

"Yes. I endure sitting next to him and his like in lectures, but I assure you, my attention is on our professors. Let me just take a quick look at this ankle. How much does it hurt?"

"Only some. Feeling a bit better already."

She turned the ankle gently, one way and then the other. Siobhan could feel the young woman studying her, probably seeing what everyone saw: a solid-bodied young man, clean-shaven, with graceful, strong hands.

"Perry, did he say your name was?"

"Yes. Sean Perry."

"I'm Virginia Reeve."

"Pleasure to meet you, Miss Reeve. Nothing broken, I'm pleased to say. May I help you up?"

They gripped each other's hands — Siobhan was so used to planting her feet wide as a man's, she didn't have to think about it — and then they were standing next to each other. They were around the same height, Siobhan larger and heavier, a slightness to the young lady that went beyond how much space her body took up. Almost as if she wanted to take up even less space than she did, though that might have had something to do with the darkness around them, the looming atmosphere of the docks, her obvious suspicion.

"May I walk you to your residence?" asked Siobhan, forcing gallantry.

But this Virginia Reeve's eyes were locked on her, raking over her chin, her throat, and back to the hand she held. And Siobhan's heart began to hammer. Did she know?

"You're . . ." began Virginia.

In fear, Siobhan interrupted, words spilling carelessly from her lips. "The greatest healer it's ever been your good fortune to meet? I know! Isn't that a piece of good fortune? For you, I mean. In your time of need." Even as she heard herself stumble over her words, she knew the blustery confidence didn't sit well on her, but she did not know what else to do. Run? She'd given the young woman her name — Sean's name — but she wasn't a threat, was she?

Virginia Reeve took a step back, considered her words, looked around to see if anyone else was listening. They were alone. She said, with obvious care, "I believe you and I have a great deal in common."

With equal care, Siobhan framed her response. "What makes you say that?"

"Oh, nothing in particular. At first glance, I'd say you seem like . . . a very kind young man. But the journey I'm about to go on, unfortunately, no men are allowed."

"Indeed?" she ventured, careful but curious. "What kind of enterprise?"

"An expedition to the frozen north."

"You don't say." Narrowed eyes, a thoughtful pause. "How interesting."

"An expedition of women."

Careful now. "As you said, I would not be allowed."

"Someone very much like you would be. Someone with a sharp eye, medical training, the ability to adapt. If you happened to know a young woman with your skills, she would be most welcome."

"Women are not permitted to develop skills like mine."

"That is a shame. One could be excused for arguing that equal potential for knowledge exists in both sexes," Virginia said.

"I have no female friend as you suggest." The very idea of such an expedition was outrageous. And Siobhan wanted desperately to be a part of it. It would mean giving up her lectures for the rest of the semester, but that was no great loss; only her apprenticeship remained after this, and if she were paired with an eagle-eyed doctor who saw through her guise, she would lose everything.

Could she go? Sean would encourage her, of course, and their parents had already shown themselves capable of supporting their children even in the wildest pursuits.

Virginia was watching her, waiting, her face open and trusting.

Siobhan took the leap. "I do, as it happens, have a sister."

Virginia's eyes instantly brightened. "Do you indeed."

"And this sister . . . I have taught her everything I know. I dare say she would do as well as I on such a trip. Perhaps I could extend your invitation to her."

"I would very much appreciate you doing so."

"Her name is Siobhan."

"It would be a pleasure to make Siobhan's acquaintance," said Virginia.

Their eyes met.

Perry, whether she was Sean or Siobhan or neither or both, could not help but smile.

CHAPTER TWELVE:
VIRGINIA

American House, Boston
April 1853

When Virginia allowed herself to think of the Very Bad Thing, which was not often, she tried to only think of the good that came from it. She'd discovered her faith, for one thing, which was her rock, her guiding light. She would not trade that faith for anything. From that, she learned that even in the midst of the worst luck, a flower of good luck can bloom. In those dark days, she learned to be tenacious, to never give up hope. She had seen the hopeless waste away. But mostly she valued the Very Bad Thing because she knew no matter what else might happen to her in all her life, nothing else could ever be that bad.

In the safety of her rooms at American House, as she tested her sore ankle to be sure it had healed from the incident at the docks where she'd met Siobhan, the dark memory flitted across her mind like a black stallion's shadow. She reminded herself that she would not have the skills to carry off this expedition without it. Her physical strength and endurance would be tested once they sailed north — the Very Bad Thing had honed those too — but it was her sense of danger, her instinct for who and who not to trust, that snapped into sharp focus in those dark days she tried hard not to remember.

It was that instinct that had led her to trust Doro and Siobhan and invite them along on the journey. And last night, in the ladies' ordinary, she'd asked Thisbe to join the expedition as well. She seemed intelligent and bull-headed, both attributes that would serve her well on a journey. Brooks had given Virginia only days to secure three dauntless women, and she'd done it. She could not help but feel a swell of pride at that. It augured well for the journey.

The same instinct that helped her recognize Siobhan's feminine soul under her masculine trappings told her that Brooks was not entirely trustworthy. So when he appeared at her door unexpectedly, two days after her visit to the docks, she was ready for him.

Brooks had told her to expect him on

Wednesday, and it was only Monday, but she was still ready. Bubbling with anticipation in fact. She was sure he hadn't expected her to find three ideal recruits in such a short time. For once, she felt like she had the upper hand.

"Yes?" she said, stalling in the doorway, trying to force the discomfort on him that he'd clearly intended to make her feel.

"A lovely day to you too, Miss Reeve," he said with a glimmer of sass and stepped inside uninvited.

A woman from society would've pretended to succumb to the vapors at that, but he knew she was no such woman. She supposed that was the point. Mixing with higher society kept reminding her of her shortcomings. Once they went north, she told herself, that would change. In the wilds, she'd be the one who knew what to do.

Once he was in, she offered him tea, which he declined with a wave of his hand.

She began brightly, "I'm so glad you've come early, Brooks. I have news."

"I have news as well."

"I assumed so," she said. "Since you stand here. But mine first."

He raised an eyebrow and said nothing.

She plunged ahead. "You asked me to

secure three resources. I have done so. Their names are Siobhan Perry, Thisbe Westphal, and Dorothea Roset."

He must have been a superb player of card games; his visage remained pleasantly blank through all three names, without even a flicker of recognition at the third. She could not help a twinge of disappointment.

"Are you quite finished?" he asked.

"I thought you'd be glad."

"Gladness is a waste of time," he said dryly. "I came to inform you that circumstances have necessitated a change in the roster."

She reviewed the roster in her mind, silently, quickly. She already had a way of remembering all twelve: a journalist, an illustrator, a translator, and a mountaineer; one woman who knew dogs and one who knew maps; two English ladies, two medics, Thisbe from the ordinary, and herself. Had someone gotten cold feet? Who? Hope surged up in her heart that Caprice Collins had decided to stay home after all. Perhaps the tidings that Brooks bore so gravely would be, for Virginia herself, good news.

Brooks said, "One more passenger will be coming with you. Her name is Stella Howe. She will meet you with the others in Buffalo, New York."

"So our party will number thirteen?" That was bad luck, that number; she didn't have to be a sailor to know it.

"No."

"No? But that's — what am I supposed to do? I have twelve already."

As if he were speaking to a simpleton, Brooks stretched out his words, spacing them like posts in a fence. "It seems, Miss Reeve, that you will need to release one woman from the expedition."

"*Release* one? They're not passenger pigeons, Brooks."

"Tell one she's not coming," he said bluntly. "Any one you like."

"Caprice, then."

"Any one of *yours*. The three you chose. Now it's two."

A quarter of an hour before, she'd been thrilled with herself for quickly securing her recruits, and now, she wished she hadn't. If she'd only . . . but she knew the uselessness of regrets.

And just like that, she was already weighing the pros and cons of each of her three precious recruits. Who had the most essential skills? Not just who did she want to have along, but who did she need? Doro for her maps and her expertise in the ice, second to none. Siobhan was not the only one on the roster with medical knowledge, which made her slightly less valuable, but Virginia knew all the things that went wrong on a trail. And she was not being asked to strike two, only one.

And there was her answer, clear and plain: Thisbe would remain behind. There was no real alternative. Truth be told, the woman was such a wild card, the expedition might be better off without her. But she dreaded imparting the news.

"All right, then. I'll find time to break the news to her before Saturday." That was the time frame he'd given her for leaving. Saturday they would leave on the train for Buffalo; some of the women were already there in New York, and the rest were on their way. Her mind was already rushing forward into the logistics of their gathering, the inn where they'd stay, the provisions that had to be transferred, when she heard him speak.

"Make it Tuesday," he said.

"Tuesday? That's tomorrow."

"Yes."

"Why do I need to tell her Tuesday?"

"Because you leave Wednesday."

"Do I?" she challenged.

"That's correct," he answered, his voice cool.

Cool as a desert at midnight, she thought, one of Ames's favorite phrases. She noticed the words Brooks spoke were a response, not an apology.

Barely were the words out of his mouth when her mind was working again. How hard could she push back? What response was most likely to get her what she wanted? That was when she realized she didn't really need more time. More time wouldn't help and could possibly even hurt. They should really be on their way. Which was probably why the timetable had been moved up, but damn it all, why could the man not just say so? He seemed to have a deep, pronounced aversion to explanations.

So this time, she would not ask for one.

Back in Illinois, before her family set out West, she'd gone to have her fortune told by a spiritualist at a county fair. Whenever Virginia tried to ask her a direct question — *Will I find love? Will I die young?* — the woman had hemmed and hawed and danced aside. *The signs are uncertain, young one.* Brooks was like that. Or was he more like the wild horse she'd watched Ames try to break back in Laredo? No matter what angle Ames had chosen to approach, the horse seemed to anticipate him and sidestep, just far enough, with a contrary grace.

145

Whether he was a horse, a spiritualist, or some combination thereof, Virginia knew what Brooks really was: a pain in the ass.

But she'd be shut of him as soon as the expedition began. Which, according to what he'd just told her, was only two days away.

Keeping her manner calm so as not to show how much he'd rattled her, Virginia said coolly, "Well, I suppose I'd best prepare, then."

Not to be outdone, the man answered, "However much preparation you undertake, Miss Reeve, I doubt you will ever truly be prepared."

She gave no answer, but as she shut the door behind him, Virginia sighed. She did not trust the man, nor did she ever want to see him again, but in this, his words had the ring of truth.

She would never really be ready for this challenge.

She was going anyway.

CHAPTER THIRTEEN: VIRGINIA

Massachusetts Superior Court, Boston
October 1854

The murmurs in the courtroom are rampant today, rapid, rippling currents that remind Virginia of the spot where the Laramie River meets the North Platte River, just beyond Fort Laramie. The rivers in Wyoming are well-known for their swiftness. So, too, the whispers of gossip in a Boston court. Virginia can't make out most of the words, but she hears something that sounds like *What's next,* and after that, she just hears those words over and over again from a dozen mouths, two dozen, the whole vast room. *What's next. What's next? What's next.*

In a swirl of black robes and seeming indifference, Judge Miller finally arrives — probably having kept them waiting on purpose, she decides, not feeling generous of spirit this morning — and nods to the bailiff to start the proceedings. The bailiff

147

nods in turn to the prosecutor.

The prosecutor, with his usual flair for the theatrical, booms, "The prosecution calls Thisbe Quinlan to the stand."

Virginia gives an inner groan. She should have expected this. On some level, she did expect it, she realizes. Everything comes back to haunt her eventually, it seems. Today, it feels like the entire world is peopled only with ghosts, that all those who have ever walked the earth are still here, and the dead outnumber the living by multitudes.

If this is the worst it gets, perhaps there is hope for her. She never harmed Thisbe, not really. She only withdrew something that, it turned out, was not hers to give. Was it such a sin? When the real reckoning comes for her in heaven, she's confident that this sin isn't one she'll be called to account for. Then again, her reckoning on earth seems to be much more immediate. That one worries her.

Thisbe looks smart, with a new hat undoubtedly purchased for this occasion. She has a distinct air of self-satisfaction. Her cheeks are rounder, her waist thicker, since Virginia last saw her in the ordinary. The change looks well on her. Her hair is pinned up in an intricate system of braids. Thisbe has taken her time today preparing to be looked at. Hand flat on the Bible, she swears her oath with her chin, indeed her whole head, held regally high. She is not entirely the same creature Virginia once knew, she decides, nor is she entirely different.

The prosecutor says, "Thank you for joining us to give testimony today, Miss . . . Quinlan, is it?"

"Mrs. Quinlan," she says. "I was joined in marriage only last month."

"Congratulations to you."

"Thank you. I am quite a fortunate woman, in this and many ways."

Thisbe's name was not Quinlan when they met, Virginia remembers now. Funny how life has gone on in their absence. The world did not screech to a halt when they left Boston for Buffalo on the way to Sault Ste. Marie, nor when they set sail on the *Doris,* nor when they leaned into the killing Arctic wind in the vast, unknown expanse. It merely continues wheeling now that they are back. Babies were born, people grew and changed, others died, young or old. In the wheeling of the world, Thisbe got married, and this is just another fact.

"And can you tell us how you know the defendant, Virginia Reeve?"

"I can tell you that woman is a charlatan

and a liar," she says, her eyes burning with righteous fury.

Though she has not exactly answered his question, the prosecutor urges her on with great relish. "Can you tell us more about why you say that?"

Thisbe says, "She made me certain promises. Which she did not keep."

"Promises such as?"

"She invited me to go on this little excursion of hers. This trip to the Arctic, all peopled with women, as if women were not too delicate for such a risky undertaking."

Even without looking, Virginia can feel the five survivors bristle, and her heart is bathed in warm love for them. Her affection for them helps her deal with her anger at the liar before her. Thisbe is here to destroy her, yes, but she will not succeed. She cares far more about what the five think of her than what Thisbe thinks, though she cautions herself against hubris. Whether she wants to hear what Thisbe will say does not matter. The jury will listen, is listening. She does not let herself glance over at those faces. She knows what she'll see.

The prosecutor asks, "She invited you?" His questions flow easily, gently. No doubt they have rehearsed.

"She said she did. I told her I would,

150

though I wasn't ever sure I was going to. Against my better judgment, I thought I'd go at the appointed day and time, you know, to see whether there was anything to it. Perhaps it was a fleecing, and if so, I wanted to warn other women against it. Against her. She can be quite persuasive, you know."

"Can she?" laughs the prosecutor.

Virginia sees a cloud cross Thisbe's brow, a grim set to her mouth under her smartly styled hair. Conflicted, Virginia silently cheers the prosecution's witness on. Of course, Thisbe doesn't want to be made to look foolish. If the lawyer wants her cooperation, he needs to treat her with respect. Then again, how much more cooperation does he need? She has already come here and testified to the offer Virginia made her. An offer made, then rescinded. It doesn't matter that the offer was made in good faith, nor does it matter that Virginia was forced against her will to rescind it. Thisbe is here to make Virginia seem like a liar. In that, Virginia suspects, she will succeed.

Judge Miller, one hand casually extended toward the prosecutor, breaks in. "Excuse me. That was, you might notice, a question. Is it a question you expect the witness to answer?"

"No, no," the prosecutor hastens to add.

"Let me be clearer, please."

"Please."

Virginia looks at the judge with a smidge more respect than before. Is he . . . trying to be fair? That would be a pleasant development, though she doesn't trust it. More likely he just likes to needle attorneys who appear before him no matter which side they're on. Impartiality doesn't require the absence of mistreatment, only the application of equal mistreatment all around.

"Here is the question, Miss — Mrs. — Quinlan," the prosecutor says, visibly working to regain his composure. "So this Virginia Reeve persuaded you to join her so-called expedition, but at the last minute, you changed your mind?"

"I did not. Not every woman is a vapid flibbertigibbet who changes her mind, sir." She is bristling now, giving the prosecutor the full force of her glare, and Virginia knows this is not in the script. If Virginia dared, she would look at the jury to guess if they see what she sees. She does not dare.

"I see. You did not change your mind. But you did not go on the expedition. Could you explain to us what happened?"

"Yes." She nods and gazes around the room slowly, establishing control. "Only the day after she invited me on this expedition

— now a fool's errand, as even a blind man could see — Virginia Reeve told me there was no longer room for me and I was not welcome to participate."

"No reason given?"

"None."

"And what do you think her reason was?"

"Cruelty doesn't need a reason," snaps Thisbe. "A woman who has no respect for rules, for promises, is no true woman. She is some other kind of creature."

"What do you think would have happened had you gone?" A foolish question on the face of it but as clear to Virginia as an alarm bell. Thisbe went off script, but now the lawyer is wrenching her back on track, which means they have planned her next answer.

Thisbe says, "I might have died, too, like half her expedition."

The courtroom erupts, and the judge bangs his gavel. If their voices were the clashing nexus of two rivers before, now they are a thundering waterfall.

This is what Thisbe's really here for, thinks Virginia. To say what the prosecution wants said. She's doing a bang-up job, it seems. Another hand to steady the coffin. To drive the nail.

After he gets the room halfway hushed

again, the judge points his gavel at Thisbe and says, "Mrs. Quinlan, let's keep your answers to the scope of what you know."

"But I do know it, sir!" she protests, eyes blazing again. "This woman, the defendant, told me she was leading a group of twelve women into the North to search for Franklin. Here are six, including herself. Where are the other six? Have you thought to ask her?"

The courtroom roils again; the gavel bangs again. The judge says, "Let me remind the witness that she is here to answer questions, not ask them. Is that clear to you, Mrs. Quinlan?"

"Yes."

Judge Miller aims his gavel at the jury, lowers his brow, and intones in a serious voice, "The jury will disregard Mrs. Quinlan's claims that are outside her experience."

But who can disregard something so salacious? Virginia is only on trial for one murder, but one is enough. Caprice will stand in for all the others. Caprice is the one who matters. She would be thrilled by that, Virginia thinks, if there were any way for her to know it. Caprice always did believe in her own importance the way other people believed in God.

Thisbe should be grateful she did not go. Thisbe looks healthy and happy, Thisbe is married, Thisbe has not lost toes or ears or her whole damn life the way other women did. The way Caprice did. *Bugger Caprice,* thinks Virginia, allowing her anger to express itself in profanity. She'd gotten out of the habit. Ames would disapprove of her relapse.

She makes herself focus. Sucks in air through her nostrils and forces it out through her mouth. In the Arctic, she learned to breathe differently. It took her months to get back to the normal way. But at least in this respect, she thinks, normal was a possibility.

She looks at Thisbe. She breathes. *Be like a stone,* she tells herself. Like a stone, she endures.

The prosecutor fingers his chin and tilts his head as if considering, though of course he has planned what to say.

"Thank you for your honest testimony today, Mrs. Quinlan. The court is most appreciative."

She nods, sober, with only a touch of the preening attitude Virginia remembers from her days in the ladies' ordinary. Virginia lets herself wonder who Mr. Quinlan is, how Thisbe met him, how their love unfolded, if it was indeed love. *Why not speculate idly about the affairs of others?* she thinks. She needs something to occupy her thoughts besides her own impending death.

"One final question," says the prosecutor, and something about the way he says it makes Virginia think that this bit, perhaps, might not be planned.

Thisbe says, her voice just a little too loud in the quieted room, "I'm an open book."

"Very well. If you could say one thing to Miss Reeve now, what would it be?"

"But I wouldn't be confined to one thing, sir."

"Pretend you were."

"But she's sitting right there. I can say what I like."

"Fine," he says fussily. To Virginia, it seems like he's regretting the decision to ask. "Say what you like, then."

"You did me wrong, Miss Reeve," says Thisbe, but even by the end of the short sentence, her voice seems to lose its resolve.

Virginia can't respond to her, makes no motion, but the longing is strong; she wants to hold Thisbe and stroke her hair. Even though the woman has damaged her standing with the jury, even with no real information, Virginia still wants to comfort her. As many bad decisions as she has made, as many times as she has forced herself to choose practicality over sentiment, there is something in her that will never be able to ignore someone else's suffering.

"I wanted to go," Thisbe says, this time more mournfully, softly. She is the first of the witnesses to look Virginia in the eye, and what Virginia sees is unbridled sadness. "I wanted to go."

CHAPTER FOURTEEN: VIRGINIA

Charles Street Jail, Boston
October 1854

Hours after Thisbe's testimony, once she finally finds a fitful sleep in the dark, uneasy silence of the jail, Virginia dreams of Ames. It's the first time in a long time that she's done so. On the expedition itself, she thought of him often, wondering what he might think of her adventures, but he'd been absent from her dreams. It is only now that she is back in relative safety — though she is not safe, not by a long shot — that his face and voice come to her.

The dream is a confusing, erratic mishmash of reality and imagination, though no worse than a full dose of reality would be. Dreaming what actually happened would be enough of a nightmare. Her mind can think of no punishment greater, no invented guilt more terrifying than his actual death, for which she blames herself just as much

158

as she blames herself for what happened to Caprice.

Would either of them still be alive if they'd never known her? It had been Ames's choice to reach out to her in 1850 with his offer. After she broke with her family and they put about the lie that she'd eloped with a Roman Catholic of whom they did not approve, Ames was her only friend, but more than that, he was her partner. She admired him for so much: his intelligence, his grit, his absolute fidelity. He was, pure and simple, a good man.

If Ames had turned his back on her in the beginning, Virginia thinks as she lies on her prison cot, his life would likely not have been so different. He'd already been a guide before they met. Without her help, he still could have led hundreds of people to California in safety, even though they'd been a great team together, even though she was the one who made the women comfortable and soothed the children and animals and even once, memorably, talked the gun out of an irate rancher's hand. Ames perhaps would not have had quite as much success without her, it was true, but she knew him well enough to know how outstandingly capable he'd been. Even without Virginia, Ames would have succeeded.

But at the end, his last decision, just six months ago, she could have changed that one if she'd tried.

He'd put sentiment first. And she had let him.

Now when she considers the pattern — what happened to Ames and what happened to Caprice — she wonders if the world might be better off without her. If this knot of powerful people have their way, that is exactly what will happen. She will be hanged by the neck until her spirit, her soul, is no longer in this world.

She could fight, but why? If the Collins family wants her dead as a punishment for Caprice's death, and they have enough money to hire this dragon of a prosecutor in front of this snide judge who has probably dined at their house and raised a glass at their parties, what shape would fighting even take?

In the dream, Ames stands on a path through the hills, smiling. No one is following; they're headed northeast, back toward Fort Bridger. It's just the two of them, scouting a side trail that has been pitched to them as a potential shortcut, a word that still sends shivers down Virginia's spine. They can take the usual, southerly path, which is wide and broad, and they know

160

what will happen if they do: they will walk through the front gate of Fort Bridger exactly seven days from now. But Ames's wife, Gloria, will only be at the fort for five more days; she visits at set times whether or not Ames can be there, as it's never possible to know exactly when he will arrive and depart.

Ames points toward the northerly path, which wends higher into the mountains, and says, *Let's try it.*

Are you sure this is wise?

Is wisdom the only force that guides our steps? he says, merrily challenging, and his grin widens.

We might still not make it before she leaves, she tells him. She has to be the voice of reason if he won't.

Then we better hurry, he says, turning his back on her and setting off at a run. *Come on!*

He makes a game of it. She plays. Virginia hikes her pack up higher and chases after him, only a few steps behind.

Faster, slowpoke, he calls, accelerating.

After a few minutes at this clip, as the climb grows steeper, they're both breathing hard. She thinks of calling out to him, thinks of asking him to pause for a moment so she can catch her breath. But she is stubborn and doesn't want him to think she's not up to the challenge.

In the dream, she can hear the rushing river. Was it that loud in life? If it was, she didn't notice it, or she only heard it subconsciously. It sounded like the blood rushing in her ears.

The path winds upward and the going gets harder, the path rockier, the boulders blinding them with their high, smooth sides. They can no longer see far ahead or behind. The world narrows to the space between stones, the dirt under their feet, the sky only visible in slices of brilliant blue directly above their heads, and neither is looking up. Their eyes are on their own feet, because that is the only safe way to traverse this kind of terrain. They are pushing themselves harder, going faster than they should. Virginia knows it, but she doesn't want to seem weak, and she lets Ames set the blistering pace.

But she lags, and that is the only reason why, when the land suddenly disappears and the steep, twisting path ends in a spray of loose gravel high above a rushing river, Virginia is still holding onto the boulders on both sides of the narrow path when Ames loses his footing and falls, his body turning circles in the air like an acrobat's on the long, long arc downward, and while in life there was only the blood rushing in her ears, in the dream, she hears his body hit the stones in the river, and in the dream, that sound is louder than her inevitable, endless scream.

She opens her eyes in the cell, its pitch-blackness obscuring the ceiling and the bars, and tries to figure out whether she has screamed aloud. The guard doesn't come, but would he either way? She forces herself to think about who is on duty tonight. Keeler. No, he wouldn't come. She can easily imagine him greeting her screams with a detached, mildly curious laughter.

But her thoughts won't be diverted so easily. Ames again, always Ames. If Ames had lived, no San Francisco newspaper article. If no article, no expedition, at least not for Virginia. And without Virginia on the expedition, Caprice wouldn't have . . . well, she tells herself, who knows what Caprice would have done in the end. But things would have been different.

In another world, a world that looks almost exactly like this one but with one or two stray, seemingly inconsequential decisions made differently, Caprice still walks the earth. She still has a toad's face and a harpy's tongue, and she and Virginia never even meet each other, living in pleasant ignorance one of the other alike.

Tonight, her eyes adjusting to the dark just enough to see the parallel lines of the bars of her cell looming only feet from where she shivers on her cot — there is nowhere to go farther away from them — Virginia wishes she had a better imagination. She would like to imagine that world. She would like to know how things would have ended up for Caprice, for Virginia, for the others. For Ebba and Althea, for Ann, and oh, for Stella. What in the world would have happened to Stella? She would like to imagine something better than the truth.

Instead, she remembers what actually happened, and there is no comfort in that. They started in such ambitious optimism. They ended up here.

Or at least, she corrects herself grimly, a few of them did.

Which are the luckier? The ones who came back or the ones who didn't?

CHAPTER FIFTEEN:
VIRGINIA

Buffalo, New York
April 1853

When they disembarked on the platform in Buffalo, Virginia coughed once in the sooty air, then blew out a long breath. She felt more energetic than she'd expected. The motion of a train was like gliding on air compared to the jolting an ox wagon delivered on a crossing to California. Her traveling costume had been chosen for comfort, but a dress was still a dress, and she looked forward to donning her more practical divided skirt soon. She was eager to meet the rest of her party and get started. There had been only one misstep on the trip from Boston; predictably, Caprice had been responsible.

Virginia, Ebba, and Althea had ridden the whole way in a first-class cabin with an empty fourth seat, one Brooks had purchased with Lady Franklin's money. Caprice had thrown a fit in Boston when she saw the accommodations — *to spend my last hours in civilization packed tight like a pickle in a jar? Are you savages?* — and immediately marched off to secure a compartment all to herself. Virginia, mindful of the scene they were causing, had simply let her go. So instead of spending hours on the train getting to know each other better and dispelling their negative first impressions, she spent those hours chatting with Ebba and Althea, enjoying the scenery as it rushed by, and from time to time quietly seething at Caprice's gall.

She should have put her foot down and insisted the young woman ride in the cabin purchased for her, she told herself. Starting from Buffalo, she would have to take the reins more firmly. But she let Caprice storm off for the same reason, she believed, that Caprice had stormed; she wouldn't have the chance much longer. The train passage was the last leg of the journey where they could safely ignore each other's existence. Even in the canoes, though the propulsion would be provided mainly by hired voyageurs, the women would have to paddle in rhythm, and it would be Virginia's responsibility to dress down anyone who failed to fall in line. On the train, she could still rest. She talked, she napped, she nibbled a pastry; at no point did she have to worry whether Caprice was doing the same.

When they disembarked in Buffalo onto the crowded platform, she regretted that hasty, self-indulgent decision. She'd assumed Caprice would be easy to spot, but she searched the crowd for several minutes and did not see her. Virginia did not seriously think the young woman could be lost, but it felt like a personal failing to lose her even temporarily, and it didn't bode well for the journey.

But then she came into sight.

Caprice wore a bright red knee-length coat of wool, thick as a carpet, with gold frog closures all up and down the front. She stood out from the crowd like a cardinal. Whatever Caprice's faults, her tailoring was always impeccable.

The porter carrying her luggage was, unusually, a woman; when Virginia looked more closely, she realized the woman wasn't a porter at all. She wore no uniform, just a simple cloth coat over her dress, appropriate for cold weather. She was dark-skinned, with watchful eyes and an unlined face, though Virginia could not guess her age. Once she set down Caprice's bags, Virginia expected her to turn and go, but she stood just behind and beside Caprice, looking at the white woman expectantly.

"A pleasure to see you again, Ebba, Althea," said Caprice.

Virginia chose to pretend she hadn't heard the slight. As the English ladies murmured their greetings, she said in a cheerful tone, "I hope your journey was as pleasant as ours."

"Yes, we were quite comfortable." Caprice indicated the dark-skinned woman behind her with a subtle nod.

"We?" Virginia was forced to ask.

"This is my companion. There was no previous opportunity to introduce you, I regret. This is my lady's maid, Elizabeth," said Caprice.

Elizabeth inclined her head to the other women, saying nothing.

Virginia could think of only one response, and it came out of her in a cold growl. "Your bloody *maid*?"

"Watch your language, please. And yes. I feel I'm making a great sacrifice to get by with only one," Caprice said, her manner infuriatingly calm, "if that's what you mean."

Caprice's dramatic fit back in Boston made sense now. Oh, she was clever. Caprice hadn't wanted a whole compartment to herself just to stretch out in; she'd wanted to bring another entire person with her, and she hadn't wanted Virginia to know about it until long, long after they'd left the city. She'd put off the confrontation for nearly five hundred miles. Now, it was upon them.

"It is not what I mean, and you know that. We're going into the bloody wilderness. Not a bloody ballroom," said Virginia.

"Language!"

"I'm sure you've heard worse. Probably said worse, too, climbing your precious mountains. You understand my point."

Caprice said flatly, "Elizabeth is my maid and my companion. I will need her assistance. If I go, she goes."

"Fine, do not go," said Virginia, delighted. "That is my preference in any case. I wish you good health and safe travels back to Boston, Miss Collins."

She turned on her heel, presenting her back to the infuriating rich girl, and did not stop when Caprice shouted, "Well, wait!"

Then Althea, her lovely brow creased in concern, put out her hand and laid it on Virginia's arm. Her glove was bright white against the navy wool of Virginia's coatsleeve.

"This is a shock," she said, "of course. But will it make so much difference? One more pair of hands? She might even be a help."

"The choice is not mine," lied Virginia, seeing a way out, one that had more than a kernel of truth to it. "If it will make the parting easier, Elizabeth may remain with us overnight. Tomorrow, when we present ourselves for the next leg of the journey, I am certain the chief voyageur will turn her away. The canoes have been fitted out to accommodate twelve women, not thirteen. There is simply no space."

Instead of speaking to Caprice, she addressed Elizabeth directly, trying to make her voice as warm as possible. "At that point, your mistress will be required to decide whether the two of you will travel back to Boston together or whether you are sent alone. If the occasion requires, do you think you could go all that way with no companion? I realize I would be asking you to do something quite extraordinary."

"Rather less extraordinary than going to the Arctic," Caprice muttered.

Virginia ignored her. To Elizabeth, she said, "Could you?"

"If that's what Miss Collins asks," said Elizabeth. Her voice was low and lovely. The emotion in her dark eyes was hard to read, but it looked more like hope than disappointment.

A few moments later, they were joined by Siobhan and Doro, who had ridden second-class on the same train, and Virginia made the necessary introductions. Doro's eyes were bright with excitement. Siobhan was more tentative, her watchful manner having more than a little in common with Elizabeth's, but Virginia was struck by her feminine grace, which she was seeing for the first time. It seemed that Siobhan wore a dress, bonnet, and gloves just as comfortably as she'd worn trousers the night the two had met. Once they were out of civilization, they'd all be dressed for comfort, but for now, they all wore traveling dresses of lesser or greater quality, depending on their means.

Still perturbed, Virginia did not speak to Caprice while they waited for the coach to the inn, nor while they rode in it, nor when they dismounted.

The inn at which they'd been directed to wait for the other women of the expedition was an undistinguished brick affair, recently built, on a quiet street. The lobby was clean and sparsely decorated. Brass lamps, wooden chairs, a youngish clerk standing at his desk who offered them a tentative smile. Virginia was not sure what she'd expected an inn in Buffalo to look like, but when she saw that they weren't the only women present in the lobby, she assumed Brooks had chosen somewhere not too disreputable, and that was all they needed.

Once inside, Virginia said to her companions as a group, "Ladies, there is no telling when next we'll enjoy having a roof over our heads for the night. Please enjoy this one."

"Well, I'm hungry from the journey," said Caprice. "Some of you ladies are too, aren't you? I'll go see about some supper."

"Actually, there is a space designated for us to gather in the back parlor," said Virginia. "Already arranged. You may find refreshment there. Again, enjoy."

"Thank you, I suppose," said Caprice without a trace of genuine gratitude, "but I do not need to be *told* to *enjoy* things." She raised her chin and folded her arms so she was cupping her own elbows, every inch of her issuing a clear challenge.

This time, Virginia would not let herself be baited. Without speaking, she turned away from the other women and lowered herself into a chair to wait.

The chair was hard and straight and made her back ache almost immediately, but she waited until all the women's footsteps had faded in the distance before she dared to adjust her position. She had just selected a better chair, one with a thin cushion tied to the seat and another to the back, when another woman came through the door.

Was this one of her party? There had not been sketches, only descriptions, in the files, and this one did not match any of those descriptions.

There was youth in every inch of her: the hesitation in her tentative step, the soft curves of her heart-shaped face, the bright strawberry-gold of her hair combed flat against her head, the two-handed grip with which she held a satchel clutched to her chest. She looked around the inn with a slightly awestruck curiosity. As she matched none of the descriptions in the initial file provided by Brooks, if she was among their party, there was only one person she could be.

"Stella?" guessed Virginia.

The girl nodded once, solemn.

So this was the girl who had changed everything, the new passenger Brooks had demanded they bring at the last minute. The reason Thisbe had been left behind. For a moment, Virginia saw red, thinking of how carelessly Caprice had assumed she could add one more to the party when she, Virginia, had been forced to pay attention to the numbers. But this girl, this Stella, should not have to suffer for it. She doubted the girl even knew what had been done to get her a berth. She looked too innocent to know much of anything, clearly far out of her depth. She reminded Virginia of her younger sister Patty, always so open and sincere, always out of her depth with her small frame and big heart. She'd felt so grateful not to lose Patty during the Very Bad Thing, though of course, like the rest of her family, she ended up losing her anyway.

"Welcome to the expedition," said Virginia.

"I hope to have a very pleasant voyage."

Pleasant, thought Virginia, was a fool's dream. The voyage might be any number of things, but anyone with a brain in her head would know that none of them would find the frozen wastes to the north *pleasant.*

Rather than contend, she nodded politely at the girl and told her where to stow her things. She hoped Stella knew what it was to work; that would make things easier once the physical demands of the journey grew. Her clothing was neither as fine as Caprice's nor as plain as Doro's. Of all the expedition's women Virginia had met so far, she was dressed the most like Elizabeth. Perhaps she worked for a rich household, as Elizabeth did.

While still mulling over Stella, Virginia felt a hand clap on her shoulder and turned to see a woman in buckskins. Automatically, Virginia smiled. A woman dressed for frontier life was a woman she didn't have to acquaint with difficulty, and that was something to celebrate.

"I'm Ann," said the woman, returning the smile. Her grin showed the effects of hard living, some teeth dead, others missing. Virginia guessed this made her look older than she really was. She also looked brutally strong, her broad shoulders straining the buckskin of her coat. This woman, thought Virginia, was a gift.

"You must be missing your dogs," said Virginia politely, reaching for the only thing she knew about the woman other than that she cared more for comfort than propriety.

"Like limbs," Ann said.

"We're glad to have you in our party. We'll be acquiring dogs in Moose Factory, I understand. Is that your understanding as well?"

"Yeah. I told 'em to try to get malamutes, though if there's only huskies, we can use those all right. All good running dogs. I'll

175

need to be looking 'em over real close. Don't want to get sold a bill of goods."

"Absolutely," Virginia agreed.

She sent the two newest arrivals to join the others inside in the back parlor and did a quick tally. Six women who'd come together in the coach, plus Stella and Ann. Including Virginia herself, that accounted for nine, with four remaining.

Thirteen, she thought again, shivering. At least it wouldn't be for long.

Virginia rearranged herself on the thin cushion and waited. Each time the inn door banged open, she straightened up, but after a few disappointments as men entered the room, she was beginning to grow impatient. She decided to walk outside. There was only one entrance to the inn; she wouldn't miss anyone by introducing herself before they came through the door instead of after.

As soon as she came out of the building into the slightly chilly afternoon air, she nearly collided with a small, dark-haired woman with delicate features who barely came up to her shoulder. The birdlike woman looked up at her, and Virginia saw her dark, flashing eyes and a thin upper lip. This must be Christabel, the illustrator. They introduced themselves, and the illustrator beamed a bright smile at Virginia.

After a brief conversation, Virginia sent her inside to join the others.

The sun had just begun to descend when the three remaining women appeared. One Virginia recognized from her description the moment she stepped down from a coach. Dove, the nurse, was as tall as a man and as broad as a ship, with a voice that carried like a copper bell through the evening's cooling air. Her skin was tawny and her coat was too light for the weather. The other two were harder to tell apart. Both were of an average size, shorter than Virginia but not as short as the illustrator, with dark blond hair and faces on the narrow side of average. The translator was listed on the manifest as Irene Chartier, but she looked not in the least French. Of all of them, she seemed the most tired, not even speaking when addressed, merely nodding along. The remaining blond woman — the imprint of middle age clearly stamped on her face, now that Virginia got a better look at her, with her wide eyes framed by round spectacles — had to be Margaret Bridges, the journalist.

She welcomed them in and walked to the back parlor with them, and once she stepped over the threshold into the room of women she would be traveling north with, she was stunned speechless for a moment.

It was a motley group, cobbled together from women who would never even have spoken to one another in the course of their regular lives, but then again, what woman here had a life that could be described as *regular*? In a way, thought Virginia, this was like the freak shows that occasionally made their way to the California frontier. These women were as strange to society as tattooed ladies and sword swallowers. She could imagine the talker giving his spiel to the crowd, selling these exotic sights — *See the Mexican nurse! See the dog woman! See the lady journalist!* — all too easily.

Every woman's face turned toward her. Everyone waited to hear what she had to say.

Virginia had led more than five hundred people from danger into safety. These women were different. These she was leading from safety into danger. God willing, once they found the men they were looking for, she would lead them from danger back to safety again.

She covered her sentimentality with bluster, and once she found her words again, she kept her speech short. She only told them how glad she was that they had all come, that on this first leg, it was still possible to send them back to civilization if they could not bear the strains of the wild, and if anyone here felt they would make a better authority than her — she did not look at Caprice as she said it — they should be advised the position was not available. There were a few uncomfortable laughs but no protests.

After the other women went upstairs to settle for the night, Virginia chatted with the innkeeper, who asked which steamship they'd be leaving on. It was the first Virginia had heard of steamships to Sault Ste. Marie. In the moment she managed to hide her surprise, but the revelation troubled her. Surely Lady Franklin would have wanted them to move through this part of the journey as quickly as possible. What reason could there be to go more slowly?

Once in bed, Virginia lay staring at the ceiling in the dark, and the answer came to her. A ship meant a manifest. A manifest meant a record. No one would know about this mission unless they came back successful. She'd bet anything that both the voyageurs here on the lake and the captain of the *Doris* had been paid not to write these passengers down in their records. They would move toward the North like ghosts. That was the bargain they'd all made.

The next morning, they were off to the lakeside before the first rays of sunlight touched the deep blue sky.

She was sure that as soon as the sun rose, the glassy surface of Lake Erie would be inspiring, but in the dark, it was disconcerting to hear the water without being able to see it.

The scene felt wild, theatrical. Even the light from the torches made her think of the footlights at the only theater performance she'd ever attended, a bawdy showcase put on by bored soldiers at Fort Bridger. Clutching their precious, small bags, her group of women came forward, dressed for the first time in their issued clothes and coats, the divided skirts swirling around their heels the same color as the darkened sky. The crowd of heavily bearded voyageurs loomed out of the darkness, giants straight from a child's storybook.

But the chief voyageur extended his hand to her, shaking it briskly, with a grin on his face. "I see you must be Miss Reeve!"

"Thank you, I am."

"All is arranged, all is arranged," he said, holding his torch high and gesturing so she could see the canoes waiting for them, already loaded and balanced, their substantial food stores heaped high in the centers of the open craft. She knew from discussions with Brooks that the stores were heavy on pemmican and flour, foods that could sustain their energy while taking up as little space as possible, and even so, they would be carrying a great deal of weight.

"I am sorry to say," she said, speaking clearly and loudly to make sure Caprice could hear, "there has been an unexpected change to our party."

"Change?"

"One member of the party has requested to bring her maid. I'm sure you'll agree there will be very little chance to dress for dinner on the lake, yes?"

His laugh was booming, but when it settled, he said, "Lovely ladies are a decoration no matter what they wear."

"But it makes our party thirteen," said Virginia abruptly. No need to dance around the point.

Caprice broke in then, her voice just as forceful and clear as Virginia's. "I'm sure some accommodations can be made, can't they? Elizabeth is not so very large, and as you can see, neither are most of our companions. Delicate little things, you see? I'm certain just one more addition won't overload these fine craft."

His eyes were on Caprice, not looking

away, taking in the tilt of her head and the firm hand planted on one cocked hip.

"Well, certainly, miss. And what do they call you?"

Extending her hand, Caprice made a girlish, musical laugh. The smooth lake's surface sent back a faint echo, disconcerting in the darkness. "Miss Caprice Collins, at your service, kind sir. With you in charge of the party, I am certain we are in capable hands."

Virginia could not believe the absurdity of what was unfolding. The voyageur bent to kiss Caprice's hand, as elegant as any gentleman in a ballroom, except surrounded by utter darkness.

"Now it goes without saying," Caprice continued, "that for the additional trouble, I can extend you some additional compensation. You let me know what you think is fair. Shall we discuss?"

And off she sauntered with the chief voyageur, leaving Virginia behind with the other women, working with broad-shouldered men to add the women's packs to the carefully stacked and secured supplies.

When next Virginia caught sight of her, just before departure, Caprice was perched in the center of the second canoe atop the supplies. She alone of all the women wouldn't even have to paddle. She grinned broadly at Virginia with the exact expression of a cat in cream.

Virginia made the conscious decision to let it go. Let Caprice feel victorious, spending her money; it would do her little good where they were going. Virginia herself was still the leader, still the one who commanded respect from the women. When they boarded the *Doris,* she was the one who would work with Captain Malcolm, and Caprice would have to fall in line. That would set the tone for their sledge journey on the ice. Not every skirmish needed to be a battle and not every battle a war.

Sunrise began as a distant glow, and as they worked, a thin gray light began to reveal the broad, silvery lake. When all the preparations were done, the women sorted out into the two canoes, the men's grumbles dying down as they set to work, only then could Virginia begin to relax. But it was a short-lived relaxation. The voyage had begun.

"Allons-y!" called the chief voyageur from the head of the forward craft, and as they lurched forward, Virginia fixed her eyes on the horizon.

They were on their way.

CHAPTER SIXTEEN:
CHRISTABEL

Lake Erie, leaving Buffalo
April 1853

Four dozen paddles cleaved the water, and Christabel Jones raised her chin to gaze out over the glistening, rippling water of the lake as their craft began its voyage northward. Christabel had sailed to America with her parents when she was too young to remember it — her younger brothers had both been born on American soil — and her travels since had rarely brought her to the water. There was something both thrilling and daunting in these shallow, open crafts surrounded by water in every direction. In her explorations searching for plants to sketch, she had undertaken more physical exertion than most women of her acquaintance, but she knew the paddling would test her.

At first, she felt nothing in her muscles but excitement. A surge of power with every stroke, a bracing cool in her throat and lungs as she caught the breath that would fuel the stroke after. An hour later, her shoulders ached. An hour after that, everything hurt so much she desperately sought escape in her thoughts, and when she let her thoughts drift loose of her body, her body receded, and she was able to deal with the pain.

That Virginia Reeve, she was a sly one. How comfortable she looked, thought Christabel, as if she sailed off toward the frozen North on a canoe every damn day, tucking her paddle into the lake with a regular, unruffled rhythm. Cool as a block of ice fresh from the icebox.

Christabel had never sat in the midst of a group of women so unusual and varied. Was she staring? She was afraid she could not help but stare. But others were looking around too, even if they pretended nonchalance. They were all going to be bound together, irrevocably, who knew how long. And none of them knew one another from Adam — or, she supposed, Eve.

With her artist's eye, Christabel caught the differences and similarities between her fellow adventuresses more quickly than some others might, and even in the brief time the women had spent together at the inn, she'd taken in dozens of details. She'd seen that the tawny-skinned woman — named after some kind of bird, wasn't she? — dressed too light for the weather. She was the most likely to have come from some southerly region. She'd seen that the journalist had an eagle eye and a ready pen, already scribbling notes when she thought no one watched. She'd noted that the Irish woman stood, at times, like a man. And there was something about that Stella that Christabel didn't like, a discordant note in the way she could go so quickly from knowing to innocent and back again.

"What do you think?" came a voice from the other canoe, unmistakably addressing her. Virginia's. Christabel turned to see the party's leader looking straight at her, her expression open and curious, even as she continued to keep perfect rhythm with her paddle.

"Well," said Christabel, "there certainly are a lot of us."

"Safety in numbers," said Virginia, then turned away, putting her attention back on the lake.

Christabel took the cue and turned her attention forward, but her thoughts remained on Virginia. The young woman — how young was she? — seemed smart

186

enough, with confidence to spare. She was plain, and it was Christabel's experience that plain women had to work twice as hard to get half as much respect as pretty ones. Those English ladies, for example, with their crumpets-at-high-tea accents, were lovely enough that the voyageurs' heads turned toward them with brief, birdlike movements of a comical regularity. The next prettiest was the young one called Stella, whom she gathered had been some kind of servant, and then Christabel herself.

Christabel was a student of faces. She'd been brought into the expedition to record its doings through drawings and sketches, and though Brooks had explained in correspondence that would often mean drawing whatever vegetation they experienced, not to mention the landscapes and views from different static places, it would sometimes mean capturing the faces of her fellow travelers. It was with that eye that she had already evaluated all the women on the expedition and decided who more classically fit the model profile — that blond Englishwoman, for example — and whose beauty was, how to put it, less conventional. Dove was the largest woman she'd ever met, six feet if she was an inch, though her face was still delicate and soft enough to be called pretty instead of handsome. These women were outliers, unusual specimens. She could not wait to draw them all. She no longer remembered her brothers' faces or her parents' well enough to draw them, which caused her pain whenever she thought of it. Time had blurred their features. Perhaps this was part of the reason she hungered to draw these women so desperately that whenever she took her hands off the paddle, her fingers twitched automatically into the position of holding a pencil.

In the center of the canoe, she'd stored her precious collection of personal belongings, the small pack each of them had been allowed to bring. Virginia had explained that their food would be provided and their clothes. Now they each wore an identical divided skirt in navy wool, full enough to look like a dress from a fair distance, though in practice, the adjustable skirts looked very different on a slip of a girl like Christabel than on a veritable giantess like Dove. Since the issued clothes were stored separately, the packs they'd brought were mostly for sentimental possessions. And they'd been warned that once the going got rough, some of those possessions, no matter how precious, might have to be left behind.

So the most precious thing she'd brought, wrapped in a protective oilskin, was her second-best copy of Maria Graham's *Book of Botanical Illustrations.* In the evenings, she imagined herself consulting Miss Graham's drawings of culen, lamb's tongue, twenty-two species of fern. Miss Graham was her inspiration. She'd traveled so far — India, Chile, Brazil — and brought back dramatic, important drawings and descriptions of flora her readers would never see firsthand.

Christabel was going about things some-what differently, not entirely by choice. While she certainly would have found a wider array of more colorful plants in the tropics, no one had offered her a place on an expedition going in that direction. So even if she would only discover lichen, moss, and scrub in the frozen North, at least she would be the first woman to draw them.

She let her gaze wander over the women in both canoes again. She would learn their ways. Lose her loneliness. Perhaps some of them she could grow close to. Probably not Ebba and Althea, who already seemed to form a complete unit of two, but someone on the expedition must be a kindred spirit. Perhaps even Caprice Collins, who must have some fascinating stories. Christabel had heard whispers in last night's gathering that she was a mountaineer, that she wanted to take charge of the expedition, that she and Virginia — the leader insisted they all call her Virginia — had already quarreled about authority and direction. Couldn't hurt to make friends with everyone, even those who weren't friendly with one another.

Her gaze met that of Miss Collins, and thinking of how they might make some sort of connection, Christabel gave Miss Collins her best smile.

Miss Collins looked through her, past her, as if she were no more present than a haint.

Christabel turned her eyes back to the vast, open lake all around them and wondered if perhaps, just perhaps, joining this expedition was an utter mistake.

Chapter Seventeen:
Virginia

Massachusetts Superior Court, Boston
October 1854

Today, when Virginia enters the courtroom, she feels a simmering anger in the chamber, a new sensation. Is there a new witness, someone to rile the Bostonians' passions, stir up their rage at the death of their hometown girl? The name on the roster is, as is becoming far too frequent for her comfort, unfamiliar. Why hasn't Clevenger prepared her? She feels much better when she knows what's coming, even if she knows it will be negative, as with Thisbe, as with Dove.

But this man's name is a stranger's, and she wonders how many more days she'll have to do this, how many more hours of sitting still and looking impassive she'll have to endure.

Her allies in the front row, those five survivors, already look like their energy is beginning to flag. The physical exertion of their journey has, she supposes, left them with scant reserves. Dark circles have appeared under Doro's eyes, their stain spreading toward her cheekbones. Virginia wishes she could comfort her, but that is not how things work these days, in this place. Later, there will either be time for comfort or not.

Now the witness comes forward, and she focuses all her attention on him. He is a thin-faced man of medium height, bespectacled. As he passes, she catches sight of two roundish spots of white scalp on the back of his head, where the dark hair thins awkwardly. When he sits, his shoulders are rounded and vulnerable, like a sad child's, but there is something hard she does not like in his small eyes. The glass of his spectacles reflects the light.

"State your name for the record, please," preens the prosecutor.

"Claudius Dalrymple," says the man.

It rings no bells with Virginia. With a subtle glance around the room, she scans the present faces for recognition but sees no signs.

The prosecutor begins, "And your occupation?"

"I am a legal scholar."

"Of some renown, aren't you?"

"One could say so," says the man, pretending modesty, but Virginia sees the falseness of it, the way he understated his credentials only so he could draw more attention to them. "I am often called to testify on matters similar to this one in the great Commonwealth of Massachusetts. By way of profession, I teach at the college."

"And by the college, you mean Harvard College, of course?"

"Of course."

The lawyer continues jovially, "And do tell us, please, Mr. Dalrymple, what is your particular expertise?"

"Evidentiary precedents in capital crime."

"Shall I translate for the less educated? Murder."

The word is loud. Even though the courtroom has no echo, Virginia can hear it repeat inside the chamber of her mind. *Murder, murder, murder.*

"Yes, murder," says the man, turning his head so the lights wink against the round lenses of his spectacles again. "Specifically, the likelihood of conviction when certain evidence is or is not present as well as the patterns currently predominant in the United States judiciary system across its states and territories. I make a study of murder, you see."

"And murderers as well?" asks the prosecutor. His voice is neutral, but his body turns toward Virginia, drawing attention to where she sits.

She risks a glance at her counsel; he seems almost bored by the testimony and certainly not inclined to object. She's not sure he could — the prosecutor's tactics are subtle today — but she would at least like him to be as suspicious as she is. The fact that he isn't is starting to look less like incompetence and more like willful neglect. She is beginning to suspect that even though his entire purpose as her attorney is to defend and protect her, he might be working toward another agenda entirely, for someone else's ends. Or is she only being paranoid?

The witness simply answers the question as if it were straightforward, genuine. "Not exactly, sir. I do not study the perpetrators in depth, nor the details of the crimes they commit. My expertise is in studying the way justice is meted out by the courts. How it is prosecuted. How it is punished."

Whispers hiss and chase one another around the chamber at that word, *punished.* Virginia has to work harder than usual not to show, in any way, the shiver that runs down the length of her spine.

"Mr. Dalrymple. We are grateful to you, of course, for your time," the prosecutor says.

She can hear him winding up to something. She hates that his patterns have become so familiar. She hates everything about him, which makes sense, but it is his familiarity she now loathes most. She should never have been in a position to know him. None of this should have ever happened. They should have found Franklin and come back lauded for it. How different things could have been.

Instead, it is this factotum who enjoys being lauded, praise that the prosecutor heaps at his feet. "We know how busy you are, how important, and so we do not plan to keep you long. Just a few questions only someone of great expertise like yourself can answer."

"I will endeavor to do my best," says the witness with the gravest of expressions.

Virginia cannot believe she has room to swallow her anger at this on top of all the anger she has already swallowed, but perhaps her capacity is infinite. If it isn't, she thinks, one day soon, she will burst.

"What I am sure many of the brighter minds in the court have been wondering," says the prosecutor, lacing his fingers together over his stomach, "is how we can be sure a murder happened when no body has been produced."

Virginia herself has wondered this countless times. She finds herself in the awkward position of being deeply curious to hear what this man will say, though it may well doom her.

"Well, I can tell you. This is not the first time a murder has been prosecuted in the absence of the body of the murdered, and I am sorry to say, it is not likely to be the last."

"It's a sad fact." The prosecutor shakes his head as if he rues the violent state of affairs in America today. As if this weren't his bread and butter. As if . . . but she can't think about him anymore. She's hanging on the witness's every word.

"Without the presence of a body," he is intoning, "the precedent indicates that a reasonable amount of other evidence, including the sworn testimony of at least one eyewitness, is sufficient to create the presumption that a death did in fact take place at a certain time at a certain location."

"So let me make sure we understand." The counsel exaggerates his motions as well as his words, drawing the jury along. He even takes a step in their direction. "You say that we can assume someone died if sworn witnesses tell us where, when, and how she died."

"Yes, that's it."

"And this applies in the case of Caprice Collins?"

"Not just hers." He sounds excited now, livelier than he has so far. "Several others, all relevant here."

"Several others in the Commonwealth of Massachusetts? Or other states you're familiar with?"

"No, no," says the witness, an odd sense of delight radiating from him that makes Virginia feel ill again. "On this expedition, I mean."

"This very expedition?"

"Yes! For example, there was another woman who did not come back from the mission —"

"There were quite a few, as I understand it," the prosecutor interrupts, his mouth crooking up at one corner.

Finally, though Clevenger has told her every time they've met that she must remain silent, Virginia cannot help but attempt to get her counsel's attention, just once. How can he not object to this? She keeps her body still, but her eyes are on him, her jaw

197

clenched, and she lets out a short, sharp hiss.

Clevenger's head snaps in her direction. His eyes go wide. He pinches his fingers together, his meaning clear: *shut your mouth.*

Part of her wants to leap from the dock and slap him, hard. Slap the teeth out of his mouth if she could. He won't stop the prosecutor from prejudicing the jury against her; he won't stop any of this. He should pay. A larger part of her, the part that believes she deserves this fate, already knows she's bound for the hangman's noose no matter what. This part sits back to watch with something very close to indifference.

The expert says, "The scope of my testimony applies primarily to the precedent that enables this case to go forward, convicting a woman of murder without the presence of the body of the person she has killed."

She chances one more hiss toward Clevenger, more discreet this time, softer. Her counsel pretends not to hear her at all, just sitting there like a statue of an overgrown cherub. He does not even blink as the moment to object irrevocably slips by.

"Please tell us," the prosecutor continues, "whether it is your considered legal opinion that there is enough evidence of the death of Caprice Collins for this defendant to be tried for her murder."

A shadow flits across the man's face so quickly Virginia knows the jury won't see it. One of the things this paid expert is paid for is keeping his cool. After a moment of recovery, he says easily, "It is not up to me who is tried for what crime. But yes, I believe there is evidence of the death of Caprice Collins. Her death is a matter of legal certainty."

"Please explain how."

"When she was taken into custody, upon questioning, the defendant admitted that Miss Collins had died. We also deposed several of the other women who sit before us today, and their accounts all agree. The time and place cannot be pinpointed with as much accuracy as we would have if the death had taken place in, for example, Boston itself, but still, because of the level of agreement and lack of dispute, this death can be considered established as the nearest possible thing to fact."

The expert gestures at the five survivors with an open hand, not dismissive and not accusatory, simply factual. "Every woman here has stated that Miss Collins died on an expedition in which they were all participants. There is some dispute as to how it happened, which is why this is a murder trial: it is up to the judge and jury to determine who is telling the truth."

"If anyone," the prosecutor says.

Someone, somewhere in the courtroom chokes off a cough that might have been a guffaw. Judge Miller glares out over the heads of the audience, seems not to find an obvious culprit, and says nothing.

"That is the nature of truth," says Mr. Dalrymple. "A slippery little creature. People can have different interpretations of the same fact, the same word, same sentence. In this case, it is a matter of life and death, but these minor disagreements, these differences in perception, happen every day. Who has not disagreed with his wife about the meaning of the phrase 'I'll be ready in a moment'?"

The prosecutor laughs as if this is funny. So, to Virginia's horror, does the judge.

Virginia does something she has not done so far in this trial.

She stops listening.

It's a foolish thing to do, she knows even as she does it, but she can't stand listening to another word, not today. This man is joking away her freedom. He is joking away her life.

She hates to think of the past, and yet it's

the only thing that makes sense to her in the moment. The deeper they get into this recollection of the expedition, the more horrors she will be forced to face, but losing herself in memories of those horrors is less painful to her than listening to men scheme to destroy her future.

At least when she remembers the past, she already knows all the traps, all the fatalities. There is a reassuring certainty in those moments of loss. Having lost these women once, irrevocably, she cannot lose them again.

She knows the time will come when she'll have to face the memory of losing Caprice.

But she can put it off just a little longer. That day is not today.

Chapter Eighteen:
Virginia

Sault Ste. Marie; aboard the Doris
May and June 1853

Despite the initial awkwardness of forcing a party of thirteen into a space meant for twelve, thought Virginia, the first leg of the journey felt almost enchanted. The weather cooperated, neither too hot nor too cold. The food was neither plentiful nor delicious, but it sufficed. They were so hungry at every mealtime that they fell upon it with great and grateful joy. Stops felt short, but the women slept like the dead and awoke rested even when they rose before the sun.

After the first few days in the canoes, the aches in their untrained muscles subsided as their bodies adjusted to the hard work. Then they enjoyed the journey more. The lakes sported great beauty and life, and on the shore, they saw new plants, new creatures, furred and feathered things they'd never seen before. Christabel and Margaret were always sketching and scribbling in any free moments, attempting to capture the wildness of their new surroundings, even before they left what still counted as civilization. Even when Christabel did not have her hands free to sketch, her joy at spotting something new was audible. Her *ah!* of pleasure became a common refrain, and the women heard it so often that sometimes they would sing it back to her, sounding for all the world like a flock of chipper ducks, *ah! ah! ah!*

Best of all, they had no trouble with the men. Virginia had feared that the voyageurs hired to transport them via canoe from Buffalo to Sault Ste. Marie would be hard men, disdainful or worse, but they were entirely businesslike. Her experience in the West was that some men took to the wilds because they were unfit for civilization. Too independent at best, and at worst, too violent. But there were exceptions, like Ames. And like her, she supposed. She felt uncomfortable in cities, but she still knew how to navigate them without much friction. In Boston, she'd felt out of place, yes, but she'd been able to take her meals in the ladies' ordinary at the American House without snarling like a feral hog or dancing *la gigue* on the tabletop.

After they disembarked in Sault Ste. Marie — the chief voyageur, Thibodeau, brushing his lips over Caprice's knuckles in farewell as they went — the women efficiently transferred their goods to the transport for Moose Factory. The practice of their regular stops and starts along the lakes had honed their unpacking and repacking skills to a sharp edge.

The same skills served them well at Moose Factory when they arrived the morning of the same day they were to leave. Brooks had paid in advance for transport on a topsail schooner called the *Doris,* and Virginia could not imagine what they would do if the *Doris* turned out to be fictitious, but it was waiting for them exactly at the contracted time and place. At first, Virginia wondered that more time hadn't been built into the schedule to allow for the transfer, but she quickly figured out why. Moose Factory was not just a wild town. It was barely a town at all. Clearly, there were no convenient accommodations sufficient for an overnight stay for more than a dozen women traveling without male supervision, and rather than compromise the women, Brooks had chosen to simply move them out of the town before the time came for them to sleep. Expedient and safe, yes, she understood, but it was also exhausting. She knew once the excitement flooding her veins drained away, she'd collapse, but the thrill kept her going for now. Everything felt momentous.

Virginia lost track of her own pack for a minute, and her heart was in her throat; she didn't have much to speak of in terms of worldly goods, but those precious letters from Lady Franklin were in her pack, and she was dying of curiosity to see what they'd say. There were four. Three for her and the fourth for John Franklin himself. That one, she would never know what it said unless and until they found him.

But today, all things felt possible.

Along with the goods transferred from the canoes to the *Doris,* a flood of other deliveries arrived for transfer over the course of the next few hours. Supplies to prepare them for the ice, as large as the disassembled sledge and as small as twelve precious pairs of snow goggles, rectangles of polished caribou antler with narrow eye slits cut to minimize light and prevent snow blindness. Virginia tracked each delivery and checked them off on the list she'd been given by Brooks to make sure they had everything they needed. Every flick of her pen was satisfaction itself.

The most rambunctious delivery by far was a full complement of twelve sled dogs, each of which Ann threw herself to the ground to wrestle, examine, and judge. She was thorough but efficient, getting a good look at their mouths, eyes, ears, paws. In the end, she judged two of them too weak to take, but the other ten were satisfactory, and ten was plenty to pull the sledge they'd be using, Ann said. Virginia gave her the funds with which to pay the Esquimaux trader. Business was briskly done.

When the dogs yipped and jogged their way up the gangplank, tumbling around Ann's ankles, a pale, stone-faced whaler stood at the top as if to block them. He was not a large man, though he had an air of authority, the voice and carriage of a man accustomed to giving orders and seeing them obeyed.

"Hold up, there," he said angrily. "You can't bring those bitches aboard. Where in blazes do you expect them to stay?"

Ann — his height exactly, with a lantern jaw that put his own weak chin to shame — responded before Virginia even saw the need. "Are you the captain?"

"Nearest to," he said. "I'm the ship's mate, Keane."

"It's been planned out with Captain

Malcolm," Ann said with confidence. "There's a cabin for 'em. Anyone has a problem with that, feel free to follow me down, and we can jaw about it in their quarters."

Then she gave some kind of a signal that made all the dogs growl in unison, low in their furry throats.

After that, with all the activity, the women did not see Keane again until after the ship had set sail.

An hour later, as the ship pulled away into the cold bay, Virginia pushed aside her concerns and fears. There was nothing else to be done. They had closed one chapter, and the next had yet to begin.

Virginia was no sailor, but as she breathed in the salt-stung air and looked out across the water, it felt like an auspicious day for sailing. Brilliant blue sky overhead, clouds scudding by in puffs like a giant's breath. She knew that no wind was just as bad as too much wind, so this amount seemed fair. But the captain would tell her, she supposed.

She saw him then, Captain Malcolm, the loud bark of his orders making it obvious he was in charge. At first she saw only his head and shoulders, higher than most, his cap a spot of stillness in the maelstrom.

When coincidence turned him in her direction, she saw that his skin was a shade or two lighter than Elizabeth's, his cheekbones high and sharp. His close-cut black beard was spotted here and there with gray, his features suggesting a combination of races she couldn't identify at a glance. As she watched, his narrowed brown eyes skimmed over her and were off again, raking the deck, searching his men.

She took a step in his direction, almost without meaning to, studying his wide face, its sharp planes. She could tell he was thickly built, even in the navy greatcoat, his posture as straight as a soldier's. Wide but muscular, a definite bulk in his shoulders and chest. He looked like he could pick her up without effort and snap her in half just as easily.

Still, she took another step toward him. They should speak.

His eyes met hers for a longer moment this time. He looked at her when he barked the order. She understood it was not meant for her ears, and yet he called so loudly, the force of his voice made her flinch.

"Fit up!" he shouted. "We're underway!"

Then he turned away again, pointing and shouting, tending and calling, going about the ship's business as if she and her women weren't there at all.

She looked out over the sailors, a motley two dozen, all ages and colors and moods. They ranged in size from men among the largest she'd ever seen, barrel-chested and hale, to a pair of young boys as slender-hipped as girls. The only thing they seemed to have in common was their strict focus on their work, getting the schooner underway. Not a one of them spared her a second glance.

She knew from Brooks that the men of the *Doris* were whalers, and she knew from Doro that whalers could be a wild lot. Men who never would have stood next to one another in society made societies out here on their own where the only things that mattered were hard work, luck, and loyalty. Some were venturesome men willing to risk everything on a rich score, and some were desperate men who'd already risked everything and lost, then gone to sea to build their lives back up again. Which were the men of the *Doris*? What had they risked, what did they hope to gain, and what would they do to gain it?

Fear came upon her then, far worse than she'd expected it to be, here on the water with the unknown all around her. She was afraid of the Arctic, yes, an area of cold terrain that would almost certainly try to kill them. She was afraid of her own lack of skill and confidence. But in this open moment, she also found herself afraid of the men on this ship, the sailors who scurried about the deck like hard-shelled beetles, men who'd made a living being tougher, sterner, more durable than other men.

She knew little of ships, but she knew that in some ways, they were like forts, and in that area, she had far more expertise. The commander of a fort set the tone for every soldier under his command. It followed that the captain of a ship was a bellwether of his entire crew. So one question weighed heaviest on her mind.

What was Captain Malcolm like?

If he was not a good man, if his crew were not good men, she had brought a dozen other women into a den of danger that she would not necessarily be able to rescue them from. Already, they were surrounded. Already, there was, if things went bad, no escape.

When she bedded down that night with the other women, her fear grew no less in the silence. The last thing Virginia did before she slid downward into an exhausted, irresistible sleep was to raise her eyes, somewhat toward heaven, somewhat toward the unknown, mysterious Captain Malcolm, both invisible above.

CHAPTER NINETEEN:
ELIZABETH

Aboard the Doris
June 1853

The worst part about being surrounded by water, thought Elizabeth Kent, was how the temptation to shove Caprice Collins overboard was a constant thrum in her blood.

The idea of doing her mistress harm had, of course, crossed her mind many times over the years. It was Elizabeth's firm belief that anyone who knew Caprice for any length of time fantasized about doing her in. She could tell the leader of their party, this Virginia Reeve, had no love at all for Caprice. Even if Mr. Bishop hadn't gossiped to the other servants, Elizabeth would have known. Something about Virginia seemed to bring out the worst in Caprice. Heaven knew there was plenty of bad there to bring out. It wasn't even buried very deep.

Of course, having served the Collins family since Caprice was a child, Elizabeth knew the girl had no chance of growing up likeable. If Caprice were generous and openhearted, she wouldn't have been a Collins, just as if Elizabeth hadn't been intelligent and reserved, she wouldn't have been a Kent. Then again, Elizabeth thought, perhaps she went too far in assuming the worst of the Collinses. When it suited them, anyone in the family might be generous, if only money was required.

Mrs. Collins herself had increased Elizabeth's wages when her grandmother first fell ill and Elizabeth had nearly buckled under the strain, fainting from exhaustion one day and coming back to consciousness under Mrs. Collins's suspicious, judgmental eye. Confessing that she'd been forced to take on other work to care for the only family she had left was her only option. Then, surprising her, Mrs. Collins had offered the increase without Elizabeth even asking. Ever since, that money went directly to her grandmother's care, and Elizabeth knew she could not have earned so much so quickly by honest work in any other household in Boston. It was a gracious act but not a selfless one. In return, Elizabeth had given up nearly everything else to keep her position.

The piecemeal jobs went first, and that was a relief, but her mistress asked more and more as time went on. Elizabeth no longer attended the Twelfth Baptist Church, as Mrs. Collins thought it too radical, and she gave up abolitionist rallies and conferences for the same reason. She'd helped with the escape of the Crafts in 1850, but by the time Shadrach Minkins needed assistance a year later, she didn't even know about his case until she read it in the papers. Her father would have been disappointed, she knew, but if he'd lived long enough, they would have shared the load. As it was, she bore it alone.

And Mrs. Collins joked — was it really a joke? — that Elizabeth shouldn't expect a reference from her if she chose to leave, as much as she'd done for her over the years. Getting a new position without a reference would be challenging to say the least, and out on the street, she wouldn't be safe alone. Then what would happen to Mimi Lolo? Mrs. Collins just chipped away at her like a block of cheese, only taking a little at a time but working at her so steadily, she'd end worn down to a nub.

Then Mimi Lolo had passed, God rest her soul, and in the daze that followed, Elizabeth found herself bundled onto a train by Caprice without having any notion where they were headed. She knew now, too late.

Caprice had likely dragged her all this way — a truly absurd distance — merely to make a point. To prove to Virginia that she could force a whole other person into the party if she wanted to. Her mistress demanded that Elizabeth be nearby in case she needed her — though for what, in this environment, Elizabeth could hardly imagine — yet during daylight hours, Caprice steadfastly ignored her. Elizabeth could swear that once or twice, her mistress had even looked at her as if she didn't really recall who she was. She'd wanted to shake Caprice's shoulders the first time it happened. She hadn't, of course. She only laid a hand on her mistress, to adjust her petticoats or help her off with the stays she still insisted on wearing though none of the other women bothered, in the rare minutes of the morning and evening when Caprice demanded her help.

In her spare moments, Elizabeth had explored the ship, finding that despite its size, the schooner offered precious little space. The storerooms were jammed from planks to rafters with goods, packed so tight the doors barely closed. There was one cabin for the captain, one for the crew, one for the women, and one for the dogs. There was a medical cabin, a galley, and a mess.

There was nowhere to be alone, and she feared anywhere she tried to be alone she'd be found by someone else, and God only knew what the intentions of that someone else might be.

But there was all that water. All around. Every minute of every day and night. And while the railing wasn't particularly low, neither was it particularly high. Certainly not high enough to keep someone from tumbling over the edge, not if the push were strong enough, especially if the wind blew in the right direction.

Dangerous thoughts of watery graves were not, however, the only ideas preoccupying Elizabeth on the journey. Another had popped into her head the first time she'd spotted that redhead Stella aboard.

She'd groaned on the inside when she'd seen Stella, whom she recognized. A bit of the groan actually escaped her mouth when she learned the two would be sharing a bunk. There was one cabin for all the women, six bunks to a wall. Twelve women would have fit. Thirteen women had boarded.

"That's quite all right," Caprice had said. "I have a solution. My lady's maid will share."

No one asked Elizabeth whether she

wanted to share. Giving her a choice would mean taking the risk that she would choose otherwise.

And so Elizabeth and Stella shared a bunk. Stella snored like a sawn log. Exhausted as she was, Elizabeth slept little those first few nights before she laid her hands on some wool to stuff into her ears to muffle the worst of the sounds. It was not only Stella's rumbling snores that kept her awake. It was the knowledge of Stella herself.

At home, she wouldn't have made a stir; she kept her head down, always. She could not risk losing her wages, not with Mimi Lolo depending on her. But they were no longer at home, were they? The rules, what rules there were, were different here. And she had the sense she was becoming different too.

Not to mention, every servant in the Collins household knew from Bishop — not that he'd meant to reveal exactly this — that Virginia Reeve had stood up to Miss Caprice. *If she could do that,* thought Elizabeth, *she could do almost anything.*

When she spotted her opportunity, Elizabeth seized it.

"Miss Reeve, please, begging your pardon," said Elizabeth, approaching the dark-

217

haired woman near the doorway to the women's cabin. She took care to keep her manner extra deferential. "May I speak with you a moment?"

"Certainly," Virginia said, her face quickly narrowing in concern. "Is everything all right?"

"Yes. Could we speak in private?"

Virginia glanced in one direction and then the other and took her gently by the elbow, guiding her toward a kind of blind corridor that, judging by the warmth radiating from its wooden planks, backed up against the ship's stove on the other side.

"Will this do? I think we're quite alone."

"It'll have to," said Elizabeth. "But please, I want you to keep the details of this conversation private. Do I have your word?"

Virginia seemed to be sizing her up, but after long moments, she said simply, "Yes."

"This Stella," Elizabeth began. "Why is she on the ship?"

"Why are any of us?" Virginia responded, her tone matching Elizabeth's, neither flippant nor angry. "She was put on the roster by our patron."

"Well," Elizabeth said pointedly, "at least one of us wasn't put on the roster, for all the difference that made."

"I'm sorry about that," Virginia said. "I'm

sorry Caprice dragged you along. I imagine you would have rather stayed at the Collins mansion or found another position."

She'd meant only to speak of the rumors she'd heard but found she could not bite back a response. "It isn't as easy as all that, miss."

"Why not? Servants leave their households and find new employment every day."

"Maybe white servants do, miss," said Elizabeth.

Virginia seemed stunned at that, slow to react. It was disappointing, really. At last, she said, "Why would that make a difference?"

"Without a reference, a new position is hard to come by. Doubly so for women of my . . . hue."

"You seem so capable. I'm sure you could strike out on your own."

"On my own?" asked Elizabeth, trying hard to keep the mockery out of her tone, only partially succeeding. "I suppose, since I don't have anyone, that would be my only option. No savings, no church, no family. My only living relative died a month ago, and either Caprice doesn't know about it, which makes her a fool, or she does know, which makes her a devil."

Virginia fell silent and then repeated, "I'm sorry."

Elizabeth was tired of white women's apologies, though at least this one seemed sincere. Still, apologies were cheap. What good were empty words? Words wouldn't get her home, wouldn't get her into a better situation. Some words had power, but these, these were hollow.

Elizabeth said, "Anyway, I didn't come here to jaw at you about sadness. I came to mention something I thought you should know."

"About Stella?"

"About Stella."

"Out with it, then. You know her?"

"By sight and by reputation," said Elizabeth. "She worked for another Beacon Hill family, the Hollidays."

"And?"

"Word had it she was dismissed for stealing, a few weeks before we left Boston. No one'd seen her since."

"Stealing, you say?"

"And before that, there were other rumors about her."

"I hope this isn't idle gossip, Elizabeth." The confidence was back in Virginia's voice.

"I do not gossip idly. But the consequences of . . . certain behaviors would be

220

magnified in our current situation."

Virginia eyed her. "Certain behaviors?"

"I hesitate to say, miss," said Elizabeth, stumbling, "but I believe you will understand when I tell you that the Hollidays have a son named Charles. Eighteen years old, rather handsome, rather . . . romantic. Do I need to say more?"

Something crossed Virginia's face. A shadow. Somehow this touched her, but Elizabeth could not tell exactly how. She'd done her duty, in any case. Now it was all in Virginia's hands.

"Thank you," said Virginia. "You do not. I am in your debt, Miss Kent." She seemed to hesitate and then drew closer to Elizabeth, her voice dropping low. "I'm sorry Caprice dragged you along on this mission. I understand you had no choice."

"We all have choices, miss," said Elizabeth, thinking of the ones she'd made that got her into this situation. Maybe she would have made all the same ones over again — she could never have abandoned Mimi Lolo — but could there have been another way? Some path that took her anywhere but here?

Virginia said, "When we get back, I'll help you. I don't know how, but I'm sure there's something. If we succeed on this expedition, there'll be a share of the money for you, I promise."

"Do you really think we'll succeed?"

There was just a moment of hesitation before Virginia said, "Yes, I think we very well might."

Elizabeth said, "You are an optimist, Miss Reeve. It suits you well to lead this expedition. But please do not make promises to me that you have no way to keep."

Virginia, head bowed, put her hand atop Elizabeth's. Elizabeth froze. The woman meant well, but what could she really do? Here or elsewhere?

Finally, Virginia whispered, "I'll try. That is what I can promise."

Elizabeth did not bother to reply. She'd flattered the woman, but her eyes were open. They were up here in the frozen North, miles from civilization, unprepared and overmatched. The men on this ship watched them with suspicion and barely concealed disdain. Once the women went out on the ice to search for Franklin, even if they managed to survive the cold, starvation would stalk their steps. Virginia might be an optimist, but Elizabeth herself was a realist.

She did not believe she would ever see Boston again.

CHAPTER TWENTY:
VIRGINIA

Massachusetts Superior Court, Boston
October 1854

Another day of uncertainty, another hollow ache of worry wondering who will testify against her next. Virginia finds herself wishing they'd just get on with it. Then she reminds herself that it might be the noose she's speeding toward, and she tells herself to let the days unfold as they will. As if she has a choice.

Today, the attorney for the prosecution is flustered, which is a novelty. This, Virginia will savor. She can barely look at her own counsel anymore, as deeply as the man's inaction affronts her; it will gladden her heart to watch this one stumble for a while, given the opportunity.

"The prosecution calls . . ." A shuffle, a rustle. The attorney looks through his papers, creases his brow, turns one paper over and seems offended by what the page shows. From where Virginia sits, that page appears blank.

"What is it?" says Judge Miller, not bothering to hide his annoyance.

"I'm just confirming the name here, Your Honor. Just a moment, if you'll forgive the delay."

"I haven't yet decided," says the judge in a voice that suggests he has. "How much longer do you think we might need to wait?"

"Only a moment — there — yes, sir, I apologize. We do not have the legal name of the witness on record."

Now she knows who's next.

Oh, thinks Virginia. *Of course. Of course they've found her.*

Of the surviving members of the expedition not sitting in the front row, Dove is probably the one she's gladdest to see. That isn't to say the woman's testimony will be favorable. Why would the prosecution bring Dove here if not to say things that will damage Virginia's case and threaten her life? To bring more nails for her coffin, hammer them in?

But Virginia desperately wants certain survivors to stay far away from this place, this trial. She must protect the secrets that are not and never were hers to reveal. She protects none of Dove's secrets. She's not even sure Dove has any.

The prosecutor is still fumbling, still awkward. "But this woman claims to have been a passenger on the *Doris,* and we call her to attest to events thereon here today."

"You don't have her legal name? What do you have?"

"Begging your pardon, I believe, sir, she is called Dove."

"I am," rings out Dove's voice, "and no one needs to beg anyone else's pardon for it. I sure won't."

"All right," the judge says, pointing his gavel at the woman. "You're being called to the stand, Miss . . . Dove."

"Thank you kindly," she says and picks up her skirts all proper, proceeding to the front of the room to sit. A crackling charge of energy sweeps through the room at exactly the same speed as her passage; one does not see women of Dove's stature every day. She looks every inch of her six feet in this room, with a sturdy, curved build that goes from broad shoulders to narrow waist to broad hips in a way that the men of the jury seem unable to look away from. Dove is larger than life in every sense of the expression.

Virginia watches Dove approach with a heady cocktail of relief, dread, and familiarity. The woman looks less changed than most of them. Her skin had already been weathered by years of sun and wind, hard living on the border with Mexico, before she joined their expedition. She did not waste away from lack of food like some of them, though Virginia does not care to let herself linger on the reason. The dress Dove wears is new and stiff, and she wears it with unconcern, as she has done most things in the time they've been acquainted. Dove has proved herself to be passionate about saving lives, but otherwise, it seems there is little that Dove cares much about.

And now Dove testifies from the front of the room, her dark eyes level and inscrutable, the toes of her sharp boots pointed just so. Unlike some of the women, she did not lose any toes on the journey, at least not that Virginia knew of. It did not seem like the kind of event Dove would keep to herself.

After she's sworn in, the prosecutor begins, "You go by the name Dove?"

"I thought we'd established that."

"One can never be too careful," the attorney intones, "when entering information into the official record."

"I'll keep that in mind for the next time I'm called as a witness in a murder trial."

"Miss Dove, please, if you could confine yourself to responding when a question is asked."

She makes no effort at all to hide her annoyance as she says, "Ask a question, then."

"You were a member of the expedition that sailed north on the *Doris*? The same one the defendant, Virginia Reeve, sailed on?"

"The *Doris* was really only part of it."

"Yes, of course, ma'am. I think we're all aware of that."

"I thought you might not be from how you phrased the question."

"A question you have not answered." His tone is almost as annoyed as hers now, though he's trying harder to hide it. "Did you or did you not sail on the *Doris* with Virginia Reeve?"

"I did."

"Yet when the prosecution put out a call for members of the expedition, you did not answer."

"I did not." Her eyes are flint.

"Why not?"

"I have more important things to do."

"Indeed! More important than a murder trial?"

"Actually, yes. I am supposed to be on my way to Crimea. You've heard there's a war there, I assume? Surely, you're aware that lives are being lost there every single day, without enough trained nurses to care for the wounded? Crimea — that's in Russia, as I'm sure you know — is where I am needed. I am not needed here."

"That doesn't seem to be your decision to make."

"Can we get on with it? Because I have passage booked tomorrow. I suppose that's how you found me, on the ship's manifest. Do you really think any information I can provide to these proceedings outranks the actual saving of lives?"

The judge breaks in, "Miss Dove, as the attorney directed you, he'll be the one asking the questions."

She swivels to eye the judge, not a trace of fear or even deference to be seen. Virginia had always hated this attitude when it was directed at her, but she has to admit there is something very satisfying about seeing it leveled at someone who could stand to be taken down a peg. She'll say this for Dove. She is a force to be reckoned with.

"And as I said to that one, I'll say to you, Your Honor," Dove goes on. "If he wants me to answer a question, he should go ahead and get to asking."

"All right, then. You have your orders,

Counsel," Judge Miller says, clearly more amused than angry.

"I'll proceed," says the lawyer, making a great effort to get himself under control and mostly succeeding. "So, Miss Dove. Let's talk a little bit about your background. You were a nurse in the Mexican War?"

The disdain on her face is unmistakable, but her voice is plain and firm. "I was."

"And your medical experience, that was what led you to join the expedition?"

"In a sense. Nursing can be done anywhere, and for my part, I got tired of war. Thought a trip into the frozen North would be a novelty at least."

"And was it?"

"Better than war, certainly, in some ways. Worse in others."

"Worse than war! Do tell!" To Virginia's ear, his theatricality is grating, but the rest of the room seems to eat it up. All but those five women in the front row, who gaze on Dove without either contempt or affection. They know her, but they won't lay claim to any more than knowing her. That is why they sit in the front row and she sits in the witness box. They are sacrificing to be here. Their time, their privacy, their conflicting loyalties. Dove has chosen not to sacrifice, at least not for Virginia's sake.

Virginia hopes Dove makes it to Crimea. Some people were simply better off at war. Dove respects soldiers, and whatever else they were, the women of the expedition had not been soldiers. Their battles were too secret, too sly. Nor had the sailors of the *Doris* acted in soldierly ways. They followed orders most of the time, but they did not unite in pursuit of a common goal the way soldiers did. And despite the hierarchy on the ship, as Captain Malcolm would have admitted with that haunted look of his, they did not truly fall into line. Not when it counted.

"In war, we were on the move," says Dove, looking out over the faces of the jury to make sure they're listening. She must like what she sees, because she goes on. "On a ship, there's nowhere to go. Especially a ship in the North. Too cold to breathe the air, even. And inside, you go a little stir-crazy."

"Crazy! That's quite an allegation."

"Not alleging anything, sir," she says as primly as a parson's wife, a parallel that had never come even close to occurring to Virginia before this moment.

"Explain what you mean, then."

"As I nursed fallen soldiers in the Republic of Texas, it wasn't pretty work, no mistaking. Blood in the dust, dirt in the wounds. Battles followed so hot and heavy on one another's heels, stopping to save the wounded after one skirmish might mean getting caught by incoming fire from the next."

"That sounds terrible, miss."

"It was," she says, but her voice sounds more like pride than regret. "But if I got tired of it, I could just up and leave. I think that was part of what kept me on the battlefield. The knowledge that I was choosing to be there. Every day, I woke up, and I chose. I chose to help those men. I chose to save lives."

"And the expedition was different?"

"As a bee from a bunting, yes, sir."

"Tell us more."

"Instead of rising every morning and choosing to serve, I was stuck. Moving, but stuck. You get what I mean?"

"Yes," he says, though Virginia doubts it. He just wants to get to the meat.

The attorney goes on, "And do you think your emotions clouded your opinion of your shipmates?"

"Not at all. On the battlefield, I had to get good at sizing people up. Still am."

"Then tell us what you think of Virginia Reeve."

"Frankly, I think she's a danger to herself

and others," says the nurse, her voice matter-of-fact.

Instant clamor.

After the judge manages to quiet the room, the prosecutor says, "Sorry about that, miss. Please. Continue. You were telling us your opinion of the defendant."

Dove continues as if never disrupted, same look on her face, hands folded in her lap like she's clutching needlework. "I think she started off this voyage with a misplaced sense of self-confidence, and once that was shattered, there was no putting her back together."

It hurts to hear Dove's assessment, but Virginia has to admit, she doesn't think the nurse's view is entirely wrong.

But Dove goes on, and what she says next hurts more, wounds deeper. "To be honest with you, she was a wreck from, well, not the beginning, but close to it."

"From when, then? When did she begin to fall apart?"

Dove looks out, seeming to savor the attention for just a beat before she speaks, an uncharacteristically coy moment. Then she says, "I suppose it was just as soon as women started dying."

CHAPTER TWENTY-ONE:
VIRGINIA

Aboard the Doris
June 1853

What surprised Virginia as they sailed north into Hudson Bay was how the day could be every temperature at once. With the evidence of her eyes she saw the mottled, jutting ice still cluttering much of the bay's surface, but her cheeks were warmed by sunlight. The cold would be unrelenting farther north. In the June gleam here in the bay's southern reaches, the air tasted of summer. When she had pictured this journey, she had seen herself and every other person swaddled in their winter slops up to the tips of their noses. But so far, some days, such precautions proved not just unnecessary but unwelcome. Some days, if you wore your wool mittens, you'd roast in them.

The third day after they launched from Moose Factory was such a day.

The women had initially been reluctant to

233

gain the deck, but the enforced closeness belowdecks had already started to breed resentments. Dove and Siobhan, for whatever reason, developed an instant antipathy for each other that rivaled Virginia and Caprice's. Ann spent every waking moment in the small cabin where the dogs were kept, and Virginia wouldn't have been surprised if she started sleeping there too, preferring the company of friendly canines to wary human women.

Today, things were starting to change, and some of the women proved themselves venturesome. Ebba and Althea could be seen strolling arm in arm about the deck, steadying each other, heads bent together in conversation. Doro stared northward from the prow as steadily as a painted figurehead, scanning a horizon she'd read about a thousand times but never seen. Her look of wonder never failed to pluck a string in Virginia's heart. Margaret, the journalist, was always observing with a weather eye. The translator, Irene, kept to herself — she was still largely a mystery — but she, too, stood on the deck with a look more joy than fear, and Virginia hoped that someday soon, she'd begin to reveal something of herself. It would be good to know what she thought of this journey, what she thought of their chances once they disembarked at Repulse Bay. They would rely entirely on her to communicate with any natives they might meet on land, and if Doro's accounts of John Rae's overland explorations were accurate, successful trading with the natives could easily make the difference between life and death.

But no one took to life on the ship with as much gusto as Christabel, the delicate, bird-like illustrator with the dark eyes. She hadn't told Virginia her story, but she'd read it in Brooks's files: one day at a church picnic, the rest of her family — parents, young brothers — had been trampled under the hooves of a runaway team of horses, and there were no other relations to take her in. She'd had to make her own way through skill and luck. A talented student under the tutelage of a local artist at the time of her parents' death, she immediately began hiring herself out for portraits and sketch work. She'd made enough of a name for herself to be profiled in the local newspaper, which must have been how Brooks found her for Lady Franklin. It was not so different from her own story in the main, thought Virginia, though highly divergent in the particulars.

But while Virginia had expected Christabel to be shy, sticking to her pencils and paper and observing from afar, instead, the young woman had leapt into the action of the ship. The ship's boys had taken a shine to her and she to them. All three dark-haired and bird-boned, they seemed to belong together somehow, the only people on the *Doris* so far to find the gap between the male crew and female passengers sur-mountable. The three could be seen scam-pering together across the deck, leaping up whenever possible onto coils of rope, inte-rior railings, the occasional crate. Their fleet feet took Virginia's breath away.

She cast her eyes about for the captain, hoping he wouldn't chastise the ship's boys or Christabel for their play, but she only glimpsed him at a distance. The broad shoulders in the dark coat, always turning away. They still had not spoken. At this point, it had to be deliberate.

But she would not chase him. They could ride all the way to Repulse Bay in silence if that was what he wanted, she thought in a fit of pique. She had other fish to fry.

One of the boys had shimmied up the mast and, to Virginia's astonishment, Christabel followed. Even in her divided skirt, heavier than the boys' fitted breeches, she somehow managed to cling tightly against the post with her knees as well as her arms. The boy below them shouted directions, directing her to footholds and handholds, and her cheeks were flushed with both excitement and exertion as she made upward progress. The other boy scuttled up after her, and then all three were in the rigging.

When the bright sun made it hard to follow their motion, Virginia returned her eyes to the deck, blinking. She saw a woman's form moving toward her, and while it was sometimes hard to tell the women apart in the thick woven coats Virginia had issued, she recognized the red-gold of Stella's hair.

"Come," she said. "How are you finding the journey so far?"

The other woman shrugged. "Cold."

"Sorry to say it'll be getting a lot colder," said Virginia, then regretted it. How far did the limits of Brooks's requirements stretch here? She had technically already brought Stella on the journey, fulfilling the letter of the law. What if instead of disembarking with her at Repulse Bay, she sent the young woman back? Immediately, she rejected the thought. She could never send one woman on a ship alone with two dozen men, no matter who that woman was, even Caprice.

Above their heads, laughter pealed.

Stella tilted her head, looking up into the

rigging, squinting against the sun. "Who's that?" asked Stella.

"Christabel. The illustrator."

They gazed up in united wonder, watching her antics. Christabel skipped as lightly as a bird along the mast, swinging her body up into the rigging and setting her small feet along the thin spars until it looked like she was flying.

Virginia turned her gaze discreetly to Stella's face. The pretty woman bit her lip, closed her eyes, opened them again. She seemed to be wrestling with something.

For her part, Virginia was still troubled by what Elizabeth had told her. Was there anything to the rumors about Stella? Was she a seductress or a thief, and if so, did it really matter out here on the water? It certainly wouldn't on the ice. But the fact that she was here at all meant that someone powerful must have wanted her far, far away, and Virginia was more than idly curious to know the reason.

Stella said nothing. Neither did Virginia.

The wind puffed and swirled around them, and Virginia heard the sail flap once, a remarkably loud sound in the vast, empty air. She looked up. The white cloth snapped hard at the mast, and if she hadn't looked up to watch it ripple at that precise moment, she would not have seen what she saw.

Christabel, falling.

Her heavy coat parted as she fell, a dark, divided flap of cloth so unlike the sail, her body no longer like a bird's, because instead of swooping upward on the wing, she simply fell straight down.

There was no other sound, not until they heard the thud of flesh arrested, with sickening suddenness, by the deck.

The next moment was long and awful and utterly silent until it got loud.

Someone howled. It sounded like it might have been Doro, possibly Althea. The howl was high, almost a scream, but deeper in the throat, darker.

"Dear God!" shouted a man's voice.

Virginia turned from Stella and ran straight to the fallen girl, arriving in unison with Dove, whose face was a stony mask. The two women got there faster than any of the sailors could muster.

It was only hours later that Virginia realized the men had moved toward the illustrator's fallen form slowly on purpose. After a fall from that height, there were no patients, only messes to clean up, blood and brains to swab away. The women had run because they hoped. The sailors — wise, seasoned — had not wasted time hoping.

She and Dove knelt closest, but she felt other women gathering behind and around them, their hushed voices murmuring and grieving, the occasional gasp of horror as another straggler joined the cluster around the small body on the hard wooden boards.

Virginia did not let herself cry, not then. She'd seen enough bodies on the trail to control her response to them. Death saddened her, of course it did, but it no longer shocked her. At that moment, she needed to manage the situation, and that meant moving the women away from the sailors to grieve in private. Up here on deck, tears would provide occasion for the sailors to shake their heads and say *Yes, see, these women don't understand. They're weak. All emotion. Fools to the last.*

So perhaps she shooed the women away too quickly. One by one, with a private whisper in each woman's ear, she ordered them downstairs to the women's quarters. She did not have to urge any of them twice. The pool of blood under Christabel's head was still spreading outward, and most had little enough experience with death that they still regarded it as somehow contagious.

She herself didn't even want to stay. But in mere minutes, there were only three of them left, the three who'd stared death in the face enough times to know him well: Virginia, Dove, and Siobhan. While Dove and Siobhan had yet to exchange a civil word, Virginia was glad to see that in a situation like this, they could set their differences aside. They discussed in hushed tones what to do with the body.

A low voice several inches above Virginia's head said, "Miss Reeve, I'm so sorry."

Those were the first words Captain Malcolm ever spoke to her. Turning to face him, she caught sight of the ship's boys who had climbed down from the rigging, their faces pale and horrified, wet with tears.

"We'll take good care of her," he said. "You may go."

Dove and Siobhan melted away, heading toward the women's cabin. The men who had dared to approach parted for them without ever looking in their direction.

Angling her head back to look the captain in the face, Virginia said stiffly, "You have my thanks. But I will not go until you tell me what arrangements you mean to make."

She knew her anger was misplaced. What had happened was not his fault, not really, not more than anyone else's. It could only be laid at the feet of Christabel herself and the cold, dispassionate wind. But she could not read him, and that fueled her worry.

Was he treating her with kindness or pity? Did he think her incapable?

His deep brown eyes, which she now saw turned down at the corners, gave nothing away. "I suppose, Miss Reeve, you are unfamiliar with death at sea."

"At sea, yes."

"Our options are limited. Once we get farther north, it'll be cold enough in the hull to keep bodies on ice."

"Bodies!" Virginia exclaimed, unable to help herself. "Today, let us only speak in the singular."

Virginia cursed herself for that exclamation, so womanly, but the body of a person who had trusted her to stay safe now lay dead on the boards at her feet, and keeping the tears back was getting harder and harder. The anger helped.

"As you wish," said Captain Malcolm. "The body will be wrapped and stored until I determine the proper time for a burial at sea."

"I wish to help make the determination."

"It is my ship," he said.

She answered, "It is my expedition."

His eyes hardened then, finally losing their sympathetic softness, and she felt a perverse pride in angering him. There. Now they were on a footing.

Then she remembered the ship's boys still watching, the deck they stood on, the blood at their feet.

She told him, in a softer voice, "I would like to say a prayer."

"At the service? Or now?"

She'd meant the service, but then she heard herself saying, "Both."

He nodded and surprised her by reaching out to take her hands in his. His hands were cold, but the firm confidence of the motion was still reassuring. He bent his head. She bent hers and closed her eyes.

"Our Father," he began, and she mouthed the familiar words along with him, her voice a hoarse whisper, only cracking when she reached *Thy will be done,* then settling back into the oft-repeated rhythm again.

Once the prayer was done, she spoke quickly, feeling the tears almost upon her. "Excuse me. I have kept the rest of my party waiting too long. I trust you and your crew to make the arrangements."

He inclined his head in agreement.

Before the pity could return to his eyes, she turned away and hastened toward the women's cabin. The women would need comfort. Only she was not sure she had any to provide.

By the time she got to the cabin, all the

women knew what had happened from the ones who were on deck, and she regretted having taken any time at all for her own grief. All she could offer them were platitudes, *terrible accident, no one to blame.* Afterward, they clustered among themselves, speaking no louder than a whisper, and boxed her out.

That night as they bedded down, her heart nearly broke when she saw Elizabeth and Stella, who she knew did not care for each other, lying side by side on their shared bunk. They'd both chosen to share their discomfort rather than move to Christabel's now-empty bunk below.

Once the lights were extinguished, Virginia lay sleepless, overwhelmed by all the ways she'd already fallen short. Not only had she let Christabel die, no one had turned to her for guidance or succor, not that she had any to give. She could not reach out to them; they did not reach out to her. A leader who could only take her flock through the good times was no leader at all.

A hand reached up and squeezed her wrist. She looked down to see who the hand belonged to. Improbably, it was Caprice's.

"We'll be all right," said Caprice, her voice disembodied in the darkness.

Virginia had no good answer. She could

not agree, because Caprice wasn't necessarily right, but she'd be a monster to disagree aloud. The other woman's confidence was born of naivete. Of course all her adventures had turned out all right. She'd traveled in a carefully crafted bubble of money and power. Inside a bubble like that, there were no true adventures.

In the end, she only answered, "Sleep well, Caprice."

In the night's long darkness, she could not help but let the worst of her thoughts, the most cynical one, in. Losing Christabel was far from the worst that could happen on this journey. When they returned, there would be questions about any other woman. Christabel had neither family nor employer waiting for her return.

Virginia lamented that Christabel had died, but perhaps some good could yet come of it. Perhaps now that they had seen how easily danger could come for them, the women of the expedition would turn to one another, form stronger bonds of trust. She had seen death give life before. It was a paradox, to be sure, but contradictions did not make the truth less true.

She knew by then but let herself forget in the darkness that Christabel might not be the only one they would lose.

CHAPTER TWENTY-TWO:
VIRGINIA

Aboard the Doris
June 1853

Christabel's burial at sea was a somber but brief occasion. Both the men and the women attended. The captain said a few words — *Known but little, gone too soon,* and the like, along with two well-worn Bible verses he recited without opening the book — and the group muttered *Amen.* Then two sailors chosen for the duty tipped the wrapped form over the side, and after a splash that was both louder and softer than Virginia expected, it was done.

None of the women lingered. Virginia alone remained on the deck with the sailors, and in just minutes, the shift in their mood was a palpable thing. Quick and frightening, like a rainstorm filling the banks of a dry creek. Shedding their somber manner like a cloak, the men were already back to business as usual; she heard one deep guffaw, then another. Perhaps their laughter was just amusement or an attempt to lift the sad mood, but Virginia heard menace.

To cover her fear, she turned to Captain Malcolm and forced out the right words. "Thank you."

"Not much to thank me for," he said, "but I'm sure you're welcome."

"You read well. The Bible, I mean."

"I preach to the men on Sundays if you'd like to attend." His hands on the railing were large, well-formed. His cap covered most of his close-cut hair, and as it had been on the first day, his beard was still tightly trimmed. Its defined line ran black and sharp against his skin, which was very close in color to the planks of the ship's wooden deck. The connection seemed fitting. He was an extension of the ship in a way, or the ship was an extension of him.

She asked, "Is that usual? For captains?"

"It is. Though I am more than usually qualified. I was studying for the ministry before I went to sea."

"Oh! Why did you leave?"

"Why does a man do anything?" he said with a tight smile, directed out over the water, not toward her. There was no mirth in it. "For a woman."

Carefully, she ventured, "You have a wife

at home?"

"No wife. And this ship is my home." His eyes returned to the inland sea. He seemed uncomfortable in her presence, his tone distant. "We were whalers, not so long ago, you may know. But this year, for the first time, we are a transport ship. Running south to north in the bay, north to south, west to east and back again, carrying supplies between the factories. Until the ice fences us in."

"When do you expect that to be?"

"All too soon. I hope it will be long after we deliver on our contract and put you off at Repulse Bay. You should hope so too. But in any given year, no one knows exactly when the freeze-up's coming until it's already here. Please excuse me. I have duties to attend to."

She watched him go and immediately caught the eye of the ship's mate, Keane, who was watching her with undisguised suspicion. He was a lean man, craggy and knobbed, as if carved from pale, weathered wood. His gaze unsettled her. Ever since the first day, when he stood at the top of the gangplank to block Ann and her dogs, he had made no secret of his antipathy. She could guess its cause well enough: old salts who believed women had no place aboard

248

ship were far more common than men like Captain Malcolm, who would transport them when it suited. She'd heard Keane singing late one night on the watch and paused to listen. His voice was lovely, his notes pure, and she might have let his talent soften her heart toward him if she hadn't listened long enough to make out the words of his song as they shifted from a sprightly, charming chorus into an entirely different kind of verse.

She had a dark and a rovin' eye,
And her hair hung down in ring-a-lets.
She was a nice girl, a proper girl,
But one of the rakish kind.

So up the stairs and into bed I took that
maiden fair.
I fired off my cannon into her thatch of
hair.
I fired off a broadside until my shot was
spent,
Then rammed that fire ship's waterline
until my ram was bent.

Then in the morning she was gone; my
money was gone too.
My clothes she'd hocked; my watch she
stole; my sea bag was gone too.

But she'd left behind a souvenir, I'd have
   you all to know,
And in nine days, to my surprise, there
   was fire down below.

She had a dark and a rovin' eye . . .

Today, he did not sing, only stared. Holding her gaze, Keane spat onto the deck, a
great hocking glob of something, and it took
all she had not to wince. But she held his
gaze in return, held and held it until he was
the one forced to look away. When she
turned, she could feel her heart pounding
away under her heavy garments, hammering like a woodpecker on a rotten oak.

Keane was on her mind when she went
down to the women's cabin and called the
women to gather. She even sent Doro to
fetch Ann from the cabin where the dogs
were kept so they would all be present.

Once the women were gathered, eleven
faces — dark and pale, wide-eyed and
jaded, hopeful and suspicious — turned
toward her expectantly. Their attention
jangled her nerves, but no matter. She
pressed on.

"We are very different women," Virginia
told them. "We have come from different
places for different reasons. But we are all

women on a ship of men. And I would like to see us stick together."

"What do you mean by that, 'stick together,' miss?" asked Stella, concern on her heart-shaped face. She was always the picture of innocence. If she was truly as innocent as she sounded, Virginia worried for her; if she was not innocent but made such a flawless show of seeming so, Virginia worried for the rest of them.

Virginia said, "My meaning is that we should be ready to render assistance to one another."

"What sort of assistance do you think we will need?" Caprice asked, her voice openly sharp.

"In my days on the westward trail to California," Virginia began, choosing her words carefully, "there were many dangers. We were in danger from hostile natives, from wild animals, from the risk of thirst or starvation, from extreme or sudden weather, from the very land we crossed. Many of those factors will not be present on this journey — I expect very few wild animals on the *Doris* — but many will."

She examined their faces one by one, not lingering long on any but taking a quick read of their attitudes. Most seemed receptive. Caprice was obviously skeptical. Dove's eyes were narrowed, but that was not unexpected. The journalist, Margaret, was taking notes, and she, too, looked less than convinced.

Virginia addressed her. "Miss Margaret, can I ask you not to write this down?"

"I'm here to document the journey."

"This is not about the journey. This is about our safety as women. So we survive long enough to have a legacy others will want to read about."

Margaret eyed her with displeasure, but she put the pen down.

Virginia told them, "Some of the women traveling westward weren't just threatened by outer dangers. The real threat to them came from other members of the party."

Again she scanned the room. Irene looked away, her eyes darting downward. Althea looked at Virginia with something between surprise and confusion. Ebba looked only at Althea.

Virginia saw that many did not understand, so she made herself clear. "Not to put too fine a point on it, but some were endangered by their very own husbands."

"Endangered how?" asked Althea, while at the same moment, Dove grumbled, "Sounds about right."

"And it wasn't always safe for them to ask

for help in so many words. So when any new woman joined the party, I took her aside and taught her two hand signals. I would like us all to know them so we can use them if we must."

Virginia faced Doro, who sat nearest to her, and said, "For example, if I saw you on the deck talking to a sailor, and you wanted to signal to me that his attentions were unwelcome . . ."

"Goodness!" exclaimed Doro. "Attentions?"

"These men are not accustomed to female company. There is every chance they will try to take advantage of the situation in ways you may find . . . unpleasant."

"Do you have any evidence of that?" interrupted Caprice. "It seems to me you are introducing paranoia into the situation. You are the one making us less safe."

Virginia shook her head, doing her best to keep her voice utterly calm. "No. That is not true. This is preparation. This is necessary."

"Well, I've traveled all over the world with hired men," said Caprice, directing her remarks to the entire group. "And not one of them ever showed me anything other than the greatest respect."

"They were hired men, you say?" said

Virginia, not too loud.

"Yes."

"And who hired them? Your father?"

"Well, yes."

"And you're sure it was you they respected?" said Virginia, making it clear with her tone that she did not expect, or welcome, an answer. A cloud crossed Caprice's brow, but she kept silent.

Virginia let the silence hang in the air for one more moment so the women could come to their own understanding, then continued. "I will teach you two signals. If our shipboard companions are as dignified and respectful as Miss Collins believes they will be, you will only ever need to use one."

She was careful not to look at Caprice, quickly turning back to Doro. "So if a sailor addresses you, and I am close enough to see you but not to hear what's being said, I might wonder if you want me to intervene. If you don't want help, you simply do this."

She raised her hand, elbow down and fingertips up, facing her palm toward Doro. Doro moved to imitate her: palm facing outward, warning her off, but in a subtle way.

"I see. It could be mistaken for a greeting," said Doro.

"That's the idea. We will know what it

means. They do not need to."

"So this" — Margaret mirrored the gesture — "means do not intervene?"

"Yes. It means essentially *don't*. Or *no*."

Virginia looked at them expectantly, and one after another after another, they raised their hands and put their palms up, almost as if expecting a childhood game of pat-a-cake. Every palm went up but Caprice's.

"Very good," she said, pretending they'd all complied. "So that's the first."

Margaret prodded, "And the second?"

Virginia turned to Doro again, reached out for her hand. "May I?"

"Of course."

"If you do want me to intervene — if the man's attentions are unwelcome for any reason at all — you only need signal this way instead." She flipped the other woman's hand, keeping the palm flat but moving it to a resting position parallel to the ground. The palm was outstretched this time, a gesture of supplication. Open. Asking.

Doro said, "So this means *help*."

"This means *help*."

The women mirrored the gesture, twisting their wrists and extending their hands flat, all those waiting palms extended in anticipation in front of them. This time, every palm went out, all twelve, including Caprice's.

255

"That's it?" asked Caprice.

"That's it."

"Seems . . . well, very simple."

"Sometimes the simplest things are the best. And as I said, nothing would make me happier than for you to never have need of a signal like this. But there is no harm in knowing it."

The women turned to discuss, and she was pleased to see that a few even made the decision to go up to the deck right away, newly emboldened. She did not want them hiding for the entire journey. She was glad she'd done it, though she did have to admit, there was a kernel of truth to Caprice's accusation. Some of the more innocent women had probably never had cause to think ill of others, regardless of sex, and now they might. But most women — certainly Dove, who'd been a battlefield nurse, and Irene, who'd lived in the wild with trappers and voyageurs — had lived in the world long enough to know and fear the evil that certain men could do. Siobhan had probably seen more than any of the rest of them, walking among men as if she were one. Someday soon, Virginia would ask for her stories.

She felt a tap on her shoulder and saw Irene, her face serious. She was surprised to realize she and the translator had not even exchanged words yet; there were so many women, and Irene kept to herself, but there was no real excuse for not getting to know the women better, especially one whose skills would be so essential.

"Irene! Can I help you?"

She put up her palm in the *no* motion. When Virginia clearly understood her, her face brightened, but she did not speak.

"I can't? So . . . I'm sorry . . ." Confused, she did not know what to say next.

Irene made a gesture Virginia didn't recognize, a circle with her hand, gesturing toward herself and away in a kind of loop.

"I'm sorry, I don't understand."

Irene repeated the gesture, again silent. A creeping dread flowed through Virginia.

"Irene, are you choosing not to speak?"

She used the gesture that meant *no,* and the creeping dread inside Virginia blossomed into something darker, larger.

"*Can* you speak?"

Irene repeated the *no* motion and let her mouth fall open. Virginia only caught a glimpse of what was there — or rather, wasn't — and had to turn away in horror.

Irene had no tongue. Most of it, if not all, had been cut out.

"I'm sorry," said Virginia, mumbling the

apology down at the wooden boards of the cabin floor. "I'm sorry."

Feelings warred within her. Disgust and horror at whoever had done this to Irene. Anger that Brooks hadn't known — had he? — that the translator he'd hired was mute. And a sinking, spiraling sense of foreboding that the woman they'd planned to depend on for communication with any natives could not speak a single word out loud.

Irene tapped on her shoulder again, and Virginia forced herself to look up. She'd been able to face the woman just fine before she'd known of her injury; as the leader, it was her responsibility to accept and adapt to the change. She wondered how many of the other women knew.

"Yes?" she asked, willing herself to be open.

Irene used the *help* gesture, then perfectly mimed drawing back a bow and arrow, then picking up and hauling the animal her imaginary bow and arrow had slain.

"Help hunt?"

Irene nodded.

"We're going to need that," said Virginia, half to herself. "When we get to the ice."

Irene pointed down at the deck emphatically.

"Now?"

She nodded, mimed herself drawing the bow again, then touched Virginia's nearest hand.

"You want to teach us to hunt? Ah. Can you shoot too?"

Irene nodded fiercely, clearly happy that Virginia was catching on.

"We could have lessons. While we sail. You can teach the other women. I don't know who's able and who's not, but all the firearms in the world won't help us in unschooled hands."

The mute woman gestured *help* enthusiastically, and while it wasn't what Virginia had intended the motion to be used for, she understood Irene's use of it perfectly.

"Thank you," said Virginia. There were so many other things she wanted to say, but she wasn't sure how to say them. She would need time to decide.

Irene pointed to her and made another motion: with a flat palm, she touched the tips of her fingers to her lips and gestured outward, almost like blowing a kiss.

"What does that motion mean? I'm sorry, I don't know."

Irene gestured as if giving a gift, moving her hands outward from her chest toward Virginia.

"Giving? Gift?" guessed Virginia. It was

like a parlor game but the strangest one she'd ever experienced. How was she supposed to know what the other woman wanted?

Irene nodded. Then she pointed to Virginia, at Virginia's mouth, and cupped her ear.

"You want a response. If you give . . . give to me. So you give me something, and I say . . . thank you?"

Irene grinned broadly and nodded once more.

"It means thank you? This?" And she repeated the motion, moving her fingers outward from her lips.

Irene's smile was all the answer she needed.

The sooner they could learn how to communicate with Irene, the better. There was so much they had to learn and not that long to learn it.

Even with that small satisfaction, Virginia could feel the beginning of a panic welling within her. The reality of Christabel's death was settling in, and now this. There would be so many other surprises, so many other things she couldn't anticipate. Any one of them could spell disaster.

She needed to get away, just for a moment. She nodded her farewell to Irene, who stepped back, head low.

A kernel of an idea sparked in Virginia's head. She ducked back into the women's cabin to grab her pack, the precious few items she'd brought on the journey for her own use, and headed for the deck.

There was nowhere aboard ship she could enjoy true solitude, but in the inhospitably windy conditions of the prow, she was able to crouch against the rail. Working carefully with trembling fingers, she spread open the first of Lady Franklin's letters and read it eagerly to herself.

Dear Miss Reeve,
So you have passed the first month of your excursion. I imagine it has not been easy. No, I do not have to imagine — I know it has been hell. Do not forget that I traveled a great deal, both with and without my husband's company, and I know the million awful sins that travel into the wilderness visits on a person. At least in the frozen North, you are less likely to have your provisions swarmed by rats. Once on the Nile, my flatboat was so overrun by rats, they ate away the greater part of my maid's quilt during the night. Filthy little beasts. Whatever the demons of your journey so far

have been, I hope rats have not been among them.

This first letter is to encourage you, Miss Reeve. Your travels have just begun. Though misery may be your constant companion, it is my fervent wish that hope rides just as close to you and your company. Whatever your personal feelings at this time, they are, in the main, irrelevant. You must keep them to yourself. Clutch them under your coat like you would a precious trinket or a spy's message, not to be thieved. Especially if they are doubts. Let no one see.

You alone are the leader of this expedition. At this moment, a man might be at the helm, but your mind, your sense of right, propels the ship forward. Soldiers and sailors, men and women, all aboard look to you.

Do not disappoint them. Do not disappoint me.

Sincerely,

J

Virginia put the letter away, fighting the wind to fold it back into a rough square and slide it back into its envelope, then stood for a moment in the silence. It was not truly silent, of course. She could hear the low-pitched shouts of men elsewhere on deck, calling, responding. The ship had its own voice too, creaking its many discomforts as its masts and sails captured the power of the wind, as its precious wooden hull fought its way north in the cold water. When she thought about it, how narrow the division was that protected them from disaster. A few feet of wood, that was all. Like the narrow wheels of the wagons that rode west, like the thin walls of a cabin in the dead cold of winter mountains, the barrier here between life and death was too fragile to bear thinking about.

All you could do was thank God that there was a barrier and do your best to stay on the right side.

CHAPTER TWENTY-THREE:
VIRGINIA

Sierra Nevada Mountains
1846

Virginia fell a little bit in love with Emmanuel Ames the moment they met, when he lifted her thin, wasted body in his arms as if she were something precious. Only dimly aware of him in the beginning, as her legs swayed and dangled limply above the snowy ground, she came into full consciousness already held by him, his body warming hers everywhere they touched.

When he proposed a unique partnership between them six months later, how could she have said no? What she needed then, above all else, was escape. Ames offered it. In the months following the Very Bad Thing, she refused to be a prop for her stepfather's misguided political ambitions. They shouldn't be out in the world, flaunting the lives they'd all clung to so tightly. Saving his life had apparently not given her a say in

264

how he spent it, but she could at least choose not to give any more of her own life in service of his.

She did not even hesitate before saying yes to Ames. She hadn't known what she was getting into, that was true, but he'd never given her cause to regret it.

She'd loved him, in her way, and she knew he'd loved her, but not how everyone assumed. She'd met his wife, Gloria, a true beauty with hair as black and shiny as a raven's wing, and she liked her. Gloria seemed to like her too. Sometimes Virginia thought Gloria was the only person, man or woman, stranger or friend, who didn't suspect Virginia of slipping her naked form into Ames's sleeping furs at night.

Virginia knew what part of a man went between the legs of a woman. She'd seen and heard it all on the trail, where people seemed to forget about the very idea of keeping things private. Possibly because privacy was hard to come by, but possibly because they had decided that privacy, like the other trappings of civilization, was no longer as important as they'd once thought.

Some corner of her wondered, yes, what it would be like to physically unite with Ames. But he was far too important to her to try. Much of what she loved about him was his utter fidelity to his wife when men all around them treated vows like kindling twigs, no good but for burning up. To her, he was alluring because he was upright. It was his very untouchability that made her want to touch him, and if he'd let her, she wouldn't have wanted to anymore.

She had never told anyone this, partly because she was afraid she'd be judged for it — was this how normal people felt, or was she an aberration? — and partly because there was simply no one to tell.

Later, she and Ames were partners, but that first time, he had been her rescuer. She still remembered that feeling, unmoored but still secure, aloft in his arms. Free of the earth as if she were floating. As if nothing, no worldly concerns, could touch her anymore.

Until the first shivers of sensation began to tingle in her neglected limbs, for a long, not unwelcome moment, she thought it was just like being dead.

CHAPTER TWENTY-FOUR:
VIRGINIA

Aboard the Doris
June 1853

After two weeks on the *Doris,* Virginia was torn. They were well underway now, settled into a routine, and the crew still viewed the women with disdain and ignorance. After Christabel's fall, some had even begun to cross themselves when a woman drew near. But perhaps that was safer, she thought, if it kept the two groups separate. She was otherwise satisfied with the progress they were making toward Repulse Bay — they were on course, so far — and with the women's preparations for launching onto the ice when the time came.

Only the captain had exchanged more than half a dozen words with her, but his goodwill was far and away the most important. When they could, she and Doro would take him aside to discuss what they all knew of the land and sea, comparing maps of

Franklin's route to the route Lady Franklin had given them to search, the area where she was sure the entire party could still be found. Alive, she'd said she hoped, though Virginia wondered how long such a practical woman could truly sustain such an impractical hope.

The more she got to know Captain Malcolm, the more he reminded her of Ames, which surprised her. They didn't look anything alike: Malcolm was tall, broad, and dark, while Ames had been wiry and pale as birch bark, surprisingly thin in his arms and legs despite his strength.

But there was something about the captain's apparent calm that spoke to her. Ames had had that same quality. No matter what came to pass on the trail, Ames had been a reassuring presence. Virginia had seen dozens of men begin to turn on one another, seeking to blame and even punish others for their own foibles, but when Ames stepped in between the potential combatants, their anger drained away like so much water on the salt flats west of Bonneville.

Because of his careful, thoughtful way of speaking and his ability to remain still in chaos, she believed that Captain Malcolm probably had the same ability. She believed it up until the first time he failed her.

The captain was escorting Virginia and Doro back to the women's cabin after one of their discussions. He'd thawed toward her somewhat but never sought her out and only seemed comfortable talking with her when Doro was present. He was obviously trying to keep his distance. There were many reasons one might do so, thought Virginia, and she wondered which was his. She might or might not figure it out before they reached Repulse Bay, she decided. She had plenty more pressing matters on her mind.

As they passed the mess, Doro said, "There's a question I've been meaning to ask you, Captain. Why do your men eat with plate?"

Virginia had noticed it too: every man on the *Doris,* from cabin boys to the captain himself, ate with sterling silver cutlery. She and the women ate with battered old forks, tossed into a heap for washing after they were done, and retrieved another fork from a similar heap when it was time to eat again.

"Ah," the captain said, "that was a gift. From those who hired us to transport your party."

"Some gift," laughed Doro.

"You sound skeptical, but it truly is. No matter what does or doesn't happen on this journey, these men have been compensated more than they might have made from their lays in a whaling season."

"Lays?"

"On a whaler, the compensation depends on the haul. Everyone receives their portion — their lays — from the harpooner to the first mate." He gestured toward the men on the deck above them, unseen, bustling, and tending to keep the *Doris* moving northward. "Loyalty may not come cheap, but it can absolutely be bought."

Doro frowned. "I still think it's an odd thing to pay with."

"Here, yes. But not for the British. On a naval vessel, officers have silver, even in the Arctic."

Virginia chimed in, "Seems a waste to fancy up one's plate for tinned stew and a few morsels of seal liver to ward off scurvy."

Meeting her gaze in the shadowed hallway, the captain cocked his head as he answered. "Don't underestimate how much it matters to people to feel human."

"I know people," she said defensively. "I've gotten hundreds of them safe where they needed to go."

"So I've heard," he replied.

A sailor squeezed by them in the hall, and she fell silent for a moment. They stood at the open door of the women's cabin, the happy chatter of its inhabitants audible. She found herself highly conscious of how near she stood to the captain, though of course the choice was not hers. The tight space left nowhere else to stand.

Instead of moving away, she forged ahead. "I suppose if you'd stayed in the seminary, become a preacher, you'd have done the same."

"The same?"

"Guided people to where they needed to go."

He gave a rare smile and nodded at that, an acknowledgment. But almost immediately after, she saw something else clouding his face. The smile faded. His eyes went to a spot some distance behind Virginia and Doro, and he said, "What is it, Mate?"

"Captain," said Keane, his voice overly loud in the small space. "I regret to tell you some men have reported belongings missing since these women boarded ship."

The captain shifted uncomfortably, his eyes gliding from the mate to Virginia and back again. Doro was standing in the doorway of the women's cabin, but Virginia could hear that the hubbub in the room had subsided. The women were no longer talking, only listening.

"What kind of belongings?" asked Virginia.

"Small things, mostly," Keane said, still addressing the captain. "Spare pair of socks, pouch of tobacco. But today, two men reported their cutlery missing."

"Heavens," Virginia said. "That, I'm sorry to hear."

Keane did not look at her, but the captain did.

Captain Malcolm asked her, "Have you had any of that happen?"

"I don't think so," Virginia said slowly, but when she looked through the door of the cabin at the gathering women, she saw she'd answered too soon. Several glanced at one another, their gazes veiled. She could not miss the import of those glances. Clearly, some of them were missing items, though they'd said nothing about it.

She felt a heavy slug of worry in her stomach. If they hadn't told her about this, what else weren't they telling her?

She also didn't like how Keane's eyes looked past her to rake the women's cabin, taking in every detail.

"We're quite crowded down here," she said, struggling to keep her voice pleasant. "Could we take this discussion up on deck?"

"No," said Keane, at the same moment as Captain Malcolm said, "Of course," and

Virginia watched the tension crackle between them for a moment before the captain spoke, saying, "As you wish, Miss Reeve."

When they got up on deck, where the weather spat and blustered under a dim gray sky, she immediately regretted her suggestion. It was more open, but there were other men milling about, and a few began to draw closer, curious. They were out of the frying pan and into the fire.

"You were saying," Keane prompted, his eyes glinting, "about whether there's been things thieved from your party as well as our crew."

Virginia bristled inwardly, looked at the women who'd followed her up on deck — most of them — and forced herself to speak in a calm tone. "It seems there may have been a small item or two. It's a very serious accusation, thievery, especially when items might just be misplaced. Small things like tobacco pouches or . . ."

"Earbobs," volunteered Althea.

"Well," the captain laughed, "haven't seen any of my men in new earbobs of late, have you?"

It seemed he was trying to lighten the mood but unsuccessfully. Murmurings and stirring passed through the clutches of sailors, and she did not know what they might do.

A voice from a knot of men close by called, "Sounds like one of the women's been thieving!"

"Now, now," said the captain, putting his hands out. "That's not what I meant at all. I merely thought it unlikely that a sailor would steal earbobs, though of course I know many of you have sweethearts at home or could sell . . ." He trailed off. They were all in it now.

"A thief is a thief," broke in Caprice, "whether he steals for love or money."

"He?" fired back a sailor. "I think it's a she!"

"Oh, do you now? Who's got evidence either way?" Caprice said loudly, tossing her head.

Virginia flinched. Of course another voice would not make the situation better. Particularly not this voice.

The sailor murmured something under his breath, something about *show you my evidence,* and the men around him laughed in a way Virginia found unsettling.

"Search the women!" shouted an unidentifiable voice from the crowd. She knew a few faces and names, but most of the sailors were still interchangeable to her. Usually, she was glad they kept their distance, but today, things were different.

Either another voice joined the first or the first one repeated — it was impossible for Virginia to tell — "Search the women!"

"Search the men!" Caprice yelled back.

"That's enough, Caprice," Virginia hissed under her breath.

"Oh, is it?" Caprice shot back, but after a look around the deck, she fell silent.

The captain shouted, his voice ringing with authority, "Enough! I will handle this! The thief should be rooted out before more goods go missing. Every man on the crew will be searched."

Hisses and grumbles toured the deck, but when the captain held up a hand for silence, they obeyed.

Then he turned to Virginia, and she caught a glimpse of true regret on his face before he set his expression back into impassivity. "For all the same reasons I have given the order to search the men, I must insist the women also be searched."

Almost immediately came a shout, "I'll volunteer to do the searchin'!" This time, Virginia saw the speaker's face, his leering grin. He was the only red-haired man on board, freckled everywhere from his hairline to the backs of his hands. "Get 'em in a line, and I'll limber up my fingers!"

The laughter that rippled around the clutch of men on deck sent a chill down Virginia's spine, even in the cold. Any one of them might put his hands on a woman now; the others thought it would be good sport, and from there, the more the merrier.

She looked over toward the women, so close by and yet so far, and saw several of them putting their hands out discreetly in small, waist-level gestures toward Virginia: *help*. She said the only thing she thought could get them out of the immediate danger, create time for this tension to dissipate.

"Fair," said Virginia, speaking clear and loud, speaking to the captain for all to hear. "I'll agree that the women be searched."

Howls and hoots sounded from the crowd, and she wished she'd been more specific from the start, but as it was, all she could do was carry on.

"There are conditions, of course," she said.

"Of course," the captain said eagerly, and she could hear in his voice — could anyone else hear it? — that he was as keen to have this situation resolved peacefully as she was. She hadn't thought before about how it must feel for him, to sail with a baker's dozen of women when likely no woman had ever set foot on the ship before. In their way, they must be almost as strange to him as the Esquimaux.

"Just as your men will only be searched by your men," said Virginia, again in as clear and loud a voice as she could muster, "our women will only be searched by our women."

There were mutterings and harrumphs but no louder protests than that.

Virginia went on, "Our medical personnel will do the searching, one by one, in a closed cabin. They will report to me anything that they find. But there will be complete privacy, no matter what."

The captain nodded, not looking at his men, only at her.

"So I recommend," Virginia said, holding his gaze, "that your men line up to be searched at the same time. Then we'll have the whole business done."

"And none can pass their ill-gotten gains from one to another," the captain said. "Straight from here to the searching places, no detours, no chance to squirrel the thieved things away. Does that meet with your approval?"

"It does," she said, almost wanting to chuckle at his formality. Ames had never been one for formality. But then again, she reminded herself forcibly, this man had nothing to do with Ames. He'd showed that by knuckling under.

"Dove and Siobhan," she said. "Do you need anything to conduct your search? Besides a closed cabin?"

"No, ma'am," Siobhan said promptly. Dove looked unhappy, but Virginia had no intention of exploring the form and shape of her unhappiness with a whole ship's muster of men and women looking on.

So she shepherded the women back toward their cabin and lined them up in the hallway outside. They mumbled and murmured to one another, but she was surprised to see how few of them took this invasion ill. Althea and Ebba seemed the least disturbed by it; likely, they knew from their husbands how hard justice was at sea and that the only way through was to keep one's head down and hope to emerge on the other side.

But Caprice. Of course Caprice could not just keep her head down. It was not in her nature. After the women formed an orderly line, Caprice elbowed her way through them until she was close enough to tug on Virginia's sleeve, then spoke in a low voice directly into her ear. "I understand we've got to keep up appearances. But you don't

278

actually think any of our women did the thieving, do you?"

Virginia found her eyes sliding to Stella and forced them back to Caprice's face. "I don't know," she said. "It makes sense to check."

"Well, you don't have to check me, obviously."

"We'll check everyone."

"Come now." Caprice's voice went silky. "That's all well and good for the others. But you know I'm not a thief. I'll go into the cabin with the searchers, and you can just tell them to keep me in a minute or two to make it look good, yes?"

"It'll look like what it is. You will go in, be searched, and come out. Like the others."

"But I'm not like the others," Caprice hissed.

"Just for now, try thinking of yourself that way."

The look Caprice gave Virginia could have done just as much as ice to freeze her solid.

Virginia waited outside with the women in the hallway to keep order while the first few were searched. As she'd thought, Althea and Ebba were the first to volunteer, and both came out unruffled.

"They're asking for you, mum," said Ebba quietly.

Had they found something already? Virginia slipped quietly inside the cabin.

As she entered, Dove glared at her, arms folded. "Didn't think this through, did you, Reeve?"

"What do you mean?"

"If you're out there," she pointed through the closed door back toward the hallway, "it'll be obvious what's happening when we call you in here." She pointed again, this time to their feet.

"Oh."

Dove echoed her *oh* in a disgusted tone and turned her back as Siobhan opened the door for Margaret to enter.

So Virginia stood awkwardly to the side as the women briskly searched the journalist, then the next few women: Ann, Irene, Doro. Caprice grumbled through her entire search, but it took no longer than the others. She was pronounced innocent and sent on her way. Virginia did not even look up at her.

Then there was Stella.

She was joking quietly with Siobhan as the nurse and doctor worked. Virginia had her back turned but heard them say something about the fit of her coat and how high the waist on her divided skirt had been shifted.

Siobhan said something in a quiet, teasing tone, too soft for Virginia to make out the words. But then she sucked in her breath sharply.

After a moment, Dove said, "Oh."

"Virginia?" Siobhan's voice was more cautious than usual.

As soon as the word *thievery* had been mentioned, Virginia had thought of Stella, but then she'd pushed the thought away. Now disappointment flooded through her. What would she do about it? What could she do? But perhaps she'd misunderstood. She forced herself to ask, "Did you find something?"

"Oh yes," Dove snorted. "But not at all what we were looking for, I can tell you that much."

"What's happened? What did you find?" Virginia looked to Stella's face, which was streaked with tears. Silently, she was crying, perhaps had been crying the whole time, but utterly without sound.

"Tell her," said Siobhan harshly.

It was so out of character for their doctor to be harsh with anyone, Virginia couldn't imagine what in the world had turned her against the girl.

"I can't," Stella said.

"Show her, then," Siobhan said, and

281

without waiting for a response, she reached over and, without ceremony or shame, loosened the string at the waist of Stella's skirt and tugged it down several inches.

Virginia gasped out loud.

Stella's belly swelled outward, low and looming. The higher-class women among them would have said she was *increasing* or *in the family way*. But the first thing that sprang to Virginia's mind was neither polite nor elegant. Instead, she thought, *Oh. Stella's stung by a serpent.*

Siobhan said, "Five months along, I should think. Give or take."

"Could be as much as seven," said Dove.

Virginia wanted to ask Stella if she'd known before they left Boston, all those weeks ago. Had Brooks? Lady Franklin? What was it Elizabeth had said — *they wanted her out of the way.* Her employers. Was this why? Not because of any suspected thievery, although perhaps, she thought grimly, that too. The affair with her employer's son that Elizabeth had told her about, that Stella hadn't mentioned, oh yes. The pieces fit together all too neatly. She didn't like the picture they made.

And what was she supposed to tell the captain? His men were already surly at the presence of women on board. Not a one of them would tolerate a woman with child, let alone, if they were still on this ship when the time came, a baby. Virginia's stomach turned just thinking of what the crew might do — to Stella, even to Virginia — if they found out.

"We're keeping this to ourselves, the four of us," she told them in a harsh whisper. "Not a word. You hear me? Not a word to anyone until I tell you."

Every day, they were closer to their destination. Now every day, they were closer to something else.

She had started this mission with twelve women. Christabel was dead, God rest her soul, leaving eleven.

But now Virginia realized she didn't have charge of eleven women. Ten women, yes. And one powder keg in a woman's shape.

That shape would grow and change every day. And one day, like a powder keg, it would explode.

CHAPTER TWENTY-FIVE: VIRGINIA

Massachusetts Superior Court, Boston
October 1854

The next witness is no surprise. So far, the witnesses have painted a picture of Virginia that damns her completely. She'd threatened Caprice Collins with death, said the butler. She was a liar who couldn't be trusted, Thisbe had sneered. Caprice's father and the law expert made the case that the rich girl had been lured away and didn't come back and that somehow, that was enough to prosecute Virginia on. Women had started dying on her watch almost immediately, Dove had told the court. Where to go from there?

So this witness next. If he had something terrible to say, wouldn't they have called him sooner? The men of the jury will believe a man in a way they'd never believe a woman. Even men who think themselves enlightened. There had been men who'd attended the National Women's Rights Conventions in Worcester and Syracuse, yes, those men existed, but she'd bet her shiniest nickel that none of them were currently present in this room. This man could speak with authority on a certain part of their ill-starred expedition. If there was damage to be done, he could absolutely do it.

From the moment he enters the courtroom, rigid as a walking stick, Captain Malcolm doesn't meet her eyes. She doesn't really want him to.

"The prosecution calls Captain Jacob Malcolm to the stand," the prosecutor intones.

He looks even larger in this environment. She knows how much space he took up on a large ship under an open sky, and in this closer space, he verges on the comical. He seems too large for the chair, too large for the room. His hands in particular are awkward. He cannot make them settle. After he swears his oath, his dark, nimble hands still move. His constant motion would make her nervous if she weren't already as nervous as she can be.

His hair and beard are trimmed with precision, his suit an impeccable navy blue. She wonders if a woman is taking care of him. In some ways, she hopes so. Perhaps he looks larger than she remembers because he is. Maybe he has put on weight with good cooking. They'd all lost pounds from their frames aboard ship, even before they set across the ice, those who made that trip. Though he has always been, in most but not every sense, solid.

The prosecutor begins, "Your name again for the record?"

"Jacob Malcolm," he answers, his gaze down but his voice clear.

It is impossible not to notice that Captain Malcolm has the darkest skin in the room. The judge, the jury, the bailiff, all are white men, as is the attorney peppering him with questions. "Captain?"

"Yes."

"And is that your military rank or an honorific?"

"I am currently captain of the *Doris,* a whaling ship out of Provincetown harbor."

"And is that all the *Doris* does?"

"I'm sorry?"

"Whaling. I ask whether that's the only purpose for which your ship sails."

"For the most part. Occasionally, she's engaged for other purposes."

"Such as?"

"Sir," Captain Malcolm says with a sharp tone, "will you please just ask me the questions you want answers to? We're wasting the time of these good people with your song and dance."

The prosecutor, theatrically offended, raises his eyes to the judge, who considers his silent appeal for a long moment, then shrugs. Judge Miller is not entirely a fair man, Virginia thinks, but neither is he as unfair as he could be. She doesn't waste a glance toward her own counsel, knowing for certain he has given up even pretending to have an interest in the proceedings.

"Very well, then, Captain, I'm going to ask you some questions about a voyage you undertook last year to transport certain passengers the length of Hudson Bay. Do you know the voyage I mean?"

"Yes, sir."

"And you did sail the *Doris* last year with a purpose other than whaling?"

"I did."

The prosecutor appears smug, as if this is some kind of meaningful admission, though Virginia can't see how it would be. He follows up quickly. "So who funded your voyage?"

Malcolm shifts in his seat. "We earned what we made."

"I don't doubt it. But you must have

started with capital. Who provided that capital?"

Without emotion, the captain says, "Our initial expenses were paid by a benefactor."

"And what did that benefactor ask you to do?"

"Transport a party of twelve women from Moose Factory to Repulse Bay. If there were any important decisions to be made along the way, I was instructed to follow the directives of Virginia Reeve."

"And weren't you suspicious of this offer, Captain?"

"I'm not sure how you mean that."

"To agree, sight unseen, to transport strange women to the wilds of the outermost frontier. Well, they could have been unwilling, for example. It's a sad truth that there are men who wish to do vulnerable women wrong."

"Unfortunately, yes, that is true," agrees Captain Malcolm, though his brow lowers in suspicion.

Virginia shares his trepidation. Where is this going?

"It seems one reads of these scandalous horrors every day!" says the prosecutor, animated now, clearly playing to the men of the jury. "The terrors that men of a beastly nature might visit on poor, innocent young ladies. Unspeakable. Sold off into . . . well, I wouldn't even use the word in a room like this, with fine people like yourselves present."

He turns away from the jury at last to address Captain Malcolm in the witness's chair. "Suffice it to say, sir, I hope you had some way of knowing you weren't facilitating white slavery!"

There are no words for the expression that crosses Captain Malcolm's face. Virginia worries for a moment that he might throw caution to the wind and do something outrageous — laugh out loud, leap forward to throttle the prosecutor — but he maintains complete control. He does not let himself be baited.

The prosecutor goes on, "Oh, I apologize. I suppose I did not put that as a question. Did you, Captain Malcolm, have some way of knowing for sure you weren't furthering the cause of white slavery? You have not shared your country of origin, but men of your . . . complexion have been known to involve themselves in those pursuits."

The captain's voice and expression are laudably calm as he says, "Sir, if slavery is your concern, you must be aware that men of your complexion have done far more harm on that front than men of mine."

A shocked hush stretches out in the courtroom for one, two, three beats and continues. For this long moment, everyone else seems as still as Virginia. She finds the feeling unsettling. At the same time, she wants to stand up and cheer.

Finally, Judge Miller clears his throat, breaking the silence. "I think we've spent more than enough time on this line of questioning. Counsel, select a new one, please."

"Of course, of course." The prosecutor bobs his head. Then he clears his throat and addresses Captain Malcolm anew. "Were you given any information about the intent of the women's party?"

"I was told they were in search of two ships."

"And that was all?"

A flash of humor, inappropriate but certainly understandable, puts a new sparkle in the captain's brown eyes. "When someone says they're looking for two ships in the Arctic, sir, everyone knows what two ships they mean."

"But your benefactor did not say they were looking for the *Erebus* and the *Terror*."

"No."

"And your benefactor did not speak with

you directly?"

"All work was done in writing, signed by a man named Brooks."

"Was Brooks his first or last name?"

Virginia feels sorry for Captain Malcolm having to answer as he does, even though she knows exactly what he will say. "I'm afraid I can't answer that."

"Can't or won't?"

"Can't. I only knew him as Brooks."

"You didn't think to ask?"

Captain Malcolm only glares silently at the prosecutor. He stares so long that the judge prompts him, "Captain, will you please answer the prosecutor's question?" At least his voice is respectful. A request, not a command.

"What was the question again?" Captain Malcolm asks.

"Did you not ask this 'Brooks' about his name?"

"I did not. Again, I never met him."

"In your correspondence, let us specify, then. What *did* you ask him?"

"About the service I was contracted to provide and the recompense for providing it. Are those not important questions?"

"Fair enough, I suppose."

"You're too kind," grumbles the captain.

Virginia's surprised that this of all moments is the one where he lets his composure slip, but honestly, how can she think she knows him? They knew each other for such a short time, in such a strange place. Neither of them could have foreseen this. That she'd be on trial for murder with him testifying against her. But here they are, the unforeseen now breathing its hot, wet breath into their faces like an eager wolf, hungry for blood.

The lawyer pretends to miss the naked aggression in the captain's voice. It's obvious, at least to her, that he's pretending to be unaware because it will benefit him in some way. Her stomach roils, her head aches. Even his pretended weaknesses are just roundabout ways to lead back to his case's strengths.

"As I'm sure you're aware, Captain Malcolm," the prosecutor continues, "the defendant has made what sounds to our ears like an outrageous claim: that Lady Jane Franklin put her in charge of the expedition. Do you know whether there is any truth to that claim?"

"I assumed it was true. It made sense."

"So Miss Reeve made that claim to you as well?"

"She did."

"But you had no particular reason to

believe her?"

He says defensively, "As I said, it made sense."

"Yet there is no real evidence."

"I suppose not."

"So you cannot support Miss Reeve's claim that her expedition was undertaken on behalf of Lady Jane Franklin."

The slowness of his response conveys his regret. "No."

"And what is your assessment of Miss Virginia Reeve?"

His eyes go to her as if he can't help it. The connection takes her by surprise. The memory. As if they were still there in his cabin, his breath warm on her ear, their bodies close. She forces her eyes away. She picks a spot on the wall behind his ear and dedicates herself to it.

Judging by his tone, Captain Malcolm seems to regain control of himself, his voice polite and distant as he says, "Assessment? I'm afraid I don't follow."

"Was she an experienced sailor? A pleasure to have on the ship? A thing of beauty and a joy forever?"

With each question, the captain's brow grows stormier, and though the prosecutor seems lighthearted, Virginia knows he has built his assertions with great care. Even if the captain says nothing at all, his lack of agreement with the implied compliments here — none of which truly apply to Virginia, to be honest — will stand as a black mark against her.

Captain Malcolm says, "I found her pleasant enough company."

"Company?" repeats the prosecutor, and Virginia winces at the insinuating note in his voice. The captain should have anticipated that trap, and certainly, it would have been better for them both if he had. But she feels a pang of tenderness toward him. This is not where he belongs. There's too much at risk. What might he lose if he puts a foot wrong? Everything, she supposes. And he is not even the one on trial.

The prosecutor asks a few more questions, and the captain answers each reluctantly, with no great panache. He struggles forward, clearly out of his element. It's a shame, because the lawyer is so obviously deep in his.

At least, after a particularly clumsy exchange on the topic of where and when exactly the women disembarked from the *Doris,* the prosecutor says with great satisfaction, "Thank you, Captain. That will be all."

She is not sure whether Captain Malcolm

tries to catch her eye as he rises to leave the courtroom. She has torn her gaze from the spot on the wall and allowed herself to look at the five survivors again, her human rosary beads, checking one and the next and the next. Doro, Althea, and so on. Looking over their sleek hair and their neat gowns. Each wears a dress that is delicate and modest, but to Virginia, what they wear looks like armor. They knew they would hear things here that would make them want to melt, cry, shrink away. Yet they're facing up to what happened. She must force herself to face up too.

When she turns her head to look, Captain Malcolm has already left the courtroom. She has missed her chance. Not that it matters, she tells herself. Not that there ever was a chance to miss.

Has he done her any great harm, the captain? Not here. He is a man of honor. He could not have dodged questions put to him in a court of law. He said what he needed to say, no more.

A swirling mix of emotions swamps Virginia as they walk her back to her cell. Anger and fear, yes, those have been her constant companions throughout the trial, but other feelings swim and surface alongside. Relief. Surprise. Even gratitude.

If Captain Malcolm truly wished her ill, she thinks, there were so many things he could have told them.

CHAPTER TWENTY-SIX:
VIRGINIA

Aboard the Doris
July 1853

Both mittened hands on the starboard railing, Virginia breathed deep. Three weeks into the voyage north aboard the *Doris,* more than a thousand miles north of Boston, the night air tasted of frost and tin. The calendar might say summer and the clock might say night, but weak daylight still swept the deck long after they were too tired to stand, and it felt to Virginia like they'd sailed into their own past, back into the heart of winter. Breathing out was a relief. If all went well, they were halfway to Repulse Bay, but what were the chances things would go well? She needed to be prepared one way or the other.

The frenzy of suspicion that Keane and his allies had whipped up around the missing objects had abated, but Virginia still felt the undercurrent. Virginia reported that no thieved goods had been found on any of the women, which was true. Captain Malcolm, his face chagrined but his words clipped, informed her that one of the missing silver forks had turned up in the pocket of a green hand named Haskell, and he'd been punished as appropriate. Virginia did not ask what the appropriate punishment was, but she assumed it involved lashes, and she was happy not to have witnessed it firsthand.

Unfortunately, she now had a bigger issue to consider.

There was a phenomenon on the trail where people faced with too many decisions simply lay down and died. Ames had told her so. He'd claimed he'd seen it more than once — in the long stretch after Fort Bridger, just past the high pass near Cochuga, and three times in the summer droughts all too common west of Bonneville — and he was scrupulously honest about such things. He never told tall tales or gave untrustworthy guidance in the mountain lands. He knew such a thing would break her heart.

These people died right at the crossroads, Ames had told her, dead center. Not because they ran out of food and water, though that lack was a factor. And not because of weather rushing them into a decision that they were afraid to regret. No, this phenomenon was about the impossibility of the choice itself. Right or left? North or south? Press on or double back toward home? And in these cases, with infinite time to decide but too much riding on choosing right from two unknown options, that was when people simply collapsed under the decision's weight. Bodies stayed behind as souls wafted upward. They died rather than make a choice.

That was why, when Ames sought her out and offered her a new life as a guide, Virginia had shed her past to say yes. She wanted to spare travelers those choices. Her first journey to California had been unusually hard, yes, but the greater part of it had been typical. Her party had been made up of desperate, inexperienced people, in well over their heads. Everything else, including the Very Bad Thing, was part of the story but not the whole.

Now that she knew Stella was with child, Virginia was at her own crossroads. In some ways, of course, there was nothing she could do. The fact could be shared or withheld, but it could not be changed. She'd sworn Dove and Siobhan to secrecy, and though she trusted Siobhan to keep silent, she wasn't at all sure about Dove. If the news spread through the group of women, it was only a matter of time until it spread further. That was where the danger lay. Every day, like clockwork, she resolved to tell the captain. Every day, like clockwork, she failed. She simply could not form the words.

She had given others bad news countless times, of course. On the trail, she'd broken news of deaths — *your husband isn't coming back from the hunt, your child didn't survive the snakebite* — and held strangers while they sobbed their grief out in her arms. She'd ordered people to leave behind their most precious possessions. One memorable winter, when there was no way to move forward through a pass, she had turned three dozen people around and taken them all the way back to Fort Bridger. But this, this was different. A baby, for the love of heaven. To bring a small, helpless human into these frozen wilds. No good could come of it.

She could not take a pregnant Stella with her onto the ice; she could not leave a pregnant Stella on the ship alone.

She should tell the captain. It wasn't that she never had the opportunity. They spoke several times a day at least, and his manner toward her verged on friendly. Every time they spoke, she could feel the secret under her skin, knowing he'd want to know everything that went on under his command, the same way she did.

But after a week, she'd let her silence harden. If she told someone — it had become an *if* — she would wait until they were closer to disembarking at Repulse Bay. Since there was nothing they could do anyway, she told herself, until then.

A woman drew near to her, and though a scarf was drawn around this woman's face, Virginia recognized Doro instantly. Others might venture out on the deck, even at night, but who would willingly seek Virginia in the coldest, most barren place on the ship? Only Doro.

Both of them looked out toward the North at the enormous boulders of ice rising from the harbor, bobbing and veering dangerously, pushing them toward shore. They had entered the exact situation Doro had warned Virginia about all the way back in Boston: if they continued to hug the shoreline, they'd be in constant danger of scraping the hull on the bay's bottom. They could not afford to run aground.

"This ice . . ." said Doro, and when she trailed off, Virginia felt it in the pit of her stomach immediately. Doro wasn't one to mince words. That she felt the need to do so now was a very, very bad sign.

Virginia rose. "Let's go."

"Where?"

But Virginia did not bother answering. Doro was smart. She'd figure it out on the way.

And indeed she did, once they'd turned down the corridor and approached the closed door of the captain's cabin. Doro straightened her cap over her hair as Virginia raised her knuckles, rapped once, then again, and waited.

"Who's there?" shouted a voice, drowsy, annoyed.

"I apologize, Captain, but we must speak with you."

"Miss Reeve?" The voice was definitely thick with sleep, but it didn't take long for the sound of footsteps to ring out.

The door opened just enough for the captain's face but not his body to appear. "Yes?"

"We need to talk to you. About the ice."

His eyes went back and forth between her face and Doro's, and whatever grim set he saw there convinced him.

"Can we come in?" asked Virginia.

"No. I'll come out."

"It's no time to stand on ceremony."

"Isn't ceremony," came his muffled voice

through the door. "Common sense."

She realized they'd likely come upon him in partial dress. Even in the cold, one must change into new clothes from time to time. Virginia found herself wondering whether the captain stripped all the way down before putting new clothing on and assumed he probably didn't; she and the other women tended to slip their bodies out of one dress into another as quickly as possible, leaving only a bare minimum of skin exposed for the shortest possible amount of time. Then she realized how much thought she was giving to a man's bare skin, and she felt a hot blush creeping up into her cheeks, flaming against the cool air.

Then he stepped into the hallway, fully clothed, and said with a level tone, "How can I be of assistance?"

"The ice," Doro blurted.

"Yes, I've noticed it," he said dryly.

"I've read the maps over and over. As you know. All's been well till now. But we're coming up on a particularly shallow ridge," Doro said, her voice growing softer, less confident, even as she stated facts. "It'll rise up. If we stay this close to shore, we'll beach, and no mistake."

He gave Doro a long look, a challenging one. "I know the southwest section of the bay thaws last. But didn't you yourself tell me that by this time of year, it would likely be fine?"

Doro shrank from him a little, not used to confrontation. Virginia had a momentary pang of regret. She'd brought this woman out of her native element, into the true wilderness, because of her knowledge. But a woman was not just what she knew. Perhaps Virginia should have thought of that before inviting her along.

But goodness, it was far too late for that, wasn't it?

Virginia stepped in. "A man like you, a seafarer, knows there's infinity in that word *likely.*"

He rubbed his forehead with his hand, the palm paler than the skin it touched, his expression impossible to read.

Finding her voice, Doro said, "It should have been safe. The spring's been warmer farther south. But the current gyre brings ice from the north, and the winds play their part . . . We can't control the ice, only react to it."

"I'm afraid it might be too late even to do that," he answered, leaning back against the wooden boards of the hallway.

"Sail away from shore," said Virginia.

"Do you understand the risk? At a minimum, we'll need to halve our speed so that we're nudging the ice out of the way instead of crashing into it. Do you know what that does to the journey?" he asked her. "How much time it can add?"

"Doro does, I expect."

Doro swallowed, then said, "It depends. A few days, at least. Could be a week or longer — much longer — depending on how far out we go and how the ice behaves once we're there."

"You are far from our only cargo," the captain told them, straightening up. "We have other goods to deliver. And pick up. And deliver elsewhere. Repulse Bay is only the beginning. The season is too short for detours."

"But the risk —" said Virginia.

He held up a hand, his palm toward her. She thought for a moment he was deliberately showing her a signal until she remembered he had no knowledge of their signals at all. Which was the point, she reminded herself. He added, in case his gesture wasn't clear, "I will think on it."

"What's to think on?" blurted Doro. "You want the *Doris* to run aground? No? Then you have no choice."

An icy shiver ran up Virginia's spine. She could picture it all too clearly. Ice against wood against stone. A rip in the hull as it beached in the shallows, then stuck. Immovable. How long would they last then? With no way to sail home, nothing but icy water on three sides, land with no civilization for miles on the other?

"Everyone has a choice," Captain Malcolm said coolly. Then, almost as quickly as he had turned harsh, he softened. "I do appreciate your diligence and your knowledge. But there are factors at play here you do not fathom."

"Then explain them to us," Virginia said. "You might be surprised at just how much we can fathom, how quickly."

And perhaps he would have, except that they were interrupted by a series of screams, loud and high.

Women's screams.

Then all three of them set off at a run for the deck. Virginia ran as hard as she could, even though she knew she would not want to see what greeted her once she reached it.

The sound of the heavy wooden hull dragging against the sharp, hard ice was an unmistakable, wrenching sound.

When the screams began again, they were softer and even more terrifying. If they'd come from the deck, they'd stay loud. And if the screaming women were outside but no longer on deck, that left only one place they could be.

CHAPTER TWENTY-SEVEN:
ALTHEA

Aboard the Doris
July 1853

Althea had grown accustomed to the whisper of the men's uniforms, how the wool rasped against itself, though she'd never grown to like it. In the beginning, she thought she might. She thought sailing on a ship among rough and ready men might make her feel closer to James. But she just felt further away. These men were nothing like her good husband, not warm like him, not tender like him. James could bluster with the best, and he was no angel, but she knew he'd loved her. If these men loved anything but rum and profanity, she'd be hard pressed to tell it.

So when she walked down the short hall alone, when she heard the rasping of a man's uniform close behind her, she did not pause; she kept her footsteps steady and prepared her breath for a scream.

"Easy there, young lady," said the sailor in a friendly voice. She glanced back; he was ten years younger than her if he was a day, and he was smiling. "You've got nothing to fear from me."

"Who says I was afraid?" she said, still refusing to slow. She heard a burst of women's voices from the deck above, and quickly muttering, "Excuse me, please," she headed toward the sound.

She could still hear the sailor's uniform rasping as he followed her, all too close behind.

The women on deck were swathed, as always, in heavy coats and Welsh caps, but she recognized Ebba's voice. She had awoken in the night and seen her friend's bunk empty, so she'd come out looking for her. No one was sleeping well; the Englishwomen's bunks were not the only empty ones. It was light enough to see on deck twenty hours a day, and women who didn't dare venture out in the bustle of the afternoon were known to gulp fresh air in the quieter hours when most of the crew slept below-decks.

Then she saw the familiar shape of Ebba's cheek, which coaxed a relieved sigh from Althea's chest.

But Ebba had her arms crossed, her face

troubled. Althea slowed. Next to Ebba stood Dove, the woman as tall and broad as a man, with her hands in fists, facing a grimy sailor.

"I didn't mean nothing by the offer," the grimy sailor was saying. "It was a fair one. You gave me friend a tumble."

"What friend?" asked Dove, not sounding as if she cared about the answer.

"Name's Murrow."

"Says I gave him a tumble? I didn't."

"Well, he says a tumble and a larking and a good one too," the grimy sailor told Dove with confidence, "and his say-so is good enough for me."

Althea unwittingly moved her hand in the motion Virginia had taught them, *help, help,* but even as she did it, she knew it was useless. Dove was the one who needed help.

"What's going on here?" asked the man who had followed her up from belowdecks, but no one offered an answer.

Althea saw the other sailors on deck starting to turn and pay attention. If this weren't dealt with quickly, things would get bad. She put her hand on Dove's arm. "Let's . . ."

Dove twitched it away, addressing the grimy sailor again. "Your friend's word? It's not good enough for me and neither are you. And even if I had tumbled with your friend, doesn't mean I'd tumble with you."

"Aw, it do. Shows what kind of doxy you may be."

"I'll show you exactly what kind . . ."

In a flash, Dove's hand jabbed up, heel first, into the sailor's nose. Instantly, blood began to fountain.

"Bugger you, doxy whore!" he shouted through the blood. More men turned at the shout.

"Not today," said Dove grimly and turned to go.

Blood still cascading down his face, the sailor tried in vain to stanch the flow with one hand. With the other, he drew a knife from his boot.

"Look out!" shouted Ebba.

Dove ducked and turned seemingly by instinct. As the man slashed toward her, she barely evaded his blade.

"Get away from her!" Ebba shouted, putting herself between them.

"You mind yours!" the man yelled in return, and Althea's breath caught in her throat as his blade slashed toward Ebba.

The blade did not catch Ebba, but she stumbled back, then back again, and Althea stood frozen in horror as she watched Ebba smash against the nearby railing and begin to tip over, tipping, tipping.

311

Without thinking, Althea rushed forward to grab her friend, flinging both arms around her waist, but the momentum was already underway. She latched on tight and hauled, but then she felt her own feet rising off the deck, and then, with awful slowness, they both went over.

They screamed all the way down.

Hitting the cold water was like smacking into stone. They very nearly hit something harder; she was told later they barely missed hitting the boulders of ice that knocked and bumped against each other, and against the ship's hull, in the cold water.

But she remembered little from their time in the water after the first minute. At first, they clutched and kicked. Then the ice-cold water swamped their split skirts and froze their legs. They both knew how to swim, but how long could they, fully dressed, in water this cold? She managed to kick off one heavy boot. She and Ebba clutched each other, fell away, reached out again. The last thing Althea remembered from the water was a stray thought popping like a bubble: it was fitting that she die as her beloved James surely had, frozen, foolish, countless miles from home.

Then there was nothing until she was lying on her side on the deck, unable to move, as cold as death.

Later, she was told that Dove had thrown a rope in after them and screamed for the captain, who commanded the men to save them. After a mighty struggle, they'd succeeded in hauling them back up on deck. The men claimed they'd had trouble locating the women in the water and that was why it had taken them so long to effect the rescue, but Althea knew better. Had Dove not been there to sound the alarm, the sailors almost certainly would have let them drown without intervention. As it was, damage was done. If the men had moved faster, they might have been unscathed, but frostbite had set in. Siobhan had managed to save their fingers, but they were both likely to lose some toes.

At that news, Althea let out an involuntary laugh. There were so many far worse things to lose.

When she saw that Ebba had not opened her eyes, had not stirred, she was no longer laughing.

Ebba lay half-frozen, unresponsive, in the hammock in the medical cabin for two full days. Althea did not leave her side.

When Ebba opened her eyes at last, Althea gave a little cry of relief.

"Ebba! Can you hear me? It's me, Althea. Do you see me? Do you know me?" She hunched over her friend, who she had so recently thought dead. There was a deep joy, one that moved her to tears, in seeing what had always been so ordinary: Ebba, breathing.

Ebba's eyes were clouded, but her gaze seemed to fix on Althea, and she gave a faint smile.

"Don't try to speak," Althea said. "There will be time. For now, rest and get better."

Ebba reached out her hand, and though she missed Althea's hand on the first try, she caught it on the second. She squeezed. Her grip was weak.

Althea tried to lay her friend's hand back down, but Ebba would not let go. She tugged Althea down toward her, Althea assumed to bring her ear closer so Ebba could whisper into it.

"Yes? What is it?" She proffered her ear.

"I love you," Ebba said.

"Rest," said Althea.

Althea leaned to kiss her friend on the forehead, to press a kiss to her brow to soothe her, but in that split second, Ebba moved — so quickly. How could a woman so near to death move so quickly?

Their lips met, soft and shocking all at once.

Ebba's mouth lingered on hers, asking a question, giving an answer to a question Althea had not asked, had never thought to ask.

"I love you," Ebba said again, her meaning rattling the foundations of Althea's world.

Althea leapt back, almost hitting her head on the wall of the cabin in her haste to put distance between them.

Ebba looked up at her, and Althea saw the truth, a truth she had never imagined, in her friend's dark eyes.

"No," said Althea, her voice quivering. "Apologize for your presumption."

Ebba's voice was low and quiet, rasping with the effort, but it was firm. "No. I will not. I have loved you, and you know it."

"I did not know it."

"If you didn't," said Ebba softly, still skeptical, "you do now."

Althea rose, smoothing down her divided skirt, still stiff with salt from her own descent into the freezing sea. Only moments ago, she had rejoiced that Ebba was alive; now she was ashamed, confused, angry. For her dearest friend in the world to want — no, it was not possible. She was a navy wife.

315

They both were. She would act with the dignity and decorum she'd been rehearsing all these years. She did not have to be what Ebba was asking her to be, someone she had never once considered.

Ebba's voice, still weak but with a fierce note of urgency, said, "You know now, Al. What will you do?"

Scores of possible answers surged through Althea's mind. It wasn't even a choice, what she ended up saying. The words spilled from her lips, unbidden.

"I can't," she cried huskily and turned her back.

CHAPTER TWENTY-EIGHT: VIRGINIA

Charles Street Jail, Boston
October 1854

"How'd you like seeing your sweetheart, then?" asks Benson as he closes the door of her cell with a heavy *clang,* and it takes Virginia a painfully long, clumsy moment to realize that he means the question for her. His voice, for the first time, has an acid edge almost as unpleasant and sharp as Keeler's.

"Pardon?" asks Virginia, her standard gambit for buying herself a moment to think.

"That blackamoor captain of yours, the witness. Suppose you two were cozy for so long on that ship, up there in the chill, he must have missed you something fierce."

"Sir." Virginia addresses him with the frostiest condescension she can muster. "I'm appalled at your insinuation. I insist you stop making such false claims im-

317

mediately."

It is only after the words are out of her mouth and she feels the position of her body — holding her own elbows, her chin thrust high — that she realizes she is unconsciously aping Caprice. The realization brings a prickle of oncoming tears to her eyes, and she hums them away.

Benson folds his arms, glowers down at her. "Say all the fancy words you like. I know how a man looks at a woman, and that's how the captain looks at you."

"I cannot help how I am looked at."

The guard shrugs. It occurs to Virginia that he has only been kind to her because he's had some romantic notion of what's between them. Some one-sided intimacy that he imagined. Has she led him on? She has been grateful to Benson, but only grateful. It sickens her a little to look back and see — so clearly now — his true, misguided intent.

"If you're concerned for my well-being," says Virginia, "you could busy yourself finding me a thicker blanket to keep me warm at night or rustle up something more than gruel for my meals."

"Better I should be keeping an eye on you," he says with a note in his voice that chills her. So different from how he was before. His jealousy of the captain has revealed him. "You're my first murderess. We don't get those in here every day."

She feels weary as she answers, "I'm not a murderess."

"Not proven so yet, I suppose. But I've been reading the *Clarion* lately, miss. Keeler lent me his copy, and I must say it's been eye-opening. They don't stand on such niceties."

"Niceties such as the truth?"

He shrugs again, and just like that, everything warm and human that ever passed between them melts away.

She supposes only a fool would be surprised. Of course there are allegations she was whoring it up with Captain Malcolm. The world cannot conceive of any bond between man and woman other than a romantic one, nor can a woman's accomplishments ever be judged on her own merits. It is assumed that everything she had she was given because a powerful man wanted access to her. That was what the sailors on the *Doris* assumed, with their whispers and their sidelong stares. It's what the newspaper writers and readers alike clearly assume. When she's hanged for murder and buried in a potter's field, they'll probably gossip she'd been tupped by whatever lout or lowlife they bury her next to.

This isn't new, of course. That was always the assumption of the westward travelers when she and Ames had guided them through the mountains; she and Ames were a couple, because why else would a man and a woman travel together? What else could be between them?

The answer was far more complex than she ever would have been able to explain, and besides, she didn't care to bother. What she and Ames had had was between her and Ames. And she had no reason to explain it to anyone, not from the day he rescued her after the Very Bad Thing until the day six years later when he died.

She only regretted that newspaper interview. The novelty of the girl reporter had thrown her off. When the woman had asked her about Ames, she'd grown emotional. She'd admitted, *The world won't be the same without him.* When the woman asked if she was going to find a new partner and go back to guiding settlers to California, she said, *That part of my life is over. I'm waiting here for my next adventure to find me.*

And find her it had, in the form of Lady Jane Franklin, who had read that newspaper interview and offered her employment. She wondered what would have happened if she'd never said those words. Would Franklin have sent out exactly the same expedition but with Caprice at the head? If she had, would Caprice be alive today? Would Christabel? Stella? Everything hinged on those words in that newspaper. The chain of events that had led some of them to this trial and some of them to the grave had started the moment Virginia dropped her guard, however briefly, and let herself be found.

She'd always wondered if Jane Franklin knew her whole story. The newspaper had only described her career as a trail guide. That was the experience that Franklin and Brooks alike had referred to. Virginia Reeve was a leader of men and women. She'd proven she could work closely with a man for the good and health of a traveling party. And if that was all she knew, Jane Franklin had chosen well.

But did she know the rest? The uncertainty had prickled at Virginia since the beginning. It prickled at her still today. And if it came up at trial, well, this whole charade would come to an abrupt halt, and not in a way that would benefit her.

Perhaps things will turn out well after all this, but she can't see her way to that possibility. Right now, she sees no reason to hope. At least she wasn't counting on Benson to jailbreak her; the wisest course, as ever, has always been to count on no one for anything.

Lost and found, found and lost. Like the truth. Like so many lives.

CHAPTER TWENTY-NINE:
VIRGINIA

Sierra Nevada Mountains
1846

Virginia looked out on a bright white landscape that seared her eyes. Everything had been wiped away. Trees, rocks, the path that brought them here, any path that might have led them out. Invisible, impassible.

They'd been told it was a shortcut. They'd wanted to get through the mountains as fast as possible to beat the advance of winter. They'd failed. And now they would be here only God knew how long, trapped by the unforgiving, merciless snow.

At home, she had never seen anything like this. Never seen snow this deep, never felt cold all the way to the bone. California was supposed to be the promised land, but from here, it looked like hell.

Were they even in California? She had lost track. She wasn't a leader of this expedition by any stretch anyway. She wasn't yet twenty years old, unmarried, still part of her mother's household. She could only do what she was told, go where she was bid. Sneaking out to give her stepfather enough supplies to survive on after his exile, that had been her only act of rebellion. And look where being good had gotten her. Stuck here, and look at the people stuck with her — Keseberg certainly wasn't a good man, nor Foster, and she had serious doubts about Spitzer and Reinhardt. If one's actions made such a difference, she should be in a different place than they were, not the same.

She'd prayed with the Breens a few times already, and she was considering, if the weather warmed enough, dragging herself through the drifts toward their cabin again. The times when she knelt to pray with them, grasping John's hand on one side and Edward's on the other, were the only times she felt warm. The only times she forgot her hunger. Perhaps their god warmed them. Perhaps when God spoke to you, it wasn't in words you could understand, only feelings. If she got out alive, she would thank God for it and ask Him to tell her how she could serve Him best.

And if she didn't get out alive, she wouldn't have to worry about keeping that promise or any other.

The snow was beautiful, in its way. Blue from within, like the color of the veins under a pretty girl's pale skin. Virginia herself had never had skin translucent enough to see through, but her cousin Mary Catherine had, and she could hear her relatives' compliments ringing out over this cold snow. *How lovely. How delicate.* The fact that she'd left Mary Catherine behind when her family had joined this wagon party — and the much more worrisome fact that the women she could hear speaking these words were clearly nonexistent — oh, those facts were simply not relevant right now, in the face of life-changing uncertainty. If her mind was developing ways to come to terms with it, that was to be expected.

Was she going insane? And if so, what could she do about it? Perhaps the smartest thing, given how bad it had already gotten and the inevitable truth that it would definitely get much worse, would be to walk outside and throw herself facedown into a drift. If the fine snow didn't choke or smother her straight off, she would quickly freeze stiff. Then death would come for her at last. Would it be pleasant enough? Would it be over soon? Would there be pain, if she simply let the cold carry her away?

As she watched, fresh flakes of snow began to fall.

They added to the ocean of snow that had already wiped the world away. How tall must it be? Ten feet, fifteen, twenty? And now more came down. The Breens' God must be a cruel one indeed if he allowed this to happen, and yet they never seemed to rail against him. Why was that? What was the peace they'd attained that Virginia herself did not seem able to find? She wanted to rail every moment of every day. Even in those moments before the snow began to fall, in the perfect solitary quiet, she'd wanted to scream. Her fury threatened to boil, to burn her up from the inside, though it could never keep her warm.

Her tears froze on her cheeks. She wouldn't go inside, not yet. She would wait out here until she could get herself under control, even though the cold was already squeezing the breath out of her throat and she'd started to lose feeling in her left hand, specifically the first two fingers. The cold was pressing the life out of her, but the way it looked from her vantage point, there were things more important than life, at least what seemed to pass for life here and now.

She couldn't let the little ones see her cry.

CHAPTER THIRTY: STELLA

Aboard the Doris
July 1853

As if it weren't lousy enough, being cooped up on this ship, Stella felt herself growing. Expanding. Every day, she took up a little more room, when for all these years, she had been striving to take up as little room as possible.

Back in Boston, the whole time she'd worked as a maid, she hated it when people remembered her. Or even noticed her. Her mother had worked her whole life in a factory, worked there still, and Stella would have done better to follow that example, like her sisters. But once she found work as a live-in maid, it was hard to give up that comfort. In some households, she found she didn't even have to work that hard, which beat the ugly, dirty work of the mills hands down. Let her sisters spoil their beauty with long hours, their hands with lye burns and caustic dye. She could stay above it all.

But no matter how quiet she kept, no matter how small she tried to make herself, the men of the house always ended up noticing her. She could often pinpoint the exact moment as it happened. A raised chin, a curious eye. Sometimes it was a glance that lingered too long; just as often, it was a hand that roamed. The household's father, a son, a brother. It mattered little who took a fancy to her. Once he had his sights set on her, no matter what she did or didn't do in response, it was always the beginning of the end.

So she had a habit of thieving just a little bit here and there, building up a stash of goods. Items that were valuable but ordinary were the best. Diamond studs or pearl drops, for example, could be exchanged for hard coin or folding money without raising uncomfortable questions. But she was an opportunistic thief, tucking aside everything from silver thimbles to porcelain pots if the opportunity presented itself. Small things could be tucked away into the folds of dresses and secured in the lining of a knapsack, a mattress, a coat. In this way, when she was inevitably dismissed — sometimes mere days, sometimes several months after a man of the household first noticed her — she'd have something to survive on until she landed on her feet, like a cat, in her next situation.

On the *Doris,* she'd been stealing things here and there purely from habit, but so far, none of the men had noticed her in that dooming, dangerous way. Her invisibility here was a small, treasured wonder. She'd once heard that certain animals smelled different in heat, sending out a scent that brought potential mates to them for a good rutting. Perhaps now, in her condition, she sent out the opposite of that. Neither the men nor the women seemed to have much interest in her, and she relished that lack of attention, all until the day things took the darkest turn.

She'd misjudged the hour somehow and found herself arriving at the mess just as the women's shift was ending. So as she came into the tight, fragrant space, the last of the women headed for the door as the men, still looking forward to their own meal, arrived. Had she been less hungry, she would have fled then and there, but her growling, avid belly would not let her. She stood her ground and served herself a trencher.

Had there been more room and proper seating, the men would have kept their distance. But as the room filled up, there was simply nowhere else to stand, and the late-arriving men drew closer and closer to where she stood.

She ate as quickly as she dared, but she was not done yet when a man took the last space in the cabin, immediately next to her. As they all shoveled food into their mouths wordlessly, everyone hoping to be done as quickly as possible, she saw the man next to her recoil.

At first, she simply thought he was disgusted by her ravenous, graceless way of eating, but when she snuck a look at his increasingly horrified face, she looked down to see what he was recoiling from.

Blood. Her blood.

Now, at the moment she most needed help, Stella was truly alone. She'd always prided herself on taking control of things, whether that meant handling the persistent advances of her employer to her own advantage or squirreling away her mistress's lesser-loved valuables against a rainy day. This last time, when her mistress had informed her gleefully she was to be dismissed, she herself had suggested she be sent on a voyage — *because if I am still here in Boston, Mrs. Holliday, don't you think Charles will come look for me? And if he finds me, he will want to marry. I'm not sure I could refuse him if he asked.* This was not the kind of journey she'd meant, but it would do. As a child, she'd imagined herself on the deck of a ship like this, hair blowing in the wind, face thrust forward with anticipation. An adventure, a true adventure. Had Charles been the only one to notice her, she would have happily run away with him or stayed in Boston as his mistress, but when his father noticed her also, that awful clock had begun to tick, and there was no coming back from it. There was also no telling which one of them had put this unwitting passenger in her belly, but in so many ways, it didn't matter.

And now this. Bleeding in the mess, crimson blood mixed with some other, clearer liquid running down her leg onto the worn wood of the floor. She'd seen enough women in the family way to know that the kernel growing inside her was nowhere old enough to live and breathe. She should have had at least two more months, probably three. Every day since she guessed about the passenger, she wondered what would happen to her, to it, but at this moment, she wondered no more. She knew, with an awful, dire certainty deep in her gut, exactly what was about to happen.

The only question was whether there would be one death or two. The bloody puddle on the floor grew.

"You there!" she heard a man shout, far off, miles away. "Here! Help!"

A rumbling caught her ears. The men were annoyed by something. If she could gather the strength to look up, pull herself together against the wringing pain that threatened to steal her breath, her mind, her everything — yes. They were mumbling their discontent to one another because a woman walked among them, her skirts brushing their knees in the narrow space, and she did not seem even a bit sorry.

Stella swallowed down bile and looked up so she could face the woman.

It was Elizabeth.

Pain and dizziness smeared the other woman's features, and it was only the color of her skin that made her stand out.

Of all the rotten luck, Stella cursed to herself.

What was she doing here? Of all the women who could have crossed her path at this moment, why did it have to be this one? She must have been passing when the man yelled for help, dragged her here.

Stella could not form words, but there was one thing she could do. She did not want to do it. She had to do it or die.

She stretched her hand out toward Elizabeth in the way Virginia had taught them, palm facing outward. *Help.*

Then Elizabeth was by her side, offering her arm, which Stella clutched hard like a drowning woman, balling a wad of cotton in her fist.

"It's coming," she whispered.

Elizabeth said, "Do you want me to take you to someone? Or bring them here?"

"I — it's hard to move," Stella said. "But the men can't see this."

"I'll take you to Siobhan. She'll know what to do."

"All right."

Stella flung her arm around Elizabeth and almost brought her down, but the shorter woman didn't complain. She braced her feet hard, leaned over to place one hand on the table, and said in a low voice, "Let's try again."

They edged out from between the men, hearing the grumbles as they went. A roll flew through the air and bounced off Stella's shoulder; she ignored it. Elizabeth moved forward grimly, in silence. Then they were out of the mess. The door swung shut behind them, and she heard the dull roar of their celebration, laughing at the woman who'd had to be carried out, rejoicing that their precious room belonged solely to sailors again.

Still silent, still clinging to one another, Elizabeth and Stella made their way through the ship. They did it slowly, with halting steps and staggering missteps that sent them both careening into boards and rope heaps and doors that swung open under their weight into rooms they'd had no intention of entering. Every time the motion of the ship swung them off course, Stella listened for Elizabeth's determined sigh, and they moved as one back in the right direction.

Finally, finally, Stella arrived in a tiny, dark cabin she didn't recognize, and standing over her was the familiar face of Siobhan, saying, "You made it. Just rest. Just rest. We've got you."

She fell onto something that might have been a pallet and lay still, relief swirling in with the pain.

Stella barely had time to notice that Siobhan hadn't said anything at all about things turning out all right before she slipped out of consciousness, the dark curtain descending.

CHAPTER THIRTY-ONE:
VIRGINIA

Aboard the Doris
July 1853

The day and night and day that Stella labored were some of the longest of Virginia's life, and she'd had days before that would have put seasoned soldiers in the madhouse. But the limbo of Stella's labor was terrible. If the baby had been born right away, that would usher in a whole new host of problems, but the prolonged situation in which the baby was eternally *on its way* was somehow worse. Everyone knew what was happening but not how it would resolve. All they knew was that it could not end happily.

All the women came and went, offering their prayers or their hands, their support or their sympathy. If Virginia had been merely a disinterested observer, she would have found their varied reactions fascinating. Perhaps Margaret was recording them

335

for posterity, she found herself thinking. That woman was always writing something down. Were her notes accurate? Desperate to distract herself, Virginia let her mind wander.

Did Margaret note how long Irene stayed, far longer than any other, gripping Stella's hand with both of hers even when the woman was unconscious, unaware? Could she tell that Elizabeth was the only one Stella seemed to recognize, how she made a weak gesture with her hand, the *help* motion, every time the dark-skinned woman came near? Did she record Althea's brief, perfunctory stay and the way Ebba, unlike her friend, chose to linger?

At no time did the ship's doctor offer his services or his instruments, though they occupied the medical cabin without apology. Siobhan did her best, though she confessed to Virginia and Dove that her medical lectures had not at all addressed the mechanics of childbirth; Dove replied that she'd supervised a handful of labors, all in intolerable conditions. She did not say how many of the babies and mothers had survived the ordeal. Neither Virginia nor Siobhan asked. They simply turned their attention back to the patient and offered her the comfort they could.

None of the three left Stella's side. Virginia felt it was her duty, though the stink of blood made her ill. It reminded her all too sharply of butchery, the way fresh wounds smelled different from older ones, how the scent changed as rot began to set in and then again when it really, truly took hold.

Her head was swimming, a cloud of black threatening the edges of her vision, when she felt a heavy hand clasp her shoulder.

"You ever seen a baby born?" asked Dove.

Virginia did not think Dove cared about the answer, but she grasped at the conversation to take her attention off the carnage. "No. You said you'd seen how many?"

"A few."

"Is it always like this?"

"Dear Lord, I hope not," said the nurse and turned away again.

Stella had lost consciousness, and Siobhan and Dove took the opportunity to argue about her when she couldn't hear. They kept their voices down, but Virginia caught the gist of it. Siobhan wanted to try to save both the baby and the mother. Her lectures hadn't told her much, but she'd read plenty of anatomy texts, and she thought Stella had not yet lost a dangerous amount of blood. If they took care to keep the area clean and let things take their course, they could at least reduce Stella's chances of succumbing to childbed fever. Dove, for her part, thought Siobhan was a fool.

Just as Virginia opened her mouth to put in her own two cents, Stella awoke with a guttural howl, writhing in pain, her legs flailing.

How long can this last? thought Virginia, her stomach twisting. *How long can any of this last?*

It lasted far longer than any of them would have liked, and it ended in a way none of them would have wished.

At the end of the second day, when even the ridiculously long hours of sunlight began to give way to what passed for a summer Arctic twilight, Stella's hoarse screams came one upon another upon another. Between her legs, Dove held her hands out, and something landed in them, wet and dark and red.

Virginia held her breath.

After a long moment that stretched over the horizon and into oblivion, Siobhan looked up, caught Virginia's eye, and shook her head in the negative. No breath. No life. The child was not a child but already a body, no more.

Virginia spoke in a whisper, but even her soft words fell with a thud in the sudden silence. "I will tell the others."

It was only after she left the close, fetid air of the cabin that she realized she should have stayed until they knew whether Stella would survive. The other women would ask her, and she had no idea.

Halfway down the hallway, her steps slowed, too dazed to move forward. She was not at all sure she could force herself to go back.

When the big hand grabbed her arm, she was too stunned to react, and she was being pulled, stumbling, faster than her feet could plant themselves to resist.

Captain Malcolm pulled her inside his cabin and slammed the door shut, his breath a ragged pant. "Did you know?"

She had never heard such emotion in his voice. He sounded like a different man. He'd been holding so much of himself back, she saw now, and his face was alive in a way she'd never seen it: as if the next words out of her mouth could save his life or break his heart, and the entire world would stand still until she spoke.

Not now, she thought. *Not here.* She had been accustomed to thinking of the captain as an extension of his ship, as merely an instrument, and she could see now she'd done him a disservice. Or perhaps she had only seen what he wanted her to see until now. Now, she saw everything.

He prompted her, more gently, as if he were afraid he'd scared her into silence. "Virginia, did you know?"

She could not lie. "Yes."

"How long?"

"A week."

Low and certain, he said, "You should have told me."

For a moment, wrecked, she could not form words. His cabin was close and almost warm, with an unmistakable musky scent. Virginia knew it well. The smell of unwashed man, closed in, cooped up. It did not scare her, but it put her on guard.

She forced herself to meet his eyes and read the anger there. He was not wrong, she knew, to be angry at her. She was angry at herself.

"I'm sorry," she said. "I should have. But what could you have done?"

"I don't know," he said, and then again, softer, lower, "I don't know."

"The child died," she said, the harsh words a small explosion in the dimly lit, tight space.

"Eternal Lord God, you hold all souls in life," he said, not to her, and turned away from her to continue the prayer, muttering softly, his words only between him and his God. She remembered early in the voyage, after Christabel's death, when his bare hands had clasped hers in prayer. Now they both wore mittens to keep warm at night, even inside their cabins, and for this prayer, his hands clasped only each other.

Her face burned with shame. She had failed Stella. She had failed the captain. She pressed her mittened hands together, trying to pray, but her mind was too dizzied with earthly concerns.

What now? Dear God — and it was a prayer, but not a reassuring one — *Dear God, what now?*

Once the captain finished his prayer and rhythmically tapped his forehead, chest, left shoulder, right, he turned back to her. The look on his face was far more complex than anger.

"The men . . . they will take this as another bad omen. I cannot say what they might do. Two deaths in such a short time."

"Or three."

"The woman will not survive?"

"Her name is Stella," said Virginia, her voice unsteady, "and we don't know."

"Death comes in threes," he said grimly. "For them, it might be better."

"Worse for her," said Virginia, almost spitting the words. "Is that all you think of? How it is for *them*?"

He grabbed her by both shoulders. She felt the covered tip of his thumb in the hollow in front of her shoulder bone, he grasped her so tightly, and yet she did not believe he would hurt her.

"You have no idea what I think of," he said.

"Then tell me," she said, not flinching.

Captain Malcolm let go of her shoulders, but their bodies were still so close together she could smell him, the real him, not the cabin's stale air. He was salt and musk, dirt and cedar, with a faint undertone of rum.

He began, "Do you know the story of the man this bay is named for? Hudson?"

"I'm afraid I don't."

"I'll tell you the short version," he said, his voice clipped. "Henry Hudson, after he discovered this bay, had a disagreement with his crew. So they mutinied, took over the ship, and set him adrift in a shallop to die."

"That is . . . short."

"And I'm sure you see my meaning. You seem to think that being in charge of a group means you dictate their actions."

"That's not what I think," protested Virginia, but he did not stop to listen to what she did think.

"One never dictates people's actions. You only guide them. No one person can ever truly be in charge of another."

"Are you saying you can't command your crew not to hurt us?"

"I'm saying I already have. For all the good it will do."

She wanted to pound her fists against the close, close walls. She wanted to roar. She couldn't. "You're afraid they won't listen?"

"Yes."

"Can't you make them?" She knew she sounded childish but didn't know what else to say.

"You've met Keane. Do you think I can make him do anything?"

More gently now, more softly, she said, "But if you fear him, why don't you relieve him of his position? Punish him, or — there must be something you can do."

"He has too many allies," said the captain, his expression grim. "A dozen of these men have served longer with him than they have with me. When I moved the *Doris* into Hudson Bay, much of my crew chose to sign on with other whalers instead. I had to take whatever pickings I could get at York Factory, the only big trade depot on the western shore. At the time, it seemed good fortune that Keane could suggest enough men to round out a full crew. And that all twelve were big, strapping men, built for the hardest hauling. Now, of course, I see it differently."

"I'm sorry," she whispered.

He shrugged. "This is my first voyage with this crew, and one way or another, it will be my last."

"And you think that if you take the wrong action, Keane or his allies will mutiny and put you out in a shallop? Make a Hudson of you?"

"I do," he said nakedly, and she saw the fear in his eyes. "Or perhaps he won't even bother with the shallop. Perhaps he'll just shoot me through the head, claim accident, and do what he wants with you and your women once I'm dead."

Virginia stared at him. She hadn't realized the intensity of his fear, how deep it ran. It was contagious.

He said, "I'm sure it has not escaped your notice that I am not of English origin."

"It has not," she replied.

"My father's family came from free men and women, slaves emancipated after the American Revolution, and my mother's family was Wampanoag. I own my ship free and clear, and yet if any man wants to take what I have — as Keane might do — he could call my freedom into question."

"But he could not succeed," she said incredulously.

He answered, "Do you truly believe that, Virginia?"

The silence hung between them for a long time before she was able to form words, and when she did, she did not think they were the right ones, but she had no others.

"I don't know what to do," she said.

"As I said — and I know you do not want to hear this — it will be better for you if Stella dies."

"I cannot hope for that."

"I know."

All at once, her fear, like his, roared over her in a wave. "Why did you tell me? Why did you tell me any of this?"

"You've kept secrets from me, things you should have shared. But I understand," said Captain Malcolm. "I kept my distance for my own reasons. I led you to believe that you could not trust me. I am sorry."

"You weren't wrong. The fault is mine too."

"Let us set the question of fault aside. Can you promise to be honest with me?"

"Yes," she said, although she feared it was far too late.

The captain's gaze met hers, held it, asked

a question she did not know how to answer.

She looked away and told him the one thing she could not tell anyone else aboard, perhaps no one else in the world, at that moment. "I'm afraid."

He stepped closer to her then, one step, two.

"Only fools have no fear," he said.

Then she was the one stepping forward, curling her hand around the back of his neck, drawing his face down. He let her move him, bending to her, wordless.

She pressed her cheek against his and stood, feeling the warmth of his skin on hers, savoring it, the details of his solid presence a moment's respite from the uncertain world. The high, hard cheekbone. The brush of his eyelashes as he blinked. The edge of his beard rough against her jawline.

"We are all fools here, I think," she said quietly. "Only different kinds."

He turned his face to press his forehead against her temple, his breath warm on her ear. "I do not think you a fool."

She smiled ruefully. "If you knew me better, perhaps you would. But I won't be around much longer, will I?"

He lifted his head then, the spell broken, and she let her hand drop from his neck. She took two steps back, then three. When he held her gaze again, the question was no longer in it. He had his answer.

"God willing," he said, "we will both find glory in our separate adventures."

There was nothing more to say. She had promised honesty, and the honest truth was, after the women disembarked at Repulse Bay, she never expected to see Jacob Malcolm again. Their adventures would be, as he had put it perfectly, separate.

Moments later, Virginia was back in the narrow, cold hallway, dazed and uncertain.

Her duty to the women of the expedition was the most important thing. But after that, she desperately needed to calm herself and could think of only one way.

In gentle, spare terms, she told the women what had happened in the medical cabin and led them in a short prayer. Then, she did not stay. She let them assume she was headed back to check on Stella, but instead, she shouldered her pack and headed in the direction of the galley.

There was nowhere to be truly alone, but the cook rarely left the galley, so she pressed herself up against the galley's closed door. She could feel the warmth of the stove through the wood and savored it for a long moment.

She was desperate for reassurance. She

hoped that Lady Franklin, across time and miles, could provide it. No one here could, least of all herself. She should have opened the letter in early May, but she was holding it for when she most needed it; she needed it now.

Virginia broke the wax seal with trembling fingers and raised the letter toward her face in the dim, greasy light of the oil lamp. The thin paper fluttered as she devoured each word hungrily.

Dear Miss Reeve,

Two months into your journey now. If you have followed the proper course, this letter should find you passing Darkness Point. A windy, desolate place, they say. An earlier expedition ran aground there, beaching their ship, which was lost, and marooning twenty men. When they were found the next summer by another schooner, six remained.

Let us hope your luck is of somewhat more durable stock.

Your luck is, of course, not the only thing that determines whether you succeed. Your spirit and determination play a part. That is why I chose you. I chose the other women who are with you for good reasons as well. I wonder if you might be doubting that at this point, now that you have gotten to know them, now that the veneer of society has long been stripped away. You know these women now, better than anyone else could. I imagine much has been revealed. I am certain each of these women has flaws of which I was not aware.

I am certain the same is true of you.

And so, do the best you can. No expedition's path is completely smooth. You are in rough terrain. If you have veered off course, you are likely in even harsher territory and greater danger. Make good decisions. Use the strengths of your women. That is why they are with you, every last one.

My husband had more ships, more resources, more men, and yet we do not know his fate or theirs. I look to you to answer that question. I look to you to bring him home. And if you cannot, for whatever reason, I hope you can bring home news of his fate so we can trumpet his successes to the world. The world thirsts to know the truth. I cannot have them thinking he made the mistake made by the expedition beached at Darkness Point. He was not so foolish. He cannot, will not, be remembered in such a way. You will help me show them. You will polish his name to a brilliant shine. I have no doubt in my mind.

Move ever forward. It is summer now, but winter will come. Do as much as you can until that day.

Sincere regards,

J

CHAPTER THIRTY-TWO:
VIRGINIA

Charles Street Jail, Boston
October 1854

Today's food is no better than yesterday's, but with each day, Virginia finds it more tolerable. Probably because it has become habit. In the North, she became accustomed to flour paste and pemmican, and after that, nothing, then raw meat, then jerked meat, then nothing again. Whatever they call food here is at least halfway worthy of the name and arrives regularly. She never has to wonder whether there will be more.

She looks up from her gruel when Benson calls nonchalantly, "A visitor for you."

Perhaps it will be her counsel, coming to ask questions Virginia will never answer, now that she is certain he's working against her. She thinks she has figured it out. If the Collins family has arranged for him, she thinks, it all makes far more sense. Not just his indifference and inaction in the court-

351

room but his probing questions in the privacy of her cell. On the few occasions he bothered speaking to her, he pressed her to tell him what really happened. Was that for her defense? Or to hand over to those who want to destroy her? She does not bother to look up when she hears footsteps. She will never speak a willing word to Clevenger again.

Then she catches a whiff of rose perfume wafting gently into the frigid stone box of her cell. She hears the unmistakable whisper of silk on silk. How long has it been since she heard that sound? Since the parlor where she met Caprice? That was a lifetime ago, but it was the beginning of all this, and she fears she will not like the end.

The very thought makes her head feel heavy, but she forces herself to lift it anyway, open her eyes, stare out through the bars. The freckles like scattered stars, the stout body, the long, dexterous fingers. Instant recognition.

Siobhan, she thinks, her hand rising almost of its own accord to touch the cool metal of the bars between them.

The girl almost looks like a ghost. Younger, untouched, somehow like an earlier version of the Siobhan that Virginia knew. And she'd never seen Siobhan like this: decorated and adorned, fully feminine, with her hair in precise ringlets that tumble down from an intricate hat Virginia assumes is very much in fashion.

The purity of her smooth cheeks under the powder can't be real, it isn't possible, and so Virginia looks closer.

The face is Siobhan's, yet subtly not. And then she realizes who she's looking at.

The twins look so much alike, nearly identical. It's the only way the switch could work. Siobhan attended medical lectures at Harvard College and came north on the expedition. The one who stayed home and busied themselves with social calls and dress fittings, the one whose skin remains creamy and flawless, this is not the Siobhan that Virginia knew.

"Sean," she breathes.

His eyes flash wild at her incautious use of the name.

She hastens to correct her mistake, takes care in case the guard is listening. "It's kind of you to come, Miss . . . ?"

"Perry. Miss Siobhan Perry."

"I wish I could be more hospitable, Miss Perry. To offer you a seat. Alas, I haven't one at the ready." She gestures around at the bare walls and floor, and Siobhan's brother, Sean, follows with his eyes.

"I've known worse hardships."

"I imagine." She knows from Siobhan that the true hardship for him is being forced to live as a man when he — or should she say she? — is a woman born into the wrong body. She cannot imagine.

As if hearing her thoughts, Sean says, "We were sisters. She always knew it, despite what others thought, what the world insisted. Did she tell you that?"

"She did not put it quite that way, no. But I'm familiar with . . . your situation."

Sean says, "Then you understand why she couldn't come. It would expose both of us in ways that are . . . unacceptable."

"How is she?" whispers Virginia instead of answering. She doesn't want to indulge in asking why. Sean didn't have to come here at all. In an ideal world, yes, Siobhan would sit in the witness box telling her story, the one that would prove Virginia innocent of murder. Siobhan saw everything that happened between Caprice and Virginia on that last day. Her truth, if she shared it, would be the real truth.

It is sad, recognizes Virginia, that she thinks so fondly of how lovely it would be if her friend were here to testify on her behalf. In a truly ideal world, Virginia would not be on trial for murder in the first place.

354

Sean says, "Quite well. Practicing medicine. Hung out a shingle over Woburn way, general practice, establishing an excellent reputation for good care given with good cheer. The family's exceptionally proud, as you might imagine."

She thinks about how to ask her next question. It doesn't seem like there are any guards or officers close enough to overhear them, but better to be circumspect. "Living under a new name, then?"

"The name belongs to Dr. Perry now. Its original owner has no need of it."

Virginia wonders if Siobhan is truly happy with this arrangement. The switch is not exactly tit for tat. The Perry who is the sister before her, born into the name Sean, can now live as the woman she has always believed herself to be. But the new Sean is a woman too, born Siobhan, who has never wanted to be a man, only to exercise the rights a man has: to get an education, to use one's talents, to walk in the world without apology or fear. Rights that half the white population takes merrily for granted and most of the other half feels will always lie beyond their constrained feminine reach.

But her friend is, in many ways, living the life she wanted. Virginia can't help but smile at that.

"Does that strike you as odd?" says the new Siobhan.

"I am not sure how any of this strikes me," Virginia says truthfully. There is no reason not to be honest; soon she'll be either free or dead, and either way, she doesn't want her soul weighed down by any regrets or lies. "Our mutual friend is a truly exceptional person. I am glad to hear of . . . the doctor's success."

A soft, perfumed hand reaches out toward the bars, and Virginia reaches out in response. Even though this Siobhan is not the one she knows and trusts, her touch will be comfort. When the survivors first came off the ice, they found themselves casually touching one another, almost constantly, for reassurance. It was such a joy to feel skin on skin again instead of only wet fur forever scraping their chilled, half-numb fingertips. So when she sees Siobhan's hand, her concerned face, Virginia eagerly puts her hand out to be touched. Siobhan's gloved fingers lie across the back of Virginia's rougher hand so tenderly.

Speaking softly, the new Siobhan asks Virginia, "And is there anything I can do for you?"

What she needs is the other Siobhan, her Siobhan, here. To testify. To save her. But that can't happen. For the past year, Siobhan Perry has been regularly seen living her modest life in Boston, while her brother, Sean, the family told friends, had elected to take apprenticeship with a doctor in New Orleans to make a particular study of yellow fever. Siobhan Perry cannot now claim to have participated in an all-female expedition to the Arctic when countless witnesses saw her everywhere in Boston from Charlestown to Quincy Market. Both halves of the twins' charade would fall apart. Catastrophe. And after all that, what if the jury didn't believe her story of Virginia's innocence? It isn't worth it. Even Virginia, whose life is on the line, knows it isn't.

Instead of asking for what she really wants, what she needs, Virginia says, "Send the doctor my best if you two speak."

Siobhan nods. "Of course. But are you sure there isn't anything I can do to help?"

Virginia thinks of everything that has happened in that courtroom and everything that hasn't. Her lawyer, the one person who is supposed to be on her side, is a puppet for her enemies. The prosecutor is beating her down word by word, witness by witness. The jury of well-off white men and the well-off white judge only trust people who look and sound like them, and those are not the people who will ever speak in favor of Virginia. Every day, every minute, she's felt powerless. She gave up even before she got here.

But.

Even though the captain didn't exactly speak up for her, he didn't speak against her either.

Even though her own Siobhan is now beyond reach, this Siobhan is offering help. *Help.* Her wrist begins to twist in the familiar motion, independent of Virginia's mind, moving on its own.

What if she didn't give up? What if she tried?

If she really wants to live — does she? — she cannot just wait for salvation. She could pray to God for help, but that's not the God she knows. If He is to work, He will work through human hands.

The new Siobhan says again, softly and urgently, "Can I help?"

What can she do? One thing, but oh, what a thing. She can carry a message. All Virginia has to do is decide who the message should go to and what she wants to ask for.

It comes clear.

"I have a message for you to carry." She keeps her voice low and her eyes on the new Siobhan's eyes. "I can't offer you anything to carry it, but . . . in the spirit of honoring those we have in common, I would very much appreciate your help."

"Miss Reeve," says the new Siobhan in a low, lovely whisper, "I am at your disposal."

CHAPTER THIRTY-THREE:
IRENE

Massachusetts Superior Court, Boston
October 1854

It is torture to sit here day after day and watch Virginia's trial unfold, and Irene never for a minute considered doing otherwise. She recognized the darkness in Virginia's gaze when they met; it was the dark self-knowledge of a person who has once been unfettered and can never forget what happened in the feral days. She doesn't know Virginia's particular pain any more than Virginia knows hers, but those days make them kin, deep down, and she will never abandon kin.

All the survivors, the ones who are here and those who aren't, owe Virginia a debt they can never repay. Perhaps that woman Dove — off to Crimea by now, surely — believes she saved her own life up there in the North. The rest of them know better. Virginia's leadership protected some of them more directly for longer, but all of them, all of them, would have been at risk without her. Irene may not be able to do much to save her, but she can be here. She can watch. She can witness.

Today, she witnesses as, for the first time, the prosecution calls one of the five forward. "The prosecution calls Mrs. Ebba Green to the stand."

Ebba's eyes are wide. Her mouth falls open.

Irene, sitting next to her, grabs for and squeezes the Englishwoman's hand. She always sits between Ebba and Althea. They always arrive at the same time, but in the courtroom, they barely glance each other's way. The two former friends never speak to one another, never touch. When Irene's hand squeezes hers, Ebba breathes in audibly and squeezes back. She clearly needs the comfort, however brief. Irene can practically hear her heart galloping in her chest. Irene can hear better than most.

Getting unsteadily to her feet, Ebba lets go of Irene's hand and moves forward, almost lurching, putting her hand on the courtroom rail to keep herself from tumbling. She stands there a long moment. Perhaps she's not as stable as she once was after losing those toes. One never realized how important all ten toes were to balance a person's body. So small, so crucial.

Like a tongue, thought Irene. One had no idea how much it was needed until it was gone.

Irene suspects Ebba's unsteadiness isn't all about her injuries, though. The Englishwoman is delaying the moment she sits in the witness box.

But even as slowly as she creeps forward, she arrives, and in the swearing-in, she stands to face straight forward without any curve to her spine.

"Please state your name for the record," says the bailiff.

"Mrs. Ebba Green."

"You don't use your husband's name?" asks the prosecutor, sounding surprised.

"I beg your pardon? Green is my married name."

"Oh, but I thought you upper-class ladies used the Christian name as well. Mrs. — what is your husband's name?"

"Is?" asks Ebba quietly.

Was, thinks Irene.

The prosecutor mistakes her hesitation. "James? John? Henry?"

"Daniel."

"Yes. So you could also call yourself Mrs. Daniel Green."

362

"I could, should I choose to," says Ebba slowly.

"Well, have it as you like. Do you miss your husband, Mrs. Green?"

Ebba can't keep the emotion off her face this time. She is outraged. "*Miss* him? What could that matter to you?"

The judge looks to the defense attorney, who is rustling papers around — Irene cannot believe just how often the man rustles — but he does not object.

"I don't usually hurry attorneys along," says the judge, "but I'm beginning to see the need. Could you please get to the point, Counsel?"

"Of course, Your Honor. Question withdrawn, Mrs. Green, since you're having trouble answering it. So let's move forward. I'm sure you're wondering why I've asked you to testify for the prosecution, though you sit there in the front row with the supporters of the murderess as if you are proud to know her."

"Accused."

"I'm sorry?"

"Accused murderess."

"Have it as you like, Mrs. Green. I hear that is English custom."

"Get on with it," says Ebba through gritted teeth, and Irene tries to send her messages with her eyes, *Calm down, steady now, steady.*

"It's simple. I have two questions. Can you answer two questions for the sake of your friend, the *accused* murderess?"

"That depends on what the questions are, sir," Ebba says.

Irene can hear that she's trying desperately to get herself under control. Irene wonders what they know about Ebba, why she has been chosen. To what use do they intend to put her? Do they know the ways in which Ebba and Althea differ, or do they think one is as good as the other? Certainly, if Althea had been asked if she missed her husband, she would have just said yes and been done with it. The prosecution probably doesn't know that. But while a shot in the dark doesn't always hit its target, if that target does get hit, it still ends up with a hole in the middle.

"Mrs. Green," intones the prosecutor, "could you please name the twelve women of the expedition for us? There was testimony earlier from Mrs . . . let me see, yes, Mrs. Quinlan. She indicated the defendant told her that the expedition numbered twelve. We know some of them, but I think it would be helpful for our jury to hear you give the complete list."

Irene sucks her breath in at the exact moment Ebba does, and she hears and feels the rest of the group breathe in too. Doro's breath, Margaret's breath, Althea's, all five of them as one. She does not look over to see if Virginia is affected as well. She bets that Virginia is less surprised and better able to hide it.

They talked about this. Their answer was agreed upon. Now the only question is whether Ebba will, under oath, give that agreed-upon answer or another one.

Ebba says, her voice cool, "No."

"I'm sorry." He is incredulous, offended. "No?"

"No."

"Judge," complains the prosecutor, "can you compel her to list the women of the expedition?"

The judge looks annoyed, which is not new, but this time, at least his disdain is directed at the prosecutor. "I suppose I could. I choose not to. What reason do you have for wanting them listed?"

Putting his hip out almost like a girl denied a stick of penny candy, the prosecutor says, "So we know the name of every woman Virginia Reeve failed to bring back."

Irene leans ever so slightly forward in her seat. She can read the skepticism on the judge's face. She knows what he's going to say before he says it.

"Do their names matter?" the judge asks, his own answer to the question obvious in his tone. "They are not here."

Irene takes this as a good sign for Virginia, a slight nudge in the direction of justice, until the judge goes on.

"She failed them," Judge Miller says flatly. "There is one name that matters, the one this case concerns. Caprice Collins."

To his credit, the prosecutor draws the curtain over his disappointment quickly and says, "And that is my second question. I hope, Mrs. Green, you'll provide a more satisfactory answer to that one."

Ebba looks down her nose at him. She is not generally haughty, but Irene appreciates her haughtiness now. She remains silent, which is suitable, since she hasn't yet been asked a question.

Irene is far from the only one leaning forward in her seat now. She sneaks a look at Virginia; Virginia looks utterly impassive. Not uninterested but unemotional. Irene knows how hard Virginia must be working to look like she doesn't care when her heart is a fierce and burning one.

The prosecutor takes a few steps, faces Ebba, and says, "Here is my question."

He revels in the silence. She just stares.

"I only wanted to ask you what happened to Caprice," he says. "Out on the ice. Now, we've heard from the police reports that the death happened on the ice, after the women of your party disembarked from the *Doris*. All the accounts — and we've read many — agreed in the main. Caprice was alive on the ship. So we know that out on the ice, that's where she died."

Ebba opens her mouth to speak, but he cuts her off.

"No, Mrs. Green, not your turn. I haven't asked you a question yet."

If Irene could bottle the fire in Ebba's glare, she could melt ice in a heartbeat.

"So here's your chance to tell us your version of the story. Exonerate your friend. Tell us, Mrs. Green, exactly what happened on the ice, exactly what you saw unfold before your very eyes."

Ebba gets herself under control, just barely. Irene can still see the fire in her eyes, but she regains her posture, grips one hand with the other in her lap. She breathes in and out, and then she answers. "I'm sorry. I cannot."

"Oh!" His surprise is so badly feigned, Irene realizes in a rush he has planned this all along. This, it seems, is the entire point of the Englishwoman's testimony. "Why can't you?"

Ebba admits, with clear regret, "We were not there."

CHAPTER THIRTY-FOUR: DOVE

Aboard the Doris
July 1853
The thrice-damned bitch, thought Dove.

She didn't mean to find the loot. She only went through Stella's belongings in search of something that might comfort the woman after what had happened, and what was her reward for trying? A cascade of thieved items, everything reported missing and more, cutlery and earbobs and half a dozen other items Stella had obviously stolen since the *Doris* set sail.

Another woman might have taken the stolen goods to Stella herself, asked her to explain them, but Dove couldn't. Her priority was to protect herself. It always had been; that was the only reason she was still alive after years on the front. If she hadn't been sentimental about her husbands, she wasn't going to be sentimental about a girl she barely knew, no matter how sorry she felt for her.

Stella was in no state to explain herself anyway. She'd survived losing all that blood, but barely. Siobhan had stitched what had torn — Dove admired the neatness of her stitches grudgingly — and kept the incision site clean as a preacher's collar. Then, they could only wait.

A week had passed, and they'd moved Stella back into her own bunk, but she said nothing, ate little, mostly slept. That was why Dove had thought to cheer her with something treasured. But the treasured things she'd found in Stella's pack, lo and behold, were others' treasure. Now there'd be a reckoning.

Nor would she take these things to Virginia. Virginia might be in charge of the mission, but she wasn't in charge of the ship. No. The captain needed to know.

Dove's mistake, if she'd admit to making one, was confronting the captain as soon as she saw him instead of waiting for a private moment. The moment she unfolded the cloth and the silvered gleam of two nested spoons caught the air, a sailor saw too, and word spread.

She explained where she'd found the goods. The captain thanked her for it. They stood close together on the deck, heads bent over the cloth bundle. And then everything broke wide open.

"What a lovely tête-à-tête!" crowed Keane. He pronounced it *teat*.

"What is it, Keane?" said the captain through gritted teeth.

"We see you've found the thief, sir," the mate responded, his voice louder than it needed to be. He had a voice that carried. "We've got some thoughts on what you might do with her."

"I'm not a thief," said Dove hotly.

"Round up the other women!" Keane called out to the crew, and though the captain opened his mouth to belay the order, Dove saw the moment when he decided he could not.

She hadn't realized he was afraid of his men. She could tell the whole situation was on the cusp of exploding, but who would be left standing after it did, she could not be sure.

Then, Virginia was charging toward them.

"What's the meaning of this?" she said. "Malcolm? Dove?"

"I am sorry," said the captain without preamble, his throat tight, though with what emotion, Dove could not guess. "We can no longer deliver your party to Repulse Bay."

"What?" The word came out of Virginia

371

like a bark, sharp and cutting.

"I am sorry," he repeated. "The thief is among you. Such behavior cannot be tolerated."

"You?" Virginia asked Dove.

"Stella."

Her gaze flicked over to where Dove now saw the women were assembled. They clustered together like doves in a cote. What had they been told and by whom? Even Stella herself was among them, pale but upright, with an Englishwoman on either side to steady her.

Virginia drew close to the captain. "Can we discuss this privately?" Her eyes darted around, her message clear. But if she hadn't figured out yet that the captain had lost control of the crew, she would soon.

Keane grabbed for her arm. "No, miss. You can have this conversation in the presence of God and everyone instead of trying to seduce the good captain with your little mousehole."

"Watch your language, Keane," growled the captain.

"I told you this would happen, sir. Taking these women on. And here we are. Two dead in their party and a thief. Not to mention the near miss with the ones what went in the drink. Put their party off before the next death is ours."

"Put us off?" said Virginia incredulously. "In the middle of Hudson Bay? I suppose you would like us to swim."

Now the crew began to chip in. *Sounds good. Yeah. See if they float.*

"Might be we'd give you a craft. Might even be one that doesn't leak much," Keane said, his face smug.

"Not your decision, Mate," said the captain.

Behind Keane, though, Dove saw some of the larger men gathering. She recognized the one named Coffin, who had fists like sledgehammers, and an equally large seaman she'd only heard called Bear.

"Five hundred miles from where you promised to deliver us," argued Virginia, her voice clear and strident, unbowed. "Nowhere near Repulse Bay. Nowhere near the search area. Making it impossible for us to complete our mission before winter comes."

"Your mission ain't our business," Coffin growled. "Our business is staying alive."

"Would you have us do less?" Caprice shouted at the huge man, her coat a crimson splash like blood against the navy and gray of the rest of the crowd. "Abandoning us on the shore hundreds of miles from civilization? No idea where we are or where we're going?"

"If we did take you to shore," the captain said, his voice quieter, "you could go south to Prince of Wales Fort. Churchill's just beyond. Probably a month's journey, but just hug the shore, you can't miss it. All you have to do is turn south."

"Or we might turn north," Caprice said, a challenging light in her eye.

"Or we could stay on board until Repulse Bay, per our agreement," Virginia said loudly. Turning herself to directly address Captain Malcolm, she added, "And you could keep to your contract, as a man of your word."

"Like a siren she calls!" Keane countered, stepping between her and the captain, the huge men behind him moving in concert. "We knew it from the first. You said they would bring us no harm. Yet there's been nothing but harm from the beginning. Do you see now? What they are? What they do?"

Dove saw her moment and interrupted, "Not all of us, sirs."

The captain's gaze flicked from face to face, uneasy. Then, answering Dove's question without looking her in the eye, he said, "I'm sorry. The men of the *Doris* want you gone."

"But we're not all troublemakers," said Dove. "Take me, for example. I know how to get along."

"Dove!" Althea's voice was shocked. If she'd had pearls at her neck, she would have clutched them.

"Didn't mean anything by it," Dove said. "I only meant that if some of us were to stay on board, we would listen to you, Captain Malcolm. Obey your orders. Fall into line like any of your sailors. We're not all bad luck, you know."

The captain and Virginia locked eyes, and he looked — what? Pitiful? Pitying?

Virginia seemed to weigh something and make a decision. Then she said quietly, "I'll go. And Stella will go."

They all looked at Stella. She gave a small, weak nod.

"And any of the other women who want to go with us are welcome," called Virginia. To the captain, she said, "In return, we take all the supplies we brought with us, and I expect safe passage for the women who remain on board."

"You think he's in a position to make that bargain?" the mate asked, his voice mocking.

But the captain glared daggers at him, stepping forward, his hand going to the firearm at his hip. "I can make what bargain I like."

They were right on the edge of disaster, thought Dove. The aggression that had bubbled just under the surface was about to boil over. It wasn't just disapproval, what these men felt for these women. It was a deep, choking hate.

Was she foolish to stay? Perhaps. But her chances of survival were better on a ship than on the land, and she'd always been a smart one for playing the odds. Finding Franklin had been a lark. Now it was about survival.

"Who's with me?" asked Dove, stepping forward, addressing the women directly. "I will protect any woman who stays."

Caprice took one long step forward, and Dove found herself wondering which way the woman would go. She'd made no secret of her dislike for Virginia, but she was also hungry for glory, and there would be none of that going home on this ship. Their road home would be the opposite of glory.

So it was not entirely a surprise when Caprice, eyes burning bright, said, "Thanks for that offer, Dove, but I'll be trying my luck on the ice. We're with Virginia."

"We?"

"Me and Elizabeth," said Caprice without

looking behind her. It was not a question.

But the dark-skinned woman's voice trembled on a single word. "Well . . ."

Caprice turned then, smooth and unhurried, to face Elizabeth. "You think you'd be welcome returning without me?"

"No, but —"

Caprice drew closer to Elizabeth then and spoke a couple of words in her ear, fast and low. Dove only caught one, *reward,* and watched Elizabeth's face carefully. She was wavering.

Dove interrupted, "Are we going to chitchat or are we going to choose? Because I don't see much patience where I'm looking."

Caprice raised her voice one more time and said to Elizabeth, "Let's go."

And whether it was the authority in Caprice's voice or whatever Caprice had offered or for her own private reasons, Elizabeth said, "I suppose that's fine, then," and stepped forward.

As the two crossed to stand next to Virginia and Stella — Virginia's eyes stormy with emotion — Caprice reached out to tap Ann on the shoulder as she passed.

"I assume Ann is with us, right, Ann?" Her voice was almost cheerful. "Your dogs will want to run."

"Right behind you, miss," Ann said.

The crew, surprisingly, parted without comment to allow the women to make their choices. Dove drew herself up to her full height. Every woman now knew what was at stake. It was up to each of them to choose.

For a moment, Dove feared she might be left alone on the ship. Then, she would not be safe. If Caprice could make a case, so could she. So she called, "Althea, Ebba, I assume you'll want to stay on board. Respectable women like you."

Althea murmured, "Yes, of course," without looking at anyone.

Ebba's eyes were on her friend's face when she said, "We'll stay."

As they came to stand behind her, Ebba took Dove's arm and whispered into her ear, "Why did you start this? Have you no principles?"

This was not the time nor the place to explain herself, even if she'd wanted to. "Principles cost," Dove hissed back. "Too dear."

But there was no time for conversation. Choices were being made.

Next, Siobhan piped up, "Wherever the party on land is bound, they will need a medical officer. Since the nurse is not available, I'll go." She moved up to stand with Virginia and Caprice, holding her chin high.

They all chose. Neither Doro nor Irene spoke their choice aloud, but they didn't need to. Their feet showed where their loyalties lay.

The last one to make her choice, as she stepped forward, Margaret hesitated for a moment. Dove reached out a hand to her. A long beat later, the light winking against the glass in her spectacles, Margaret took it.

In the end, the split was far from even. Eight women would take to the land: Caprice and Virginia, Stella and Siobhan, Elizabeth and Ann, Doro and Irene. Four would remain: Dove, Ebba, Althea, and Margaret. Dove was too stunned to feel relief, but she was glad of the company. The crew would be less likely to mistreat the Englishwomen, who were the wives of British Navy men. It wouldn't be bad to have the journalist among them either.

Still. Likely she would just hole them up in that musty cabin and not come out until Repulse Bay. They could hire a ship home from there and make the whole miserable trek in reverse. She didn't look forward to it, but of the available options, it was clearly the better.

Then Dove counted the women, those

who would stay and those who would go. Twelve. *Shouldn't there be a thirteenth?* she thought. Then she wished she hadn't. For a moment, the dark, small body of Christabel fell through the sky behind her closed eyes.

When she opened her eyes again, she saw Caprice reach out and grab Virginia's hand, and it looked to Dove like they both squeezed.

Well, that was something, she thought. Perhaps the two of them had recognized that there was a good chance they'd die out there on the ice, especially if they turned north to continue the search for Franklin. They'd probably realized that they might as well die on good terms. And once they were out in the Arctic wilds, working together instead of working against each other might make the difference between life and death.

If they were to have any chance at all. Which Dove was not convinced they did.

CHAPTER THIRTY-FIVE: MARGARET

Aboard the Doris
July 1853

It was Mr. Emerson's voice she heard during the tense scene on the deck, telling her to stay. *Think of your legacy, Miss Bridges,* the dream voice whispered to her. *Don't put yourself at risk. Stay with your pages, your story.* She felt pulled in both directions, longing to go but feeling fear and the imagined words of Mr. Emerson pressing her to stay.

It was after the women were launched in their tiny, open craft that everything came clear to her: Mr. Emerson was a fool.

He was right, of course, that dream Emerson. If she'd gone on land, taking her journals of the journey so far, they would be as much at risk as she was, which was saying something.

But if she had listened to Mr. Emerson, she wouldn't have come on this adventure

381

in the first place. Besides, Mr. Emerson was a bit of a charlatan. He'd made her the first female editor of his journal, which was a great honor, and then failed to pay her even a single red cent for her labor over the course of two years, which was an equally great slap in the face. Metaphorical, though she would have welcomed a physical one: if someone slapped her, she could slap them back. Not that violence conducted by women was considered acceptable by men in any case, but if she'd learned anything so far on this journey, it was that when women stopped worrying about what was acceptable and what wasn't, they were capable of nearly anything.

She was fully aware she spent too much time calculating. What were the motives of the people she wrote about? Who was putting what at risk and how much? She calculated what queries to ask a subject, how much truth to put in her writing, what to publish anonymously, and what to put under a byline. For years, her byline had been a single asterisk: clear, unique, and as obscure as a bucket of tar. If she ever came back from this adventure, she'd have more and more questions to consider.

And now, she supposed, she had nothing but time to consider them. In that breathless, fearful moment, she had chosen the safe path. There was no undoing that snap decision. There would be no more adventure for her.

She'd been the first woman allowed to use the library at Harvard College; she'd read more than any person she'd ever met, man or woman, though none of the men would admit as much. Typical. She'd read everything there was to read about women adventuring. Clearly, it was inevitable that she, too, would join the ranks of women adventurers. To do otherwise would be to live life as a kind of encyclopedia: of no use to oneself, only others who pried you open and took what they needed, then shut you up and put you back on the shelf. Margaret Bridges had made the decision to be no one's encyclopedia.

Yet now, she was something worse. A book no one had any reason to read. One decision, one moment, and she had hesitated to make the bold choice. Now she would stay on that shelf forever.

What had she been so afraid of? Certainly, it had something to do with those who had chosen the ice, the members of that party. Their leader and the woman who thought she should lead instead. She knew, with the certainty of a practiced evaluator, that

Caprice Collins and Virginia Reeve were going to come to blows. She hadn't liked Caprice, who always seemed to be trying to get Margaret to write down something that glorified her exploits, but she certainly had a fire to her, one that clashed with Virginia's. A lazy journalist would have called the women oil and water. If she were writing about them, which she someday might, she would have called them something more descriptive. Snow and sun. Time and space. Spark and gunpowder. Yes, spark and gunpowder, that was good. She grabbed her book to write it, but a thought stopped her hand.

If nothing else, she could have lit their fires. She could have torn a page out of her journals one at a time and set fire to it. It would have hurt to give up the journals, but when it was the difference between life and death, of course she would have done it. This handful of women, especially if they turned north onto the ice, they would need fire.

Before she could consider any more, before she could talk herself out of it, she yanked on her cold-weather gear and gathered all three journals in her mittened hands, leaving the women's cabin behind.

Death by freezing was painless, or so she

had heard. Though she was always suspicious of those who claimed to know what death of one sort or another was like. The only people fully qualified to speak to a particular form of death were those who'd already died from it and therefore spoke no more.

Margaret raced to the ship's stern and flung each of her journals, one at a time, into the water. She could not even follow them with her eyes all the way down into the churning deep; there was certainly no question of being able to hear a splash. But what came after that, she let herself imagine. She let herself hope that each book would wend, like a tiny sailboat, across the water to its destination. Perhaps they would wash up on shore. Perhaps the women, following the shoreline of the bay in whichever direction they chose, would spot a waterlogged book and know who had sent it their way. The words would be gone by then — how and why had she ever let herself think words more important than lives? — but they would carefully dry the pages in the wind and save them for kindling.

So many maybes, Margaret told herself. Too many. She stared down toward the black water, cold and roiling, like a sea in a fairy story, dark enough to hide a monster.

But this water didn't have to hide a monster, she realized; it was a monster. And so was the ice. The entire Arctic was a frozen mouth full of icy teeth, and it would slay those women. They'd become another of the expeditions lost forever on the ice, marching off into oblivion.

And the journals were gone. Not even one word of what she knew remained. She could not even do them good now as a faithful chronicler of what had happened before they disappeared. She might have made her own fame and theirs if she hadn't panicked. She was not a woman equipped for quick bravery; she needed time to consider, to weigh, to judge. She hadn't had time, and she'd erred badly. She'd made foolish decision on top of foolish decision, and now she'd have nothing but time, all the way back to Boston, to remember her foolishness.

As she stood at the stern, cold wind buffeting her, she swore to herself then that she would be wiser next time, if there ever were a next time. If she had the chance to make it up to those women, the women she had turned away from when the moment came, she would do anything. She would turn back toward them. Support them. Give them anything they needed.

But what were the chances? Slim to none, and slim had sailed away, she thought as the darkness of the bay stretched out behind the ship to the invisible horizon.

CHAPTER THIRTY-SIX:
VIRGINIA

Charles Street Jail, Boston
October 1854

The guard who tortures Virginia with the *Clarion*'s sensationalist stories, Keeler, is reading the latest issue out loud. She is trying as hard as she possibly can to not hear. She doesn't physically cower or cringe, doesn't clap her hands over her ears. She won't show weakness. But inside her head, she is singing at the top of her imaginary lungs, nearly shouting the words of hymn after hymn, to drown him out. She pictures herself standing in a pew, wearing her best, most modest Sunday dress with the eyelet-covered buttons, hymnal in hand and her mouth as wide open as the prairie sky, music pouring forth. An imaginary organist pumps away at the pedals and stops, pounding the keys in fistfuls. An imaginary congregation in their imaginary finery crowds her on both sides, their voices raised, bass and baritone and soprano and tone-deaf howling, each louder than the next.

Inside her head, they have just finished an utterly rousing rendition of "Crown Him with Many Crowns," and Virginia is flinging all her spirit into "My Hope Is Built on Nothing Less" when a voice — a real voice — stops her.

It stops Keeler, too, who trails off midsentence, a sentence Virginia congratulates herself on not having heard.

"Excuse me. I'd like a word with Miss Reeve."

The familiar voice in her ears lands like rainwater on parched ground. The message she sent with the new Siobhan reached its destination.

Keeler, caught off guard by the fact that he should have heard this man coming long before he was close enough to touch, barks, "Who let you back here?"

"I have friends, as it happens," says Captain Malcolm. "Good men and true. Will you be a good man and give me ten minutes alone with Miss Reeve?"

To his credit, the guard's first response is, "I can't leave you alone with her, sir, for her own safety. And yours."

"Fifteen minutes."

"Sir. It cannot be done. Safety."

"There will be bars between us."

"Even so."

"I swear I'll keep my distance. All right? Just let me have twenty minutes."

"Twenty?"

"Half an hour?"

The captain leans toward him with folded money between his fingers.

Keeler fairly grabs the money, tucks it into an invisible pocket somewhere, and shrugs.

"Your funeral," he says.

Grumbling, reluctant, Keeler shuffles off down the hallway, glancing over his shoulder every now and again to see whether this man, his fists meaty, his frame broad, poses a threat to the prisoner or whether it might be the other way around. But eventually, Keeler loses interest and turns his back.

Then it's just the two of them, the bars between. His presence does not warm her — nothing can inside this frozen, stone room — but it fills her with something that makes the cold feel farther away.

"Miss Reeve," he says, and if the bars weren't there to restrain her, she'd reach out to him. Her feelings about him are not uncomplicated, but she knows this, that she would hold nothing back. The time for holding back has passed.

Her gaze locks with his, the way she did

not allow it to in the courtroom, and the power of it rocks her.

Captain Malcolm sheds the bravado he had with the guard as if it were a coat. His voice is thick with emotion. "I'm so sorry. I have regretted — and I have prayed. When I heard you'd survived, my prayers were answered. But then — this trial —"

"Don't lose sleep over me," she says, meaning to be light, but it comes out harsher than she meant it to. More like a command. As if she could command this man, as if she ever could, as if she could do anything from behind these all-dashed bars.

"I can't help it."

"Captain," she says. "You did the right thing. Then and now. And I am glad to see you."

"You are a saint, Miss Reeve."

"I'm no saint."

"But to me — to be able to forgive me — you forgive me, don't you?"

"There's nothing to forgive," she says, and this time, it does come out light. As if he were a waiter in the ordinary apologizing for bringing her the egg salad instead of the chicken salad. As if things mattered not at all. As if her life weren't on the line.

She says, "You kept your word. You said you'd bring the rest back safe — Dove, Margaret, Ebba, Althea — and you did that."

"But I should have — I could —"

"You couldn't," she says firmly.

"Virginia," he says this time, and there is a note of urgency to his voice. "I would not have presumed to come. But you called for me."

"I'm glad you answered."

His voice is still rough with emotion. "Are you truly resigned to your fate? Up in the North, you were always determined. Even when everything was against you. Everything is against you now again, but I hoped I would still see fire in you."

"Do you see it?" Now she draws closer to the bars, letting herself look at him. The luxury is dizzying. It may well be the last time she sees him, she tells herself, so why not indulge? His expressive eyes are worried, regretful, their coppery brown dimmed to a darker shade. At the same time as she's examining him, she realizes, she's showing herself. Truer than she ever has. The emotion she's been smothering all these days in the courtroom, all the anger and fear, she lets them out now, lets them radiate out of her like a light.

"Virginia," he says in response, throatily. "Tell me. What can I do?"

"I have a favor to ask. I don't know

392

anyone else who can help, but I hope you can, and I'm in dire need."

"Done."

"You don't know what it is yet."

"Doesn't matter. Whatever you need. Done."

"Thank you."

"I will do all I can to save you," he says, and she does not tell him what comes instantly to mind, because she isn't sure he could handle it, but the thought rings out in her head over and over even after he leaves and Keeler returns with a glare and her dinner: *It will not be enough.*

CHAPTER THIRTY-SEVEN: VIRGINIA

On the Expedition
July 1853

As the hooded, swaddled women huddled together on land for the first time since Moose Factory — a lifetime ago, it felt like — Virginia could not stop counting.

Twenty boxes of ammunition. Twelve sets of snow goggles. Ten sled dogs. Nine guns. Eight women. Seven slabs of pemmican. Six axes. Five bundles of trade goods, mirrors and trinkets, nails and tacks.

What else did they have? One tidy little shallop that had borne them from the *Doris* — a fine, seaworthy craft, but off the water, useless as a hatful of bent nails. One sledge, disassembled and packed away for now. It would slow them down until the ice came, at which point it would be essential, if they even found the ice before the ice found them.

Then, the things that could not be touched

or gathered, not in a physical sense. She counted those too.

One mission, compromised, a goal that might have been close to an impossibility to start with — to find a lost man, his lost company, and his lost ships out here in the vast, unmapped nothingness of the Arctic — but was now even less possible than it ever had been.

Zero hope.

But her lack of hope, Virginia decided, was not the point. She stepped back from the cluster of women and scanned the horizon, gathering herself. She could not allow her hopelessness to dictate all their fates. On the ship, she'd had hope, and here they were anyway, farther from their destination than they'd ever thought to be, almost certainly doomed to the failure of their mission. Hope had not delivered the expected result. So perhaps hopelessness would not either.

They were such rare, savvy women, thought Virginia. If they were men, they would be world striders: generals, scholars, victors of every stripe. Her eyes threatened to prickle with tears at the sentiment of it, even knowing it was so cold the tears would freeze on her face as they formed.

She could not afford sentiment.

That was why she put the choice to them,

the eight women who had chosen the land. They had put themselves at risk for the chance to continue northward, rejecting safety, or as close to it as could be found in this part of the world. They had as much of a stake as she did. Each had an equal say: one life.

"We must decide," she said to them all, "in which direction our fates lie."

Given her unmatched familiarity with the maps of where they were and where they hoped to be, Doro was the first to understand. As hard as it was to see her eyes in the furred maw of her raised hood, Virginia caught the flash of recognition in them right away.

Caprice was the next to catch on and the first to speak her mind. "You mean we can choose safety or we can seek Franklin but not both."

"Almost," corrected Virginia. "We can choose to seek safety."

"I fail to see the difference," Caprice said dryly, "between that and what I said."

"We can *seek* safety," clarified Virginia. "I cannot guarantee we will find it. There are two safer routes, one north and one south, and even those are not safe. We could freeze. Starve. Suffer attack. Break our legs falling over one hazard or another — a gully, a hole in the soft ice, a ravine, a buckle —"

"We know the dangers. You needn't list them all." Caprice's tone became more combative, not less.

"I *can't* list them all," spat back Virginia. "There are too many."

At that, Caprice fell silent a moment.

Doro spoke into the silence, raising her voice to be heard. "We have three options. We follow the coast south to Churchill, a settlement something like Moose Factory, a place from which we could join others going south, toward home."

Caprice made a dismissive sound, a *hmph* in her throat, though it was not possible to tell if she'd been loud enough for the other women to hear.

Doro went on, "Second option, we follow the coastline north instead, to Repulse Bay. Where we'd planned, Victory Point, is both west and north of there. From there, we could either wait for a ship home — the *Doris* or another — or overwinter and set out for Victory Point again as soon as the thaw permits."

"How long would that take?" asked Elizabeth. "To get to Repulse Bay?"

Doro's face clouded with doubt. "A couple of months or longer. Depends on how fast we move and when the cold comes in.

We'll actually go much faster with ice and snow under us, once we can use the sledge. Walking is the slowest possible way to go."

Elizabeth spoke again. "And the third option?"

"Northwest. As direct a route to Victory Point as we can manage. Same issues, same timeline."

It was Elizabeth who asked the next question. "If we head northwest, are there rivers to follow, maybe somewhere we could sail the shallop? What's the terrain like?"

Doro spoke a single, ominous word. "Unmapped."

"Oh."

Virginia looked from one face to the next, hunting for their expressions in the darkened shadows cast by their raised hoods. "And if we decide not to follow the shore, maybe we leave the shallop behind."

Ann said, "Nope. The dogs can pull it."

"Across the ground?"

"Across the ground," she echoed. "With supplies in it. Spreads the weight out. Unless you want to hump all that?"

She gestured into the shallop, and seven other heads turned to look. The heaps of supplies that had seemed reassuring only moments ago looked daunting if they proposed to carry them. Perspective was every-thing.

Ann went on, "Shallop makes a good cover to sleep under too. If we realize we don't need it later, we chop it for wood then. And if we hit a river . . ."

"I'm convinced," interrupted Siobhan. "We keep the shallop."

"Except if the terrain gets too uneven, both the shallop and the sledge slow us down," Doro interrupted. "That's another risk."

"As if we needed more," said Caprice.

You could have stayed on the ship, thought Virginia. *Why didn't you?* But she did not speak the words aloud. Whichever route they chose, the days that lay ahead would be so much harder than this one. If she didn't want to stoke conflicts that could present dangers as deadly as the terrain, she would need to hold her tongue. Best to start now. A good leader knew not just when to speak but when to listen.

Irene tapped Doro on the shoulder. She squinted at the horizon, then back at the shore, turned her body toward her left shoulder, and pointed out over the land-scape, her eyebrows raised.

Doro guessed what she was asking. "Northwest."

Then Irene shifted her hand a few degrees back to the right, pointed again.

Doro answered, "North."

Irene pointed in the opposite direction.

"South," Doro said.

Then Irene brushed something invisible from her heavy coat, pushed back her hood, and pointed again in the first direction. With her hood rearranged, they could all now see the grin on her face.

Doro said, a hint of wonder in her voice, "Irene votes for the northwest, it seems. And I'm with her."

Caprice said, "No."

"No?" echoed Virginia.

"I don't think we should take a vote," Caprice said, addressing the group. "We are all together. If some of us vote one direction and others vote differently but the majority rules, some may grow to resent the others. We cannot split up; there are few enough of us as it is, and this is a clear case of safety in numbers."

Virginia scanned the women's figures, reading the language of their bodies. They were nodding. Leaning. Listening.

Caprice finished, in a ringing voice, "Anyone who wanted to play it safe had the option to do so back on the ship. So let us throw ourselves into this adventure together.

We will survive together or not." Then she took a step closer to Virginia and said, "Right, Virginia?"

Grateful and a little stunned, Virginia answered, "That's right."

In the changing light, she could see their faces better, and she examined each in turn. Each had a similar, determined expression. Even Stella, who'd been worn to a shell of herself mere days before, turned her back on the rocky shore, facing toward the open, daunting flatlands.

Virginia said, "All right, ladies. Northwest it is."

The shallop already had supplies arranged down the middle like their canoe had, and Ann took only a moment to strap the dogs, yipping with excitement, into their traces. The remaining women arrayed themselves in two lines, one on each side of the shallop, slotted into place like the kitchen utensils hung on the wall of the *Doris*'s galley.

Irene reached out for Stella and gestured toward the back of the shallop. Stella's face was drained of color, and as determined as she looked, Virginia realized Irene was right. Stella should ride, not walk, if that was at all possible, as long as she was still recovering.

As they headed out, Virginia wiped any hint of concern or consternation from her face. Not that the women could necessarily see it around the shielding of her hood. But the brave face wasn't just for them. It was also for her.

Ann snapped the traces over the dogs' backs, and they began to pull, too fast at first, but under Ann's practiced hands, they settled into a speed that was only slightly faster than the walking women.

They were on their way.

That first night, they did not stop. They were tired, yes, but the sunlight stayed with them, so they could see the shape of the terrain they crossed, and it was smooth and featureless. Virginia tried not to think too hard about how unmarked all this space was, how it would be so easy to become lost if Doro weren't steadily shaping their direction.

No one asked Virginia if they should stop, but if they had, she would have forbidden it. Because moving was the thing that kept them from freezing. There might not be ice on the ground, not yet, but it already felt like there was ice in their veins.

She knew, in theory, what the Arctic cold would be like. She'd even gotten flashes of it on the ship, belowdecks where the ice-clogged water of the bay chilled the planks of the hull so thoroughly they radiated that cold inward. The heat only went so far, and one could walk around a corner from relative comfort into a sharp bout of cold that caused you to inhale sharply, but when you did, the insides of your nostrils instantly froze together. More than once, Virginia had found this happening to her and flung up her mittens against her cheeks and backed around the corner again into the relative heat.

Here, there would be none of that. Nowhere to retreat to. In the day, there was some relief, but at night, there was only cold: unending, unrelieved. Their instruments said the temperature of the air itself was above the freezing point, but the harsh slap of icy wind on their cheeks told a different story.

Hours into their walk, in the hours near midnight when the light thinned and dimmed into something that was barely a glow but still not darkness, Virginia strongly considered giving up. If she stopped long enough, there would be peace. The cold would take her away if she just let it. It could take all of them away. In death, there would be no struggle, no anger.

Because there was so much anger in her.

She'd had no idea. When she'd looked at the map of the far North and seen the word *Fury,* it had only occurred to her that this was a word for a vengeful goddess. That so many Arctic features had been named for hazards because it was a world of hazards. But now she saw its other meaning. Fury, as in anger. As they marched ever forward, she thought only of how unjust it was that she and these women were forced farther away from their goal instead of closer. What could they have done if they were helped instead of hindered? Now they would have to work twice as hard just to get back to where they should have been. Those ignorant, superstitious sailors. Foolish Stella and her thievery. The weak, fearful captain. And she did not spare herself from her anger: she, too, had been weak. She, too, could have done better. This anger burned, but it did not, on any level, keep her warm.

Of all things, it was the memory of the Very Bad Thing that helped her continue on. Because if she could survive that, she could survive this. She even would have told the other members of the party about it, reshaping its ghastly horror into a rallying cry, if she didn't think they wouldn't be able to look at her the same way afterward. Once someone knew what was in her past, they'd see her as a different person. She couldn't take that chance.

That was probably what she'd loved best about Ames. He knew everything about her, and he didn't judge her for it. To be known for oneself is a powerful gift. She felt she'd only received it once. Maybe these women would give her the same gift, she thought to herself, but then doubt swarmed over her. They did not love her now, and they would love her less if they knew everything about her. Particularly Caprice. Caprice's lip would curl in a horrified sneer if she knew what Virginia had done. The rich girl already looked down on her for living hard on the trail, traveling with a man, wearing men's trousers — trousers! — and not even seeming the least bit sorry. Imagine her outrage at the Very Bad Thing, at Virginia's role in it, which her youth at the time did not excuse.

So she would not tell them that, but in her private soul, it gave her the hope that she'd been missing. Bad could come from good; good could come from bad. She'd seen that happen before.

Virginia sent up a prayer, squared her shoulders, and kept moving.

CHAPTER THIRTY-EIGHT:
VIRGINIA

*Massachusetts Superior Court, Boston
October 1854*

Sundays in the prison are Virginia's worst days by far. There is no respite from her cell when court is not in session; the Sunday guard is a matron, an oddity. The nameless woman slides trays of food into the cell at the appointed times but does not speak or even look at the inmate. Does she disapprove? Think of Virginia as a gender traitor? If so, what part of Virginia's behavior has offended her? There are so many possibilities. But her silence makes Virginia miss the guards who engage with her, even when that engagement takes the form of hatred. When court is out of session, Virginia is alone with her thoughts, and she does not like the company.

But there is one reason to look forward to Sundays, one she has forged herself. On Sunday mornings, because she cannot go to church, church comes to her. She stands and sits as if called to from the pulpit. She opens her hands in front of her like a hymnal, like a prayer book, and sings, sometimes even out loud. For the postlude, she hammers out an approximation of organ music on the hard edge of her cot, though if her hands touched actual keys, she would make only noise, not music. Afterward, she doesn't always feel better, but at least she doesn't feel worse. And distracting her busy mind is a welcome, necessary break. Ever since she decided to try, to ask Captain Malcolm to help her take control of her fate, her emotions have been flooding her body. She almost misses those early days in her cell when all she felt was the cool, reassuring virtue of resignation. Hope, when it alternates with fear, hurts more.

Monday dawns, though she cannot see the sunlight to welcome it, and even though she knows she will be led forth in chains, her whole body leaps forward eagerly to move beyond the cell's walls.

When she arrives in the courtroom, she looks out at the five survivors, as is her practice, but today, what she sees surprises her. She sees something she hasn't seen in their gazes in a long time.

Hope.

What is it? she wonders. What do they know that she doesn't?

She looks at her counsel, who doesn't bother to look at her, and she risks a glance out into the sea of spectators. She does not spot Captain Malcolm. There are more people than she remembers, but she has been intentionally avoiding looking at the crowd these past days, so there's no telling when it grew.

Then the bailiff calls the name of the next witness, one who wasn't on the list her counsel had gathered at the beginning of the trial. If he knew this was coming, he's kept it to himself.

"The prosecution calls to the stand Levi Brooks."

Brooks! In her roiling thoughts, which should be consumed with the same hope her friends are feeling, she can only focus on one overwhelming thought: *so Brooks was his* last *name all along.*

Somehow, it feels powerful to know that. They have been trading in names, she and he, since the day they met, and his was always kept back. *Caprice Collins,* the first name he said to her, that fateful, fraught name. *Dorothea Roset,* the one he'd never intended to give her, that she'd tracked until she solved the mystery. *Stella,* the name

408

he'd never even told her, the fact of a body all that mattered to him from his comfortable perch in civilization. Names added to lists and struck from them. Names of the living and the dead. And now, Levi Brooks. *Levi.* Knowing his name feels like an ingredient in a wizard's incantation. Those two short syllables feel like a place to put her anger, store it away, for now. Two syllables, just like the word *fury.*

But there is no more time to dwell on his name, because here comes the man himself, striding to the front of the room with familiar, steady confidence. He has the swagger of the voyageurs, but he's so different from them he looks almost like a different species. The tailoring of his trim black garb is impeccable. Unlike the women he sent north, he has not changed in any way since the journey began, and why should he? He is not an adventurer, just a factotum. They left civilization, endured the wild, created their own pocket nation, struck out into the unknown, fought their way back to civilization again. They have evolved. He, with the rest of society, has remained.

Passing the long rows of courtroom seats, stepping into the witness box, he does not look out of place. He looks ready. Virginia keeps her face utterly still, but inside her mind, she is pouring anger toward him, sending it out in an invisible wave, willing it to disappear inside his rigid, arrogant body. He does not even glance in her direction.

He is here. Brooks is here. She doesn't know how they could have found him, forced him to come, but he is here. Is it Captain Malcolm's doing? This wasn't what she asked him to do, but did he manage it somehow? Brooks can back up her story. Whether he wants to or not, he has no choice. Brooks will change the course of the trial, and someone will believe her at last. She is desperate to have someone, anyone, believe her.

He is sworn in and identified, all without incident. Virginia finds herself leaning forward in her seat while she waits for the prosecutor's next question.

"And where do you hail from, Mr. Brooks?"

"Australia."

Australia, of course. Another realization. Lady Franklin's lackey was acquired during her days in Van Diemen's Land, on the other side of the world. Life in America was famously easy compared to the hardscrabble life of the former penal colony Australia. A well-off patroness like Lady Franklin would have had no trouble convincing him to follow her to the other side of the world if it suited her purposes. And it has, all these years. But now he sits in front of the court, compelled to tell the whole truth and nothing but. It will be hard for him, she thinks, but he has no choice.

Yet he looks no more worried than he ever has in her experience. She felt like he always thought himself superior. Clearly, he still has that thought in his head.

"You've come a long way, sir," says the lawyer.

"America is my home now."

"As it should be. The land of opportunity."

"Exactly."

"Opportunity," the lawyer muses, and Virginia can feel him winding up like a child's toy with a key in its back. Once he's wound up, he'll let fly with his next question. What will it be?

He goes on, "We brought you here for an opportunity."

Brooks looks mildly curious. "Well, I do hope it's a worthwhile one. I've taken a great deal of trouble to appear."

"Your testimony will be extremely helpful in setting the record straight. Now, I've been told that this defendant — Virginia Reeve — has claimed that a man named Brooks was acting on behalf of Lady Jane Franklin to send her on an all-female expedition to the Arctic."

"A what?" Brooks interrupts. "Female expedition?"

"Yes, sir. I know, it sounds preposterous, but we are doing our due diligence here. The young lady's life hangs in the balance, and though we believe her fully guilty — and all the evidence so far has pointed in that direction — it is our solemn duty to be sure justice is done."

"Of course. You're very conscientious."

"I'm a man of the law." The attorney nods gravely, enjoying plaudits. Virginia's own attorney, of course, does nothing more than shuffle his papers. Looking at either of them will infuriate her too much. At the moment, she cannot decide which she hates more.

She turns her attention back to Brooks, who still sits comfortably in the witness box as if it were a box seat at the theater and he is watching a mildly interesting but not too lively play.

The prosecutor says to Brooks, "She claims that you are that man."

"Levi Brooks? She specified the name?"

"As it happens, no. She couldn't give your Christian name, only the last name, Brooks."

"I see," he says slowly, as if to suggest he

doesn't. "Then how was I chosen for the honor of testifying today?"

"We asked the local hotels within a five-mile radius to show us their records from a set of specific dates. All the hotels, mind you, from Porter House all the way down to some of the less reputable houses by the docks. All complied, without exception. I imagine you're eager to hear what we found."

"Well, yes, I'm sure I'm not the only one."

The prosecutor continues, "You, sir, were the only person with the last name Brooks to stay in one of these hotels during the period when the defendant claims to have met the mysterious Brooks. Accordingly, it could only be you — if the mysterious Brooks exists at all, of course."

The realization hits Virginia like a punch to the gut. No, it was not Captain Malcolm who brought Brooks here. She should never have fantasized that he did. She should have realized it sooner. Right away. As soon as he walked in. But her optimism, her completely misguided optimism, blinded her. She hadn't been listening.

Brooks is testifying for the prosecution, not the defense.

His voice mild, his manner almost distant, Brooks agrees, "Of course."

"So please, Mr. Brooks, we need your utmost cooperation in solving this mystery. Can you provide the confirmation that the defendant is eager to have you give? Can you tell us that you met this young woman and helped her arrange her travel and the travel of the women who accompanied her into the northern wastes?"

Brooks's pause is mercifully brief. He does not try to keep them in suspense. He has that mercy at least.

In a clear, steady voice, he says, "Sorry to say, here in front of the court, seeing as there's so much interest in it, but I've never met the woman in my life."

In the stunning silence after, Virginia doesn't know what she expects. Lightning, God, to strike him dead? Nothing strikes. He simply tells the baldest of bald-faced lies, and the world keeps on merrily turning.

Was there even any truth to the story about asking the hotels for their rosters? Or was that just a fig leaf concocted by the prosecution? Has he been paid for his lies, or does he give them freely to sever Virginia, once and for all, from his employer for the sake of keeping the Franklin name unsullied by this failure?

"You may step down," the judge says to

414

Brooks, his voice almost friendly, warm with kind regret. "Thank you for your service."

She looks at the survivors in the front row and realizes none of them ever met Brooks. They must have been excited because his name was read out, but even Ebba and Althea never met the man, only Virginia herself. They could testify that they'd corresponded with someone named Brooks, but they could testify to Lady Franklin's name being used as well, and yet no one could prove Lady Franklin had really sponsored their travel. The coin was untraceable. Letters would be inconclusive, even if they'd kept them, which she knew they hadn't.

And her own letters that might have served as proof, well, she knew exactly what had happened to them.

As Brooks leaves the court without even glancing her way, she curses him under her breath for his cleverness. He and Lady Franklin had been three steps ahead this whole time. From the very beginning, it seemed. Keeping her at arms' length and everyone else even more distant, their connection indirect. Perhaps Caprice had met Brooks — she alone among them might have — but a fat lot of good that does Virginia now. The Collins parents, too, had likely met him, but since they want Virginia dead, they won't be the ones to come forward with evidence that would set her free.

Franklin and Brooks are in control. And with that thought, there is only one question that nags at her.

Why is Brooks here at all? In America, let alone Boston? His testimony is damning but not defining. What is the point of his presence when he could have avoided this entire charade by staying far away? There must be a reason, and the fact that she has no idea what it is burrows down into the base of her skull and rests there, awkward and heavy.

The five survivors still sit there in the front row, and the hope is gone from their faces. In its place, she sees nothing but disappointment. She holds the gazes of her friends, her compatriots, and wonders how many more times she will see them. How many more times she will be led in shackles to this room where her fate will be decided.

Our Father, she prays, *whatever happens, and I fear the worst will happen, I pray only that when my judgment comes, you receive me with forgiveness into your holy kingdom.*

But why should God prove more merciful than anyone else in this world? Than this judge, than this jury? God, after all, like this judge, like these lawyers, like every single juror who holds Virginia's fate in his hands, is a man. With precious few exceptions, she has not known men to take her part or smooth her way. She can only think of two men who've ever truly helped her when push came to shove: Ames and Captain Malcolm. And even so, both of those precious two also failed her, each in his own fashion. If God guided her safely out of the Very Bad Thing and home from the Arctic, she owes Him praise for that, but it doesn't mean that He, too, won't fail her when the reckoning comes.

World without end, she prays. *Amen.*

CHAPTER THIRTY-NINE: VIRGINIA

On the Expedition
July and August 1853

Quickly, the party established a reliable rhythm. During the day, instead of stopping for meals, whoever was riding in the shallop — most often Stella — would pass around each woman's ration of pemmican or meat. They ate walking. Every third night or so, they did stop for a nighttime sleep, overturning the shallop and huddling tight together underneath for warmth. The dogs snuggled among them, their warm fur better than any blanket, their reeking breath becoming a familiar comfort.

Irene had the job of constantly scanning the horizon for game, and when she spotted a pack of caribou or a smattering of wild sheep, she rapped on the shoulder of the nearest woman, who gave a soft whistle of warning to bring everyone to a halt. Three to five women were sent in the direction of the animals while Ann quieted the dogs, and they did not get underway again until the animals had either scattered or been successfully brought down. Irene was a crack shot from the beginning. Elizabeth was steadily gaining in aptitude, quickly establishing herself as a natural talent. Virginia and Ann both had excellent aim but lacked skill in staying quiet enough not to disturb the animals; Stella was the opposite, all stealth and no precision. Caprice preferred not to hunt, which Virginia was willing to overlook for now; while they'd become friendlier, she was still somehow uneasy with the idea of the mountaineer putting her hands on a loaded gun.

As the days grew short enough that an hour or two could actually be called night, if it was absolutely necessary in order to make camp, they burned a lamp of precious whale oil for enough light to see by. On the occasions when a larger fire was needed, especially when roasting game, they had to find kindling. The dogs made a game of picking up dry sticks, but to get the fire started, something finer was needed.

So each delved into the precious pack that she'd brought with her, and if there was paper or delicate fabric to be burned, they burned it.

And it all went up so quickly. A letter of Stella's she declined to share the nature of, though Virginia spotted a letter *C* in the signature before the licking flames devoured it. A worn hair ribbon of Elizabeth's. Siobhan paged carefully through her single medical text, plucking out pages she felt would be least useful, one on exotic tropical diseases, another on social diseases like chlamydia. Sometimes she read them aloud to amuse the women before committing them to the flames. In turn, every contribution went up with a golden, liquid light.

For Virginia's first turn, she offered up the first letter she'd received from Lady Franklin, which she had long since committed to memory. The wind was rough that night, and though she had hoped to use the letter and the envelope on separate occasions, it took both to get the flame to catch.

Too soon, Virginia knew her turn would come again, so one morning, she stole a few moments of privacy, plucking at the red wax seal with numbed fingers. It was well past the time that Lady Franklin would have wanted her to read the third letter, but her journey had become something Lady Franklin had never foreseen. This was her decision. It was one small way she had of asserting that she was in charge of what would happen next. Lady Franklin could not help or hurt her now. Only the other women here. Only nature. And, of course, Virginia herself. She could still choose well or badly.

She unfolded the fragile paper, hands shaking, and read the third letter for the very first time.

Dear Virginia,

I may call you Virginia now, may I not? I imagine I hear your assent. We have been through a lot now, you and I. In the reality in which I write this, we met only yesterday, but you are in the third month of your journey, which means a great deal of time has passed and many miles in that time.

I am with you in the only way I can be. I wish I could have been with my husband in this way.

You know by now, I think, that I am not just writing these letters for you. I am writing them for me. The process of poring over maps, plotting out courses, measuring miles against months, is like a balm to me. I imagine you and your ship in each of these places, and I imagine my husband and his ships there as well. The broad expanse of the straits, the piled ice that lines each shore, the buckled, hazardous ice fields that surround King William's Land. I can see you silhouetted there in my mind's eye, and more importantly, I can see John.

I encouraged him to go. You may not know that. Our experience in Van Diemen's Land ended poorly, and he needed a new post, a way to prove himself, Jo I made sure he had this one. He went there because I wished it. Now I wish his return. So you see it must be so.

Did I do right, sending you? Is it a fool's errand? Some part of me hoped to prove that women's intelligence and fortitude could compare to men's, but I fear there was a flaw in the design of my experiment. No matter how many women you have with you, there is no real safety in numbers, is there? Your will, your leadership, are still subject to the whims and desires of men. Ah, the desires of men. The words I could write to you on this subject would fill far more than the stack of paper sitting here beside me. But you know that as well as I. And I fear your education on the matter grows every day.

Virginia, I owe you an apology. I did not want to close you in on a ship with men who think women inferior, only there is no other kind. They are raised to think themselves superior in every way. I chose you because you have proved yourself more than capable, a true survivor, and a woman like that does not trifle with who thinks what of whom. She sets her goal and accomplishes it. That is all I expect from you, and if you stay true to your goal, then no matter what happens, you will have succeeded.

Am I feeling sentimental? It seems so. Then I will end on a note of a personal nature. Virginia, I am sorry for your hardships, both those you have endured and have yet to endure. May the latter category be far less than the former.

Yours very truly,

J

Two nights later, they burned the envelope, nurturing the flame into a fire that roasted a brace of rabbits Irene had brought down nearly single-handedly. Ann excused herself to toss morsels to the dogs, and the other women huddled shoulder to shoulder around the fire, devouring the warm meat with gusto. This close to the roaring flame, they could remove their mittens just long enough to eat, and once the animals' skeletons had been gnawed down to bare bone, every woman licked and sucked the rich grease from her fingers with a thorough, eager tongue.

The fire had died down to embers, and the women were arranging their shallop shelter for the night when Doro took Virginia and Ann aside.

"I can unfold the map to show you," said Doro, "but I don't want to lose my fingers."

"Tell us, then," said Virginia, Ann nodding alongside. She could barely form words in the evenings, let alone thoughts and certainly not strategies, but Doro would not have brought an idea to her if it weren't worthwhile.

"On one of the Rae maps, I think I've found a spot we should stop. A cache."

Ann leaned in. "What is that?"

Doro said, "A cache. A place to set aside food and supplies for future expeditions or for the same expedition if it's coming back the same way. John Rae came up this way more than once and found that he and his group were able to bring in more game than they needed to feed themselves — not the way it usually goes, obviously — so I think there may actually be something to find in this spot."

424

"Shall we go, then?"

"It does take us off our intended course."

"By how much?"

She squinted and seemed to be calculating in her head. Virginia had done the same countless times for familiar distances, but up here, she would not dare to guess at a path. It would be like taking a pickax to a patch of ice, not knowing how deep it went or what lay underneath.

At last, Doro said, "About three days, I think. To get off our course, check the cache, and get back on. We'll join the trail farther up, of course. So maybe we lose two days, two and a half."

"Worth it in your opinion?"

"Worth it."

"Well then. Let's go."

Doro smiled, a rare smile for her in these days. "In the morning."

"In the morning," Virginia echoed.

As they turned away from the last glimmers of light from the fire's embers, the ghost of Doro's smile remained.

Three days' hard travel later, they found the cache.

"I see something," Caprice said, pointing off into the distance.

Virginia squinted. She didn't even see a

smear; she saw nothing. But she said, "Let's go," and gestured for Caprice to lead them in the direction she wanted them to go. If there was no hope, there was no reason to go forward. Without hope, they might as well lie down on the cold, stony ground to die.

As they closed the distance, she began to see it. A faint gray line at first — how did Caprice even spot it? Perhaps her eyes, experienced as they were at reading the territory of snow-covered mountains, adjusted more quickly to the light that seemed to blind the rest of them. As they got closer, the object grew, defined itself as a thick mark of dark gray against the mottled, lighter grays of the landscape. A cairn, likely made of stones piled high, not quite as tall as a man.

It stood out clearly with its regular, artificially precise angles, the first man-made thing they had seen in days. Wait, far more than days, she thought, tallying up what passed in this part of the world for sunsets. Two weeks at least. She would have to ask Irene to tell her how many days they'd been on land. Of all of them, the mute woman had the most unerring sense of time.

Virginia's heart quickened, which was a

painful, squeezing motion in the cold. She could not afford for her heart to gallop out of control. But the excitement brought that perilously close to happening. She forced herself to look at the exploration as an exercise. What possible things could a party find in a cairn in the far North? If this were merely an exercise, if her life and the lives of the women who'd trusted her didn't hang in the balance, then she could calm her racing heart.

In a way, she wished Margaret had left the ship to come with them so there would be a record. Then again, perhaps nothing good would happen here, in which case a record would only cause pain. Would the records the journalist had written so far praise her or condemn her? How would it all work out, if it did? She supposed that depended on whether they found evidence of Franklin's whereabouts. The world, and most specifically Jane Franklin, would laud a success and ignore a failure. They had kept the door to success open by heading off in the direction of Victory Point, still in search of the Franklin party, instead of making for Repulse Bay. But the odds were still very much against them. They were a long way from succeeding.

"Something's wrong," she heard Siobhan

say, and the women's footsteps slowed.

"What is it?"

"It's too regular," Siobhan said. "Those aren't stones."

As they approached, once the shapes came clear, they lost their concern in the face of curiosity.

The cache was not made of stones but a pile of tin cans, stacked a bit higher than all their heads. The labels had worn away, but the seals remained.

"Is it food?" someone asked.

"They just look so . . . wrong," said Elizabeth, echoing what Virginia supposed they were all thinking.

"No, not wrong," said Stella in a thready voice. "Althea told me once how the British packed their ships. Tons of supplies like you wouldn't imagine. Because they were headed into a wasteland."

"So it is food. That we could eat," Caprice said.

"Wait." Stella reached out, holding her palm in front of Caprice's eager form. "The other thing Althea said was that a few years after the *Terror* and the *Erebus* sailed, the man who'd won the contract to furnish it out was barred from doing business with the government again. Seems his cans didn't preserve as well as he'd claimed."

"So the question is," Elizabeth said, "are these cans from Franklin's expedition or another?"

"Likely another," said Doro, at the exact moment that Caprice said, "Well, no way to know for sure."

"Even if we could open them up," said Stella, "I'm not so sure I'd try one."

"Oh, I'll try it," said Caprice, oddly merry. "You wouldn't believe the things I've eaten on mountainsides. Local stews, the occasional eyeball from who-knows-what animal, whatever it was, it kept me alive. I've got an iron stomach by now. So hand it over."

Irene had a can in one hand, and as she was nearest Caprice, Caprice reached out for it; Irene yanked it back before she could wrap her glove around the metal.

"Oh, come on," Caprice said gruffly.

Irene shook her head. When Caprice feinted toward her, the mute woman whipped her hand back and hurled the can as far as she could throw it, which was indeed far. It clanged once against a stone and disappeared somewhere in the endless hillocks and buckles of variegated brown and gray.

With a glare and a shrug, Caprice walked over to the stack of cans next to the cairn and grabbed another tin. "Someone needs to try."

"I'm not so sure," said Virginia.

Caprice said fiercely, "Don't be ridiculous, Reeve. We can't leave them behind if they might be valuable; we can't afford to take them if they might kill us all. So the only logical thing to do is for someone to open a can up and tuck in. And I'm volunteering to do it. No one in their right mind, no one who cares about the future of this expedition, can say nay."

But what Stella had said weighed too heavily on Virginia, and before she really understood what she was doing, she'd reached over and smacked the tin out of Caprice's hand.

"No!" said Virginia. "I forbid it."

Unlike the high-flying can Irene had hurled, this one rolled across the landscape unevenly, wobbling on its dented side, until it came to rest on a tiny hillock. This one, they could still see.

Caprice's eyebrows leapt up in amusement. Her expression turned mocking. "Oh, do you? Do you *forbid* it, Virginia?"

"I am the leader of this expedition," said Virginia. "A fact of which you are well aware. Without someone in charge, all we've got is chaos."

"I don't see much difference from chaos in what we're doing now. Do you? We've found nothing. We're nowhere."

"We're making progress."

"We're dying slowly," Caprice nearly shouted, her voice growing louder still. "Maybe you consider that a success compared to dying quickly, but I sure don't."

"Caprice. Keep your voice down."

"Oh, should I? Do you get to decide what we all say as well as what we do?"

"I'm not the one whose family treats their servants like slaves." The words slipped out before she had time to consider their wisdom or lack thereof. Once they were out, she wished she could take them back. This was neither the time nor the place. Elizabeth was looking back and forth between the two of them, visibly horrified.

With a snide, distant air, Caprice said, "Do you mean Elizabeth? Elizabeth is free to leave my family's employ whenever she wishes. I wouldn't recommend right this minute, of course."

"Is she so free? Did she want to come on this journey at all? Did you even ask her before you hauled her a thousand miles into the unknown?"

Both women turned to Elizabeth, whose gaze flickered toward Virginia in quiet desperation but then fixed back down on the ground.

The flash in Caprice's eyes could have been either anger or fear. Either way, almost as soon as Virginia noticed it, it vanished.

Then, Caprice waved a hand dismissively. "You know the truth? She's no worse off than you or me. Women are all slaves of one sort or another."

"How can you say that?" Virginia was aghast. Surely, the woman must see the difference. She hadn't realized it herself at first, how much more constrained Elizabeth's choices were than her own, but as soon as Elizabeth had pointed it out, she understood. All her life, Caprice had lived in a household with servants, had been their mistress. She must understand they were not all the same. Didn't she?

"You think I'm free?" challenged Caprice. "I'm not. I do what my parents tell me up until they marry me off so I can do what my husband tells me."

"Poor you," Virginia returned, her voice dripping with sarcasm. Anger heated her blood. She was surprised it didn't heat the air around them, warm it until it felt like true summer, not just the North's version of it. She felt that much fire. "It must be so hard to get everything you want."

"Everything I want? You know nothing about me."

They were both shouting now, completely out of control, heedless of the horrified women watching them in silence.

"I know you're spoiled and childish and the only reason you're on this voyage is because I was forced to bring you along for the money," spat Virginia.

"Money isn't everything."

"That's what people with money say."

Caprice answered, her voice harsh with anger, "You never gave me a chance! You saw a woman of means and decided because I was lucky, I couldn't also be good."

"And have you been good? Have you contributed, worked hard, put yourself at risk for the other women here?"

"It's come to exactly that, hasn't it?" said Caprice. "And I will."

Then she drew her knife.

Instinctively, Virginia leaned back, putting herself out of reach.

Then, Caprice took the blade and began stabbing down into the nearest can. The sound of the blade piercing the metal fell somewhere between a thump and a shriek, and every time it repeated, Virginia winced.

Caprice paid no mind. She stabbed the can over and over, more than a dozen times, until it yielded up its contents. Then she put her mouth against the tin and slurped directly from it. Virginia was terrified she'd cut herself on the metal. She looked over to Siobhan, who clearly shared her worry and readied herself.

They all watched Caprice in horrified silence. Or at least in Virginia's case, it was horrified; how did the other women feel? Did they admire her, even a little bit, for taking the risk? Were they bold enough to follow her lead?

No one did.

"Well then," said Virginia. "You've made your point. Now we can go."

"Go? Without the cans? You can't be serious," said Caprice, gesturing at the cairn, taller than she.

"I am in charge, remember," Virginia snapped. She could feel control slipping away. "If you wanted to be out from under my thumb, you could have stayed on the ship. Played it safe, ridden along, headed home to Pop-Pop and Mummy. But no. You're on land, headed for Victory Point. Which means you think we're going to accomplish something here. What is it?"

"We're accomplishing something just by setting foot in this part of the Arctic. First women to do so."

"First white women," Stella added quietly from her position on the sledge. As she got stronger, she'd begun to contribute more. She looked to Irene, who nodded encouragement. "The Esquimaux were here. Are here. They've forgotten more about surviving in this environment than we'll ever know."

"When they write the record books," said Caprice, "no one will put an asterisk by our names because of the color of our skin."

"You think we'll be in the record books?" asked Virginia with surprise.

"We could be. If you don't screw it up."

"You think that's what I'm doing?"

Caprice said frostily, "I'm just reminding you of your tremendous responsibility."

"Don't you fret your little head about that," said Virginia. "I remember that you're my responsibility every damn minute of every damn day."

"Language!"

"When I get back to Boston," Virginia snapped, "the very first thing I'm going to do is buy myself a parrot. And I am going to teach him to pipe up 'Language!' at regular intervals to annoy any and all around him."

"I don't an—"

"And I will name him in your honor."

From the look on Caprice's face, a slightly stunned expression, she thought she'd struck home with her barbs. But it was something else entirely.

The rich girl bent over and vomited.

The contents of her stomach splattered with an awful sound, everyone around her shocked into utter silence.

Caprice stood back up with a green, grim look and wiped her mouth with the back of her hand.

Only a moment later, she bent over to retch again.

In Virginia's gut roiled a combination of grim satisfaction and sickly uncertainty.

What was it now? Had the contents of the tin or something else sickened Caprice? Virginia couldn't abandon an unwell woman in these wastes, even Caprice. Besides, she had no desire to answer for a disappeared heiress upon her return.

That seemed unlikely, though. Caprice had a constitution of iron and a will to match. If Virginia had to lay odds on who would survive all this without a scratch, Caprice would be a good bet. Heaven knew, in her weak, overwhelmed moments, she had given the rich girl poor odds to survive this expedition. She had said it to her face. But personally, she thought Caprice was the toughest of them all. Irene had better wilderness skills but could not lead, partly because she could not speak, partly because she did not want to. Siobhan didn't know enough about the North. Elizabeth was strong but not naturally venturesome, though she gained new skills every day. And Doro, poor Doro. Her knowledge of the Arctic had been essential on the journey so far and would be even more essential going forward, but could her body keep up with her mind? Virginia couldn't know for sure.

Caprice, though. She had the skills, the youth, the fire. She wouldn't give up just because things seemed impossible, Virginia told herself. Caprice would be fine.

Wouldn't she?

Chapter Forty:
Virginia

Massachusetts Superior Court, Boston
October 1854

The first words Mr. Mason says to her, even before she sees his face, are the two words she both can never hear enough and has already heard far too many times: *I'm sorry.*

She'd been praying for hours, wrestling with something much like a pain in her chest, that wringing-out feeling of hopes growing and hopes dashed. It felt as if something green were forcing its way out of her, and the only way she could forget the pain was to pray.

She lost track of how long she'd been there, knees dully aching on the hard blue-stone, and when she heard the guard announcing a visitor, she did not look up. She had been disappointed so many times. So many times, she'd caught her breath when a visitor was announced, always wondering if it could be someone she expected never to see again, hoping it wasn't and yet unable to embrace that hope fully.

"I'm sorry," he says, and when she hears the unfamiliar voice, she finishes her prayer, *Thy will be done, Amen,* and then looks up with battle-wearied eyes.

The man is unfamiliar, but she's pretty sure she knows who he is. The pain of hope in her heart, that green shoot, pushes up harder toward the sunlight.

"My name is Thomas Mason," he says, "and I'm your new attorney. I'm sorry it took me so long to arrive. There were some complications untangling you from Mr. Clevenger's representation. He did not go willingly, but now the deed is done, and you will deal only with me for the remainder of the trial."

"Thank you. That's good news," says Virginia.

There is no smile on his face. "To be frank, I wish it were better," he says. "I fear the time when I could have made great strides in your case may be behind us."

Virginia stands, her legs creaking as she puts weight on her feet for the first time in hours, and almost falls. She puts out her hands and catches the cold metal of the bars to keep herself upright. The bars are so cold. They are always so cold.

Thomas Mason is around her height, not a tall man but with a strong jaw and broad frame that give him a larger man's presence. His nose is sharp and angular, his mouth wide. There is a warmth and sympathy in his eyes that makes Virginia's mouth go dry. Whether or not that warmth is real, it is compelling. She wants to be sure of him, but at the same time, does it matter whether she is? He has to be better than her last counsel, and there is no way she'll have the chance at a third.

"Are you a friend of the captain's?" she asks.

"Captain Malcolm engaged me, yes," says Mr. Mason. "We are old friends, from before his seafaring career began."

"And what do you mean? About it being too late?"

"I cannot object to anything that has already happened," he says. "I cannot cross-examine witnesses who have already been dismissed. If I'd been here at the very beginning, certainly I would have argued the case's very jurisdiction. Why Massachusetts, when the body was not found here?"

Her head spins. She counters, "The body was not found at all."

"Of course, of course," he agrees smoothly. "But I could have argued that

440

because Caprice was known to have departed the United States by crossing the border at Sault Ste. Marie, if the case is to be tried in an American court at all, it should have been tried in Michigan."

"Would that have been better?"

"The state of Michigan has abolished the death penalty," he says, and the kindness in his voice almost undoes her.

Struggling to speak, she forces words out, mindful that she doesn't know how long she has with him. "So there are many things we can't do. What can we do?"

"We are entering a new phase of the case, Virginia," he says. "They have called every witness they plan to call."

"How do you know?"

"We know."

"So what comes next?"

"Our witnesses. Our strategy."

Somehow, Virginia's dizziness overtakes her, and what she hears coming from her mouth are the very last words she intended to say. "My last attorney was not keen on letting me take the stand."

To his credit, her new attorney seems unfazed by this revelation. "Really. Did he give you a reason?"

"He said I wasn't credible."

"I'm not sure I agree with that," he says,

and her heart lifts a little. His manner becomes more businesslike. "What's most important is that I don't think it matters. We can't very well just roll over and admit that everything they've said is true; we need to counter it. Which you can do. You're a well-spoken young lady."

"Around here, I may as well be a foreigner."

"That's as may be," he agrees. "But what we need here is doubt. You're familiar with the standard of guilt in American courts, I assume?"

"This is the first American court I've ever set foot in," she says, "and I dearly hope it will be the last."

His lantern jaw tightens visibly, and she realizes her mistake. Whichever outcome results from this trial, that will almost certainly be the case. Either she'll walk free and live an exemplary life hereafter or, once her legs swing in the air as she dances from the hangman's noose, she won't set foot in a courtroom or anywhere else.

"In any case" — she hastens to cover her error — "I'm not the attorney here. Tell me. What is the standard of guilt of which you speak?"

"It comes from England, actually, but it holds here. The presumption of innocence:

'innocent until proven guilty.' A gentleman named Blackstone said it another way: 'It is better that ten guilty persons escape than that one innocent suffer.' "

She thinks about this for a while and does not know what to say. Which category does he think she fits in?

"You've suffered," he says.

"And you believe in my innocence?"

"Your guilt, to me, is like your credibility. Not important for my purposes. Your innocence is preferable but ultimately irrelevant."

"So you think I did it, and you'll defend me anyway?"

"Not at all," he says, almost cheerfully. "I'd like to believe you're innocent, but it doesn't matter what I believe. I was hired to serve the law. I'm required to give you the best defense I can, so I will."

Still too stunned to speak, she tries to digest this. Her new attorney doesn't even believe she's innocent? What about Captain Malcolm, who hired him — what does he believe? She realizes he has no idea what really happened. He'd seen her with Caprice on the *Doris* early in their acquaintance, their frequent clashes, jealousy, competition. Maybe he thinks her a murderer but knows men like him have committed similar sins when in dire straits. Maybe his willingness to hire her counsel is a sort of hope that someone else would do the same for him.

Now Mr. Mason tells her, "You can plead guilty if you want. They might reduce your sentence. Argue leniency if you're truly repentant."

"But I'm not repentant," she blurts.

"I simply want to give you a realistic sense of your options."

"I can't repent what I didn't do. I didn't kill her."

This time, when he speaks, he doesn't meet her eyes. "And that's the other thing you can do, which obviously, you already grasp. Maintain your innocence. And if that's your gambit, then, our path is clear."

Her stomach wrings and twists as she says, "And what is that path?"

He tells her, "We let you speak for yourself."

Without a moment's hesitation, she replies in a firm voice, "Good."

Whether it is truly a good thing she doesn't know. But what she knows is that she must speak on her own behalf. Even though there are plenty of reasons for her not to. That way, whatever comes of it, her fate will belong to her. She cannot stand the idea of being totally helpless, of standing aside while the real decisions are made about her fate. She would rather participate and lose than stand back and win.

She hopes, of course, that those aren't her only two choices.

Are they?

CHAPTER FORTY-ONE:
VIRGINIA

On the Expedition
October and November 1853

Winter fell upon them like a hammer. One morning after sleeping in a huddle under the overturned shallop as usual, they awoke to find an inch of snow had turned the world white while they slept. After that, they added a layer of canvas to their nighttime shelter so any morning snow could be shaken off quickly before they got back on their way. Irene had taught them that trick. She'd also been the first one to realize it was time to put on their snow goggles, which narrowed their vision to a mere slit but kept them from going blind from the sun's glare reflected on the snow. Now that they were well and truly on the ice, thought Virginia, the whiteness seemed to go on forever.

Yet someday, it had to end, didn't it? Miles from here or just over the next ridge. There had to be somewhere that was not this place. Somewhere that Franklin and his men, if God smiled upon them, might still be.

Virginia hoped that they would get there, but days like this, she wasn't sure they would. Doro assured her that they were making progress toward their destination. While she was not entirely sure how long it would take them to reach the search area designated by Lady Franklin, she thought it could be measured in weeks, not months. If they could get there before the bone-chilling cold prevented any forward motion.

The good news was, with the ice coating the landscape beneath, they'd assembled the sledge, which sped over the miles far faster than the shallop had. And unlike the shallop, the sledge could haul all the women and not just their goods. It didn't matter if one of the women was feeling weak, slowing her pace, and forcing the others to match her steps to avoid leaving her behind. The dogs were the only ones that mattered, and they were untiring, fearless. Day after day, week after week, the dogs took them northwest, closer and closer to King William's Land.

The other good news was that Caprice had recovered quickly from whatever sickness had struck her back at the cache. Whether she'd been sickened by what was in the tins or not, no one could be sure, and they'd left the cans behind in their worry, so it hardly mattered now. She later confessed to having eaten some weeds the day before that she'd dug out of the snow, too hungry to resist, too selfish to share, which in the end was a blessing. Whatever caused it, Caprice bore up far better under the sickness than Virginia would have expected. She was pale but determined. Without complaint, she'd forgone her ration for two days rather than take a chance on vomiting it up.

They were all keeping a weather eye on their food supply. This far north, the hunting grew poor. During an unseasonably warm turn, they had paused for several days to hunt in earnest. They shot and dressed as many animals as they possibly could, drying meat of all varieties on racks next to a bonfire: rabbit and venison, anything they could find. Irene had laid traps that brought down a host of lemmings, and she'd dressed the furs with ruthless efficiency along with drying the meat, so each of the women now had a spare pair of mittens to wear while their other pairs dried. With practice, Elizabeth's talent at shooting had surpassed even Irene's; she took down more animals than anyone else with her patient, precise aim. But the cold had clamped down like a fist again, all too soon. They had not seen game in a week. The women, by agreement, severely constrained their rations. The dogs ate more generously — Virginia worried Ann overfed them, more tenderly solicitous of their appetites than she'd ever been of her human companions' — and the heap of supplies visibly dwindled on the long days.

The women, eating twice a day at most, had grown lean. Virginia wished they'd had likenesses made at the beginning of the journey so she could compare the dramatic changes. They'd be a sideshow. *Come see the amazing transforming women! From hips and bosoms to skin and bones in mere weeks!* Irene, already thin, was the least changed of the party. Virginia suspected she had gone longer periods on less generous rations before, given how unaffected she seemed by the hardship. The change in Stella was the most dramatic; her moon-shaped face had thinned and hardened, and Virginia was stunned one night in the firelight to see she no longer reminded Virginia of her younger sister, Patty. Enduring one disaster hard on the heels of another had stripped her of her innocent charm. While still beautiful, Stella now had the face of a woman with no illusions left. With a start, Virginia realized that the woman she now resembled most closely was Virginia herself.

As they moved north and west and the temperature fell and fell, the land gradually began to slope upward. One day, Doro called a halt at a flat patch of territory that abutted a sharp hill, the beginning of a far steeper climb.

The women tumbled down from the sledge in quiet compliance, stretching their legs, solicitously checking one another's welfare. The dogs yipped and circled Ann, who patted and stroked them, praised their smarts and strength as if they could understand every word.

"This is it," said Doro.

Virginia looked around. If they continued north, they'd be heading into more challenging territory; she was not even sure if the sledge could be used on ground that looked almost mountainous. To the west, the smoothness of the snow gave it away: a frozen lake lay underneath.

Caprice, who'd always had the best eyesight, squinted toward the east and said, "Is that what I think it is?"

They all squinted in the direction she pointed, though the narrow slits in the snow goggles blurred their vision, and it was Irene who answered by tapping Caprice on the shoulder and giving a vehement nod. *Yes.*

"What is it?" asked Siobhan.

"Woods," said Caprice.

Doro turned to Virginia. "What do you think? Do you agree?"

"Yes," said Virginia.

"What is it?" Siobhan, always the most willing to voice her questions, asked.

Virginia told them, "We'll stop here. This is where we'll spend the winter."

And so it was. There were fish in the lake, at least for now, and unless they could find the open polar sea before winter — deeply unlikely, said Doro after consulting the map — this was the best place to make their camp. It was not yet so cold that they couldn't continue, but in the rockier territory north, there was no certainty; they might not find a spot this ideal again. The steep terrain to the north would help block the worst of the wind. The nearby woods were equally important to survival and not just because they might harbor game to be hunted. The trees, too, would help them. Without wood, there would be no fire. Without fire, they would not be able to melt ice for water. Even a very small amount of food each day would keep them alive, but if they did not drink, they would die.

During the Very Bad Thing, Virginia remembered, water was much less of an issue. The one thing they'd had in limitless supply was snow. Snow could be melted in one's mouth without much danger, or one could warm it in their hands to give to a child or weakened adult to drink. Virginia had done both many times. Here on the ice, that was not an option. In the deepest winter, taking off a mitten could mean losing a hand. When death by freezing was only a degree or two away, putting ice in one's mouth to melt it could bring a body's temperature down, and it didn't take a scholar to understand what the result could be.

The first night, they erected a tent over the sledge, with the dogs tucked in among them like blankets, but as soon as the sun rose into the sky, Irene sprang into action. She rummaged among the tools deep in the supply pile and came up with something resembling a saw, and as she set to work on a patch of hard-packed snow and ice, Virginia was shocked by the breadth of her smile.

Irene cut large blocks of snow, humming under her breath as she shaped and smoothed them, and then began to stack. The women who watched her began to see what was happening, and they turned to one another in wonder. Was the mute woman doing what it looked like she was doing?

She was building them a house.

It was the kind of round house the Esquimaux built, Virginia realized, with no space whatsoever between the bricks and a low, half-circular tunnel as entrance. Once the building was complete, Irene invited them in, indicating that she would build a second one that the dogs could have to themselves if Ann wanted, but for now, they would sleep close together here, since their bodies would grant each other warmth that the shape of the house would keep from escaping.

The first night inside the house, it was so warm Virginia began to cry. She cried even harder when she realized the tears on her cheeks did not freeze.

As the winter grew colder and the days shorter, by necessity, the women grew comfortable in the dark. There was no point in wasting fuel to see one another's faces; they each knew them as well as — or better — than their own. Instead, they told one another stories, and Virginia especially began to look forward to that moment each day when they all settled down, lined up like cordwood, and one woman — whoever had decided to begin that night — inhaled audibly in the darkness.

The stories they heard from one another in those endless weeks of winter were like a whole separate adventure. Adventures in the plural, really — the amazing things seen and done by an extraordinary group of women who had lived extraordinary lives. Stella had them laughing until their sides hurt with the tale of an uppity rich woman who ran through the house shouting at the servants to hunt down the source of a disgusting smell that seemed to invade the whole building when in fact she had a brown smear of her tiny, awful dog's shit stuck to her own expensive heel. Siobhan, almost as hilarious, spun tales of the follies and foolishness of her fellow medical students and the outrageous things she'd seen dressed as a man that she'd never be allowed as a woman. She'd been a visitor, a spy, in a whole other world.

Elizabeth, in a tentative voice full of wonder, described a panorama she'd seen one Wednesday afternoon in Amory Hall. She'd found five cents in the street and feared someone might take it away if she didn't spend it, so she'd done so right away. She lost herself in the lush, detailed images of *The Grand Panorama of a Whaling Voyage*

454

'Round the World, the surge of the music, the huge and soaring pictures of the ships, so vast they felt as real as the real thing. That was why, when she'd set foot on the *Doris,* it hadn't scared her, she told them; she already felt she'd stood on the deck of a topsail schooner, inhaling the cold salt spray.

But it was Caprice's story that took their breath away.

I saw myself an angel in rainbow light, she began and told them of an Alpine phenomenon called the Brocken spectre, when a person's own shadow is reflected off the snow at a certain angle by the rising sun and appears as a huge, looming presence in the sky.

My own long form rose into the sky, said Caprice, her voice musical in the darkness. *I feared it was God's judgment come upon me at first; then I feared it was Satan who taunted me so. My punishment for daring too much. My very spirit ripped from me and cast up into the clouds. I watched to see in which direction my enormous shade would travel — up toward heaven or down to hell? — and held my breath so long my consciousness began to dim at the edges, the brightness of the Alpine sunrise turning black like a burnt crust of toast held too close to the fire.*

When she fell silent, no one broke the

silence. No breath was even audible in the dark. They were prisoners in her palm, eager for the next word, caught in the power of her spell.

Then in a different tone, as light as spun sugar, Caprice said, *But it was no such thing. The sunlight crested the peak. My shadow disappeared from the sky all in a breath. My spirit flew back into my body, where it has remained to this day. I never saw Brocken spectre before or since.*

When her turn came, Virginia told the story of the first time she guided a party to California with Ames, the long-awaited moment when the clouds parted above them and the sun shone onto the settlement in the valley, revealed as if God were showing off His handiwork. She did not tell them about her own first voyage. No matter how long the winter was, she doubted she would ever share that tale. The purpose of the stories was to buoy the women up, not terrify them.

In those moments in the dark, during the stories before sleep, Virginia could let herself forget the bad days she knew were coming. She knew the food would grow more and more scarce over the course of the winter. She knew the air around them would grow colder than they could even conceive. She knew that the days would grow shorter and shorter until the daylight was a thin, milky cast for a couple of hours a day and everything else was darkness.

There would be many reckonings in the days to come. She knew what the first would be and with whom. Virginia and Doro, out of Ann's earshot, had already discussed the fact that expeditions like theirs, wintering over with no certain prospects for feeding themselves, almost always turned to the dogs. The women needed transportation, but they needed food more, and if they didn't survive the winter, there would be no one to transport when the thaw came.

But for the moment, she let herself relax and treasure the warmth. Worrying about the future would not improve anything in the present. She simply lost herself in the pleasures of the moment. The sound of other women's voices, trusting and tender, in the darkness. The pleasant, drowsy feeling of knowing sleep was not far off. Her own well-being, whatever measure of it God decided to grant her, as long as that might last.

CHAPTER FORTY-TWO:
VIRGINIA

Sierra Nevada Mountains
1846

In the throes of the Very Bad Thing, during the worst of those miserable days, Virginia could not stop people from dying. There had been deaths even before the snow had marooned them in the mountains, even before they realized the sum total of their mistakes had added up to doom for the entire party. Halloran had failed to outrun the consumption that drove him to seek California in the first place; a handful of others had fallen victim to accidents along the way. Those deaths had felt different. If they were anyone's fault, they were not hers. But the deaths in the mountains, she felt responsible for somehow, though she was far too young and powerless to take any true leadership of the party. Each one felt like a personal failure, a defeat she could have somehow prevented if she'd only taken different, better actions along the way. It took her a long time to let go of that feeling. While the Very Bad Thing was still happening, it had its icy fingers wrapped around her throat nearly every minute of every single day.

But there were things she could do to escape it. To help. To make a difference, for others and herself, and every day, she ticked them off on her fingers to make sure they stayed on her mind.

Exercise her fingers and toes to fend off frostbite.

Tend to the children, all the while pretending good cheer so they would feel less of the aching, desperate fear that most of the adults had grown too overwhelmed to hide successfully.

Make a game of hunger.

Make one good effort to find new food, whether that meant scraping down through the ice to find the bark of a not-yet-stripped tree, or sitting silently as far away from camp as she dared in the hopes a lone squirrel or rabbit might happen by, or turning something that had never been intended as food into some minor, sad form of nourishment. The only book they had left was the family Bible, and she'd taken a knife to it, separated cover from pages, to get at the glue on the inside of the spine. It had no taste, but there was a chew to it, a texture. Five of the children happily jawed away at it for over an hour.

The other thing she did, which no one else wanted to do, was go back and forth between the lake camp and the Donner camp, keeping the path from vanishing under the snow. By appearing in both camps regularly, Virginia decided, she could stay on everyone's mind. As if there weren't enough real fears to keep her awake and trembling, she'd developed a pathological fear that she might get left behind. If relief parties ever did come — and at this point, that felt not just uncertain or unlikely but impossible — she had a terror that they would come, sweep up the children on sledges, then come back for the adults, but because she was neither truly one or the other, she'd get left in camp to fend for herself. She was less weak than most — that would be another reason to deny her escape. And yet. Wouldn't any rescue party try to help as many as they could? Where was this fear coming from, and what could she do to banish it? If she knew what it was, she thought that might mean that she could overcome it, but for now, there were no easy answers.

Earlier in the winter, they'd tried to walk

out and seek help, four of them: Virginia, her mother, and two hired hands, a driver named Milt and their cook, Eliza. Her mother joked grimly at the time that Eliza might as well help in the search since as it was, there was no food left for her to cook. It seemed funny to say so until another snowstorm blew up and they had to abandon their trek, giving up and turning back. When they returned after four days, in their absence, even the rotting oxhides that had formed the roof of their cabin had been eaten. Even less funny considering what had been left to eat after that, which was only sometimes cooked, fuel growing almost as scarce as food as the snow piled high around them.

The next time a party went for help, Virginia begged to be included. She still carried a burden from the failure of the first party. If only they'd turned right or left at a different moment, would it have mattered? It had only been the poor timing of more snow that had forced them back; this time, wouldn't things be better? Besides, this time, one of the men had made them snowshoes.

Sarah Fosdick, the married daughter of the Graves family, heard Virginia's pleas to be included and took her aside. Bending down, she looked Virginia in the eye and said, "You are not coming. The die has been cast. What we need more is someone we can trust to care for those who remain behind. Rally spirits. So take all the energy you are wasting begging to come with us, and save it to keep the rest of the party alive."

Somehow, even those wise words did not keep Virginia from protesting once more. "But couldn't I be of more use —"

"No," said Sarah, her voice harsher now, her hands gripping Virginia's shoulders. Virginia would never forget how she could feel every one of the woman's fingertips, sharp and steady. The flesh had grown so scarce on her upper arms there was nothing to shield bone from bone.

Sarah went on, a rasp in her voice, "Do what you can. God be with you. I have every hope we'll bring back help. If it is at all possible, we will do it, I swear. But absent that — when all is uncertain — the only person you can count on is you."

She pressed a kiss against Virginia's forehead. It was dry and painfully cold and felt nothing like a kiss at all. Her lips had no more spirit or give than a thumb. That put more fear in Virginia than anything Sarah or any of the others could do or say.

She watched the snowshoe party depart

over the mountains. She watched until the dark outlines of their bodies vanished into the white. She paid particular attention to the slender form of Sarah Fosdick, setting a crisp pace, her body unbending even with the strain. In the end, every form, even Sarah's, disappeared into the white distance, swallowed whole.

Virginia had tried and failed, and she had hated how it felt to fail. But she hadn't known what it felt like to stay behind, to not be part of the group that tried. To wait while important decisions and actions were underway elsewhere, her fate in others' hands, trusting those others to do what was right to bring her back from the brink of death. Now, she knew how that made one feel.

Like even more of a failure.

CHAPTER FORTY-THREE: ANN

On the Expedition
January 1854

Ann knew as well as anyone that when explorers had to choose between their own lives and the lives of their dogs, they chose themselves.

But for all her days and weeks and months on this expedition, Ann told herself grimly, she was not really an explorer.

It was funny, she thought. She could tell she was well on her way to death. She had been exhausted and starving for so long, you'd think that every day would feel just as awful as it possibly could, but today, she felt a little better. That was how she knew she would die soon.

She'd never been on an expedition herself, but she'd been told the tales of dozens. Maybe a hundred even. Men coming back, telling her all the places the dogs had gone, but so rarely returning with them. Ann would much rather have seen the dogs again than the men. Every last one.

Ann raised her eyes to the horizon. Was it even a horizon, what she was seeing? Sometimes it was hard to tell apart the snow from the sky.

These ten dogs, dearer to her than any human, she could not sentence them to death. Nor did she want to sentence the women to death, but she knew their own choices were coming soon, and she could not risk them making the wrong choice.

She'd given the dogs her portion of meat every day — she couldn't remember the last time she'd eaten — and fed them from a secret trove of jerked meat she hid inside her clothes. While the women were put on a strict ration, they had not appointed a guard to watch the stores and make sure no one stole. When things got desperate, she was sure this would change. She would take her moment to act before it did.

Her eyes returned to the far-off point in the distance, farther than she could see.

The horizon was a smear of white, the gray-white of the clouded sky only a shade lighter than the white-gray of the snowy ground ahead.

When she released the dogs, they leapt and nuzzled her. The one she called Spotter made a playful bark, but she motioned for silence, and after that, they nudged and rubbed against her without sound. They tucked their heads under her dangling hand insistently, competing to be petted and stroked, fixing on her with their bright blue eyes. There was nothing in the world more beautiful than that blue.

Steady now, she told herself.

Ann had stolen one more thing, one more time. She hoped the women would forgive her. Particularly the doctor, whose kit she'd stolen it from. She had never been a habitual thief, not like Stella. The food for the dogs and the medicine for herself were the only things she'd ever filched. But even though she knew what she had to do, she was afraid. It wasn't death she feared so much as pain.

One at a time, she gave each dog the command to go. She could tell they wanted to stay with her, but when she repeated the command, even the most reluctant — Spotter — turned his head away and struck out in the direction she sent them.

South and east.

Ann removed her glove. The stinging, numbing cold licked at her fingers immediately. She had to act quickly or be lost. With as much speed as she could muster

466

while the tears welled in her eyes, she raised the phial, uncorked it, and gulped the contents in one swallow. She hoped she had guessed the contents right. Either way, this would all be over soon. But dying in agony and dying in peace were different things, and she knew which one she wanted.

She lay down with her eyes on the horizon, aiming her face in the direction the dogs had gone. Dark smears against the snow, they flung themselves wholeheartedly into their unknown future. In her way, she did the same.

The feeling spreading inside her was cool and painless. She'd chosen well, she thought. Luck was on her side, or whatever passed for it in this situation.

Only two dogs were still visible at all, off in the distance.

Her dogs, her treasured dogs, she could almost feel her own heart freezing. How soon it was too late. Unlike Virginia Reeve, she was not the kind of woman who prayed, but in this moment, she did hope. The dogs' survival was far from guaranteed, but their chances were better as a pack. She imagined them bringing down caribou and foxes, hares and raccoons. She envisioned them running south and east and south again, turning the journey they'd already made inside out, back to where the white land began to turn brown and then green. If nothing else, once they reached the shore of Hudson Bay, they would be found and welcomed. But in the miles between here and there, much could happen. Perhaps they would find a group of Esquimaux and join their nomadic family life. *That would be lovely,* thought Ann. She pictured them tumbling over the ground with children, their mouths open in wide dog grins, pink tongues lolling.

The picture in her mind was beautiful. She lost track of the far horizon, rejecting the visible, embracing what she'd imagined.

Thinking of the dogs warm and happy, Ann gave a soft, almost inaudible sigh.

The sigh died in her throat along with her.

CHAPTER FORTY-FOUR:
CAPRICE

On the Expedition
January 1854

If anyone else had found Ann, the whole party would have been wakened by a scream. Irene was unlucky enough to discover her body, so instead, she woke up only Caprice and Virginia to show them what had happened. It was possible, thought Caprice, she'd only been included because she slept between Virginia and the door, but once she was awake, there was no going back.

Together, they saw the tracks of the dogs disappearing over the horizon. They saw Ann's sightless eyes. They wrapped her body and carried it farther away from camp so it would not confront every woman who came out of the ice house, but Caprice told the other women they should keep it close so they could quickly act to give Ann a proper burial. That was not in fact why she wanted to keep the body close, but it would do as a reason.

And it was Caprice who broke the news to the rest of the women, as a group. Virginia opened her mouth over and over to say something — something reassuring, something firm, something that acknowledged the shock and pain they were all feeling — and yet no sound ever came out, only air wet with her breath. Doro thumped her fist against her thigh, over and over, her eyes shut tight against the world. Siobhan stared at the ground; Elizabeth looked to the sky. Stella alone looked right at Caprice, her gaze steady, her eyes dry. No one asked any questions.

Then Virginia turned her back on the women and walked toward the lake. Caprice hustled after her, concerned she might step onto the lake's frozen surface just to test it or even try on purpose to break through. On the worst climb of her life, a failed summit attempt on Mont Andraes, Caprice had seen suicide become contagious. When people felt trapped, it was the only sure escape route, and there was no telling who, in a weak moment, might be tempted to take it. If Virginia laid herself down and died, it would likely spell death for all of them. They'd had their differences, but

Caprice knew by now that losing Virginia would break the remaining spirit these women had. The combined loss of Ann and her dogs would bend them to the breaking point. They would not be able to endure more.

Caprice balled her hands into tight fists under her enormous gloves. If her hands had been bare, she would have been able to feel her fingernails biting into her palm, but as it was, in the enormous mittens, she could not even close either hand all the way.

She approached Virginia slowly from behind, not sure what to say but certain she had to say something. She wasn't even sure the other woman knew she was there until Virginia said, "And what do *you* want?" She bit off her words like the leathery jerked meat they'd all tired of ages ago.

Caprice said, "We need to discuss what to do with her."

Staring over the frozen water, Virginia said, "What can we do? Leave her in the ice until the thaw comes. We can't bury her in the land, and we can't bury her at sea."

"People in our situation — they don't always bury bodies."

"Of course they don't. What did I just say?"

"That's not what I mean," said Caprice

471

carefully. She had no desire to do what she was talking about, but she had to bring it up. It was a possibility, if a disturbing one. They weren't desperate enough yet, but they could easily become so. It would behoove them all to be on the same page before that happened.

"Then say what you mean."

"She let the dogs go because she didn't want us to eat them," said Caprice, forcing out each word against the cold air that threatened to freeze her lips shut. "And you know what? We probably would have."

Virginia didn't look at her. "You're so sure?"

"Yes. Certain. I wish Ann hadn't done what she did, of course I wish that, but about the dogs, she was right. She knew these next months could kill us. That we could die of hunger if we don't make hard choices. And now we have —"

Virginia wheeled on her then, raising her hand to bring across Caprice's face. Caprice's move away was equal parts dodge and stumble, her limbs slow from cold, and the few inches she moved made the difference. Virginia's mittened hand clouted Caprice on the side of the head, but through her thick hood, scarves, and Welsh cap, she barely felt the blow.

Virginia's voice, though, sent fear whistling down her spine.

"If you so much as mention that possibility again, I will kill you myself," Virginia said. "Don't think I won't."

"Virginia," said Caprice in disbelief. "I'm just trying to —"

"I don't need you to try," Virginia fairly snarled. "I need you to shut up and keep your head down until you get sick of real work. I'm sure that's coming soon. We'll hunker down. We'll survive the winter. Then whatever happens next, we'll find a trading post or another ship to leave you on, and I won't have to see you for the rest of my life."

Caprice crossed her arms. "You keep on like this —"

"Like what?"

"You keep on like this, pushing us away, refusing to let anyone help you do anything, even when you need it, and good God, Virginia, you're not going to have much life left to live."

"Language," responded Virginia automatically in a taunting tone. "Don't you dare take the Lord's name in vain."

"Profanity isn't the only thing God hates."

"How dare you presume to know what He hates or loves?" Her voice was full of anger but not just anger — there was fear there, and desperation. She sounded far too close to a breaking point. Caprice wondered if perhaps she was already there.

"I'm trying to talk in words you're going to understand." Caprice wanted to soothe her, but she knew Virginia was in no shape for soothing. She had to speak boldly, without apologies. Only the unvarnished truth could help now. "Everything else seems to fall on deaf ears. I hoped that by talking to you in the only language you seem to understand, the words of God, you might actually hear me for once."

"I hear you." But her words were without emotion.

"But are you listening? Are you taking it to heart?"

"What difference does it make to you?"

"I want to survive!" Caprice almost shouted. "I think my chances, all our chances, are best if you survive too. But I'm not even sure you want to!"

In a small, almost inaudible voice, Virginia told her, "I'm not sure of that either, for what it's worth."

Lowering her voice so the other women back by their shelter would not hear it, Caprice said, "We chose the risky path when we could have been safe. We all had our reasons. We took our chance. Now none of us may make it out alive. But that doesn't excuse any of us, especially you, from trying."

"That was well put."

"Try not to sound so surprised."

Virginia said, with a little more spirit, "I'll try."

"And by the way, mountaineering wasn't just idle sport." If they were being completely honest at last, Caprice had something to get off her chest. "I know you think I'm a dilettante. I know you think that money insulated me from everything. But just because there were guides who watched me summit the mountain, that doesn't mean I didn't do all the work to summit it. No one carried me up there on a litter. It was cold and dirty and hard, and I did it, damn you, Virginia, I did it. And you don't get to look down on me just because my background is different from yours."

"I'll tell you what," said Virginia, seeming like herself at last. "I won't look down on you for having money if you don't look down on me for not having it."

"That's fair," said Caprice. "And I owe you an apology."

"For what?"

"I judged you. It wasn't fair. But all my life, everyone's told me to be a lady, and that was the most important thing. Even while I was climbing mountains. I did it with a full skirt and a broad-brimmed hat and a picnic basket. Not because I thought I needed those things. Because I'd been told that was the only way."

Caprice chanced taking a breath of the cold air, but she wasn't done yet, and when Virginia didn't stop her, she rushed to continue.

"Then you showed up. Reaching for your own sandwiches and saying whatever you wanted. Handing out divided skirts and not even blinking at Ann when she showed up in Buffalo wearing breeches. I'd been told the world would end if men outside my family saw the shape of my legs. And you didn't care about that. And the world didn't end. I was angry because you didn't have to act like a lady. You just lived as a woman."

Caprice moved to the edge of the frozen water to stand next to Virginia. She smiled, though she knew Virginia couldn't see it; she hoped the difference could be heard in her voice. "So let's get through the winter. Together. And when we bring Franklin home, you'll be rich then, and we can be high society rivals back in Boston. Won't that be fun?"

"It'll be a delight," Virginia answered. "I've

never had a rival."

"Even if you had, I'd be a better one."

Caprice reached out with her mitten as if to grab Virginia's hand, but neither could bend their fingers inside the thickness of the material. They touched their hands and let them drop in the same instant.

"Let's go back to the others," said Caprice. "You won't have to say anything."

"You're not going to, are you?"

"We're going to get through this. What is there to say?" asked Caprice. She did not wait for an answer, gliding back toward the ice house and the other women.

Behind her, she heard Virginia following.

CHAPTER FORTY-FIVE:
VIRGINIA

Massachusetts Superior Court, Boston
October 1854

When the day comes to testify, Virginia is surprised to find a visitor has been sent to her without being announced: Althea, bearing a new dress in her arms. Her straw-gold hair is plaited and knotted in upon itself like some exotic basket, pulled just as airtight. The look on her damaged face is inscrutable. At a signal from the guard, she stuffs the gown in between the bars, muttering to Virginia in a rush, "Put this on, put this on."

Virginia acts first, knowing her questions can wait, and besides, she is used to not having her questions answered by now. Action first, always.

"Turn your back," Althea barks, uncharacteristically sharp, and Virginia snaps to attention before she realizes the words aren't meant for her. Althea's speaking to the guard. Virginia glances up to see him obeying — with conspicuous slowness, yes, but still obeying, which is really all that matters in the end.

She shucks her worse-for-wear serge, relishing the change of sensation on her skin, even though the air is outrageously cold. She stands in her underthings for only a moment before yanking the new dress on. Althea hasn't brought new unmentionables, and Virginia couldn't imagine stripping down to her skin anyway. She's not sure which idea appalls her more: the idea of seeing her own flesh bared or allowing someone else to see it. Bare flesh still feels so profane: exposed, vulnerable. She shudders even letting the image flit across her galloping mind. Though to be fair, that is not entirely the Arctic's fault. She got a taste of all that during the Very Bad Thing, which has been very much on her mind. Last night, she even dreamed of watching Sarah Fosdick walk away from her on those snowshoes. In the dream, she'd run to catch up, run and run and run, and she almost had her hand on Sarah's shoulder when she awoke.

Up goes the dress over her arms, her chest, her back. Wordlessly, Althea reaches through the bars to button up her fastenings. Parts of Virginia have to touch the bars in order for Althea's fingers, not as nimble as they once were, to reach. The sound of her breath is the only thing she hears at first, and then there's Althea's breath, and the guard's, all three of them tense in the silence.

Finally, the last button slides through the last buttonhole. Althea steps back, and so does Virginia.

"Thank you."

"It's nothing," says Althea, though she must know that it isn't. It's something. Virginia just isn't sure what.

The dress is finer than anything she's used to, and that worries her, but she doesn't ask questions. It is too late to do anything differently. Besides, the new fabric distracts her, which is good. She has less time to worry about what she will say and what they will all think of her when she is busy smoothing down every seam, settling every wrinkle, shaking out the folds of a new skirt to see how it falls around her. Perhaps someone very intelligent — was it Mr. Mason? Althea? Someone else? — has anticipated just how the dress will affect her. Or perhaps they just want her to look exactly the right amount of nice.

And once she's been in the dress for a few minutes, she knows it's exactly right. The richness of the fabric feels different against her skin, it's true, but it does not appear so different to the outer eye. It isn't a plush velvet or a rich sateen. It is good cotton, but only cotton, and it makes her look a little younger, with its blue and green sprigs on an ivory ground. For a moment, it makes her think of snow, but she brushes that away. It will not make anyone else think of snow. It will make them think of spring and growth and joy. She hopes she lives to see another spring. Whether she does could depend entirely on what she says in the courtroom today.

Apprehension grips her, an icy hand on her throat, as she approaches the courtroom. She loses herself in a prayer, silent and fervent, and all thoughts of fabric and expectation and the guard's averted gaze drain away. The moment is between her and God, and He knows what she wants most. What she fears. What's most important. Why and whether she cares. She lets herself drop into His waiting arms, and just like that, the fear falls away. Whatever is going to happen is in His grasp now. She will tell the truth she needs to tell in order to live with it, and if that means her remaining life on earth will be short, she will look forward to her eternal life with Him in heaven.

It is the only way she can take another step. Only her faith bears her up.

"Godspeed," says Althea softly.

Virginia only nods solemnly, but as the guard opens the door and swings it shut behind Althea's retreating back, it occurs to her she might never see this woman again.

"Althea," she blurts.

The Englishwoman turns. "Yes?"

Unprepared, unsteady, she asks the first question that comes to mind. "Are you glad you went?"

Althea's mouth moves as if she wants to smile, quirking up at one corner, but then it flattens out again. Her eyes flick toward the guard's face, then back to Virginia's, then down to the cold stone floor.

"We'll never be the same," says Althea.

Then Virginia can only watch as her friend — are they friends? Were they ever? — takes her leave.

Not long after, Benson comes to unlock the door, as he always does. He cuffs her hands, as he always does. She shuffles into the hall as she always has, her feet dragging slowly on the stone.

Then something happens that's never happened before.

In the courtroom, Virginia takes the stand.

She has seen so many other figures do the

same — hated ones and loved ones, people she regarded with suspicion and affection — but it is different from here. She hadn't realized how different it would be.

From the raised witness box next to the judge's bench, the courtroom is a sea of faces, and the most important faces are looking right at her. She went over them so many times, reading those faces, loving them. Doro, Althea, Irene, Ebba, Margaret. She realizes now, when she counted those survivors, she should also have counted the others who still lived. Dove, for example, who had been dragged in to testify and disappeared again as quickly as she'd come, off to go where she's needed. Siobhan, for whom the risk was too great to sit in that row but who now lives her chosen life. And herself, too, thinks Virginia. She should count herself as a survivor.

She survived the Arctic. She survived the bitter cold and the crushing ice and the lack of food. She would, God willing, survive this.

"Please swear," says the bailiff, and Virginia swears, and two curious forces hit her chest at once: a draining wave of relief and a heavy thud of fear. She has gotten what she wanted. She gets to speak for herself at last.

So why does she feel so conflicted? Probably because she cannot be sure that what she says will change anything. Which makes her doubt whether she should bother saying anything at all.

She is in control of her answers. That much is hers. She has no power over the results. She can't control the judge, the jury, the questions her counsel will ask her, whatever questions the prosecutor will ask.

Control what she can. Let go of the rest.

She was never good at this, not on the trail or even before. Her life has hung in the balance before but never quite in this way. She has been in danger from the hazards of the trail, jagged mountains and ravines of ice, the open waters of a fierce bay. She almost laughs at the inadequacy of that list, a mere sampling of dangers. So many things have come within a hairsbreadth of killing her. Hunger. Anger. Fear. The sky. The snow. The sea. Men. Women. Mistakes. Regret.

Right now, it feels like she's most in danger from herself.

Virginia smooths down the sprigged skirt of her new gown and looks out over the assembled audience. She sees so much naked antagonism there it takes her breath away.

She looks down at her clasped hands so she can regain control of herself, and then, she lets herself look at the five survivors she can see.

Irene. Althea. Doro. Ebba. Margaret.

Ten flinty eyes watching her, not without kindness, not without hope. If they had no hope for her, they would not be sitting there. She meets their gazes, each in turn, feeling her entire fate hovering in a pocket limbo as she waits for the questioning to begin.

She looks out to see if Captain Malcolm is here. A foolish hope, she decides. Or is that him in the back? No, but then she lets herself imagine that the stranger is Ames, though that is a ridiculous feat of imagination. She knows Ames is dead; she saw him die. If she hadn't, she wouldn't be here today. The man in the back is not Ames. But if he is the ghost of Ames, so be it. He will keep her honest, as he did in life.

Finally, Mason approaches. She is relieved to see her counsel looking grim and intelligent. She can tell he knows what's at stake here. That was one of the many failings of her previous counsel, one of the things that gave him away: he never seemed daunted by his burden. Mason does. That may not mean he can lift the burden, but at least it means he's aware of it resting on his shoulders.

"Miss Reeve. I understand this is all very challenging for you, and you've been held over in jail without real evidence of wrongdoing for several months already. I'll endeavor to keep my questions as brief as I can."

"Thank you."

"So let's begin at the beginning, for the sake of these good people's understanding. Why did you go north?"

"I was hired to do so," says Virginia, because it's the truth.

"By whom?"

"By Lady Jane Franklin." Whispers circulate around the court. The claim's been made before from the witness box, but she supposes hearing it from her lips is somehow different.

"And what did Lady Jane Franklin set as your goal?"

"To find her husband and his lost ships."

"Did you succeed?"

She still regrets having to admit it. "We did not, sadly."

"I'm certain your adventures on the ice were both inspiring and daunting, and though I'm sure the good people here would love to listen to them, unfortunately, in a trial like this, we must stay focused on our capital business."

This doesn't seem to call for a verbal answer, so she simply nods to show her agreement.

"So I will ask you the question at the core of this trial. Virginia Reeve, did you kill Caprice Collins?"

"No, sir," she answers and is proud of herself for the conviction in her voice. She is glad he used the pointed word *kill* and not the more elegant construction *feel responsible for the death of*. She would have had to answer that one in the affirmative.

"In your own words," he says soberly, "please describe to us the last time you saw Caprice Collins alive."

This will be the hardest part, she thinks. More than the prosecutor's pointed questions and accusations. More than the dark corners of the past she's been dragged into thus far. There is no more delaying it, putting it off, sweeping it under. It's time to look this demon square in the eye.

She tells them about the day Caprice fell into a gap in the ice and never came out.

What she tells them, her eyes held level over the heads of the assembled, breathless crowd, is both the truth and not the truth.

It is the story they all agreed on, up north. The fact that there is so much truth in it makes it remarkably easy to tell.

Virginia's voice is steady. Her hands do not tremble. Perhaps her calm will be used against her, evidence she has no real emotions, but she can only tell it the one way. All her regret and pain, she will keep on the inside.

Tonight in her cell, alone, she will cry over the truth. For now, she feeds an eager courtroom the lie.

CHAPTER FORTY-SIX: VIRGINIA

On the Expedition
January to April 1854

In the long, dark months of winter, the women went days without leaving the ice house. Some days, it was too cold to risk exposure, even for moments; some days, they simply could not stir themselves from their huddle. On the first day of January — Virginia counted on Irene to keep track — they went down to one ration a day instead of two, and as a result, their energy flagged even more, leaving little to go on.

There was a particular horror to the relentlessness of the Arctic, thought Virginia. Everything seemed to be without end. In the winter, it was the dark that persisted; in the summer, the same was true of the light. One never knew how long anything would last: a snowstorm, a bout of good hunting, a high ridge of ice. The uncertainty was probably exciting to true explorers. If she had discovered nothing else on this journey, Virginia had discovered she was not a true explorer. Her personality, her skills, were far better suited for the work she'd been doing in her precious few years of partnership with Ames: guiding people over territory that was strange to them but familiar to her, ensuring their every footfall landed as safely as her own.

She missed that certainty almost as much as she missed Ames, which was still a lack so intense it sometimes took her breath away.

For months, the only events memorable enough to distinguish the days were bad ones. Early on in March, they sent out a small group — just Elizabeth, Doro, and Irene — in search of food, hoping that the char might return to the lake or the hares to the woods. They suspected it was too soon but they tried anyway, thinking it was better than just waiting inside the ice house to die. The three women were tied together at the waist with a rope so they could not be separated, and the remaining women lost a night of sleep when the three who'd gone out did not return until the morning.

Elizabeth and Irene were only chilled to the bone and quickly recovered, but Doro had lost her goggles on the failed hunt.

She'd been so snow-blind and disoriented that she didn't realize her Welsh cap had gotten soaking wet on one side, then frozen. By the time she returned, the ear underneath was so badly frostbitten Siobhan had to cut away what was left, using precious morphine from her kit to blunt the pain. She did not have enough to take the pain away entirely, but she did her best, as did Doro.

After that, they didn't venture more than fifty steps from the ice house for the rest of the month, and that only with ropes to lead them back in case they lost their sense of direction. Had there been more rope, they would have gone farther; fifty steps did not even get them to the shore of the frozen lake. Sometimes, they continued to tell stories, but most often, they lay in silence, conserving their energy, lost in their own dizzied thoughts.

On the sixteenth of April, an anniversary none suggested celebrating, they heard the first falcon wheeling overhead. They had not heard or seen a single bird since November. The rapture of it sent them all scrambling out into the snow, whooping with laughter. The sun had not yet risen, but they searched the sky for more birds, a promising omen. Immediately, someone suggested

491

a hunt — Virginia would never remember who — and they tied themselves together on two long ropes in case they stumbled. Virginia approved consuming the day's ration early to give them the energy to trek, and they moved out together into what looked like a perfectly typical, clouded-over day. The terrain was high and uneven, their feet slipping on snow and ice, but half-grim, half-giddy, they charged on.

Two hours later, hints of a warm, soft breeze tickling their cheeks, they had bagged a dozen lemmings, small and wriggling. It was all they could do not to eat the furry creatures raw. Irene dispatched each with forceful, spare motions and packed them to cook later over the fire. They went on with their search.

Using the compass, Doro kept them on a straight heading, making sure they would not be dependent on unfamiliar landmarks. The lemmings would not feed them for long, so they continued. Every rise and fall of the land meant they could be greeted with disappointment or thrill at any time, and driven by tension, they peered out through their snow goggles and hoped. Then, they were rewarded. When a stream came into view, to a woman, they shouted with unfettered joy.

The stream lay under a cap of ice, but in the rushing water underneath, they found a feast. The fish lay sluggish near the bottom of the stream. If the water had been warmer, they could have simply thrust their hands in and yanked dozens of fish right out. As it was, it took a while to find the net, affix it to its frame, and then begin scooping fish slowly and carefully, hoping not to frighten off the ones destined for the next sweep of the scoop.

They were all so focused on this pursuit, smiling silently because they did not know whether sound would scare the fish away, that they did not see the storm rolling in.

When they had finally caught as many fish as they could carry, each woman filling her pack to the brim, they turned their attention back to their route home. Virginia heard their simultaneous intake of breath.

The snow began.

Virginia gestured for them to circle close so they could hear one another. "Do we stay or go?" she asked. "You know the dangers."

They did, and they considered them in silence. The earliest giddiness that had fueled their hunt had evaporated. Now that snow had begun, there was no knowing when it might end. It was smartest to rush back on the reverse heading that had led them here, using the compass. Their best hope was their only known shelter. If they stayed out too long in the gathering cold and the snow blanketed them, stillness meant death. They all knew.

"Let's go," said Caprice. "Virginia, why don't you let me take lead position for a while? My eyes are good in snow."

Caprice had often volunteered to take lead position on hunts, and something had changed about the way she put herself forward that gladdened Virginia's heart. Caprice had not insisted or wheedled or flaunted her mountaineering experience. She had simply asked if she might have a turn, please, and after a few polite repetitions of the request, Virginia saw no reason not to say yes at last.

And Virginia was glad for the respite. It was exhausting, making all the decisions, dictating everything. If Caprice wanted to lead, at least in this way, for a change? The release was actually welcome. They would go forward all together regardless of which one was actually at the head of the line, which in the middle, which at the end. How much could it matter if she was looking at Caprice's back for a change instead of the endless white landscape ahead?

Unfortunately, it mattered very much.

On the walk to the stream, Virginia had been in the lead, roped to Irene, Doro, and Siobhan. Caprice had been at the head of the second rope, tied on with Stella and Elizabeth. They simply switched the order of the ropes, so Virginia was fourth now, and Caprice tied the knot to connect the two ropes before they set out into the swirling white. Doro passed the compass to Elizabeth so she could call out the bearing from time to time, making sure they didn't veer too far off course.

There was no telling how long they'd been walking when it happened, but Virginia was still feeling the novelty of not walking in the lead. The jagged rises seemed higher, the valleys lower, somehow. Instead of the featureless white before her, there was the bright red of Caprice's famous coat, a scarlet blot on her vision, followed by the two dark forms of Stella and Elizabeth. There was something she enjoyed about that.

But then she blinked, and when her eyes opened again, she saw only white.

What? she thought.

She felt a hard tug for a moment, pulling her two steps forward, then nothing.

"Caprice!" she shouted.

The wind was strong, and the snow blew

in her face, and through the narrow slits of her goggles, she saw nothing. No dark shapes, no red, only blinding white.

Virginia dropped to her knees.

"Down!" she shouted to the others, praying they could hear her over the howling din. She heard a crack. Was it thunder? It sounded like a breaking board but couldn't be. "Down!"

She felt what she hoped was the two women behind her dropping to the frozen ground, lying flat to spread their weight out as they'd planned to do if something went wrong.

Something was going wrong.

Tiny droplets of ice spat in her face. She searched her thoughts for an explanation. There was only one, but she rejected it. The vanishing, the yank, the end of the pressure. No, no. Let her be wrong. Let it be something else.

There should have been rope in front of her, regardless of what else had happened. The knot that Caprice tied should have held.

It hadn't.

They must have veered off course, not checking their bearing as often, and stumbled into some kind of hole. She would have to look. To find out how bad it was. She didn't want to.

They lay there with the snow hammering down on them for so long that Virginia knew a layer of snow had built on top of her. She felt someone kick her then, and the kick might just have saved her life. If no one had tried to get her attention, if they'd just let her lay there, she might never have gotten up again.

But Irene, who'd been behind her in the line, kept kicking at the sole of her boot with her own boot. Was the snow beginning to slacken? Women's voices called from somewhere below, trying desperately to keep their panic down. She was the one who had taught them not to panic. She tried to hold onto the pride of that for a moment, but it slipped away almost instantly. There was no time for pride.

Then the snow did clear, a final swirl of white sparkle zipping through the air like smoke from a genie's lamp, and the bright sun reflected off the ice blindingly again. Her snow goggles had gone askew when she fell to the ice, and she could feel that her upper cheek had gone numb. If she lost the eye, she told herself, she might as well find the gun at her belt and shoot herself in the head with it. Though a good Catholic would never do such a thing. Her faith had given her strength when she most needed it, both during the Very Bad Thing and her years as a trail guide. Right now, her faith felt like a taunt, a tease. Why would any god allow these things to happen? Was it the devil at work? Did God simply not care? Or was the fault in Virginia? Had she failed, in this endeavor, to prove herself worthy of His love?

"Caprice!" she shouted. "Elizabeth! Stella!"

Now she could hear a faint repetition of two syllables, over and over, like some kind of far-off bird. But it was not a bird. It was a voice, warped somehow into a lower register.

Suddenly, she understood the syllables. *Stay back. Stay back. Stay back.*

And she recognized the voice.

Caprice.

"Caprice!" she screamed. "Where are you?"

"Stay back!" came the answering call from somewhere low, sunken. "Back! Don't fall!"

Inching forward on her belly again, Virginia crept forward with dread, just a very little bit at a time. When she felt the ice fall away under her fingertips, she jerked her mittened hand back as if she'd been bitten.

"Caprice!" she called down. With one

hand, she held tight to the ice's lip; with the other, she chanced lifting her goggles for just a moment, and in that moment, she saw all three women in a deep, narrow crevasse. The narrowness of the crevasse was probably why the fallen hadn't died on impact; the walls themselves had slowed their fall, bouncing them back and forth, depriving them of momentum all the way. Caprice's bright red coat shone like a beacon from the cool glow of a faraway blue.

"Don't be an idiot," called Caprice, screaming to be heard. "Stay back."

"You're the idiot," Virginia snapped back, but the fear in her blood was rising. The three women were so far down she could barely see them. Did they even have enough rope to reach?

"I'm sorry," Caprice said.

"No," said Virginia, because there was nothing else to say, and then again, "No."

Caprice and the other women in the ravine busied themselves, and Virginia realized what they were doing. She turned to do the same.

"Untie yourselves," she said to the women behind her. "We're going to haul them up."

Siobhan said, "I'm not sure we can —"

"We *will*," shouted Virginia, and Siobhan did not protest again.

When Virginia peeked down into the ravine, a woman's head was closer than she remembered. What had changed? Stella had made her way up to Caprice's shoulders. One end of the rope was tied around Stella's waist; she had tied the other around a fish from her pack as an anchor and tossed it up to Virginia.

"She's lightest," shouted Caprice. "Take her."

There was just enough rope to reach. Virginia untied the fish — comical, but she had never felt less like laughing — and knotted the two ropes together, testing the knot over and over to make sure this one would hold. She lay down and braced herself, feeling Irene's hands around her ankles, knowing Siobhan was anchoring the entire chain.

She peeked back at the other women, but their faces were unreadable under layers of leather and fur. There was no time to ask how anyone felt. Feelings could not, did not, matter. All that mattered now was what they did.

"All right, brace yourselves," called Virginia. Did her shouts echo in the narrow chasm that held, or was that pure imagination? When she called *three, two, one, now,* she heard the faint ghost of her own words, popping like a bubble in the air before the far horizon swallowed each sound whole.

Every inch was hard fought. There were many moments when she thought pulling Stella up would pull the rest of them down. Then they would be lost. But in the end, they edged back and back and back until Stella's hands slid over the ridge and she lay gasping, whooping, on the ice.

"You're soaking," said Virginia.

"The walls are wet," said Stella, panting, clearly spent. "Keep working."

They tossed the free end of the rope down to repeat the exercise, and the women up on the ice, five of them now, braced again in a human chain.

They pulled and pulled. Virginia had literally not thought far enough ahead to wonder who they were going to pull out of the hole.

Then she saw the red coat, a bright blot on her vision. For a moment, it was all she could see, that crimson on white, a flag against the endless background.

Always thinking of herself, she thought and reached out for Caprice's hand.

Only it wasn't Caprice.

"She insisted," said Elizabeth, tears frozen on her face.

"We'll get her next," said Virginia.

But they didn't.

While the women readied themselves to

pull again, Virginia shouted, "You're next, Caprice. Hold tight!"

There was no response.

Against her better judgment, Virginia crept forward and stared down into the sheer, wet crevasse. The thin Arctic light, filtered by the ice, glowed blue.

"Are you injured?" Virginia shouted down.

"Only my pride," joked Caprice.

"Stop that. Stop," said Virginia. This was no time for joking.

Once she was secure again, belly-down on the ice, she began to feed the rope down into the hole, hand over deliberate hand. Foot after foot of the rope disappeared into the gap, vanishing, swallowed up by white like everything else was in this godforsaken, hungry land.

"Ready?" she shouted.

Caprice shouted back, "No."

She edged closer, though it was unwise, to see what was going on. When she did, her throat closed up.

Caprice reached up toward the rope, but its frayed edge dangled at least four feet above her outstretched hand.

Elizabeth had stood on Caprice's shoulders to reach the rope. So had Stella. Now there were no other shoulders left to stand on.

Unless some sort of miracle transpired, Caprice was dead, even while she spoke and laughed and gazed upward at the far-off gray of the sky.

Behind her, Elizabeth said, her voice a sob, "She knew. She knew it wouldn't reach."

"What can we do?" Stella asked.

Virginia said, choking out the words, "I don't think we can do anything."

Caprice called up, "Tell everyone to stay back. It's melting. Everything's melting."

Now that she'd said it, Virginia could feel that the snow under her chest was wet. It was soaking her furs. The cold had tried to kill them; now it was the warmth, minor though it was, that could spell their doom. The irony was that the warmth up here, in the daylight, meant the crevasse might cave in, but down there in the darkness where the light didn't reach, Caprice would freeze to death before she could die of starvation.

Virginia could hear and feel someone else trying to crawl closer, and she called back, "No! Stay back. It's not stable."

She turned her attention back to Caprice and stared down into the abyss. Incongruously, Caprice was smiling.

"You know what I wish, Virginia?" she said. "I wish we'd had more time to insult each other."

It took her a moment to understand what Caprice was really saying.

Then Caprice shouted, "You'd better go. The cold. Keep moving."

"No," Virginia said. "We can't leave you."

"Virginia."

"We can't!"

Caprice yelled, "You're too close."

Virginia no longer slid forward toward the yawning gap, but nor could she move away. Caprice's false cheer was gone; without her coat, she was already turning cold, the blue all around her now reflected in the blue cast to her lips, her cheeks, her limbs.

"Don't give up," shouted Virginia, her voice breaking. "Please. *Please.*"

Somberly, as steadily as she could given the shiver that had already seized her body, Caprice looked up at Virginia.

Then she raised her palm in one of the two signals Virginia had taught her what seemed like a lifetime ago. Not the outstretched palm of supplication, of asking for help, but the other one. The forbidding palm, the warning motion. The one that asked the viewer to stay away.

No, said the signal. *Don't.*

The warm wind howled. The snow blew. The danger wasn't just how close they were to the chasm, where any of them could fall in, especially Virginia, who dangled treacherously close now. The danger was coming at them from all directions. The danger was west, east, north, south. Their only hope, and a slim one at that, was to get back to camp while there was still some light to show the way and heat themselves back up inside their snow house as quickly as humanly possible. They might not even make it if they tried, but if they didn't try, there would be six deaths today and not just one.

While Virginia stared down toward her friend, whose fists were clenched tight and turning a ghastly white already, snow blew harder. Virginia felt a tug at her ankles: the chain of other women securing her, making sure that she would not fall in.

Caprice locked eyes with her and uncurled one fist to repeat the motion, palm up, this time over her head with all the force she could muster.

Don't, the motion said, and this time, Virginia heard it loud and clear.

Don't stay for me, Caprice told her. *Don't endanger them. Don't die because I'm going to.*

A hollow ache inside her, snow and regret stinging her eyes until they burned with it, Virginia obeyed.

She backed across the ice, crawling, until it was solid enough to stand. The women looked to her for a command, and she could not give it, not with her voice. She spoke with her actions. She tested the rope and began to walk, back in the lead.

Virginia turned back only once. She could barely spot where the disaster had happened. The hole in the ice where Caprice had disappeared was surprisingly small to have swallowed so much.

It didn't seem large enough to tear a gap in the world.

CHAPTER FORTY-SEVEN:
VIRGINIA

Massachusetts Superior Court, Boston
October 1854

After Virginia tells the story of Caprice's death — a story that, in her courtroom telling, includes the deaths of both Elizabeth and Stella, with a rope that never reached far enough for any of the three to grasp — Judge Miller abruptly adjourns the session for the day. While he does not verbally note that several women in the courtroom are openly sobbing, including the bejeweled Mrs. Collins, Virginia suspects this is the reason. She's sure it will be held against her that her own eyes are dry.

She notices, idly, that the guard sent to fetch her back to the jail is not one of her usual escorts. Thinking about whether her story landed like the truth on skeptical ears distracts her.

It is not until she finds herself alone with the uniformed man in a long, dark, unfamil-

507

iar hallway that she thinks to question who he is and where they are going.

Virginia's distraction turns quickly to panic, and she realizes the only reason she has followed this man, a complete unknown, toward an equally unknown destination is his familiar uniform.

The corridor grows longer and darker. Or perhaps it just seems that way now that she expects, at the end of it, to find nothing good.

But they are no longer alone. A dark figure joins them. The man in the guard's uniform checks her wrist cuffs and her ankle shackles and then shoves her forward toward the dark figure.

"Be good," the supposed guard says to Virginia, his voice flippant, almost amused. To the man, he says, "You know how long you have."

Virginia does not know how long that is. How long does this new, unknown man have to damage her, to abuse her, alone in the bowels of the jailhouse? This one has not even bothered with a uniform.

But then she sees his face in a shaft of light, the undistinguished features, hard to describe. She recognizes the tense body, its broad shoulders. She realizes the kind of abuse she's in for isn't what she feared.

There may still be damage, but it will come at familiar hands.

"Brooks," she breathes.

"Miss Reed," he says in return, emphasizing the last name with a particular sharp delight. "So you have begun your testimony. A bold choice, that."

"I did not factor your thoughts into my defense strategy, as you were not present. Are you here to help?" She knows he's not, but if he's here to needle her, she'll indulge in needling him back. What, at this point, does she have to lose?

"It'll be a real loss when you're hanged," he replies. "You are an infinitely interesting young woman."

It's hard to keep a straight face, but she manages. She won't give him the satisfaction of seeing he's rattled her. "You're so confident? Even though I'm innocent of the charges?"

"Whether you are innocent is completely beside the point, Miss Reed. You know that as well as I do. What matters is whether you can convince the jury of your innocence. And do you think that's likely?"

If she were not shackled, she would slug him in the nose, and even with the shackles, she finds herself rushing toward him, her hands rising in the air.

He steps back smoothly, avoiding her charge, and then grabs the short chain between her wrists. With one sharp twist, he shortens it so she can't pull far away enough to hurt him. He does not hesitate. He's done this before, she realizes, with rougher criminals than she.

"There's that legendary temper," he says. "What is it the *Clarion* calls you? The 'Arctic Fury'? I wish they'd gone with 'the Northern Borgia' — that was one of my other suggestions — but *fury* does have a certain ring. An apt one, I assume."

To hell with this, she decides. She glares at him and tries to angle her leg away to kick him. He anticipates her move and twists her wrists until she is between his body and the wall, and his face is so close to hers she can feel his hot breath, and she cannot get away no matter what she does. In their very first meeting, she had wondered whether he was an envoy or an enforcer. She sees now that his skills transcend both categories.

"We don't have long," he says. "Let's not waste time. I'm authorized to make you an offer."

"Authorized by Lady Franklin?"

"I'll say this for you," he says, almost snarling, "you don't give up."

"You are correct," she says, though what

510

she thinks is *not anymore.*

"Perhaps, sometimes, you should." He eases the pressure on her wrists but keeps hold of the short chain, so they are close but not touching. "Now listen to the deal I'm willing to offer. We can make all this go away."

He pauses, perhaps wanting her to ask what he means, but she stays silent, betting he won't be able to contain himself.

If she'd have bet, she'd have won.

He goes on. "The trial, the possibility of being hanged for your crimes, all of it. With a financial settlement for you to go back to your beloved California or anywhere you'd like to go."

"Australia?"

"If you want," he says without emotion.

"Do it, then," she says, like a dare. "Make it go away."

"But we need something in return."

"What." Not a question but a demand. When negotiating with the devil, one must know what devil's bargain is offered. She realizes now that this is why he came back to Boston, why he allowed himself to be found and called as a witness in the trial. Why he didn't stay away. Jane Franklin had sent him to make her an offer.

"We'll send you an interviewer from the

Clarion. And you will tell that interviewer precisely the things that we advise you to say. No more, no less."

It comes to her then, when she considers his earlier comments about her nicknames, and now this. Obviously, the Collins family is pulling strings at the *Clarion,* shaping the coverage of her trial to paint her in the worst possible light. They have their fingers in every single pot, this family. The selection of her defense counsel, though she had at least thwarted them on that front eventually. Social connections with the judge and jury. And now, the newspaper.

No wonder it feels like everything is against her; everything is.

She remembers how she felt before she started struggling against her fate. Perhaps she should go back to that. Perhaps, like Caprice did in that ravine, she should just wait to die. Only Caprice could not have survived more than an hour or two. Even once it's a certainty, Virginia's death will take much, much longer.

To Brooks, she says, "What exactly would I say?" This keeps the door open. Besides, she's curious. And not eager to go back to her cell, not today. She does not want to be alone with her thoughts just now.

"Tell the world that Lady Jane Franklin

sent you."

"I've been saying that for weeks."

"She will back you up."

Magical words, and ones she'd have thought she'd give anything to hear. At the same time, something tingles within her, an instinct. Something must have changed. Franklin could have made this offer at any point; why is she making it now? What isn't Virginia seeing?

Brooks goes on, "She'll say she was unaware of your predicament earlier, and now that she knows, she is proud of your journey and even more impressed with the knowledge you brought back."

"And what is that knowledge?"

"That you discovered the fate of Franklin and his men."

"Oh, did I? And what did I find?"

"Evidence that they perished of poisoning on their ships, which were frozen in the ice in a remote location."

"Really! Poisoning, more than one hundred men? Some nefarious sailor took them all down with — what? Cyanide in their rum ration?"

"We've found out that their food supplies were tainted," he says.

She feels but does not show a shiver of familiarity. She does not have to believe him to know that this is the truth.

He goes on, "The cut-rate contractor who stocked the ships has been exposed. That was all they had to eat, so they ate it, and they perished. That man is the man who killed them."

"So I say this to the interviewer from the *Clarion,* and Lady Franklin owns up to sponsoring the expedition, and what? You make this trial go away? How?"

Brooks says grimly, "It may surprise you to know we've had the power to make this go away all along."

It does not surprise her. Not in the least. All that surprises her is that he's willing to say it out loud. Again, she wonders why they want her cooperation now. They have placed little value on it so far. Her value has gone from nothing to everything, like a plot of rocky California land that hides an untapped vein of gold, and she has no idea why.

The anger wells up again. "So my life is ruined, my friends are either dead or disgraced, but at least if I tell an outright lie before God and man to benefit the woman who abandoned me, I won't be unjustly hanged for a crime I didn't commit? Pardon me if I don't shout hallelujah!"

He says, "And she'll pay you the reward.

Twenty thousand pounds. Everything you were promised."

"Just me?"

"Just you. You're the only one who can give her what she wants. So I suggest — strongly suggest — you do."

She cannot decide in the moment. Her head spins. She needs more time, and however much time he gives her cannot truly be enough. "I'll consider it," she says.

"Please do. You'll be called again tomorrow morning. If you're willing to do what's required, simply tell your counsel to request a private audience with the judge. We will take it from there."

She can't help asking one more question. "My defense — Mr. Mason — he isn't working with you, is he?"

"Oh no, of course not. His involvement is an interesting wrinkle, but as you can see, not enough to change our course."

"It is *interesting,*" she says frostily, "that you regard shoving me toward the gallows as merely executing a plan."

"We needn't shove you toward the gallows, Virginia. You're doing a fine job of getting there yourself."

"I didn't kill her," she says hotly, feeling her temper slip away again.

"So you've claimed. Take your chances if

you want. See if the jury will believe you. But making you an offer isn't the only thing I've been authorized to do, Virginia."

Creeping dread comes upon her. "What do you mean?"

"If you don't play along — agree to the interview with the *Clarion,* say what we want said — there will be other consequences."

She should have guessed this, she realizes. They are not taking chances on her, not anymore. They're not just going to offer her a rich reward and assume she'll fall into line. The best wagon drivers know that when an animal shows itself stubborn, it's wisest to ready both the carrot and the stick.

She has one secret that not even the women of her expedition know. Jane Franklin knew it, and now it seems obvious that Brooks does too. She can only assume revealing her secret is the consequence he speaks of. It is not a secret she wants revealed, but if it is, at least she is the only one who will suffer for it.

Virginia spends a long night alone in her cell thinking of Caprice's death and what happened after. She thinks of the promises she made. She cries, now that there's no one here to see, as she faces up to the choices that brought her to this place. So many secrets, held on behalf of so many others.

Tomorrow's choice only matters to Virginia. And only she can decide how to make it.

CHAPTER FORTY-EIGHT: VIRGINIA

On the Expedition
April 1854

The days immediately following Caprice's death passed in a kind of haze for Virginia. Somehow, no one could have explained how, they fought their way back to the ice house and collapsed there in a dejected, exhausted heap. After a few hours' rest, perhaps they could have stirred themselves, but what was the point? They were doomed anyway, Virginia thought. If Caprice couldn't survive this wilderness, who could?

But the instinct to survive was strong. And when the fire died out, Virginia found herself, with some surprise, moving to relight it. That was when she discovered Lady Franklin's letter to her husband was the only paper remaining in her possession. When the thaw advanced, they would likely discover twigs or leaf scraps to dry out for kindling, but who knew when that would come? Nothing could be counted on.

Before she burned the letter, Virginia intended to read it. It wasn't hers, but how much did that matter now? More than likely they would all die out here on the ice, and no one would know what she'd done with her final few days. If that was the case, she was not going to deny herself anything, even her curiosity.

Her mittens made the letter nearly impossible to open, but as she was finding over and over again on this journey, sometimes the distinction between nearly impossible and truly impossible made all the difference.

She tore the envelope in half and handed half to Doro, who began to work the stove. With her teeth, she pried off the wax seal, spat it out, and focused on the spidery, inky words on the page.

Dear Virginia,
Of course this letter is not for my husband. He is dead. I know that. This letter, like all the others, is for you.

Yet I am disappointed to find you here, fingers trembling. Did you open the envelope with care or rip it in a rage? How do you feel, Virginia, your eyes raking over the words you thought were never meant for you? How did you decide to violate what I told you clearly was not yours?

I can only deduce you have given up hope.

I suppose I cannot blame you. You are my mirror, as I have said. Though I am still disappointed to find us mirrored in this way. I chose you because I thought you would never give up hope. You did not before. The fact that you have now brings you one step closer to death, and I fear that your expedition, like my husband's, is doomed.

Virginia, I fear you will become careless now. That is what happens when hope is gone. Where you are now, any mistake, any error, can be fatal. I fear your hopelessness has sentenced both you and your expedition to death. Please, in the name of God, prove me wrong.

And if you are opening this letter because you have found the remains of John's expedition — if you know now he is dead because you have seen it with your own eyes — I have one more favor to beg of you.

Look at his bones. Look at the ship. Look at what the expedition left behind.

If you see any evidence that he and his men turned to the solution to which you and your family were driven, never tell.

J

When she saw the letter was addressed to her, she sucked in her breath. Sentences later, she had to remind herself to let it out. Breathe in, breathe out, she told herself. The air under her hood was warm enough to breathe without pain, and the world around her, its danger, receded as she read.

Lady Franklin had known.

When she'd addressed Virginia by her real last name at their first meeting, Virginia had believed it could be an honest mistake. But it hadn't been honest, and it hadn't been a mistake. Lady Franklin had been signaling that she knew Virginia's whole history, not just her life as a guide, and Virginia had let herself believe otherwise.

But now she knew.

This grand experiment of sending women to the north hinged on Virginia, and now that she knew Lady Franklin's reasoning, the experiment seemed to come from a completely different root. If Lady Franklin didn't like how things turned out — and she wouldn't, Virginia thought grimly — she could write off the women's ramblings. She could disown the entire operation. That was why she only worked through Brooks. Stayed in that hotel under an assumed name. Sent her with a captain who had African and native blood, capable and respected on the waves but easy to push to the margins on land. Now it all fit together.

This was all about John Franklin's precious reputation. All to keep the world from finding out that he and his men had turned cannibal at the end. Virginia had thought it was about putting women forward in a new way, showing their competence and their power; now she realized it was because women were easier to disown, deny, discredit. Especially, given her history, Virginia herself.

Virginia did not know how long she stood there in the deathly cold, half an envelope and one sheet of paper pressed in her thick mittens, hating Jane Franklin.

A small but unmistakable happy whoop from Doro meant the fire was lit. The sound brought Virginia back to the world.

She could think about hating Jane Franklin later. There had been some wisdom in her words too — Virginia hated that, how often the infuriating woman was right — but there would be time to think about that later.

Now was not the time to think. It was the time to act.

In the light of the fire, they discussed what came next. Would they go on searching for Franklin or turn back? In honor of Caprice, Virginia did not call a vote, but consensus was reached quickly.

The search for Franklin was over. Only half the original expedition remained, and they could not afford to lose any more. Now the only goal of the six surviving women — Virginia, Doro, Siobhan, Irene, Stella, and Elizabeth — was to save their own lives.

CHAPTER FORTY-NINE:
VIRGINIA

Massachusetts Superior Court, Boston
October 1854

When court is called back into session, Virginia's choice is clear. Brooks had left no room for ambiguity. She can resume her testimony and leave her fate in the hands of the jury, risking exposure of her greatest secret, the Very Bad Thing, or she can throw herself on the mercy of Lady Franklin, lie for her to protect her husband's legacy, and walk away not only free but rich. If she trusts Lady Franklin to keep that promise.

In the end, that's what makes her decision. Lady Franklin has not proven herself worthy of trust.

So Virginia does not tell her counsel to request a private audience with the judge. She knows Brooks will not be in the courtroom to see what she has chosen — it would be too odd for him to appear, and his face would be recognized — but she pictures him receiving the news that she will not do his bidding.

She hopes he chokes on it.

So she gives the rest of her testimony under Mr. Mason's gentle questioning, detailing her regret over Caprice's death, their path back to civilization, and finally, her shock and horror that when she went to the Collins house to offer condolences to Caprice's parents, they seized her and demanded her immediate arrest. She testifies that she has spent months in jail, alone and cold to the bone, waiting for her trial. She is glad he does not ask her what she will do if she is found innocent. That might be the straw that breaks her; she cannot picture herself being set free, back out into the world, nor can she imagine what she'll do if she gets there.

After Mr. Mason states that he has no more questions, letting Virginia's downcast eyes and rounded shoulders speak her sorrow, the courtroom is hushed for a long moment.

But then the prosecutor stands with clear relish, breaking the somber mood.

He approaches Virginia, a smirk on his face that only she can see. During this whole farce of a trial, she has seen him dancing and ducking, beaming, snarling, the range of his pretended emotions worthy of the stage. She does not enjoy seeing his arch expression turned on her, but at least she's prepared for it. The prosecutor must know that Brooks tendered her the offer and she has refused it; he would have to adjust his questions if the questioning were to continue. One way or the other, their reckoning has come.

"So, Miss Reeve. I will not dillydally with pleasantries; we are all waiting to hear you answer specific questions about your past actions, and I think you know which ones I mean. Let us begin. Please explain how you found yourself in the Arctic."

"Finding my way there was the easy part."

"We are not here for comedy, Miss Reeve."

"I am keenly aware of that, Counsel," she says, making a concerted effort to blunt the mocking edge of her tone.

He sighs theatrically and says, "In the interest of keeping the peace, even in the face of antagonism, I will proceed. You testified under your own counsel's questioning — wait, I know there's been a change. I have trouble keeping track — what's the name of your new counsel?"

"Beg pardon, please, Your Honor," says Mr. Mason. "Is this a productive line of questioning?"

"I very much agree, Mr. Mason," the judge says, proving that he at least can keep track of one change. "Back to the point, Counsel."

"Of course, Your Honor, of course. You testified previously that Lady Jane Franklin hired you to undertake this polar adventure."

"No."

"No?"

"It was not a polar adventure," she clarifies. "We were not asked to journey as far north as the pole."

"I stand corrected. But in the main, let us confirm: you did say Lady Jane Franklin engaged you?"

"Yes, I did. Because that's the truth."

"And do you have any proof of this?"

"I have my word," she says and regrets it instantly.

"Be that as it may," he replies dryly with a long look at the jury. "The court desires tangible proof. Do you have any documents that she signed? Payments she made to banks on your behalf, drawn on her accounts? A record of contact between the two of you?"

"No," she says, discovering the unwelcome truth of the words as they pass her lips. "When she initially contacted me, she used a false name."

"Goodness! Now why would she do that?"

"You could call her as a witness and ask her."

"Oh, Miss Reeve, I assure you, we've tried." He flaps a hand, acts put-upon. "You see, I was told of the claims you'd make, so we reached out across the pond to the estimable Lady Franklin. Would you like to hear what she wrote?"

Virginia would not, because if Lady Franklin had written something that made Virginia look innocent of wrongdoing, she wouldn't be hearing about it from the prosecution. The counsel wouldn't have this look of simmering, simpering pleasure on his face.

The prosecutor went on. "I have here a letter from Lady Jane Franklin. In it, she answers our inquiry by categorically denying any contact with or knowledge of this young woman. I quote her letter in part: 'It mystifies me why this young woman would pretend a connection with me. I suppose she is one of the many shameless fortune hunters who wish to wring benefits from association with my famous predicament. I assure you all I only wish to be left alone. I have made my peace with my husband's disappearance, God rest his soul.' "

Of all the untruths that Lady Franklin has packed into the quoted portion of the letter, this is the lie that truly upsets Virginia. The idea that Lady Franklin could calmly accept and acknowledge her husband's death. Outrageous.

"So. The fine lady says she has no connection to you. Do you care to change any of your testimony so far?"

"I do not."

"Very well. Judge, may we enter this letter into the record?"

"You may."

"Consider it so entered. I do not want to waste anyone's time reading through the less essential parts. Instead, I will return to questioning the defendant so we can expose the truth as quickly and effectively as possible."

Is anyone believing this tripe? Virginia wonders. She refuses to look over at the jury for fear they will look credulous. She may not be able to remain steadfast in the face of those looks, so her gaze falls on the faces of the five instead. Ebba is looking at the judge; Althea is looking at Ebba. Doro is absentmindedly smoothing the thick coil of dark hair over the right side of her head, where the missing ear used to be. Irene and Margaret have poker faces. She wonders if they have sat in courts before. It was not a matter they ever discussed.

"What else can you tell us," intones the prosecutor, "about the reason for your journey north? Whoever hired you, if you were in fact hired, what was the reason for your decision?"

She thinks about what to say before she says it, but she doesn't mince words, nor does she change the facts in any way. She's been sworn in, and she takes that oath seriously, like every other one she's ever taken. "I had formerly conducted business in leading settlers safely westward to California. When I left that field, I wished to explore a new portion of the world, and when the Arctic presented itself, I believed God was calling me to use my skills in pursuit of this new goal."

"Now, when you say God was calling you, do you mean you hear His voice?"

"Not in the way you mean it, sir."

"How do I mean it?" He looks amused, which she finds insulting beyond belief.

The anger rises in her, so very hard to suppress. Clutching the sprigged fabric of her skirt in her palms, wringing her fury into it, she mostly succeeds. "Sir, I believe you mean to make me sound insane. If I were to claim that I hear God speaking directly in my ear, you would make a Joan of Arc of me."

"You feel you're the same as Joan of Arc?"

"No! What I said is that you . . . but let's leave that aside." The burning joy in his eyes shows her that she cannot let herself get drawn into his game. She must be the most levelheaded, most reasonable, most trustworthy young woman who has ever sat in this witness box. If she's anything less, she fails.

Calm, calm, she tells herself. The five. A motley crew, to be sure, though here in these four walls, they are clean and bright. She wishes she could speak freely to these women, tell them how much she appreciates them. How they keep her going. How much it means to her that they come here day after day, sitting with gloved hands in their laps and their ankles crossed, constant.

"Miss Reeve, are you attending? Miss Reeve!"

She forces herself to look at him without appearing startled. She's already damaged herself by not hearing him. *Look calm,* she has to tell herself. *Look like you don't care.* But is that the right course of action? Everything is wrong. Everything is a mistake. She can feel her chances slipping away.

"Well, I can understand why you might

not respond to that name."

A sinking feeling swims its way up into her throat. As bad as the last time she saw Caprice, as bad as that moment on the ship when she first saw Stella's swollen belly. In moments like this, she is suspended between before and after. There will be no going back to before. She savors the last scrap of it and tries not to choke on what's to come.

The prosecutor says, "Your name isn't Virginia Reeve, is it?"

"Of course it is."

"Because you changed it."

Virginia says nothing.

The prosecutor goes on, "You're wise not to object. I have the papers, of course."

Mason jumps in to respond, his voice thick with grit. "Excuse me, what bearing does this have on the case?"

Virginia's eyes fly to him, but there is nothing she can do. She should have told him, but he never would have let her speak if she'd done so. She hoped the truth wouldn't get out. She should have known it would. Didn't it always?

The prosecutor says, "Here is the evidence for the court, a document from California Superior Court, 1850. The legal name is, yes, Virginia Reeve. Miss R — well, miss, would you mind reading the name that it was changed from?"

"I would," she says, and she is surprised she has any calm left to muster, but muster it she does.

"Judge," says the prosecutor wearily, with one of his theatrical sighs, "is it necessary for me to compel the witness?"

The judge says, in a steady voice much more terrifying than the prosecutor's play-acting, "The witness will comply."

The prosecutor slips the paper under Virginia's nose, but she does not look at it. She knows what it is. Maybe she shouldn't have bothered filing a court document, but at the time, it had felt important. Momentous. A clean break between the grim past and a promising future. And here that past was again, a hand on her throat, an arrow in her gut.

"The name, please?"

Without looking, Virginia says, "Virginia Reed."

The defense lawyer says, "And what difference does that make? That she changed her name a few paltry letters? Judge, can we move on to a different line of questioning?"

She does not look at the judge, and she doesn't need to. There is barely a pause before his answer. "I anticipate the prosecutor has a reason for this. We'll see where it goes. But not too much more, Counselor."

"Almost there, Your Honor," says the prosecutor and slips another piece of paper onto the stand. She doesn't look at this one either. "Our next document for evidence. Miss Reed, do you remember writing your cousin a rather extraordinary letter?"

The sick feeling in her chest spreads down to her stomach and up to her throat. Her face feels frozen in place, and by the Almighty, she certainly recalls what that feels like. In the Sierra Nevada Mountains. On the ice fields of the Arctic. The people who knew her in her first freezing are so far away, yet here comes her past, twining around her ankles like a snake.

"Miss Reed?" the voice comes again, and the prosecutor leans so hard on her true last name she wants to slap him.

Instead, she says with no emotion in her voice, "There is no telling what is extraordinary to some."

His eyes sparkle with delight. Perhaps she misstepped, but heaven knows, there are precious few right steps here. Too late to run, too late to hide. Neither the truth nor a lie will help her. There is no help. She's beyond it.

The lawyer says, "Oh, I think we'd all agree, this one is quite extraordinary. Is it ordinary to have a private letter to one's cousin published in the likes of the *Illinois Journal*?"

She shakes her head.

"A verbal response for the court, please."

"No, I suppose it is not ordinary."

"Why do you think this publication was so interested in your correspondence?"

"If you have an opinion," Virginia says dryly, "why don't you go ahead and share it?"

Judge Miller interrupts. "Miss . . . I don't know, Reed or Reeve or whatever you call yourself, we are not interested in his answers to your questions but your answers to his. Kindly answer."

"And what was the question again?"

The court reporter reads back, " 'Why do you think this publication was so interested in your correspondence?' "

Again without looking, her voice empty as a jar, Virginia says, "There was public interest in what happened during my family's journey west."

"Indeed?"

"Judge, does that count as a question?"

"Oh come now," he says. "This is getting drawn out. Counselor, please tell us the relevance of this questioning."

"Gladly!" The counsel is preening now, a

peacock in full fan, basking in the collective gaze of dozens. "Miss Virginia Reed, for those who do not recall the name, was a member of what has commonly become known as the Donner Party."

The gasp of the courtroom is not even a gasp. The whole place melts down in a shocked rush of air. Someone in the back gets up and bolts out the back door, which slams behind him.

The disarray is so total that the judge bangs his gavel over and over, but they do not stop. People are fanning themselves, swooning, muttering to their neighbors with shocked expressions. She is glad she cannot make out any of the words. She cannot even look at the five. Will they desert her now that the truth is known? That she was trapped in the mountains with desperate people, people who consumed the flesh of others who died because it was that or die themselves. It's an ugly truth, a shocking one, and that is exactly why the prosecutor has chosen this moment to unearth it. Even if she had not gotten up on the stand, he could have used it, but it played so much better with her up there for all to see. She shouldn't have taken the stand. She had to. Either way, it's done now.

"Recess! Adjourn till tomorrow! Take the

prisoner to her cell!" The judge has to shout to be heard, and even then, the din doesn't stop. As the guard grabs her to comply, he's rougher with her than he's ever been. She suspects that tomorrow, she will have a perfect line of bruises along her upper arm, four fingers on the flesh that faces outward, a fat, hard thumbprint of purple just above the inside of her elbow.

"Wait!" cries a voice, and she wrenches herself in the guard's grasp to see who has yelled.

It is the prosecutor, that bastard.

"I move," he shouts, the room not quieting but his voice just rising and rising, "that in light of this new information, the prisoner be stripped of the privileges she has enjoyed during this trial. The private cell, the visitation rights. They must stop. She is dangerous."

In the mayhem, Virginia cannot see the judge's face clearly, but she can see that he stands behind his bench with one fist anchoring him to it, and as his other hand bangs down, she can hear the strike of the gavel as clear as the report of a gun.

"Be it so enacted," the judge says. "Guard, you hear? Strip the defendant of her privileges."

He can't mean it. He must not know what

he's saying. To throw her in with the other criminals of this prison, especially if they find out what's just been said — her history as an alleged cannibal — it's a punishment beyond anything she deserves. Not that deserving has anything to do with any of this.

As the guard drags her back to the jail, half on her feet, half off, she thinks wryly of how clever the prosecutor is. She suspects he didn't even really care whether she kept her private cell. He wanted the visitation rights gone. Now that she has a competent lawyer in Mr. Mason, they have to be kept separate. Well, the prosecutor's gotten that and everything else he asked for.

In a completely different part of the jail than she's used to, on the ground floor near the main entrance, the guard swings a door open to a much larger cell and shoves her inside. The door clangs shut. There are other women here — she can smell them if not see them — lurking in the shadows.

But she doesn't look. She walks straight to an empty cot and lies down on it, still wearing the new dress. It seems like days, not hours, since she put it on. She plans to sleep in it, but as it turns out, she doesn't sleep. She turns her face to the wall and ignores any and all voices in the half dark around her. At least they remain only voices, for now.

Hours later, on the cusp of sleep, Virginia claws at her neck. First, she blames the new dress, but that isn't it, she has to remind herself. It doesn't button up as high as it feels like it does.

That constricting feeling isn't the neck of her dress. It's her body anticipating the feeling of the noose, which she's imagining drawing tighter and tighter around her throat.

CHAPTER FIFTY:
VIRGINIA

On the Expedition
May and June 1854

Even though the thaw had not yet come, they decided as one not to wait for it. No one wanted to continue in the search they knew was futile, not at this cost, not anymore. It was time to make for Repulse Bay. The six remaining survivors abandoned everything they could not carry on their backs and started their eastward trek.

They did their best to make time, grueling mile over grueling mile. Without the dogs, in a different season, and headed over ground they'd never traversed before, everything was different. The ice was buckled and ridged, utterly unpredictable. Some days, it felt like they covered more territory vertically than horizontally, made more progress toward the sky than the horizon.

But all in all, at the end of each day, Virginia still sent God a heavenward prayer of thanks. They were moving. They were eating, if only a little. They were not yet dead. In a land that seemed to actively desire the death of anyone who dared to cross its surface, one more day spent living seemed a minor miracle. She hoped to string enough minor miracles together to meet their goal and make it back to civilization. Was she hoping for too much?

Two weeks in, volatile spring storms hit them in earnest, and during the day, the wind was so brutal they could no longer talk to one another. They did not untie themselves from one another for any reason. They slept fully dressed with their ropes still tied tightly around each woman's waist. They did not even leave one another's company to perform bodily functions, but truth be told, these functions had become few and far between. Stella was the one to propose the solution to a problem none of them wanted to admit having and told every woman to wear her rags day in and day out so they would catch any liquid. Though they had had so little to drink, they rarely urinated, and when they did, they produced concentrated golden droplets. At least that was what Virginia did, and she did not care to discuss the matter so frankly with her fellow travelers, so she made assumptions. She knew sisters who told each other everything. These women were her sisters now, and she would tell them almost anything, but she did have limits.

She muttered a prayer every time they summited a hill and she looked out on a new field of ice, buckled and pockmarked. Would this be the one where they lost another member to the deep, invisible crevasses? She missed Caprice. She never would have expected that she'd miss her. But when she closed her eyes, she still saw her last glimpse of the rich girl's face, drawn and beginning already to go blue, her hand raised in that solemn, unmistakable signal, *Don't*.

At night, when they huddled together to rest, they stared blankly at one another, wordless. She could not even see the other women's faces clearly, but she'd memorized them, chanted their names like an incantation across those endless miles of walking on the ice. Doro. Elizabeth. Stella. Siobhan. Irene. Back on the ship, they'd left Ebba, Althea, Dove, Margaret. As far as she knew at least, ten of them were still alive out of the original thirteen. Why did it feel like they'd lost so many more than that? Because every loss was total. Every woman was precious in an uncountable number of ways.

Even, or maybe most of all, Caprice Collins.

Caprice had never been kind, and she had never been flawless, but toward the end, she had become dear. And now she was gone.

How many more of them would survive, find Repulse Bay, board a schooner back to civilization? She could not imagine these women back in the world, not after what they'd been through. Were Elizabeth and Stella meant to go back to toadying up to well-off women, following orders and completing tasks, when they'd proven themselves capable of so much more? Were Ebba and Althea meant to return to England and sit with their feet up on cushions, ringing porcelain bells to call their own servants? Was Irene meant to attach herself to another man who would abuse and mistreat her for lack of better options? And what about Virginia herself — where did she belong? Nowhere.

She hoped they would live long enough to face the conundrum of their futures, but she was not at all sure they would. The best thing that could happen would be that they'd be faced with impossible choices.

More likely, they wouldn't be left alive to choose.

Long before the sun rose, the women rose and started out again across the ice.

So blind was Virginia, so focused on putting one foot and then the other in the snow ahead of her, that she didn't understand for a long time why she could hear shouting.

"Stop!" She finally heard the word. "Stop!"

Who was calling, and where from? It had to be one of her own women. She would have to stop, as much as she hated to. She tugged on the rope, one, two, three times. She felt an answering tug. All forward progress ground to a halt. Virginia turned.

She could only see the vague shapes of the women around her. They were so difficult to tell apart in their furs.

"Look!" Siobhan was shouting. Her voice, thought Virginia, sounded unusually strong and powerful, in a way it hadn't for days.

She followed the woman's pointing mitt and gasped when she saw where it led.

There were shapes on the horizon. Were they cairns? No, they couldn't be. Patches of ground showing through the melting snow, at last? Not that either. The shapes were moving. Toward them.

Then she looked down and saw tracks in the snow. Tracks made by feet other than their own.

As the other party neared, she began to be able to make them out. Six people, moving. The same as their own party, at least in number. In what other ways were they alike or different?

A noise she did not understand came from just over her left shoulder. She was too rapt, staring, to turn toward its source. She could not look away from the approaching hunters.

They were hooded, swathed in furs, with something like snowshoes strapped to their seal-fur boots. She couldn't see the color of their skin or any other details of their faces, but from their relative sizes and the way they moved, the party seemed to include both men and women. Several had misshapen bodies, lumps in their fur. She blinked to clear her vision. No, she had mistaken the meaning of their shapes. Members of the party had dead game strapped to their bodies. A brace of rabbits at one figure's waist, a full-size deer roped across someone else's back. They had been hunting. Successfully.

If they had weapons, they did not raise them. Virginia's eyes sent a signal to her brain to produce tears of joy, though her eyes were too weak and dry to comply with the order.

That noise again. This time, Virginia

forced herself to turn. The noise came from Irene.

All at once, Irene broke out running toward the new arrivals, heedless of the ropes until they yanked tight and Elizabeth and Doro on either side of her tipped and fell into the snow.

But when they fell, they laughed, because Irene was crying, making an incoherent sound, and a medium-sized form freed itself from the line of hunters — they were easily identified as hunters now — and flung her arms around the fallen woman.

"Irene!" shouted the fur-dressed woman in a joyful voice.

Irene sobbed back a sound of happiness, of relief, of a thousand other things Virginia couldn't understand or name. In the sound was everything.

We're saved, thought Virginia, her lips moving silently in a prayer of thanks. *We're saved, we're saved, we are saved.*

Once the roped women were hauled to their feet again, still laughing, the leader of the hunting party addressed himself to Virginia.

"Who are you?" His accent was not recognizably French or English, and his words were direct.

She was not sure how to answer, and

546

without exactly deciding, she told him, "We were explorers."

"Where are you bound?"

"Safety," blurted Virginia. "We will follow you anywhere safe."

To his credit, the man did not laugh. "Safety in numbers they say. Let's share camp tonight. Will you?"

"Yes. With gratitude."

He drew out the conversation no longer. He gestured to his people, who formed themselves into a kind of wedge alongside and around Virginia's party, and they all moved forward in step together.

Virginia noticed they were not backtracking in her party's footsteps, but neither did they go due forward along the bearing they'd been taking. At the end of that path, what would have awaited her? Perhaps safety, perhaps not. They would take a different path now.

She put her head down, narrowed her eyes against the sunlit brightness, and let herself be led.

After an hour, the man signaled for them all to pause, and his mittens disappeared into the folds of his fur covering. Irene gestured at him, mittened hands flying.

"Yes," he said. "We have enough to share."

And by a miracle, he was passing around

squares of fish, not dried but fresh, bright pink and slippery. Virginia crammed her square into her dry mouth, and the saliva that sprang up to make the meat slick as she chewed felt like as much of a gift as the food itself did. She had not thought to ask for food. She was no longer fit to lead. Her mind did not wallow in the realization, did not fall into an obsessive loop of blame. She simply thought, *I am not fit to lead, I know that now,* and when they resumed walking, her thoughts went back only to putting one foot forward, then the other, until they could at last reach a safe destination.

The destination turned out to be a small stone house on the edge of a river, encircled by ice houses like the one Irene had helped them make.

"The stone house was built by southerners," the leader of the party said. "You may stay there if you want, but it is cold."

"Please, we are grateful for any shelter. Put us wherever you please."

The head of the party divided them up between the ice houses, untying Virginia's women from the rope, and there was a long moment when it became clear they were not all going into the same house. They did not want to leave one another, not after so long together. But just as clearly, none of the houses was large enough to hold the entire party. They were lucky there was shelter for them at all, given that they were interlopers.

Virginia, Stella, and Elizabeth went into one house with the leader and two others; Doro, Siobhan, and Irene followed others into a different house.

Once they were inside the ice house, which was, like all such houses, bigger on the inside than it seemed on the outside, the man opened his hood, and Virginia was shocked to see his skin was dark, darker even than Elizabeth's.

Elizabeth laughed, a warm sound Virginia had forgotten the sound of. "And how did you get here, sir?"

With a smile, the dark-skinned man said, "Some years ago, the clever men ran north. I am so clever I ran farther than anyone."

Elizabeth laughed again. The charm of it was a balm on Virginia's soul. After Caprice died and they lost their way, she was not sure any of them would ever laugh again.

"But there will be time for stories," he said. "Let us eat and get warm."

"We're grateful to you," said Elizabeth. "We can't pay . . ."

"I would not abandon anyone on the ice, not even strangers," he said. "The day may come when we need others to feed and warm us. We will be the strangers then."

And it was warm, blessedly so. Their bodies in the small space were already heating it. Virginia thought she had not been this warm since they left the *Doris,* and probably not even then. Perhaps she had not been warm since Boston. One of the other men had removed his gloves and scooped a few chunks of ice into a spirit stove, melting it into water for them to drink.

The man introduced himself as Jasper, and the woman who had greeted Irene handed around raw strips of dressed rabbit, and when Virginia felt strong enough to speak, she asked Jasper for their story.

"We're headed back to Repulse Bay," he said. "We had been part of a group traveling up Back's Great Fish River, but there was a disagreement, and we're the ones who didn't want to stay."

He gestured to the young woman who was animatedly chatting with Stella. On her other side sat a man who looked at her raptly, either her husband or something close to it.

"And you knew this camp?"

"He did," said Jasper, gesturing to the other man. "I'm glad to see it's here."

Stella asked, "And once you return to

Repulse Bay? What will you do then?"

"We don't have a plan," admitted Jasper. "Some of us may stay there and find work. Or sail on a ship, perhaps. I hear the whalers are starting to come into Hudson Bay. We'll be there in time for the start of the season."

"But none of you will return south?" asked Stella, and the note of hope in her voice made Virginia pause.

"There is no need to," Jasper said. "Not for me. My life is here."

"What kind of life is it?" asked Elizabeth, and Virginia heard the same note in her voice she'd heard in Stella's. A brightness, a curiosity. A note of hope she hadn't heard from either of them in months. Perhaps ever.

Jasper said, "A hard one. A free one. The only one I ever want to lead again."

At that, both Stella and Elizabeth smiled.

Virginia saw instantly that she would lose them too, in a different way than she had lost any of the other women on the expedition but one that was just as permanent.

They stayed at the camp for five more days. Jasper suggested they wait for the full moon to make the trek to Repulse Bay; more light would mean less likelihood of turning from the right path. They could not afford any more mistakes, not even with the hours of daylight lengthening and the thaw finally imminent. As they'd found on the day three of them fell in the ravine and only two came out, the cold was far from the only thing in the Arctic that could kill.

During the five days, Virginia took each of the women aside to ask them their plans. Elizabeth and Stella, as she suspected, wanted to stay. Doro, eager to return to her father's business, had no desire to remain in the North; she seemed to regard the entire suggestion as somewhat ludicrous. Siobhan, though she was tempted by the greater freedom, felt she would prefer her life back in Boston where she could pursue her dreams as long as she pretended to be someone she wasn't.

It was Irene's choice that surprised Virginia the most. She approached her while she was talking with her friend, using string pictures to communicate. When she asked Irene if she wanted to stay, Irene shook her head strongly in the negative, taking Virginia by surprise.

"Why not? You traveled through these lands with your husband, didn't you? This is territory you know. Your friends are here."

Irene grabbed the hand of her friend, made sure she was watching Irene's face, and moved her hands in a flurry Virginia couldn't understand.

"Are you sure?" the woman asked Irene.

Irene made a single motion in front of her own mouth, and this time, Virginia could read both the intent of the motion and the words Irene was shaping without speaking aloud: *Tell her.*

In halting words, the friend explained that Irene's husband had been a dangerous drunk — as so many men were on the frontier — and he was the one who had cut her tongue from her mouth in a violent rage. She spoke too many languages he didn't know, made him feel too small.

"What happened to him?" asked Virginia.

"He took his knife and cut out her tongue. She took his knife and cut out his heart," the woman said.

Irene nodded with satisfaction.

The woman went on, "Her husband had friends here. She does not want to remain. Even if it is very unlikely she would ever see those particular men again, she wants to put that life behind her. She answered the advertisement to lend help where it was needed, and she was not sure how she would feel being here again. But now, she knows she cannot stay."

"I understand," said Virginia, who did not fully understand but knew something about turning one's back on the past in hopes of a better future.

On the fifth day, they all left the camp together, moving toward Repulse Bay, though not all would go into what passed for the city. Every moment of the hike toward Repulse Bay felt so, so different from the rest of their journey, Virginia thought. The motions were the same, yet there was something entirely new about this. Possibly because she knew where they would part ways. Possibly, she thought ruefully, just because this time, they knew their destination.

When Jasper told them they were close enough to Repulse Bay to reach it that day, after the midday break for food, Stella fell into step next to Virginia. She kept her voice low so others wouldn't hear.

"I wanted to tell you. Before we part ways. I'm so grateful," said Stella.

"For what?"

"I would never have known what I was capable of without coming here," said Stella. "Following you onto the ice. Breaking away from all the things in life that I thought defined me. Out here, with you, I realized I can do almost anything."

Virginia said, "Anything. You can do anything."

"Not anything," she said, and the look on her face broke Virginia's heart. "I can do anything but go back."

Virginia grasped her hand and squeezed, feeling her strength through the double layer of mittens. When they met, Stella had reminded her of her innocent little sister. Later, she'd reminded Virginia of Virginia herself. Now, with her look of optimism and her thin shoulders squared, Virginia realized there was no one else she resembled. Stella now looked only like Stella.

"Crossroads," called Jasper, and the party drew to a halt. The hunters who had saved them drew aside to allow the women of the expedition a private moment to say good-bye, and Virginia was grateful.

For the last time, the six of them gathered into a tight circle, arms around one another, heads together. They made a pact never to tell anyone what had happened, not for any reason. To talk about Stella's and Elizabeth's fates would be to invite someone to come after them. Only if others believed them dead would they be truly safe.

They would be lost, from Virginia's perspective and from the world's. But from their own, they were free.

The group parted then, the hunters heading southward toward a camp they knew, a place they could continue to live wild, make their own way.

Virginia, Doro, Irene, and Siobhan turned toward Repulse Bay. An hour later, Virginia realized she could hear the sounds of lively chatter in the distance, the squawk of seabirds, sounds she thought she might never hear again.

The sound of a ship's horn reminded her of the *Doris,* and a sick feeling roiled her stomach. Part of her knew the only way she would ever leave the Arctic alive was on a ship. A different part of her could still hear Stella's screams echoing off the hull of the *Doris.* She would never board a ship again without hearing those sounds inside her mind.

Now that Virginia had tasted water again, the tears in her eyes became real. She did not wipe them away from her cheeks.

They would go home failures, yes. But they would go home.

CHAPTER FIFTY-ONE:
VIRGINIA

Charles Street Jail, Boston
October 1854

In the morning, dim light creeping across the bluestone floor of the communal cell like a sick, weakened forest animal, Virginia hears the newspaper before she sees it. When it slides between the bars, it falls to the floor, landing with a noise somewhere between a rustle and a thud. First, she thinks of the rustle of her first counsel's papers, his name be cursed, but by the time the thud strikes, she's fully awake, eyes open. She sees the newspaper then.

She recognizes the voice of Benson growling toward her before she sees the toes of his shoes.

Virginia has never held with the activities of spiritualists, never thought a person's aura could be read, but when she looks up at Benson, she feels contempt pouring off him like water. Earlier in the trial, he was more gentle and affectionate than Keeler, but now that he has turned, he seems more dangerous. Today, he is like an illustration of the word *contempt* in a child's lesson book. It would be amusing if she weren't so worried about what contempt might drive him to do.

"They hanged Washington Goode, you know," says Benson. "They hanged that Professor Webster, what killed Parkman. Newspaper says nothin' keeps a woman from being hanged just the same as a man. No tender mercies for the fairer sex, they say."

Virginia is done holding her tongue. "I don't ask to keep my life because I'm a woman. I ask to keep my life because I'm innocent."

"Same as Goode said, far as that goes," he says, unmoved. "Webster finally confessed, hoping for a lesser sentence, but Goode said he never did it. Right up until the noose wouldn't let him say a word more."

Delightful man, this. She cannot believe she ever thought him kind.

"I sure did hope you wouldn't hang," he says. "Seemed a waste. But now that I know who you are, well, hanging's too good for you."

Fear zings up her spine; does he mean to

harm her? Would he do it with witnesses present? She supposes witnesses of this kind can be bought or ignored easily enough. They were no longer people, not in here, not any of the women behind bars, herself included.

"Be on your way," comes a voice from behind her.

"Delilah," Benson growls back, whether it is a name or only a description, she does not know. "Think you can tell me what to do, can ya?"

"It's merely a kind request," simpers the doxy. "I'd very much appreciate your departure. We'll see you again soon enough, Mr. Benson, won't we?"

The guard seems irritated but says nothing else before he leaves. The sight of his retreating back fills Virginia with relief.

"Thank you," says Virginia.

"Didn't do it for you. Just don't want him thinking he can boss any of us," says the doxy, rubbing her arms briskly to warm herself before crossing them over her half-exposed chest. "Plus, he's cutting into my beauty rest."

She saves Virginia the trouble of deciding whether she should converse by turning away, her face toward the wall.

Alone. She's surrounded by women. A

dozen in this cell alone. How many in the jail? The city? The Commonwealth? Yet she feels far more alone here than she ever did up in the Arctic, even when she was one of only six souls for miles around.

Benson has left the newspaper, so she pulls it out to read.

It occurs to her, almost as an idle whim, that she could kill herself. Probably none of these women would stop her. She could crumple up these pages and stuff them down her throat. One by one or all at once. She thinks about it so seriously, her fingers tighten around the paper, and she hears it crinkle. She could cram one page between her teeth, atop her tongue, then another and another. Eventually, she would choke.

What he wants her to read is the first page, and she skims the article quickly enough to see that the names of the murderers he cites are right there. It is possible he only learned them today. The reporter is reaching into the past to predict the future. Virginia remembers that there was a far more famous murderer named Tirrell, tried here in Boston seven or eight years ago, whose case turned out very differently. Caprice had told the story of his ridiculous trial during the months in the ice house when they shared nearly every story any of them could think of, and she stunned them silent with the tale of the supposed sleepwalker who slit the throat of his troublesome mistress — *nearly took her head clean off, he did* — and got off scot-free. *Of course the papers don't mention him,* thinks Virginia. His lawyer trumped up a story about sleepwalking, got family and friends to testify, spun the tale that even if he did do it, he couldn't be held responsible for doing it. A jury of his peers, probably with troublesome mistresses of their own, agreed. He lived.

To distract herself, she turns the paper's remaining pages, letting her gaze settle on other articles, anything that talks about anywhere but here.

Something catches her eye. The word *Arctic.*

Yet the article does not mention her or her trial. It's a small item, only a few lines long, deep into the inside pages. An Englishman named John Rae has returned from the Arctic and claims he knows what happened to the Franklin expedition. The name tickles her brain: Doro had told her all about him, his many journeys up the Coppermine and the bay and the Great Fish River, his unmatched knowledge of these Arctic lands. The results of his report to the committee will be published soon, the article says, but at the moment, all that is known is that he has brought back proof of the death of Sir John Franklin.

Poor Lady Franklin, she thinks first and then feels shock at her own sympathy.

Next, she feels the old unease in her stomach, that creeping sensation she felt back on the expedition when she read Lady Franklin's final letter. All the woman's words had been lies. In her letters, she had encouraged Virginia, called on sisterly solidarity, claimed to believe that in Virginia's capable hands, anything was possible. All to mislead her, make promises she had no intention of keeping. She was trying to beat John Rae, Virginia realizes now, sending this ragtag group out like a wild, muttered prayer. If Virginia had succeeded, yes, perhaps she could have become the older woman's protégé, someone Lady Franklin could dispatch to the places she herself could now only go in spirit. But she had not succeeded.

She looks back down at the newspaper, letting her finger rest on those few lines of type, words that could make an enormous difference. She had blamed the Collins family for this whole trial, for trying to kill her to exact revenge for their daughter's death while she was in Virginia's charge. But were they fully responsible? How much of the blame lay at the Collinses' feet and how much at Lady Franklin's?

This was it, she thinks, tapping her finger on John Rae's name. This is what changed, why Brooks brought that late-breaking offer from Lady Franklin. They must have found out this news was coming. If Virginia had agreed to lie, it would have been her word against John Rae's, and if Lady Franklin threw her weight behind Virginia's story, it might have enough strength to win. Lady Franklin had famous friends like Charles Dickens who would lend their voices to hers. It might have worked, thinks Virginia now, especially told with flair. The surprising newness of the story, the sheer novelty of it. Women doing this thing that no man before them could manage to do, under the direction of the woman whose husband's fate had finally been determined. But Virginia valuing the truth over her biggest secret, over her own life, has blown their plan to smithereens.

And now that Virginia had refused to lie for Lady Franklin, to protect the one thing the woman valued above all price or reason — her husband's reputation — she was of less than no use to the Englishwoman. The nagging feeling turns into something worse.

A shimmering, uncertain anxiety. A question to which Virginia has no answer but dread.

Now that Lady Franklin knows Virginia won't give her what she wants, what else will she do?

Accordingly, if Lady Franklin has now left the Collins family to their own devices, without her protection or interest, what desperate action might they take?

Chapter Fifty-Two: Doro

Boston
October 1854

"Doro, you have a visitor," says her father's voice, and she hears the disapproval in it. She has never heard these words from her father, not in the thirty-two years of her life, and she can't make sense of her feelings about hearing them now. Too little, too late. It's like a mockery of courtship: a man appearing at the door, asking for her, waiting patiently while she descends the stairs. Is it a man, actually? Her father didn't say. She only knows that whoever waits for her, there will be no romance to it, no seduction. Someone will want something from her. Only by descending and confronting the visitor will she find out whether it's something she wants to give.

Her father is still holding the door when she enters the room, and how old he looks is like a punch in the gut. The time she was gone seems to have aged him several years. Now, standing in the dim light, his head down, waiting, he looks half in the grave.

Standing in the door frame is a woman, a stranger, older than Doro but not quite as old as her father. Her clothing is uniformly dark, but Doro spots the quality of the silk right away. Doro has only ever used silk so fine for her little embroidered globes, and then only for the smaller ones, because the shop around the corner gave her their useless scraps for free. This woman's heavily ruched and bustled dress must use seven, eight yards of that silk under a cloak of wool nearly as fine. She's a rich woman trying to look poor and failing.

There is a familiar look to the width at which her gray-green eyes are spaced. Doro remembers eyes like that. She saw them for the last time on the ice. This woman is more beautiful than her daughter, but those eyes give her away.

Doro turns to her father. "Papa," she says. "Do you know who this is?"

The woman interrupts in a brisk, ringing tone. "I did not give my name. My business is with you alone, Dorothea. May we speak in private?"

Doro's eyes meet her father's, and the look in his eyes sickens her further. He

566

doesn't know what this stranger wants, but whatever it is, he wants Doro to know he disapproves.

But he nods his head to Mrs. Collins with respect and immediately shuffles off, turning his back on Doro without a word. She wonders, not for the first time, if his mind is going. It was only the two of them for so long before she left, and he has not been the same since she returned. She hadn't told him she was going; it wasn't until she returned that she figured out that the stranger who'd spoken with her father the week before she'd met Virginia had been Brooks. Brooks had intended to invite her on the expedition. When her father had demanded a steep sum to let her go, Brooks had declined to pay. Then Virginia had come for her, and her father had lost Doro anyway, with no money to show for it. Without her, he let the shop go and let many of his clients slip away. If she'd been gone another six months, he would have been in the poorhouse. Her guilt at his decline is inseparable from resentment: he should not be her responsibility, and yet because he raised her, she owes him a debt she doesn't know how to repay.

She watches his retreating back until the silence stretches out, fills up the room, settles over both her and her visitor in a thick, unnerving haze.

"What do you want?" she asks Mrs. Collins finally.

"I'll allow your rudeness," says the older woman in a frosty voice, "assuming your manners were iced right out of you by your Arctic ordeals. But I believe it's customary to invite a guest in."

"Because of you, my friend is on trial for her life, which she may well lose because of your vindictiveness. For a crime she did not commit. I don't want you in my home."

"It's not yours, really, is it? It's your father's. And from what I understand, it won't be that much longer either."

So that's it. The Collins family knows about her family's financial situation, the painful secret that drove her north in the first place, though the Arctic trip did not solve the problem as she'd hoped. Probably that same Brooks fellow, who'd lied to the courtroom about knowing Lady Franklin or Virginia, had told them. She can hate him without knowing him, she decides, based on what Virginia told her and what she saw with her own eyes. She wondered what reward he'd reaped for lying like that in front of God and the law.

In a flash, Doro knows what Mrs. Collins

is going to ask of her. The mere idea fills her with disgust.

It also might be her only choice.

Apparently deciding to make herself at home, Mrs. Collins begins to remove one glove. The sight of a glove coming off, exposing skin, still fills Doro with dread. She smothers a gasp.

"Are you quite all right?" asks Mrs. Collins.

Without missing a beat, Doro says, "I think you know I'm not."

"Very well. Since you seem eager to get to the point, I'll oblige you."

Doro should thank her and doesn't.

Mrs. Collins draws off her other glove and seats herself on the only chair in the room. "Dorothea, your testimony is on the schedule for tomorrow."

"Yes."

"And you will say . . . what?"

"Why should I tell you tonight? You can just hear it for yourself tomorrow."

"I have not decided yet whether I will be in the courtroom," she says. "I don't think you realize how much it wears on me. All this talk of my daughter's death. I expect her murderer will be punished, but I fear she won't be, and I must confront that fear every single day as I enter the courtroom."

"You struggle with your fear?" asks Doro with venom. "Think about how Virginia Reeve feels."

"Miss Roset." She shifts her form of address, as if that will help her case, and does not point out that Doro is using Virginia's alias instead of her real name, the name that implicates her in other crimes entirely. "I'm sure you know why I'm here."

"I assume you have a proposition for me."

"As I said, I worry that the guilty party will not be punished."

"Justice is always done, isn't it?" says Doro.

"I worry. It's a mother's worry. You perhaps don't understand, but I assure you, your mother would have."

Horrified, Doro answers, "You know nothing about my mother."

"I know that mothers will do anything to protect their children. And that is what I am here to do. Even though I know the jury is very likely to rule correctly and lay the blame for my daughter's death at Virginia Reed's feet where it belongs, I am concerned they might need one more . . . let's say nudge, in the right direction."

"And what form," Doro says with great effort, "do you see this nudge taking?"

"A very lucrative financial offer. One that

will save your father's shop. And make the two of you rich enough that you'll never have to work again."

On the inside, Doro is stunned. On the outside, she remains calm. It is with that calm that she says, deliberately inflammatory, "Oh, I see. You want to pay me to lie so you can see my friend hang?"

Offended, Mrs. Collins draws herself up. "I did not say any of that."

"You did," she says, "without those words. Because you're a dodge and a lousy human being."

"Careful," says Mrs. Collins, a note of true menace in her voice.

"Why now?" asks Doro. "Why didn't you try to bribe me earlier?"

The rich woman sighs. "We did not feel it was necessary, and truth be told, perhaps it is not even necessary now. Now that the truth is out about Miss Reed's background, the jury likely will feel just fine about condemning a cannibal. But Mr. — excuse me, the other concerned party in the case — feels that the very last impression the jury and judge gets will make a difference to how the situation resolves. You are the very last witness on the docket. If your testimony gives the right impression, a sentence of guilt — the sentence she deserves — will come more easily. And we are prepared to compensate you for it, as I said. Handsomely."

"What do you want me to say?" asks Doro, stalling.

"I don't have an exact script," she says. "Only you know what really happened up there."

"If I tell what really happened, I don't think you'll be very happy with me." Even as she says it, a small uncertainty creeps into her mind. Does she actually know what really happened? She saw everything before and after, but did she really *see*?

As if she can sense Doro wavering, Mrs. Collins asks in a less confident voice, "Did you see my daughter die?"

"No."

"Tell me what you saw."

"She fell. In a storm. The five of us were on a rope — we tied ourselves together in that weather — and she fell."

"Which five? You, my daughter, Miss Reeve — Reed, I guess I should say now — and who else?"

"The rest didn't come back." It's the lie they all agreed on, and she's not going to break that confidence, not even now, not even when she's considering breaking an even more important one for the sake of the money that could save her father's shop, her family's future. Stella's fate, Elizabeth's, Siobhan's, these are not for the courtroom to know. Everyone has assumed every woman not sitting in that front row is dead, but it's far from the case. For the first time, she wonders if they did more harm than help to Virginia, sitting there in the front row to comfort her. What did they signal to the jury? All this time, instead of thinking *these five women believe in her, they support her,* have all these men been thinking, *why only five?*

"And where were you on the rope? Who was in the lead?"

"Caprice."

"Why? Shouldn't Miss Reed have been in the lead, given she was the leader?"

"She'd agreed to let Caprice have a turn."

"Perhaps she knew there was danger and wanted my daughter put in harm's way."

"No, that wasn't it at all."

"Listen to what I'm saying," Mrs. Collins says more intently, laying her bare fingers on Doro's sleeve. "When you tell the story, you could tell it that way, couldn't you?"

"Lie and say she put Caprice in the front to risk her life on purpose?"

"You could tell it that way."

She stared.

"For the right price," says Mrs. Collins.

"That's the third time you've mentioned compensation," comes a gruff voice from the other side of the room, and Doro almost jumps. Her father is standing there watching the two of them. Obviously, he's been listening. She had not even considered that he would do so. How thoroughly she forgot the rules of civilization in the months she was in the North. The rules are that men can do whatever they want. And so her father has.

Mrs. Collins has turned her attention completely to Mr. Roset. "Would you like me to tell you exactly the size of the compensation we're proposing?"

Doro's father says, "I would."

She names a truly outrageous number, and Doro's throat goes dry.

It would be enough. More than enough. She could secure the shop with it, and with that, her father's life. Maybe even his respect. *Wouldn't that be something,* she thinks, her hand rising against her will to stroke the knob of skin where her right ear used to be. All her study of the ice, her brave undertaking in the Arctic, her devotion to him all these years, and the thing that will finally earn his respect is her willingness to tell a harmful, even fatal, lie.

"Not enough," says Doro's father.

"Come again?" says Mrs. Collins, not sounding like a fine, high lady at all but any slattern on the docks.

Doro's father says, "You're asking my daughter to take a risk for you. Lying in the witness box, that's a grave act. Even a sin before God, some might say."

"God took my daughter from me," says Mrs. Collins. "I do not care for matters of religion at this time."

"The law, then. Have you no respect for that? You're asking her to violate the laws of the Commonwealth and the nation."

"For a settlement large enough to ease both her conscience and yours. And I am prepared to settle the funds on you here and now."

She withdraws a packet from under her cloak, heavy with coin. Doro knows without looking that she is offering them gold. Real, true gold.

"Not enough," says Doro's father again. What is he playing at?

"This is what I have," says Mrs. Collins, annoyance coloring her voice now. "Careful of greed, Mr. Roset. What's the saying the lower classes are so fond of? Pigs get fat, and . . . ?"

"Hogs get slaughtered," supplies Doro's

father, unruffled.

Doro looks back and forth between their faces, the fine lady and the former seaman, standing inches and worlds apart. They seem to have forgotten she is in the room at all.

With a sharp, ready voice, she reminds them. Looking straight at Mrs. Collins, she says, "Your necklace."

After a moment of hesitation, her father agrees. "Yes. That's a nice sweetener. It'll do."

Mrs. Collins puts her hand on her throat, touching the necklace in question, which is a rich triple strand of pearls interrupted with elegant beads of jet. "But this was a gift from my husband, one he had made for me after our third child was born. I could send you other jewelry. This one is dear to me."

"More dear than your daughter's memory?" asks Doro's father, his voice dark.

The woman glares daggers at him while she puts her fingers up to the back of her neck, apparently reaching for the clasp. Her fingers fumble and slide. Finally, unable to unclasp the necklace herself, she says, "Dorothea. Come here. You want it, you take it."

Doro puts her cold fingers on the back of

the rich woman's neck and undoes the fine gold clasp. The necklace comes away in her hands, still warm from the other woman's flesh.

It feels like a live thing, thinks Doro, and she has chained herself with it. She has promised to betray Virginia for coin and gem. Virginia took her north, expanded her world. Trusted her when no one else did. How can she repay that with lies? She transfers the necklace to one hand, holds it between them, pearls spilling out between her fingers and dancing in the air.

"I'm not sure I —" begins Doro.

Her father cuts her off. "You will. Virginia Reed will be sentenced to hang one way or another. This grieving mother is simply going to compensate us for speaking up in the name of justice."

Perhaps he's right, Doro realizes. Staying silent won't save Virginia, not now that the truth has come out about her past. A past Doro didn't know about. She thought she'd known Virginia, thought they'd shared everything, and now it seems clear that Virginia had been hiding her true self all along.

"Let's go over the specifics," Mrs. Collins says, touching Doro's arm gently again. "To create the impression you need to create."

It seems like the only possible way forward. Part of Doro screams against it even as she says it, but the screaming part stays silent. The complicit part is the part that speaks.

"All right," she says to Mrs. Collins. "Let's."

CHAPTER FIFTY-THREE:
VIRGINIA

Massachusetts Superior Court, Boston
October 1854

Because Virginia is no longer allowed to visit with her attorney, the first time she sees him after the revelation is when she is led, chained, into the courtroom for the final day of testimony.

Mason falls into step beside her, matching her speed so they advance together toward the dock this final time.

"I'm sorry," she tells him, softly enough that only he can hear.

"I want you to know, Virginia, you are not giving up." There is a glint of humor in his eyes but also defiance. "Because a defeat for you is a defeat for me, and I do not accept defeat."

"I rather think the defeat for me will be more . . . final."

"True," he says, his hushed voice gentle. "I don't mean to put my fate ahead of yours. But we are not yet done. Until the last, I must at least put on a good show."

"Show away," says Virginia.

He goes back to the bar, and she climbs up into the dock.

She lets a dying candle of hope flare up in her. Her stepfather was tarred with the brush of participating in the Donner Party — he even killed a man with his own two hands, no one disputes it — and now he is a politician. Sir John Franklin lost half his party and ate his own boots in the Arctic wilderness, and a few years later, they sent him back into that same land with ten times as many men. Presidents have been generals, leading men into battle, fighting with guns and swords; men who have endured are seen to have succeeded. It is the testing of their mettle that makes them even more fit to lead.

But has it ever worked that way for women?

Perhaps, she tells herself, hoping against hope, she will be the first. She is not a fool, but there is something in her that wants to be a fool today if it gives her hope. Caprice hoped, she remembered, and Caprice was not a fool.

Alone now, Virginia turns to look at the front row of the courtroom, and what she sees there slams the optimism out of her in half a breath.

The five are now four.

Her rosary, her beads, they've come unstrung. They don't even sit in their usual order. Instead of five stoic, silent faces — *pretty maids all in a row* — there are only four ordinary, individual women, each in her own attitude of disarray. Althea stares straight ahead, her eyes glassy with tears. Margaret balls her fists, and Virginia can see the knot in her hard-set jaw. Ebba looks down at her hands, then reaches out to lace her fingers into Althea's, and though Althea's face does not change, she grasps the outstretched hand like a lifeline. Irene gleams like a marble statue, showing no more emotion than stone.

They know what it means for one of them to be gone. Even though she is being called as a defense witness, if she were going to defend Virginia, she would have sat with them this morning and been called from the spot in which she's spent the past two weeks.

She could not face them this morning. And they all, every one of them, know what that means.

It's Doro.

The bailiff calls Doro's name from the

back of the room, and here she comes walking. The lawyer smiles at her because he does not yet realize what it means, that she's coming from that direction. Only the women of the expedition know, including Doro herself, who walks oh so slowly up the aisle toward the witness box, passing the others. Is it Virginia's imagination, or does she, just slightly, slow her step as she passes?

Virginia stares straight ahead, pretending to be untouched, pretending she is not terrified.

She is terrified.

The prosecutor cannot even hide his grin. Virginia's entire arm burns with the desire to slap that grin off his face. Her hand even twitches up, beginning to move, but she catches Mason's eye, and he shakes his head the smallest of fractions. She lays her hand in her lap. How would things have been different if he'd been her counsel from the beginning instead of that first, incompetent young man? If she had told him the truth about her past before he put her on the stand? If she'd told the lie Lady Franklin offered her the world for, she'd be safe now, and rich. But no use in wishing things had been different. Now she just wishes things would be over.

Doro seats herself in the witness box and tries to meet Virginia's gaze. Virginia looks past her, through her, denying her the connection she so obviously seeks. If she meets her friend's eyes, she will burst into tears. She has given up on trying to save herself, but she can at least not give the jury more evidence that she is filled with shame and regret.

Doro's dark blue eyes flicker as she gingerly steps up into the witness box. Her windburned cheeks, as red and ruined as Virginia's, are powdered smooth now. For a moment, Virginia wonders who has powdered her. But there is only one possible answer. Doro, above all the others, was susceptible to a bribe. *Her father's shop,* Virginia thinks. On the ice, all that mattered was survival. Those long, cold months in the ice house, they had been a small society unto themselves. But back here in civilization, life is complicated again.

The bailiff asks Doro to raise her right hand, and she raises her left, then her red cheeks flush even darker at her mistake, and she switches hands. She has no composure. Somehow, Virginia doesn't think it will make her less credible as a witness. If the jury wants to believe Doro, they will.

In a deeply flounced, modest tartan in

shades of copper and cream, Doro is better dressed today than she's been since their return to civilization. Her lovely dress is buttoned all the way up to cover her throat; she looks proper, civilized. Virginia knows it's no coincidence. If she looked out into the courtroom beyond the front row, she expects she would see the Collinses. Their hands have wrought this. They have chosen their weapon and shaped her, and there's no mistaking where she's aimed.

Virginia's lawyer stands, readies himself, and speaks to the witness with confidence. "So tell us, Miss . . . Roset, is it?"

"Yes."

"And you're a mapmaker's daughter, Miss Roset, is that right?"

"I work in my father's map business, yes."

"And in what capacity were you asked to join this expedition north?"

"I know a great deal about the geography of the Arctic," Doro says, her voice clear and proud.

"And who ran this expedition?"

"Virginia," she says, indicating Virginia with a sharp jab of her chin.

"You mean the accused, correct?"

"Correct. Virginia Reeve."

"Objection," says the prosecutor. "We

know now that is not the defendant's real name."

The judge says, "I think we're all aware. The reminder is not necessary."

"My apologies," the prosecutor says.

"Don't be sorry. Just be quiet."

His mouth opens for another apology, but wisely, he closes it.

Mr. Mason, still unaware Doro is no longer on the side of the defense, plunges ahead.

"And were you given any information about who planned the expedition? Who funded it? Whether there was some greater power behind Virginia?"

"She said Lady Franklin was behind it," Doro says, "but I had only her word on it. I never saw hide nor hair of the lady herself."

A shadow crosses the lawyer's face. He'd expected a different answer; he needs a moment to decide how to react to this one. "But she swore to it that she'd been sent by Lady Franklin."

"She did. But there was no evidence."

His brows knit together now. He's starting to catch on.

"But you trusted Virginia, yes? With your life."

Her expression wobbles on her face for just a moment, doubt flickering across her features, but she quickly regains control. "I did then. But so did a lot of women who never came back."

Hot whispers begin to circulate throughout the room. Mr. Mason looks at Virginia, then the women in the front row, then back at Doro. He makes a calculation.

And then he gives up before Doro can do more damage.

"Thank you, Miss Roset. I'm sure this hasn't been easy for you."

She simply gives a grave, sober nod, like a queen would give a commoner.

"No more questions," he says.

"But I have plenty," says the prosecutor, rising, and Virginia's heart sinks. Unlike her counsel, he is fully prepared. He knew this was coming, and he's ready to take advantage.

"Miss Roset," he begins. "To my ear — a rather experienced ear, mind you — it sounds like the defense's lawyer was surprised by your statements."

"I wouldn't presume to guess," says Doro unsteadily and falls silent.

"Of course, of course. I'll only ask you about your own thoughts and feelings from here on out, I promise."

She nods, but her eyes still look unsettled. The prosecutor goes on. "I won't ask you to give an account of the entire expedition."

"Thank you."

"But I'll read an itinerary that was provided to the police, and you tell me if you agree with it in the main. All right?"

"All right."

"You traveled from Boston to Buffalo by train, rode in canoes to Sault Ste. Marie, from there crossed overland to Hudson Bay at Moose Factory, where you sailed north on the *Doris*. All correct so far?"

"Yes, sir."

"When you disembarked the ship, you proceeded overland to where you hoped to look for the Franklin expedition. Still correct?"

"Yes."

"And of the five women who have sat here in the front row this entire trial, you were the only one who took to the ice, correct?"

"No." She points. "Irene was there."

Irene does not react, but the prosecutor moves on before the moment can land with the jury.

"I will be clearer. You are the only one among the women with the power of speech who fits that description."

Doro's voice is softer this time. "Yes."

"Wintered over with Virginia and that portion of the party?"

"Yes."

"Because it took place on the ice, none of the other women can tell us anything about the death of Caprice Collins. I'd like to ask you to be more forthcoming."

Clearly unsteady, at least to Virginia's eyes, she says, "I will certainly try my best, sir."

Virginia expects more questions about details, laying a series of events down for the eager audience, but he does none of that. Instead, he simply goes for the throat. "Miss Roset, did you see Virginia Reed kill Caprice Collins?"

Doro hesitates.

Virginia's eyes are on Doro's face, and she knows the lie Doro has been paid to tell. *Yes* is all she has to say, and that coffin the Collins family has been sizing for Virginia will finally have all the nails it needs to seal shut.

Even now, she cannot be angry with Doro for her weakness, for giving in to the temptation. In Doro's position, it is entirely possible she would have done the same thing.

But she is not in Doro's position. She is in her own, the position of defendant. As she watches her friend prepare to hang her, she realizes the only thing she wants right now is not to die.

Virginia has been so careful to appear unaffected this entire time, and what difference has it made?

The prosecutor repeats his question. Doro's gaze slides away from his face to Virginia's.

Virginia raises her hand. Not high. Just high enough for Doro to see from the witness box.

She puts her palm out, toward Doro.

Help.

Doro freezes. Her eyes skitter over to the remaining four, Virginia's pretty maids all in a row: Irene, Althea, Ebba, Margaret. Virginia locks eyes with Irene first, and she sees an immediate flash of understanding in her keen gaze.

Irene's palm goes out in imitation of Virginia's, aiming her motion at the same target, Doro in the witness box. *Help.*

Then Althea, then Ebba, then Margaret. All three make the gesture, looking mutely at Doro, making the only plea they can, their hands out in solidarity with Virginia.

Help. Help. Help.

In that motion, in the single, silent word it represents, the survivors speak volumes.

Virginia hears it, and she knows Doro does too.

They're saying *Please don't do this.*

They're saying *Don't lie.* They're saying *We understand why you wanted to, but this is too much, too far. Don't sell out the woman who kept us alive on the ice, who keeps our secrets even when it might mean her death, the woman who brought us back.*

Help, they tell her. *You're the only one who can.*

Doro swallows.

She puts her fingers to the high collar of her uncomfortable, fancy dress, and she tugs so hard the top button comes off in her fingers. She flings it to the floor. She gulps a deep breath through the new gap in the rich fabric, and her whole manner changes. A new feeling is clearly surging through her. It bears a strong resemblance to joy.

The judge says, "Miss Roset, will —" but gets no further.

Doro interrupts, "No, I did not see Virginia kill Caprice, because she didn't. I was paid to say otherwise by Lydia Collins."

The room explodes.

Thank you, mouths Virginia silently, moving her palm from one signal to the other, extending her hand with its back parallel to the floor. *Thank you.*

There are tears in Doro's eyes, tears making tracks down her cheeks. She tosses her

590

head back and looks up to the ceiling to try to stop them; the tears run into the hair at the sides of her head, including the whorls of hair she has fashioned to cover the missing ear. Wet and sad and coughing with emotion and . . .

Smiling.

She smiles at Virginia. Virginia smiles back, her eyes equally wet. *Thank you,* she thinks.

The judge bangs his gavel, but the shouts of the crowd do not even slow.

All four of the women in the front row are extending their hands too, grateful to Doro for relenting, their palms echoing and multiplying the message, *thank you, thank you, thank you, thank you.*

Over the din, the prosecutor shouts, "Liar! Reprehensible woman! How dare you sully the name of an upstanding, gracious lady with your lies."

Now the room quiets somewhat, though not completely. They look around for Mr. and Mrs. Collins but do not find them. If they were here, they slipped out in the madness.

"Quiet!" shouts the judge, banging his gavel three times. "We must hear what Miss Roset has to say."

This finally begins to do the trick. The

audience quiets, hanging on every word of what comes next.

"I am not lying," Doro says over the continued murmurs, her voice clear and high. Virginia can hear the tension only because she knows her so well. "I can prove it."

From a pocket tied to the outside of her dress, she draws out coins of gold and lets them fall in a shower over the edge of the witness box. They bounce and scatter on the courtroom floor.

The courtroom goes mad with panic, their shouts wilder this time, their sounds meshing into a rippling, cascading roar.

Judge Miller bangs his gavel with the fast, hard cadence of a woodpecker, *rat-tat-a-tat,* and shouts, "This is your final warning! Anyone else interfering with these proceedings will be held in contempt! Bailiff, clean up this mess!"

"Do not compromise the evidence," shouts Mason, leaping to his feet. "Enter it into the record. Every coin speaks to the truth of the witness's story."

The judge should probably shout him down, thinks Virginia, but even he is overwhelmed, watching the scene unfold with undisguised awe.

The bailiff's eyes are round with wonder

— no doubt this is more wealth than he's even seen in one place, let alone touched with his own hands — as he scrambles to pick up the coins from where they've bounced, rolled, settled.

But even as this outrageous thing is happening, something even more outrageous is underway.

In the witness box, standing tall, Doro is unbuttoning her dress.

The judge's gavel bangs. Althea is clutching Ebba's shoulder, and their mouths both open in mad, shared laughter. Irene's hands fly to her own mouth, cover it. Only Margaret watches calmly, her face merely open, curious, ready. The prosecutor's face is slack-jawed and, for once, completely silent.

When the fifth button of her collar is undone, Doro slips her fingers between the parted tartan and draws out a strikingly gorgeous necklace, three ropes of perfectly matched pearls with an occasional gleam of jet beads emphasizing their beauty. An enormously expensive necklace. A unique one.

One that Virginia distinctly remembers seeing on the neck of Mrs. Collins, and she knows she's far from the only one.

"Further evidence!" Doro calls. "Now you are all witnesses. Perhaps you think the gold proves nothing; it could have come from anywhere. But this," she says, holding it up for the whole courtroom to see, high above her head and theirs. "Only Lydia Collins could have given me this necklace. And she did so to make sure the defendant would hang for a crime she didn't commit."

The simmering shock of the courtroom boils over. Whispers become shouts, laughter, even hoots and shrieks.

The judge says, almost howling now, "If you cannot control yourselves, we will adjourn until you can!"

They cannot. No one can. Even the survivors in the front row, as still as they've been this whole time, are allowing themselves to show their shock, fury, wonder. Still holding the necklace aloft, Doro sends a triumphant smile their way. It is a question, and with smiles of their own, they answer.

"I call for a mistrial, Your Honor!" shouts Mason, but no one appears to hear him in the din, the judge least of all.

On the inside, even while she laughs, Virginia weeps to wonder what might happen next. The newspapers, she thinks, will have a field day with this one. She sends up a silent prayer that Caprice, in the afterlife, can somehow feel the ruckus her death has stirred up. She would have loved it.

Because Caprice was never appreciated enough in life. Who knows what she could have done, who she could have been? Instead, she was a bright spark that burned out early. Like so many other sparks Virginia knew. Like Tamsen Donner. Like Christabel Jones. Like Emmanuel Ames.

Virginia can only hope that when the dust settles, she herself will be allowed the chance to live on without burning out.

As wild as the scene is, as much as a disaster as it appears, all this is temporary. The wheels of justice, such as they are, are still turning. Doro has broken the trial wide open, but who's to say it won't close back up again? That the rich family that hates her won't find a way to right the ship?

But the blossom of hope is bursting in Virginia's chest again, that green shoot, those unfurling petals. When she looks at the faces of the women who have turned their hands up in motions she taught them, advocating for her even without words, she is powerless against it.

For a moment, she allows herself that hope. Perhaps, as the end of this trial unfolds, God will grant her a second — or would it be third? — chance.

CHAPTER FIFTY-FOUR:
VIRGINIA

Superior Court Judge's Chambers, Boston
October 1854

The guard who fetches her from the court-room is a stranger, and he steers Virginia down an unfamiliar corridor of the court-house. The last time this happened, the stranger — a different one — had taken her to Brooks. She hopes that will not be the case again. Even though she still has her hands in cuffs and won't be able to strike him, she knows she won't be able to resist trying. She is done keeping herself in check. She has nothing left to lose.

"Where are you taking me?" she asks the guard.

He ignores her as if she hasn't even spoken, which is what she thought he'd do. Still, there is something satisfying about having asked.

She is not out of the woods yet. A funny expression, that, she thinks. In the times of greatest danger of her life, when there were woods, they helped extend her life, not do her in.

The walk seems even longer than last time, and she has plenty of time to reflect on everything that has brought her to this moment.

Of the thirteen women of the expedition, not all of them made it back, but some stayed away by choice. Their failure to return was not a failure. Virginia, too, could have stayed away. She could have stayed in the North with Stella and Elizabeth. She could have melted back into the world anonymously like Siobhan. She could have fled the country entirely like Dove.

If Virginia had known what would happen when she returned to Boston, would she have come back? If she'd known that when she went to Caprice's house to give condolences to her parents, they would seize her and demand her immediate arrest? That she would spend months in jail, alone and defeated, waiting for her trial?

She still would have come.

Because just as surely as Stella and Elizabeth could never go back to civilization, she could never stay in the Arctic. To her, it would always be the place where she'd failed to save Caprice, the way she'd failed to save Ames on that trail just to the west of Fort Bridger.

She would save the women she could and regret the loss of the ones she could not. It wouldn't have occurred to her to save herself.

Just like she'd never seriously entertained taking Lady Franklin's final offer to lie on the stand. Reputations were just words and thoughts. Society cared about them, but Virginia could not. They didn't matter the way people mattered, the way lives mattered. She would not compromise her principles for Sir John Franklin's reputation or her own.

"Here," says the guard and shoves her unceremoniously through a doorway, then closes a heavy oaken door behind her.

She is in a dark chamber, more luxurious than any room she's seen since her first stay in Boston, when she flitted from fancy parlors to luxurious hotel suites without knowing how small her world would someday become. Rich, burled wood makes up bookshelves, a desk, the backs and legs of several chairs. The color of the wood reminds her of the deck on the *Doris,* of how she once thought that Captain Malcolm and his ship seemed to be crafted of the same material. She wonders if the captain has been observing her trial. She wonders if he cares what happens to her.

Another door opens on the opposite side of the wall from where she herself came in. The sight of the figure coming through it comes as a complete shock.

It's the judge, fresh from the courtroom, alone.

"Please." He gestures to the nearest chair, a comfortable-looking leather affair, square-backed and elegant. "Sit."

Virginia is too stunned to do anything but obey. He himself takes a seat behind the desk, sweeping his dark robes out of the way with both hands before he sits, reminding her of how women in broad skirts do the same. She's never seen a man do it. But of course, she's never been in a room with a judge.

Alone, she thinks.

He slides a folded newspaper across the desk to her, letting go of it so she can pick it up with her own hands, and waits for her to do so.

She looks up at him before she reaches for it, eager as she is; she wants to see his expression. She might as well not have wasted her time looking. He has none.

Virginia picks up the newspaper. She feels her own face trembling, shifting, changing shape against her will as she reads.

What he has handed her is neither the *Clarion* nor the *Beacon* but another newspaper, one Virginia has never seen before. Something called the *Bugle*. Seeing the unfamiliar pattern of the slightly smeared print shakes something loose in her head, and she's not sure why it's taken her so long to think of it: if the Collins family had influence at the *Clarion,* pressuring the editors to write negatively about her case, might someone also have their thumb on the scales at the *Beacon,* using their influence for a positive angle? She only knows one journalist. But that journalist, Margaret, has been sitting in the front row of her trial ever since the day it began. If she ever gets free of here — and today she has reason to hope she might — she'll find a way to express her gratitude.

But this newspaper, the *Bugle,* is not even from Boston. It appears to be Canadian. And the *Bugle* has a great deal to say about the shocking news that a party led by John Rae, the latest of so many parties sent to search out John Franklin, has returned with news of the party's fate. The snippet Virginia had spotted in the Boston paper was just the beginning; this article takes up most of the front page, with the shocking headline

600

GRIM REPORT REVEALS FATE OF FRANK-
LIN PARTY: MEN RESORTED TO LAST RE-
COURSE.

"It is a newspaper from Montreal," says
the judge, his voice steady, giving nothing
away. "It quotes a report from the London
newspaper, the *Times*, that not only has
John Rae found evidence of the deaths of
the Franklin expedition but evidence among
their remains of cannibalism as well. The
world is shocked."

She can think of no reaction appropriate
to the news. It is sad, of course, but what
else is there to say? They are all dead now,
the eaters and the eaten. No one lives
forever but Jesus, and even he had been put
to death once, by those who hoped his death
would serve their own ends.

All she says to the judge is, "Oh."

"I thought you would want to know."

"Thank you."

"Before you go."

"Beg pardon?"

"I thought you would want to know that
before you leave. Since you are so interested
in the Arctic. Whether you went there or
not at Lady Franklin's behest."

"I did," she says, but softly, mildly, almost
as if she doesn't quite believe it herself. It
doesn't matter anyway. The flower of hope

is blooming in her again. He has not brought her here to punish or castigate her. She knows it for sure now. She lets herself believe.

"With the revelations of wrongdoing brought forward by Miss Roset," he says, "this trial is no longer a fit exemplar of justice. The proceedings will be stopped immediately. And without pressure from the Collins family to try the case again, I sincerely doubt the Commonwealth of Massachusetts has any interest in spending more funds and time on a trial with no physical evidence whatsoever. Without pressure from them, I doubt it ever would have been pursued in the first place."

Stunningly, he produces a small key. She knows from the shape and size of it exactly what it's for. It's the key to the handcuffs she wears around her wrists.

"Godspeed, Miss Reed," he says. "You may go. You may not have heard it in the din, but your counsel requested I declare a mistrial. I'll be granting that request."

She stammers, "Shouldn't I be present for that?"

"Do you want to be present?"

She considers this. It has been a long time since someone has asked her where she wants to be and even longer since she had the sense that her answer actually matters.

"No," she replies.

"It's my courtroom," he says. "I make the rules. And this time, I say the defendant can go."

"Where should I go?"

"How in the name of Hades should I know?" the judge says. He seems on the verge of laughter until he sees her stricken face. It hadn't occurred to him that she might actually want an answer to that question.

He unlocks her cuffs himself, managing to hold the cuff gingerly and turn the key in the lock without ever touching her flesh. His hands are steady. When the metal falls away, she finds herself already standing a little straighter.

"Congratulations on surviving, Miss Reed," says the judge, not unkindly. "Now go find a way to live."

CHAPTER FIFTY-FIVE:
VIRGINIA

Boston
October 1854
Where will she go?

She still does not know the answer when she steps into the bracing Boston air, the new dress she wore to testify now covered by an old coat the warden had given her, apologizing that the coat she'd come in with could not be located. It seems fitting, she decides. Even though Elizabeth had worn the crimson coat in those last weeks north, then given it to Virginia to wear back to Boston, it never really belonged to either of them. It always belonged to Caprice.

The question again, thinks Virginia. It cannot be answered. It must be answered. Where will she go from here?

When Ames died, she could not, did not, accept the loss. Running to the ends of the earth was a foolish way to try to escape a loss that could not be escaped, but what other ways had been open to her? How was a woman supposed to grieve catastrophe?

She is about to turn around and step back through the door of the jail, hiding for a few more moments in safety while she plans her next action, when she spots a familiar figure only steps away. Tall and broad, his dark hair topped by a woolen cap, he turns his warm brown eyes in her direction.

Captain Malcolm.

In five steps, he is at her side but stops short of touching her.

"I'm sorry," he says.

She tilts her head back to squint up at him in the winter light. "For what," she asks, "in particular?"

"This time? That I'm the one who's here to greet you and not your friends. Everything happened so fast — I don't think they know yet."

"So why do you?"

"Mason," he says.

"Oh." It makes sense, but still, with her head reeling from her sudden release, she is struggling to make sense of how she feels about him here, so unexpected.

"But don't worry. I sent a message. So they don't leave."

"Leave where?"

"A friend of mine owns a tearoom near

here, and he's been hospitable. They gather there every day after the trial adjourns. Sometimes I join them. They're extraordinary women, Virginia."

"You don't have to tell me that," she says. "I know."

"I understand," he says, his voice gentle. "Last time, I failed to deliver you where I promised to. I want to follow through this time. May I, please?"

Instead of answering, she walks, because she can. The air is cool but not cold. He falls into step beside her.

She closes her eyes and opens them again. The streets bustle with bodies, walking fools, people who've never been the places Virginia has been and would never understand what she did there. It all seems impossibly loud and frenetic. All these people are probably thinking of what they think matters, but so many of those things, Virginia could tell them, don't matter at all.

They walk three blocks without speaking until he says, "Turn right here, and then in two blocks, left." But even before they get to the next turn, he blurts out, "I'm sorry. None of this was fair. What happened on my ship wasn't, I know that. I can't apologize enough."

"Don't."

"And not just that. You've been through so much. What happened on the ice. What happened to the Don— what happened before that, when you were younger. You didn't deserve any of it."

"Deserve has nothing to do with it. Do you want to know what I learned?"

He squirms a little under her bright gaze, but then he says, "Tell me."

Virginia says, in her quietest voice, "Experiences like that teach you the harshest truth there is."

"What truth is that?"

"If you believe that no one deserves to die," she says, "you have to acknowledge that no one deserves to live."

His eyes open a little wider as he considers this. Then he nods.

He does not move to console her, and that is what makes up her mind. He understands there is no consolation. If he understands that, she thinks, he might understand her. That might be the beginning of something.

He had reminded her of Ames once, dear, much-missed Ames. If there is anything she has learned from this experience, it is that respect and friendship go further than anything else in the world. Even to the ends of the earth. Even into what feels very much like hell. She has been there and back, but returning by herself would not have been a return at all. The company on the journey was the only thing that truly mattered.

A few blocks later, she spots the sign for the tearoom, and when she raises her eyebrows at him, he nods. She isn't used to speaking much. She wonders if she will ever be as talkative again as she was before she went north. So many words during the trial, so many voices. She is tired of them now. But mere feet away, there are voices she wants very much to hear.

Captain Malcolm gestures to the short set of stairs leading down to the tearoom door.

"They're waiting for you," he says, and as plain as the words are, she's not sure she's ever heard a more beautiful sentence.

As Virginia steps down toward the entrance, she calls behind her to Captain Malcolm, "If you'd like, come in." She does not wait to see whether he follows her. She's too eager for even the shortest delay.

It takes a moment for her eyes to adjust from the bright outdoor sun to the tearoom's dimmer light, but once they do, the sight is everything she could hope for. The room is mostly empty, with only a light sprinkling of strangers, all caught up in their own conversations. No one looks at her, and she relishes the feeling.

Then she sees their familiar faces. The five survivors are seated in a cluster in front of a brick fireplace that blazes orange, silhouetted in its glow. Doro, tugging on the torn collar of her dress, fidgeting. Margaret, the light of the fire flashing in the glass of her spectacles, a look on her face and a hand extended like she's explaining something complicated. Irene, her head cocked to listen to Margaret, wearing an indulgent, half-aware smile. Ebba and Althea, sitting hip to hip on a loveseat, one whispering in the other's ear, both with a contented air. She does not even know where to start.

She does not have to decide. In only a moment, Doro leaps to her feet and throws her arms around Virginia, sighing out her happiness on a sound instead of a word. Irene is next, flinging her arms around them both. Quickly, Margaret joins, then the others, until they are just a knot of arms around bodies, laughing, not caring who looks, not caring who sees.

She wants to ask them everything. Now, she thinks, there will be time.

As she stands before the comforting light of the fireplace, Virginia sighs. The orange glow falls on her cheeks and forehead, her shoulders, her hair.

Without letting go of her companions, she

turns her face toward it like a sunflower.

In this moment, in this place, at long last, she is warm.

AUTHOR'S NOTE

When I first considered writing a book about an all-female Arctic expedition in the nineteenth century, I feared it might be too far-fetched. Any such expedition would have to be funded by an extraordinary figure: a rich woman with an axe to grind, who had sacrificed at least one loved one to the Arctic, who had lost faith in other expeditions' ability to get the job done and so was ready to do something completely unheard of.

As a gift, the historical record happened to offer up a woman who fit that radical profile: Lady Jane Franklin.

Once I learned more about the lost Franklin expedition and the search for its survivors, I found clear historical precedent for many of the story elements I had in mind. Lady Franklin not only had the motivation and the funds to send an Arctic expedition of her own design, she reached out to

Americans for help — up to and including then-president Zachary Taylor in 1849, as well as a New York merchant named Grinnell, who financed two unsuccessful expeditions. She also sent letters addressed to her husband with some of the expeditions she funded. She even considered undertaking a polar expedition herself, as the most adventurous female traveler of her time. The meeting I imagine for Virginia and Lady Franklin at Tremont House in these pages is completely fictional, but the litany of exploits Lady Franklin recites — sailing down the Nile, riding a donkey into Nazareth, etc. — is drawn directly from the pages of history.

(Speaking of Tremont House, experts will recognize that the first ladies' ordinary in Boston is believed to have been located there, not in American House, as I have chosen to place it for Virginia's convenience.)

The deeper I got into researching the 1850s, the more accounts I discovered of extraordinary women on America's various frontiers, exactly the type of women who might have leapt at the chance to involve themselves in an adventure. Mountaineers like Lucy Walker, journalists like Margaret Fuller, battlefield nurses like Sarah Bowman (also known as "the Great Western"), each one was a spark of inspiration that I folded into the party of thirteen women represented here. Virginia Reed was only thirteen at the time of her family's famously ill-starred journey to California, and I have taken a few liberties with her story, but her letter to her cousin was indeed published in the *Illinois Journal* in December 1847. Some elements of Virginia's story in these pages come from Sarah Ann Murphy, nineteen years old at the time of the Donner Party's travails, also a survivor. To my knowledge, neither ever served as a guide on the California Trail.

I also took some minor liberties with the exact dates of the spring thaw of James Bay and Hudson Bay in 1853, as well as some of the details of the terrain. The timeline of the *Doris*'s journey is roughly plausible, but British ships in search of the Northwest Passage generally approached this area from the north (via the Bering Strait on the west or Baffin Bay on the east, which was the route followed by Franklin's ships, the *Erebus* and the *Terror*). U.S. whaling ships began to ply their trade in Hudson Bay beginning in 1860, so Captain Malcolm's exploratory foray into the bay is just a little ahead of its time.

Among the invaluable nonfiction accounts that helped me fill in details of my characters' fictional Arctic explorations were Paul Watson's *Ice Ghosts: The Epic Hunt for the Lost Franklin Expedition; Fatal Passage: The Story of John Rae, the Arctic Hero Time Forgot* and *Lady Franklin's Revenge: A True Story of Ambition, Obsession and the Remaking of Arctic History* by Ken McGoogan; *When the Whalers Were Up North* by Dorothy Harley Eber; *The Arctic Journals of John Rae;* and *Sir John Franklin's* Erebus *and* Terror *Expedition: Lost and Found* by Gillian Hutchinson. The lyrics of Keane's song "The Fire Ship" are excerpted from a version of the shanty transcribed in the Jack Horntip Collection online. The character of Captain Malcolm was inspired by the legendary whaling captain Absalom Boston of Nantucket.

Mistakes are my own.

READING GROUP GUIDE

1. Virginia frequently finds herself caught up in reflections on the past. Do you think her relationship to the past is healthy? How have you dealt with difficult memories?

2. What were your impressions of Virginia's defense attorneys? Do you think she should have testified?

3. Lady Franklin chooses Virginia to lead the expedition partly because of Virginia's experience leading groups of people. How does she demonstrate this leadership? Is it enough for the journey at hand?

4. What is the source of Ebba's regard for Virginia? Why does she decide to follow her after essentially being told to stay home?

5. Virginia wonders several times which group is luckier: the ones who came back or the ones who didn't. In her place, would you struggle to decide? Who do you think the lucky ones are?

6. Which of the varied crew did you find the most interesting? Who did you think presented the greatest danger to the mission as a whole?

7. How did you feel about Virginia and Caprice's early interactions? Did you agree with Virginia's decisions to let things slide, expecting Caprice to eventually fall in line? How would the story have changed if she pursued the conflicts sooner or more thoroughly?

8. What do you see as the final danger the expedition encountered? Which roadblock ensured that they would never, as a whole, come back safe and sound? Were there any missed opportunities that could have prevented disaster?

9. When the women's party divided, whose choice made the most sense to you? Who

surprised you the most? Did you think any of them chose wrong?

10. In her musings, Virginia makes a distinction between serving as a guide in unsettled land and being a "true explorer." What challenges separate these two similar endeavors? Which would you rather do?

11. At the beginning of the story, would you have expected Caprice's actions in the crevasse? What changed for her?

12. Virginia thinks, "They would go home failures, yes. But they would go home." What do you think of this assessment? What does it mean to fail?

A CONVERSATION
WITH THE AUTHOR

Early in the book, Virginia seems determined to rid herself of the past. As a historical fiction writer, I doubt you share that attitude. How do you consider your relationship to the past?

Well, I don't have a past nearly as traumatic as Virginia's, for one thing! But I suppose I have reinvented myself a few times over the course of my life so far, so we do have that in common. In the broader sense, I do rely on the resonance of past history with current conditions to give my readers one more way to think about modern society. How far have we come since the nineteenth century? Very far in some ways and not nearly as far as we'd like in others.

For such a formidable journey, the women's party seems initially scarce on

adventurers. **What motivated that distribution?**

The exact makeup of the party was one of the hardest things to get right in the early going. What finally unlocked it for me was to make sure that each woman had a real-life counterpart, an inspiration from the mid-nineteenth century I could point to and draw from. And some of those women were doing startling things, like climbing mountains or saving soldiers' lives on a battlefield, but others were setting themselves apart in different ways, like drawing plants no one else had drawn before.

How much research do you do *before* you begin writing a book? If you come up against a fact you don't know while writing, do you leave a placeholder or take a research break?

I definitely prefer to do as much research as possible before diving into the serious drafting of a book, but for various reasons, that didn't happen on this one. So I was still researching while I was writing, which I definitely don't recommend! But there was just so much to learn about the Arctic, what the women were up against, what the conditions would be in all these locations, that was the only way I could get it done. When I was writing *The Magician's Lie,* my first historical novel, I used to stop writing in order to find a fact; that book took me five years to finish. I don't do that anymore. Placeholders are the only way I can keep forward momentum.

You develop a tense interplay between the courtroom scenes and the scenes of the expedition. Did you write both narratives simultaneously as they appear in the final book, or did you interweave them after they were both complete? How did that shape the story overall?

That was easier than I thought it would be, actually! To reference *The Magician's Lie* again, which also unfolded in two timelines, I really struggled with fitting together all the puzzle pieces to form one cohesive narrative for the reader — Arden's story. But this time around, as I was writing both the murder trial timeline and the expedition timeline simultaneously, they just sort of fell into place. My somewhat outrageous decision to include one chapter from the point of view of each woman on the expedition actually helped dictate a lot of that structure — once I knew who died when, obviously her chapter had to come before that point, and I locked in the whole jigsaw before I was done writing the first draft. And it didn't change during revision, which is kind of remarkable.

Which of the women from the expedition would you most want to meet in real life? What would you talk to her about?

Oh, I've got a real soft spot for Caprice, insufferable as she can be. I'd let her tell all the stories she wanted to tell about climbing half the mountains in Europe. I don't think I'd even have to ask questions — she would just monologue freely until her tea went cold, then she'd ring for more and keep talking.

Each time the expedition loses another member, you somehow introduce a new kind of sorrow. Which was the hardest to write? Was there anyone you were tempted to save?

The hardest was Ann, because she's the only one who completely chooses her fate, and she does it for this noble, painful reason that no one else but her would choose. She was also the only one who I had to kill twice. I'd written a different death scene for her early on, but as I got deeper into the first draft, I realized it was way too similar to what I ended up writing for Caprice. I briefly thought about letting Ann off the hook, but I knew how I wanted the numbers to come out, so she still had to go. And it turned out to be, I think, one of the most moving scenes.

Virginia traces the course of her fate squarely back to the newspaper article about her career as a trail guide. Do you believe there's always one fateful choice in life that can be treated as the source of everything afterwards? How does that shape your life?

I do think we have turning points in our lives that we look back on and recognize as significant. The *what if* of it all. I don't think there's just one, and I think that you can make a thousand different choices at a thousand different points in your life and still turn out basically the same. But without question, there are forks in the road, and taking the left side of the fork means you'll never know what would have happened if you'd taken the right.

The trial takes a hard turn when Virginia's past is revealed. How do you think we're all shaped by the ways we describe the past? Would Virginia's life be different, for example, if she stopped thinking of the Donner expedition as the Very Bad Thing from her past? Are those stories more important to us individually or to the people around us?

I think if Virginia hadn't been running away from that past she would never have made the choice to go to the Arctic, for better or worse. If she'd been honest with herself about how deeply it scarred her to see civilization fall apart in that way, she would have run farther away from adventure, not toward it. The real-life Virginia Reed, from the accounts I've read, settled down into a more traditional family life, got married, had children. Was she making peace with her past or avoiding it? I have no idea. But how our pasts affect how other people see us, yes. That's a big part of what I wanted to address. On the expedition, if Virginia's past had been common knowledge, I think her fellow adventurers definitely would have treated her differently. But by the time the survivors were there to support her during her trial, that revelation didn't change anything. They already knew everything they needed to know.

What have you learned about writing, now that you're publishing your fourth novel? How has your process changed since *The Magician's Lie*? What has stayed the same?

As I mentioned before, I've learned a lot about not letting the forward momentum of your writing grind to a halt in order to do your research! And it's funny, after *The Magician's Lie*, I told myself I'd stick to writing books told only in straightforward chronological order — so *Girl in Disguise* was that way, but the first half of *Woman 99* has all these in-depth flashbacks that form an earlier timeline, and then in this book, I'm just flinging timelines and POVs all over the place. Whatever serves the story, that's what I'm going to do.

What's next on your to-read list? Anything that might hint at your next project?

I'm always reading three or four different books at once, so some might be more relevant than others! I can say that I'm in the early stages of deciding what my next work of historical fiction will focus on, and I may have checked out a few library books on nineteenth-century New Orleans.

ACKNOWLEDGMENTS

As always, you wouldn't be holding this book in your hands if not for my agent, Elisabeth Weed, at the Book Group and my editor, Shana Drehs, at Sourcebooks, both true powerhouses. So grateful to you both for your guidance, support, encouragement, and enthusiasm.

Publishing a book takes a village, and the Sourcebooks village is firing on all cylinders (to mix metaphors just a touch). My thanks to Dominique Raccah, Heather VenHuizen, Stephanie Rocha, Jessica Thelander, Margaret Coffee, Valerie Pierce, Kirsten Wenum, Molly Waxman, Caitlin Lawler, Chelsea McGuckin, Sabrina Baskey, and Carolyn Lesnick for all their hard work, transforming my raw words into this beautiful book and getting it into the hands of readers.

I'm also grateful to Hallie Schaeffer at the Book Group, the team at Tessera Editorial, Jenny Meyer for handling my foreign rights,

Michelle Weiner and the team at CAA, intern extraordinaire Elizabeth Sander, and more booksellers, librarians, and Bookstagrammers than I have space to include here.

The company of fellow authors on this journey makes all the madness worth it. More writers than I can name here bring joy to my life; those who made particularly essential contributions to this novel and my mental well-being while writing it include Shelley Nolden, who always holds my feet to the fire; Therese Walsh and the incredible community of Writer Unboxed; Marie Benedict, Kristina McMorris, and Allison Pataki whose gracious blurbs and generous cheerleading are so appreciated; the members of the Fiction Writers' Co-Op, who tell it like it is; and my fellow historical novelists from the Historical Novel Society, who make every time and place feel like home.

ABOUT THE AUTHOR

Raised in the Midwest, **Greer Macallister** is a novelist, poet, short story writer, and playwright who earned her MFA in creative writing from American University. Her debut novel, *The Magician's Lie,* was a *USA Today* bestseller, an Indie Next pick, and a Target Book Club selection. Her novels *Girl in Disguise* and *Woman 99* were inspired by pioneering nineteenth-century Pinkerton agent Kate Warne and intrepid journalist Nellie Bly, respectively. A regular contributor to *Writer Unboxed* and the *Chicago Review of Books,* Macallister lives with her family in Washington, DC.

The employees of Thorndike Press hope you have enjoyed this Large Print book. All our Thorndike, Wheeler, and Kennebec Large Print titles are designed for easy reading, and all our books are made to last. Other Thorndike Press Large Print books are available at your library, through selected bookstores, or directly from us.

For information about titles, please call:

(800) 223-1244

or visit our website at:

gale.com/thorndike

To share your comments, please write:

Publisher
Thorndike Press
10 Water St., Suite 310
Waterville, ME 04901

631